FAR FROM HOME

Children of the Promise

·CHILDREN OF THE PROMISE·

VOL. 3

FAR FROM HOME

·DEAN HUGHES·

DESERET BOOK COMPANY · SALT LAKE CITY, UTAH

FOR TOM, KRISTEN, AND STEVEN

Library of Congress Cataloging-in-Publication Data

Hughes, Dean, 1943–
    Far from home / Dean Hughes.
      p.   cm. — (Children of the promise ; v. 3)
    ISBN 1-57345-406-0
    1. World War, 1939–1945—Fiction. 2. Mormons—History—Fiction.
I. Title. II. Series: Hughes, Dean, 1943–   Children of the promise
; vol. 3.
PS3558.U36F3   1998
813'.54—dc21   98-27381
                                                          CIP

Printed in the United States of America   18961-6409

10 9 8 7 6 5 4 3 2 1

I

Alex and Anna's days together in Windermere were nearly perfect. But a honeymoon now, in August of 1944, was like a pastoral landscape in rich, warm colors painted over the surface of a battle scene, all in black and red. Alex never lost his awareness of the deeper reality, the one that waited just beyond the dreamscape they were creating for each other. Anna was beautiful, and lovely to be with, but she was also ephemeral, and so her loveliness brought him as much pain as it did joy.

Lying close to Anna, Alex went to sleep rather peacefully each night, but then the nightmares would begin: the thumping sound of machine-gun fire, explosions, bodies torn apart, and always the color red, in flashes and streaks and spatters. He would sit up sweating and gasping, shaking, and Anna would hold him and stroke his hair until he calmed. Then he would sleep again, but warily, half awake and afraid the dreams would return. The days were exquisite, Anna's softness impossible to get enough of, but the truth was always looming. Alex would soon go back to his unit, and after that he would return to the continent: to battle, to the scenes in his nightmares. What he never told Anna, but what he couldn't forget, was that if he kept making parachute drops, his chances for survival were poor.

Clinging to this time together, of course, only frightened the days away, and Alex and Anna were soon taking the train back to London, where Anna was to stay with her parents. At the Stoltzes' apartment Alex packed his bags as though he were carrying out a script someone had written for him. The reality that had been lurking, trying to assert itself, still seemed unthinkable. Later, when he stood with Anna on the platform amid all the people and noise and the heavy smell of coal dust in Victoria Station, he clung to her until the last second, and still something in him kept insisting, "This can't happen."

"I'll try to get a pass if I can. Maybe I can get to London for a weekend."

"Oh, yes. Or maybe I can come there. Even if I can only see you for an hour—or a few minutes." She pressed her face to his chest, his uniform, and she began to sob.

"I'll let you know. I'll write as often as I can. Please write to me every day. I need some way to . . . " But he didn't know exactly what he meant. He felt as though he were slipping into darkness. His tears were falling on her hair.

"Don't worry. I won't miss a day. We'll tell each other everything. It won't be like before."

"Anna, I love you too much. I don't know how I can do this."

The conductor was making his last call. Alex kissed Anna one last time, felt her body fit against his, and it all seemed too much to give up. But he turned, threw his duffel bag on the train, and jumped on after it. Then he stood on the step, looked back, and said, "Go ahead, Anna. Don't wait and watch the train."

But the train began to roll, and Anna stood there watching him. She was wearing a little print dress, with daisies—one she had worn when they walked by the lake in Windermere—but no lipstick, no makeup, just her own flushed prettiness and her soft blonde hair around her face. She waved and then brought both hands to her cheeks, her blue eyes magnified in her tears, and then she slipped out of view.

Alex thought the pain couldn't get any worse, but halfway to Aldbourne his desolation struck him full force. He had never felt this alone in his life, not even at the beginning of his mission or during those hard days in Georgia at basic training. He sat in the noisy, jiggling train, with people all around him, and he felt as though the dark had swallowed him. He thought of getting off at the next stop, going AWOL, and running back to her. The idea seemed entirely reasonable, and it was only something automatic in him—a sense that he had no choice—that kept him moving forward instead of turning back. But he didn't think of the flag or the defense of freedom. Abstractions were for people back home who got the war from the radio.

The camp at Aldbourne was nothing more than Nissen huts with their rounded corrugated steel roofs, set in rows on a soccer field. The village was quaint, picturesque, with cottages built of rock, a single pub called the Mason's Arm, a little collection of stores at the center, and, all around, green hills and pastures divided by stone walls. In peacetime it would have been a sleepy country village, but now the narrow road through town was filled with troop trucks and Jeeps, and when Alex walked past the pub, with his duffel bag over his shoulder, he saw that it was full of soldiers from his regiment. The whole village seemed a garrison, not an English town, and he hated the feel of it.

Alex had hoped to report to Lieutenant Summers, but he found out that Summers was a captain now and the new company commander. A lieutenant named Lewis Owen had been transferred from D Company and was the new platoon leader. He was sitting at a little desk just inside one of the huts. When Alex saluted and gave his name, Owen stood up and shook his hand. "Thomas, I'm glad to get you back," he said. "I've heard what you did in Normandy."

Alex didn't want this. He still didn't understand what had

happened to him on the morning of D-day, when he had fought so ferociously, but he really doubted he could repeat that performance, and he hated to have it expected of him.

"I've been using Corporal Duncan as the temporary squad leader, but now that you're back, you'll take over again, and Duncan will be your assistant. You still don't have a full squad. We got three replacements in, and now, with you, you'll be up to ten men—about the same as our other squads. You may pick up one or two more at some point."

"That sounds fine, sir," Alex said. A year ago the combination—he and Duncan—would have seemed impossible, but now Alex knew that the two of them would work fine together.

"Can you jump yet?"

"The doctor said I shouldn't for another month or so. I only have 'light duty' papers. But if we make a drop soon, I'd rather go than get left behind."

Owen grinned. "I like your attitude," he said, "but I can't ask you to do that."

"It's not that I'm eager to get back into battle," Alex said. "It's just that when I do go, I want to be with my own unit."

Alex couldn't have explained all his feelings about that. Three men from his former squad were dead, killed on D-day, and two more had become serious casualties. So the squad was hardly the same. But the troopers he had fought with—his friend Curtis Bentley, and Duncan, Campbell, Gourley, Pozernac—these were men he had faced death with. When he went up against the enemy again, he wanted the same guys alongside him. "How soon do you think the next drop will take place?" Alex asked.

"No one knows. Rumors go around every day. Twice now we've been scheduled to go, but our infantry troops overran the planned drop zones and made the missions unnecessary. Right now Patton is pushing across France so hard that the Germans are constantly falling back. No one needs us."

Alex followed the war news carefully. He knew that Allied

troops could reach Germany before winter, and Russia was driving hard from the east, now having taken Warsaw, Poland. The Allies were also making progress in Italy, approaching the German Gothic Line, and the Seventh Army had landed in southern France. Meanwhile, German cities were being pounded into oblivion by Allied bombers. If Hitler had any sense, maybe he would see the handwriting on the wall. A group of German generals had already tried to kill Hitler that summer, and they had almost got the job done. It seemed crazy that German citizens didn't rise up and demand a halt to the war, but reports were that Hitler was killing anyone who opposed him and tightening his grip on the country.

"Don't worry. We'll be back in it," Owen said. "From what I hear, ol' General Taylor is going nuts. He says the Screaming Eagles are the best division in the army and we shouldn't be sitting around in England. You know how generals are. They don't add stars to their shoulders when their men are sitting around in garrison."

Alex liked Owen already. He was a big man, with a beefy neck and jowls, and he had a way of hunching his shoulders when he talked so he looked like a boxer ready to throw a punch. But he seemed to be a decent guy, and realistic. Alex could always tell the citizen soldiers who had come to do a job but looked forward to getting back to their lives: college, or a farm, maybe a family. The career guys—Regular Army—were the ones more anxious to earn rank by showing off for the big brass.

"Are we doing much in the way of training now?" Alex asked.

"Oh, sure. Field problems. Marches. Target practice. Just no jumps. We don't have the airplanes for that. But we have lots of replacement troops—green as horse manure—and they need work. In a way, the veterans need it too. You can't let men sit around all day. Everyone's on edge as it is."

"I don't care about this 'light duty' status I'm on. It wouldn't look good if I got out of marches and night problems. I've got to earn the respect of the replacements."

"Thomas, that's exactly what I wanted to hear you say. But don't push yourself too fast. I don't want you to go down with an injury that would keep you out of action."

"All right. But I'll try to get back into shape."

"I understand you just came back from your honeymoon." Owen's big cheeks rolled into plump balls. His front teeth were divided a little, giving him the look of a big kid. "I hope you're not too softened up."

Alex smiled. "I'll be all right," he said. But that wasn't what he was feeling. As he walked from the hut, he wondered about himself. Why had he taken on a military manner so readily? Why had he been so quick to give up his light-duty status? He hadn't planned that; in fact, he had come back wondering whether he wouldn't be better off to miss the first jump his regiment was likely to make. But something was changing in him quickly, a sense of the soldier's life coming back, and he did want to be with his men, not left behind. When he thought of Anna, however, he wondered whether he had sinned against her. Above everything else, he should do what it would take to stay alive.

As Alex walked between the rows of Nissen huts, he was amazed at how easily he could tell the experienced men from the replacement troops. He recognized a lot of faces, of course, knew the men from his own company. But he also saw the difference. The replacements looked like American boys he remembered from home: a bit of a swagger in their walk, confidence, even arrogance, in their eyes. The veterans weren't necessarily grizzled old warriors; they were almost as young as the replacements. But they seemed resolute at best, and sometimes distant. Alex remembered how these same men had bragged and bellowed—and cut their hair in Mohawks—on the night before D-day. All that was gone now.

He found an empty bunk in the hut he was assigned to,

and he began to unpack. There was a mustiness in the place, and the smell of men. The humidity was high inside, even though the air wasn't all that warm. He thought of his week with Anna, just the two of them in the cottage they had rented by the lake. How could he go back to living like this, with a bunch of soldiers? He could tolerate the language, the crassness; but the absence of everything gentle and delicate seemed to rend life in half and leave out the things that brought the best out of him.

Alex was settling in when his squad came tromping through the door. Duncan bellowed out a welcome and then announced to the other men, in his southern drawl, "Okay, boys. Now you got yourself a real squad leader. I'm jist happy to let him take over, too." Then he reached out and grabbed Alex's hand.

Alex shook hands with the other men he knew, joked with them, and took some teasing about his honeymoon. Campbell said, "Bentley told us you married the prettiest girl in the world, and we all have to look for second best from now on."

"The trouble is, there's no close second," Alex said. "You'll have to settle for a regular girl—a human being."

"That's all right," Duncan said, "I don't want no angel. She might want to limit my beer intake."

Gourley and Pozernac were both from Philadelphia and had gone through basic training together. They hardly looked like twins, with Gourley half a foot taller and light-haired, opposite of Pozernac, but the two were always together. "I'm glad to have you back, Deacon," Gourley told Alex. "I like to be around a guy who gives away his cigarettes."

The replacements didn't come forward immediately, but once the noise calmed a little, Curtis waved them over, and he introduced them one at a time. There was a young boy from Maryland, not more than five-foot-five, named Earl Sabin. Another stout, serious young man, with glasses—Royce Withers—was from Chicago. He had been a chemistry major at Northwestern before he got called up. Delbert Ernst looked a little older but probably wasn't more than twenty-two or so. He was from Tennessee and sounded not just southern but "country." "He speaks the mother tongue," Curtis said. "But not in its purest form, the way it's spoken in Georgia."

"Nass to meet yuh," Alex said, trying to sound southern. Then he shook hands with the last boy. "My name's Howard Douglas," the soldier said. He seemed pleasant enough, but shy. He didn't really look Alex in the eye. He wasn't a lot taller than Sabin, but he was built much stronger.

"Howie's from your part of the country," Duncan said. "From Boise." Douglas nodded, and then he sat down on the bunk next to Alex's. He began to unlace his boots.

"Is that right?" Alex said, and he wondered immediately whether he might be LDS.

But Duncan answered that question. "He ain't a Mormon, but he might as well be. He don't drink or smoke, and he's scared of girls."

Douglas looked up and smiled, just a little, but he didn't respond. He didn't really look like Gene—Alex's little brother who had been killed a few months before in Saipan—but something in that faint smile called back an image: Gene as a boy, when he always seemed to say much less than he was thinking, when a little slice of smile would suggest that some irony, some realization, was in his head, even though he felt no need to share it.

"Have these guys been giving you a hard time?" Alex asked him.

"It don't bother me," Douglas said, without looking up this time.

The other men were gradually scattering toward their bunks. Duncan was complaining that all the training was unnecessary, too hard, too rigid—or something of that sort. But he sounded like his old self, just happy to have something to beef about.

"How long have you been in the army?" Alex asked.

"Since last winter," Douglas said. "I finished jump school right before I come over here."

"Have you lived in Boise all your life?"

"Pretty much. I was born over by Baker, Oregon, but my ol' man ran out on us, so my mom moved back to where she was from—with me, my little brother, and two big sisters."

"What were you doing before you joined the army?"

"Just this and that. I quit high school and did some farm work for a while. I know how to weld a little, too, and I've run heavy equipment on road construction jobs."

Alex thought maybe he had asked enough. Private Douglas was nice enough about answering, but not eager. So Alex walked over and chatted with Curtis. Curtis had heard all the same rumors, that the 101st would be dropping into France or Belgium soon. "Are the guys all hoping to get going right away?" Alex asked.

"I can tell you haven't been here," Curtis said. "We got briefed last week. We were supposed to make a drop the next day, on August 19, into Chartres, France. They fed us like it was our last supper, and we all got packed up and trucked out to the airdrome, over in Membury, and then we heard on the radio that the Third Army had taken Chartres. So the generals called the whole thing off. All the new guys were disappointed—or at least they said they were—but the guys who were in on D-day partied most of the night. We don't want to go back any sooner than we have to."

"I feel the same way."

"Is it different for you now? Being a married man?"

"Sure."

"You don't have to be a hero this time, Alex. Just keep yourself alive."

"I didn't try to be a hero last time."

"I know. I don't think any of us understood what we were doing until it was all over."

Alex nodded. Some soft swing music had been playing on a radio somewhere, but now a jovial male voice, British, was ranting about something. "Is that Lord Haw Haw?" Alex asked. "They wouldn't let us listen to him in the hospital."

"Yeah, I know. But he doesn't bother us, and he plays better music than the Armed Forces Network or the BBC."

Lord Haw Haw was a turncoat Brit who broadcast for the Nazis, from Berlin. He tried to work some psychological warfare on the Allied troops, but no one took him seriously.

Alex walked back to his bunk and sat down again. Douglas was lying down, apparently not ready to make the hike to the showers just yet. "I knew a lot of Mormons in Boise," Douglas said. "I even dated a Mormon girl for a while."

"Did she try to convert you?" Alex asked.

"I guess that's what she had in mind. She tried to get me to go to church with her, anyway. That's when we broke up." Douglas laughed, softly.

"Well, it's nice to have someone around who knows what sagebrush smells like."

"Yeah, when I was a Boy Scout, we used to throw it on our campfire—just for the smell it made when it was burning."

"It's good you like to camp. We'll be doing some of that before long. You can even dig your own bed."

Douglas smiled more fully this time, and when he did, Alex thought he looked like a Boy Scout, or just a boy. "Everyone says you were hell on wheels last time over there," Douglas said.

Alex didn't want this reputation. "Actually, I wasn't there very long."

"How bad is it?"

It was a simple enough question, but Alex remembered how much he had wondered about that before he had seen his first action. The problem was, it was worse than he had expected, but he didn't want to tell Douglas that. "If you keep your head, play things smart, it doesn't have to be so bad."

"That's not what you did, was it?"

"Well, I wasn't so crazy as it might sound. We put down cover fire, and we worked under it. We did everything by the book. We just outsmarted the Germans a little. And we got lucky."

"I heard you got the Distinguished Service Medal. You got it with you?"

"No. I put it away as soon as I got it."

"Pretty nice to have, I guess," Douglas said. "A guy could impress the girls back home with something like that." He laughed. He had taken off his shirt, and his khaki undershirt was stained through with sweat.

"How old are you, Douglas?" Alex asked.

"You can just call me Howie. That's what everybody always calls me. I'm eighteen now. When I signed up, I was still seventeen."

"When we jump this next time, you stick with me," Alex said. "I'm not going to get myself killed. Just do what I do and you'll stay alive. If we play our cards right, we won't get any medals at all—including the Purple Heart."

"All right." Howie sat up. "I'd better get me a shower before it's time to eat."

Alex watched him leave the hut, and he wondered what might be in store for the kid. He also wondered why anyone should have to leave his boyhood behind by going off to war.

Duncan was back from the shower by then. He was still buttoning his shirt when he walked over to Alex's bunk. "So, are you all healed up?" he asked.

"Pretty much."

"Can you jump?"

"I'm not supposed to, but I guess I will."

"I wouldn't if I was you. I'd hold off just as long as I could. You got that right. You earned it." Duncan sat down on Howie's bunk.

Alex, who was facing him, looked at the floor. "I'll tell you what I told Lieutenant Owen. If I'm going back, I want to go with you guys."

Duncan stared at Alex for a long time. And then, finally, he said, "I can't believe I ever hated you so much. You're some guy, Thomas."

"Or stupid," Alex said, and he smiled. But then he asked, "How's Owen going to be?"

"He's all right. All the officers believe too much in all this . . . " Alex saw him search for a word to replace the one he had planned to use. "You know, this Mickey Mouse training routine. They march us around like Boy Scouts because they're afraid we'll have too much time on our hands if they don't. Then they go off and drink whiskey at the officers' club while we drink warm beer if we can get any."

"But does Owen know what he's doing?"

"Better than most. But he ain't Summers. There ain't many guys like Summers in this man's army."

Alex knew that was true. The guy hadn't *sent* anyone into battle. He was always out in front, leading the way. "What I wish," Alex said, "is that the war would end, and we could go home."

"Do you have bad dreams?" Duncan asked.

"Yes."

"I do too. A lot of the guys do." All of Duncan's joviality was gone now. He rested his elbows on his knees. Alex had never expected to see him look so solemn. "I heard your little brother got killed."

"Yeah."

"How are you doing about that?"

"Not too bad, I guess. My sister saw Gene not long before he died. She said he seemed to know something was going to happen. He told her he figured it wasn't so bad to die, since he believed there was a heaven. It helps me to think about that. But he was just a kid when I saw him the last time. In my head, he's still back home. That's when I'll miss him, I think—when I get home."

"I guess that's right—what he said about heaven," Duncan said, and he wasn't joking. For a time neither spoke, and then Duncan said, "Look around when you go to mess. About half the guys from our regiment are gone. Some killed. Some missing in action. Some too shot up to come back, like Rizzardi. Some all messed up in the head, like Huish. And we weren't in it that long."

"That's one good thing about the airborne. We get pulled back before the next drop. Those infantry guys have been in the middle of it from D-day straight on through."

"Sure. But no one takes bigger chances than we do." He grinned. "We're the Screaming Eagles—the toughest guys in the army. We drop behind the lines and fight our way out." But there was irony in his voice. All the men still believed that stuff—to some degree—but the idea had lost its thrill.

"They did whip us into shape. We're better soldiers than most."

"I don't doubt that. But I had it in my head that we'd be out there marching in a parade or something, with a band playing and flags waving. I don't know what I thought. I didn't picture all those days in foxholes, with artillery coming in on us."

"I missed that part."

"I know. But you ran straight at a machine-gun emplacement when no one else wanted to stick his nose out of the ditch."

"You guys all went with me."

"Sure. But only because I saw you and Summers out there, putting yourselves on the line."

"Well . . . we all did what we had to do."

Duncan rubbed his hand over his wet hair. He was still a big man, but he had lost weight since the early days, back in 1942, and he had aged. He had never seemed serious back then. "I'll tell you something I've thought a lot about," he said.

"Just before we got pulled back, I saw some German prisoners walking down a road. It hit me like a ton of bricks: they were just regular guys, like us. You know what I mean? Just guys who got drafted or felt they had to sign up. I think that's bothered me more than any single thing—you know, since we got pulled out. You used to always say that, back in basic, that they were just people like us. I hated you for that."

"I've lived there. I just—"

"Thomas, I can't do that. I gotta hate 'em. I try not to think how I felt when I saw those guys. I can't go into battle with that on my mind. I heard a story from a guy in a pub in London— just some dogface from an infantry unit. He got shot through the hip over by Carentan, where we were. He said the Germans were cutting guys' throats, just so they wouldn't have to take prisoners. He saw a whole bunch of our guys alongside a ditch over there somewhere, their throats cut through."

"Our guys did some of that too."

"Yeah, I know, but . . . they're worse than us, aren't they?"

"I don't know."

"I think they are. I think we can pray to kill them. Our chaplain here at the camp said a prayer like that one time. He asked God to let us be 'instruments of fury' so we could 'smite the evil forces.' I remember those words exactly. I've been saying some prayers lately, just on my own. And I always say that."

"I do think Hitler is evil," Alex said. "I like to think that I'm fighting him—and what he's trying to do to the world."

"But not the rest of the Germans?"

"My wife is German, Duncan. You can't find finer people than her and her family."

"Yeah, but they went against the Nazis, right? What about all the ones that support Hitler?"

Alex thought for a moment, and then he said, "Look, Duncan, it's not going to do any good to talk about this. We do have to kill them—until they stop trying to kill us. That's just the way it is. But don't think about it. We'll just do what we have to do."

"I've got to hate them to kill them. I told you that."

"And I still don't want to."

"But I saw the way you killed before. You weren't holding anything back."

Alex knew that. And he didn't really understand himself. He only knew that he hadn't satisfied his own desire to be righteous, somehow, even in battle. He didn't know how to kill and carry the spirit of the Lord with him at the same time. And he didn't know how to take Anna with him.

Somewhere, in another hut, a radio was still on, and Alex could hear the song that was playing: "I'll never smile again until I smile at you."

It was a stupid song, and untrue. He could still smile, and everything was going to be okay. Still, he rolled on his side, pressed one ear against his pillow, and pulled his blanket over the other. He couldn't hear the music now, but the words continued in his head.

2

Most of the POWs marched with their eyes straight ahead, but Wally Thomas watched the angry Japanese citizens who lined the street. The people were fanatic in their rage. Guards had to hold them back. Some spit at the prisoners, and occasionally someone lobbed a rock. Wally wasn't so much insulted or scared as he was curious. How could these people hate him so much? He assumed that American bombers had attacked their country, and he understood that he was the enemy, but he couldn't imagine the opinions these people must hold, to feel such wrath toward him. Maybe a group of Japanese prisoners would be treated the same way back in Salt Lake City, but he couldn't picture it.

The walk was not long, but the prisoners were weak from their long voyage from the Philippines. Wally, like most of the men, had been a prisoner of the Japanese since April of 1942. It was now August 1944. The men had been held in squalid camps in the Philippines, where they had been forced to work under unthinkable conditions, with little food. A huge percentage of the prisoners had died of disease or malnutrition. Wally had no idea what that percentage was, but he was certain that more than half his squadron was now dead. Some had died only recently on the "hell ship" that had brought them to

Japan. Wally was in a group of one hundred, including his friends from Salt Lake, Chuck Adair and Art Halverson, and his friends Don Cluff, Ray Vernon, and Eddy Nash. Now they were being marched to a train station. That much they knew. What they didn't know was where they were going or what they would do when they got there.

But Wally was hopeful. Shortly after arriving in the port, the prisoners had been given a hefty slice of brown sourdough bread to eat. The bread had actually made Wally sick, since his system wasn't used to it; still, it seemed a promising sign. Maybe the prisoners would eat better here. The men had spent sixty-two days on the ship, counting time docked in Formosa, and all their focus had had to be on surviving the heat and filth and hunger. But Wally, like all the other men, had clung to the hope, which was mostly just speculation, that conditions would be better in Japan. Rumor had it that the men would mine coal, and the theory among the prisoners was that anyone doing such hard work would have to be fed well. There was also some sense in Wally that the Japanese—not the guards he had dealt with for two years—were refined people. It seemed that such a people, in their own country, would be respectful to prisoners of war. Now, watching the hostile faces, hearing their screams, he had to wonder what would happen to him and his friends.

The men reached a train station, where they were herded onto waiting passenger cars. This was a big improvement over the cattle cars he and the others had traveled in before, but the technique was the same. The guards kept driving more and more of them into a single car until all hope of comfort was lost. But Wally had found a seat, so he couldn't complain.

Before the train began to move, a translator stepped into the car. He was a young man who had spoken to the prisoners before. He had been raised in California, and he spoke a perfect American dialect. "I'd recommend you guys keep your blinds down," he shouted. "As you saw out there, people don't like you much around here. You're better off if no one sees you."

Again, Wally tried to take something positive from this. The voice was almost friendly, familiar. Maybe conditions were going to be better in the camp they were heading to, wherever it was.

Chuck was sitting with Wally, crowded into the same seat. Back home, when they had played football together at East High, they wouldn't have fit into the space so easily. But neither one was much more than a skeleton now, so their hips didn't take much room. The men smelled powerfully of the disinfectant that had been sprayed on them as they left their ship, and all of them were still filthy with sweat and grime. But maybe they would be allowed to clean up soon. That and more food were the two things the prisoners kept talking about.

"My guess is, the war isn't going well for Japan," Chuck said. "That's why the people are so mad."

"We're probably bombing all the time over here by now," Don said. He and Art were crowded into the next seat, and Eddy was sitting across from them. The five had become inseparable during the time on the ship.

"I just hope our pilots know where we are," Chuck said. "I don't want to get killed by an American bomb."

Art nodded. "Maybe so, but I hope we hear lots of bombs dropping. I want this war over before Christmas."

It was what the men always hoped, always promised each other: that they would be home before the year was over. But Wally didn't know. What he had learned, above everything else, was to take one day at a time. If he thought of endless days ahead, and constant drudgery, he became overwhelmed with discouragement. So he tried to keep his mind on the present, to get through whatever hardship he had to face that day, that moment, and let the future take care of itself.

"If we can eat a little better here—and have a cleaner place to live," Chuck said, "we can last it out, no matter how long it takes."

But Wally was trying not to trust in better conditions. If he built his hopes up too much, another setback might knock him down too far. It was best not to rely on those kinds of hopes.

No one knew how long the train ride would last, so the men slept as best they could in the aisles or crowded into seats. But in the middle of the night the train rolled to a stop and guards ordered the prisoners out. There, in the darkness, Wally saw a sign: "Omuta." He had no idea where that was, but he soon found that it was a large place.

Guards lined the prisoners up and marched them through the city. The long hike lasted the rest of the night. By daylight the men were weary, but they had learned through years of experience to put one foot in front of the other and keep going even when they were dead tired. On the outskirts of the city, in an industrial area, they passed slag heaps and the entrance to a large coal mine. "We must have heard right," Chuck whispered to Wally. "I'll bet that's where we're going to work, and there's the camp down there."

Wally looked ahead. He could see a bay in the distance, could smell the ocean, and near the water was an area that was blocked off with high walls. It looked like a prison.

The men were marched to those walls, and then in through the front gate. It was a misty morning, bleak, and the gray walls seemed ominous. Inside were rows of barracks. They looked relatively clean, but Wally noticed there were quite a few guards and very few prisoners. It occurred to him that at this early hour, barely daylight, the men must already be at work.

What followed next was a ritual Wally had seen many times before. The guards lined the men up, made them strip, and then searched them and their clothing for anything they could steal. But the prisoners had been shaken down a hundred times before, and there was next to nothing to take from them now. The guards then ordered the men to carry their clothes to an area in the compound where fifty-gallon drums of water, over fires, were being brought to a boil. The guards motioned for them to toss their clothes in.

Don threw his clothes in and laughed. "Those body lice are finally getting what they deserve," he told Wally.

The guards brought clippers then, handed them out to the prisoners, and motioned for the men to cut each other's hair and beards. One of the guards said in English, "Cut very short. Then go for bath."

Wally felt an amazing surge of joy. These were such little things: to be freed of lice, to cut his long hair and beard, to have a chance to bathe. But he couldn't hold back the feeling any longer. Things were going to be better here. There was reason to expect an easier time through the rest of the war.

"Bath" turned out to be the wrong word, however. It was only a wash. Still, it was a wash with soap, and then the group was split in half and sent to two barracks. The buildings were clean, if crowded, with three large sleeping rooms and a small front room. Wally ended up in one of the big rooms with a total of fifteen men, his friends among them. They would sleep on the floor, on mats, but small straw pillows were supplied, and a comforter was issued to each man—which was certainly a luxury. Compared to some of the conditions Wally had experienced, this didn't look too bad.

What followed were physical examinations, and then every prisoner was photographed. Wally was told that his identification number was 1151: *"sen-byaku go ju-ichi."*

"No names," the guard told the men. "Must know your number."

They were then lined up and issued new clothes: a forest-green coat and trousers made from flimsy cloth; a g-string instead of underwear; a white, short-sleeved shirt; a cap; and a pair of rubber-soled, split-toed shoes. They were also given heavier clothes and an overcoat and told to fold those and put them away in their rooms. The prisoner's number was stenciled on each item. The men also received wooden number tags. They were told they must hang these on a peg outside their rooms when they were there. Any time they left, they had to hang the tag on a peg to indicate where they had gone: to chow, roll call, or the toilets.

All that seemed easy enough. What Wally still wondered about was the food, and, of course, the work. He hoped the guards would be decent and that working underground wouldn't bother him too much.

When mess call came that evening, Wally was very hungry. He and the other men were called out for *tenko*—roll call— before they could go to the mess hall. They stood in formation and waited, but nothing happened. It was a muggy day, and the men were tired from the all-night train ride the night before. But the guards merely left the men standing at attention for the better part of an hour. Finally, an authoritative-looking man, small but powerfully built, walked to the front of the compound. He was apparently the head guard for their section of the prison. "You must count," he shouted.

It took a moment for the men to realize what they were expected to do. When a guard pointed to a man at the end of the first row, he shouted, "One."

"No, no. *Ichi!*"

During their time as prisoners the men had learned to count in Japanese. They counted off briskly at first, but at "eighteen"— *ju-hachi*—a man hesitated. Someone prompted him, and he shouted out the correct word, but by then a guard was rushing toward him, yelling. Wally was so accustomed to such yelling that he didn't think much about it. He was looking down the line, trying to see what number he would have to come up with. But the guard stopped in front of the prisoner who had hesitated, and he slammed him with his rifle, sending him sprawling to the ground. By then another guard had joined him. The two kicked at the prisoner, striking him in the ribs and stomach.

Wally knew the guy—a man named Stewart. He had been

a big man at one time, but he had suffered more than his share of sickness and was worn down more than most. He couldn't take a lot of beating. But no one moved; no one spoke. To do anything that showed rebellion, even a reaction, was to bring down wrath upon themselves. That much everyone knew.

Wally watched, saw Stewart pull himself up, slowly, and stand again, bent forward. And now a lot of things were clear. There was no way the men could count all the way to fifty without more mistakes, so more men would be beaten. That was the immediate reality. What ran much deeper was the realization that nothing had changed. These guards were going to be as brutal as the ones he had known in the Philippines. Wally felt the air go out of him.

He felt concern for poor Stewart, but beatings had become such a part of his life that he couldn't work up a lot of emotion over seeing one more. He wasn't even that frightened of making a mistake and receiving his own beating. He had survived plenty, and he knew he could do it again. What he felt was disappointment. He should have known better. It had been stupid of him to think that things might be different here.

Wally stood his ground, came up with *niju-roku* for twenty-six when his turn came, but listened, without moving, as another man, this one behind him, was brutally beaten by the same two guards. He understood the game exactly. The guards wanted to make it clear from the beginning who was boss. The Americans needed to be humiliated, and two beatings were apparently enough, in their judgment, to establish that. If not, they would have beaten others—for any trumped-up reason.

When the men were finally marched to the mess hall, they filed through the food line, and Wally could see the others, not riled by what they had just experienced—too accustomed to it to let that happen—but more subdued, certainly feeling the same disappointment that he was. At the same time, there was the anticipation of food and maybe some lingering hope that it would be better than what they had been given in the past.

The meal was a bowl of rice and a bowl of thin soup. The rice was better cooked than some they had eaten, but there was not much of it, and the soup was mostly water. It seemed unlikely, too, that the men would get much opportunity to scrounge extra food, so this would be very little to live on.

By the time the men sat down at the tables, Wally could see it in all their eyes: the disillusionment, the sadness. No one said much. They simply ate what they had, but they were sinking into themselves, looking for strength, or maybe some state of hollowness that would keep them from feeling.

A man with a stubbly beard stepped with a limp to the table where Wally was eating with his friends. He was an American prisoner who apparently worked in the mess hall. "Hi. My name's Chet," he said. "It ain't no feast, is it?" He smiled. He looked fairly healthy, with more meat on his bones than most, but men who worked in mess halls usually managed to eat more than others. He was, however, missing most of his teeth—a problem with a lot of the prisoners.

"Is this the same every time?" Chuck asked.

"Afraid so. They put a few little chunks of meat in the soup now and then. But not very often."

"What do we get in the mornings?" Wally asked.

"Same thing. And they give you a cup of rice to put in one of them little *bento* boxes. You take that to the mine with you."

"How's the work in the mine?" Chuck asked.

"Well, it's hard work. It's a long hike over to the entrance, and then they run you on a train, down and way out under the bay. The train is open, and the ride is colder than an ice box, summer or winter. This here mine was condemned before the war. It's falling in all over the place. Sometimes they'll send you into places that are caved in and make you dig 'em back open."

"How long is the work day?"

"Twelve hours or so, counting the walk back and forth. They get you up in the dark, and most of the year they bring you back in the dark, too. You don't see the sunlight very often."

Most of the men had quickly finished their food, and now they were staring at the bowl, or at the table, saying nothing.

"Do we get any days off?" Wally asked.

"Every tenth day you're supposed to be off, but sometimes you get stuck on a special crew that day. If you do, you're looking at twenty-one straight days before you get a rest. Everyone sleeps on that day anyway. That's all there is here, work and sleep."

Wally didn't want to hear anymore, and he knew the others didn't either. He could look at them and see what they were feeling.

"How long have you been here?" one of the men from the next table asked.

Chet turned around. "About a year. Come from the Philippines, the same as you guys. A lot of the men here come from other places, though. There's lots of Limeys and Aussies, along with us Americans."

"So how did you get this job, here in the mess hall?" the same man asked.

"I got hurt in the mine last winter—broke my foot real bad. I wasn't worth nothing, so the Japs let me work in here. But this might be worse than the mine. The guy who runs this mess hall—an American Navy Lieutenant named Langston—he's worse than any Jap." Chet called the man a filthy name. "Watch out for the guards here, but more than anyone, watch out for Langston. He'll catch you with your cap on in here—or some stupid thing like that—and take away your food for a day or two. Or he'll report you to the guards, and they come and beat you. The men here are going to kill Langston someday if they get a chance. I'm surprised they haven't gotten him before now."

"What about—"

"I gotta get away from here. I can't get caught standing around talking. You'll know soon enough. This ain't no worse than most of the camps back in the Philippines, I guess. Not so many die because there ain't so many kinds of sickness. But you'll never work harder in your life. Down in the third level of the mine the tunnels run with water up to your ankles sometimes, and the guards are just waiting for a chance to catch you wasting time." He hesitated, and then he added, "I don't mean to be the guy that brings bad news, but you might as well know what you've got to put up with." He walked away.

The men at the table returned to their silence, but in a few minutes a prisoner at the next table leaned over. "We talked to a GI back at our barracks. He was down with some kind of sickness and couldn't work. He told us pretty much the same story, but he did say we get paid a little every day. It's supposed to be enough to buy a cigarette once in a while."

This seemed very good news to some of the guys, but it meant nothing to Wally. What he hoped was that the money would add up, and maybe there would be a way to spend it on extra food.

After the men ate their rice and drank their soup, they returned to their barracks. The interpreter came around and told them they would be receiving training early in the morning, so they'd better get a good night's sleep. Wally didn't have to be told twice; he knew that was true. But still, when he lay down on the floor next to Chuck, he found himself unable to drift off. He was dead tired, but reality was setting in, and he found himself struggling.

"I wonder how much longer I can do this," he said, the words almost involuntary, like a sigh.

Chuck didn't respond for a time. Finally, he said, "That's what I was thinking."

"I guess we take one day at a time," Wally said. "Like always." He was worried he had said the wrong thing.

"What if the war keeps going for years?"

It was the worst of Wally's fears. Whenever he thought of the distant future, he pictured himself back in Utah, eating with his family, sleeping in a nice bed. That's what kept him going, and some period of months, not years, was always the

time frame he imagined for that return to his old life. But at the
first of the war, he had never thought it could last this long, and
he actually knew little about what was happening now.
Sometimes the guards in the Philippines, with their limited
English, had made claims about great Japanese victories. On
the other hand, rumors would spread that the Allies were on
the verge of finishing Japan off. Wally had no way of knowing
what was true, but when he felt himself getting worn down he
would admit the possibility that he might have years to go, and
then his confidence would vanish.

But he knew better than to admit his doubts to his friend.
Chuck didn't need that right now. "Every camp I've been in
looked bad at first," Wally said. "But we figure out ways to make
it all right. There's always a way to scrounge food, or get a little
extra sleep. Something. We just have to learn the ropes."

"Do you like corn on the cob?"

"What?"

"I was just thinking about sweet corn. My dad used to raise
some rows of it in our backyard. That and tomatoes. Home-
grown tomatoes. Sometimes I used to pick me about six cobs of
corn and a couple of those huge tomatoes, right off the vine, and
I'd make me a whole meal out of it. Boil up the corn, slap a lot
of butter on the ears, and go after 'em. Get the butter all over
my face. And eat those big tomatoes, just like eating an apple."

"With salt?"

"Yup."

"What got you thinking about that?"

"It's August. That's when the corn and the tomatoes would
come on."

"Did your mom can a lot of stuff in the fall?"

"That's all she talked about. I had a cousin from up in
Willard, by Brigham City. They had big peach orchards. We'd
drive up there every year and buy a couple of bushels of those
great big Elberta peaches, and Mom would bottle 'em. She'd

get all of us helping her. I didn't like that so much, but I sure liked eating the peaches all winter long."

"My mom always put up a lot of jam. Strawberry. Raspberry. Apricot. How would you like to have a big old slice of bread, hot from the oven, with lots of butter and homemade jam?"

"I'll take two, if you don't mind. And could I also have a great big glass of milk?"

"Yeah. Milk. Sometimes I forget there is such a thing."

Art was lying on the other side of Chuck. Wally hadn't known he was awake. But now he said, "How would you like to drive in a car, stop at a hamburger joint—"

"With your girl?" someone in the room asked.

"Well, yeah. That would be nice. But right now, I'm just thinking about the food. I'm ordering me a big hamburger with mustard and ketchup and pickles and onion and lettuce, and a big slice of tomato. When I bite into it, the juice and ketchup and stuff get all over my hands."

From the far end of the room another voice said, "With a chocolate milkshake and an order of fries."

"Hey, if we're going to eat," Don said, "we can do better than a hamburger. Let's order a big ol' steak, about an inch and a half thick—nice and pink on the inside."

A couple of the guys slept through all this, but most had something to contribute. They wanted a slice of cherry pie, with ice cream, or maybe mom's fried chicken.

When the feast finally ended and the men fell silent, Wally knew that most of them weren't asleep. He could hear them breathing but not yet drawing the long steady breaths of sleep. He knew they were thinking, trying to accept these new circumstances and deal with them. But they were also thinking about food, about family, about whatever it was that had kept them going for the past two years, and making sure they didn't lose sight of it—or the smell of it—because they were going to need all their strength, all their resources, to get through this next ordeal.

3

On that dreadful August morning when the train had carried Alex away, Anna had stood on the platform and watched his car for as long as she could see it. Only then did she realize that she had no plans, no idea what she was going to do with the rest of her day. Nor was there anything she could think to do. Finally, she made her way out of Victoria station. She didn't feel like going home yet, so she strolled toward Buckingham Palace and into St. James Park. She had stopped crying by then, but a dull sense of gloom had set in. So many long days were ahead of her now.

It was a warm, bright day, but she felt an absence—not the anguish she had experienced as she let go of him, but a frightful emptiness. She walked the path along the lengthy pond and then continued on to Whitehall. As she passed 10 Downing Street, she wondered about Winston Churchill, perhaps in his nearby "war rooms," perhaps making decisions that would affect Alex's life, and hers. It seemed that a few people in the world were making all the decisions for everyone else now. She wondered what would happen if all the weary soldiers simply decided to quit fighting.

At Trafalgar Square she had intended to catch the Underground, but the thought of going home still didn't appeal to her, so she kept walking, now along Haymarket to Picadilly Circus. As always, the place was full of soldiers—especially Americans. Most were on leave, and at this hour of the day they looked like tourists, but at night the West End always turned wild, the pubs and Soho brothels filling up as the cinemas and theatres emptied out. Drunkenness seemed the most appealing state for these soldiers. They were kids, for the most part, and they were far from home. To Anna there always seemed something pathetic in their merrymaking, as though they were just going through the motions, behaving the way they thought soldiers on leave were supposed to behave. They should have been back in Iowa or Oregon or Texas, holding down jobs, or farming, maybe married to their high-school sweethearts and starting families.

She had already walked a long way, and she knew her mother would wonder about her, but the day looked imposing, so Anna kept going. She took her time, gazed into shop windows, watched people on the streets. Some buildings had been razed; others were damaged and boarded up; but London was functioning. She followed Regent all the way to Oxford Street, and Oxford to Baker. By the time she reached her building, she was worn out, but even then she hated to go inside. Still, she trudged up the stairs and used her key to enter the flat. When she did, her mother immediately called from the kitchen, "Anna, where have you been? I've been worried about you."

Anna stepped into the kitchen, but she didn't answer.

"Are you all right?" Frieda Stoltz asked, in German.

"Yes. I'm fine." Anna was trying to use English with her mother—to help her learn.

"Where have you been?"

"Walking."

Sister Stoltz came to Anna, put her arms around her. "Oh, Anna. I know how hard this is."

Anna gave up the English and said in German, "All over the

world men are having to leave their wives. I'm only one of millions. How can I feel sorry for myself?"

"If millions have sore hearts, that doesn't mean your heart hurts any less."

They were standing in the kitchen, and the bright light was filling the room. Anna was thankful for that. At least this wasn't one of those gray London days, like so many that lay ahead. "But I can do this. I'm not weak."

"You're the strongest girl I know."

"No. I don't think so." Anna finally stepped away from her mother. She wanted to go to her bedroom.

"With Peter gone from us, you've kept me going, Anna. If it weren't for you, I would sit at this kitchen table and cry all day."

"No you wouldn't, Mama. You're stronger than any of us." The little kitchen smelled of boiled potatoes, of cabbage, from the night before. For so many years the Stoltzes had gotten by on very little. Times were not much better for them now, even though Brother Stoltz was getting paid to do some translating for the SIS—the British intelligence agency.

"I hope Peter is the strongest," Sister Stoltz said. "He will have to be."

"He *is* strong. He'll be all right." But Anna was not actually so sure of that. When the Stoltzes had escaped into France, Peter hadn't made it across the border. A day never went by without her wondering where he was—or whether the Gestapo might have found him.

"Alex will be all right, too," Sister Stolz said. "God brought the two of you together. It's what he wants."

Anna walked to the hall that led to her bedroom. "I'm going to write Alex a letter," she said. She had promised to write every day, but she hadn't planned to start already. The idea to do so was mostly an excuse to go to her bedroom, to be alone.

"Yes. That's good. He'll want to hear from you as soon as possible."

So Anna went to her room and closed the door. She needed to change her clothes. She knew Alex loved her dress—the one with the daisies in the print—so she wanted to keep it nice for him. But she sat down on her bed, and she wondered whether her mother was right, that God wanted Alex to come back to her. In the early days of the war, while hidden in the Hochs' cellar in Berlin, she had pleaded with the Lord that she could come out into the light of day and find her way to Alex. Those desires had been granted; she had to remember that and be thankful. She needed to remember, too, that it was she who had wanted to marry and not wait. She had told Alex that if she lost him in the war, she could wait through mortality so long as she knew she would have him forever. But now, sitting here alone, forever seemed very far off.

Finally she got up and changed. Then she got her stationery from her dresser drawer. She sat in a wooden captain's chair by the window, in the pleasant light, and she placed the writing paper on her lap, with a German/English dictionary underneath for a writing surface. She knew she would need the dictionary to check her spelling—and sometimes just to think of the right word.

"My Dear Alex," she wrote, and without warning, tears filled her eyes. She leaned back to keep them from dripping onto the paper. She told herself she didn't need to cry, and then she dipped her pen into a little bottle of ink and began her letter:

I watched you go away from me today, and only then did I know what it would mean. You are half of me now, and I don't know how to live, only half myself. Do you know what I try to say? I want you to feel as I do, and also I don't want it. I want no pain for you the same.

Alex, do not worry about me. After today, I will be fine. I will make myself busy. I will trust and hope, and I will think good thoughts of you. In those bad years when we could not write letters, I always believed we would see each other again. This time is better. We can know each other's thoughts. Please write me every day. Please tell me what you think about. And then we are together. Then I am not only half myself.

It is a sunny day in London. I walked a very long time, all the way home from the train station. All that time, I felt very sad. But now I feel a little better. That is because I can tell you I love you, and I know you will have my letter soon. In bed tonight, I will miss having you close to me, but I have already found more happiness than many do in a whole life. I am thankful for that, and I say to you auf Wiedersehen and I love you. I will write again tomorrow and will not be so sad by then.

With all my love,
Anna

A few days later, Anna got a letter from Alex. She took it to her room and opened it carefully with a little penknife. What she read was what she wanted so much to hear:

Dearest Anna,

I got your first letter today. It meant so much to me. Your English was great, but don't feel that you have to write in English if it's easier to say what you want to say in German.

I guess I'm back in the swing of things. We have some new boys in my squad who seem like pretty okay guys, though awfully young, and of course, it was great to see Curtis and Duncan and the other men. Lieutenant Summers is the company commander now, which is great. He's the best soldier I know. He and I sat down and chatted for a while yesterday. He feels like we'll be heading into the action before very long. I think I'm getting myself ready for that. At first, I didn't want to be here, and that's all I could think about, but I know that this war has to be fought, so we might as well try to get it over with. I don't like anything about war, but I don't see any way out of it, either. Sometimes I want to avoid going back into battle, but if I don't go, some other guy has to, and why is that right?

Anna, I understood exactly what you meant in your letter. This life here in the camp doesn't seem right to me. I go through the motions, but I feel as though I'm not really here. Part of me is with you—the best part of me. Men are odd creatures when no women are around. It's like they lose touch with everything cultivated and refined. I see it in myself. I never felt so good in my life as I did during that time we had together on our honeymoon. I want to come back before too long and feel that way forever. Maybe that isn't

possible—not entirely—but I know I will always be a better person with
you than I am away from you.

Some think the war in Europe will end by Christmas—or even sooner
than that. Maybe I'll make a jump and get pulled out, and then it will be
over before I have to go back. Let's hope and pray we'll be back together before
very long at all.

If our regiment doesn't get pulled out right away, I can possibly get a
pass for a weekend. I'll let you know if that can happen. Maybe I'll see you
soon. Until then, know that I love you. I lie on my bunk at night and long
for the touch of your skin, and all day little glimpses of you jump into my
head. You really are the most beautiful girl I've ever seen; that isn't just some-
thing I say. And you're also the best—so considerate and good, so strong
and wise and funny. God must love me very much to have given me you.

Love, Alex

Anna read the letter over and over. Each time she told herself she would put it away, but she could occupy herself only a
few minutes, and then she would open it and read it slowly
once again. She read it all evening, then awoke in the morning
and read it one more time in the early light of day before she
got out of bed.

* * *

Bea Thomas was sitting at the kitchen table. When she had
come home from the plant that afternoon, she had found a letter from Anna, her new daughter-in-law. It was a touching letter, full of love for Alex, and love for the Thomases, whom she
had never met. Sister Thomas could hardly stand to think that
this lovely girl lived in London, so far away, where the two
couldn't even meet each other. Sometimes Sister Thomas worried that Alex would not return from the war, and he would
never have a chance to have children with Anna—and the
Thomases would never know this girl as part of their family.

Sister Thomas heard footsteps on the stairs, and then, in
another few seconds, looked up to see her daughter Beverly
step through the door into the kitchen. "Look. This is from

Anna," she told Beverly. "It's all in English, and just so sweet it breaks your heart."

Beverly took the letter from her mother and sat down at the table. Sister Thomas watched her as she read. By the end, there were tears on Beverly's cheeks. "I wish I could meet her," she said. "She looks so pretty in those pictures Alex sent."

"She sounds nice, too, don't you think?"

Beverly nodded.

"She'll be here one day, Bev. And she and Alex will have beautiful babies. I just can't wait for that."

"Me too."

"What's wrong, honey?"

Beverly looked across the room. The refrigerator had just kicked on, and it was vibrating noisily. The Thomases were luckier than many, to have a refrigerator, but the old thing wasn't cooling very well anymore, and there was no way to buy a new one. "Do you know Janet Pedersen?" Beverly asked.

"I know Vivian—her mother."

"Janet's brother, Lowell, died in the war. He got sick from being in the jungle."

"Did the Pedersens take the news really hard?"

"I don't know. Janet didn't come to school today. Our teacher told us."

"Maybe you ought to go see her."

Beverly seemed surprised. "I don't want to," she said. "I wouldn't know what to say."

"But if you wrote her a little note and took it over to her, I'm sure that would mean a lot to her. You've been through it, so you understand how she feels."

Beverly seemed to consider that, but she didn't respond. Instead, she asked, "What happened to that friend of Wally's? Mel? I heard you talking about him with Dad last night."

"He's home. He's all right. He got his leg hurt quite bad, and he has to use a cane for now, but he's finished with the war, and he's going back to college. He stopped by to see us at the plant, and we had a nice chat. He's happy to be home."

"What hurt him?"

"He was with the engineers, in France. He was helping build bridges and things like that. I guess one of his partners stepped on a land mine, right next to him. The other boy was killed." Sister Thomas knew exactly what Beverly was worrying about, and she didn't want that. "Have you got a lot of homework tonight?" she asked.

"No. I already did it."

"Your dad has to work late. What do you say we go to a show?"

"Really?"

"Maybe we can get LaRue to go with us. What's playing over at the Marlo?"

"Mom, it's Wednesday. We never go to shows on weeknights."

"Well, then, it's about time we did. Go look in the paper. See what's playing. If we have to, we'll go downtown. Maybe we'll even eat out tonight."

"Eat out?" Beverly was grinning. She was beginning, lately, to look more grown up. Sister Thomas had noticed she was finally starting to "develop." The two of them had already had their little talk about the way a girl's body would change during puberty—and Sister Thomas had tried to be a little more open than she had been with Bobbi or even LaRue. But Beverly had an innocent quality about her, so different from LaRue. She never talked about boys, never pleaded to go to dances, and she had too little of what LaRue possessed in abundance: self-confidence.

Beverly found the newspaper in her father's office, where he had read it early that morning. She and her mother spread it out on the kitchen table and turned to the movie section. They were looking at their choices when they heard LaRue come through the front door. Beverly called out, "LaRue, do you want to go to a show? On a *Wednesday* night."

LaRue walked around to the kitchen. "What's going on?" she asked, obviously surprised.

"We're going out on the town," Mom said. "We thought we'd kick up our heels a little."

LaRue laughed. "I'm going to the club," she said. For the past few months LaRue had been volunteering at the United Service Organizations club—the USO, as people called it—downtown in Salt Lake City, not far from the train station. She would usually go two or three times a week. President Thomas wasn't very excited about the idea, but LaRue made a big thing out of "working for the war effort," and it was hard to argue with that. What worried Sister Thomas was that LaRue might let her school work go if she went to the club too often. School had only started the week before, on September 7, but already LaRue had seemed rather lax about her homework.

"Oh, come on, LaRue," Beverly said. "Couldn't you call and cancel? You did that once before."

LaRue smiled. "I don't know. What's playing?" She was wearing a pretty pleated skirt, red and blue plaid, with a red V-neck sweater and a white blouse. It was typical dress for the girls at school, but LaRue, with her pretty coloring and her striking hazel eyes, made any outfit look dazzling.

"*Cover Girl* is playing at the Marlo," Beverly said. "Rita Hayworth and Gene Kelly."

"I've seen it," LaRue said. "What's playing downtown?"

"Hey, this sounds good," Beverly said. She giggled. "*Manhunt* at the Rialto. Listen to this." She read from the paper, "'Teenagers! Bold as their scarlet lips, reckless as their racing young blood—heedless of danger—disdainful of conse- quences!'"

"That sounds *good*," LaRue said. "I'll bet Mom would like it, too."

"I don't *think* so," Mom said, but she was laughing. "Here's what sounds fun to me: *Greenwich Village,* at the Centre Theatre. Carmen Miranda. Don Ameche. William Bendix. *In* technicolor."

"Oh, Mom, those Carmen Miranda shows are *so* stupid. Her and her fruit basket for a hat."

"Yes, but it's"—she looked down to read—"'a footloose, frivolous, fancy-free musical, full of fun and fascination!'"

LaRue rolled her eyes, but Beverly said, "Come on, LaRue. It'll be fun. We're going to *eat out,* too."

"I know what I'll do," Sister Thomas said. "I'll call Grandma Thomas. Maybe she'll go with us. We'll make it a night out with the girls."

"If Grandma will go, I will," LaRue said. "She's more fun than both of you two put together."

As it turned out, Grandma Thomas was only too happy to go along. She even offered to drive her car. She and Grandpa didn't drive much these days, so they usually had gasoline rationing coupons to spare. Mom sent LaRue upstairs to do her homework, and then at six Grandma Thomas picked the "girls" up in her Hudson. It had been a new car just before the war, and it still looked like new now. Sister Thomas only worried about Grandma's driving. She seemed to forget what she was doing when she got talking, and she drove way too fast.

Grandma wanted to eat at the Hotel Utah, and she had dressed accordingly. She had on a black crepe dress with a fancy little silk peplum around her trim hips. But Sister Thomas knew, even if they could get in without a reservation, they would never have time to eat at the Empire Room—not if they were going to get the girls home at a decent hour. So they settled on doing something Beverly loved—and Grandma could hardly believe. They ate at the lunch counter in Woolworth's.

LaRue and Beverly ordered hamburgers and vanilla malts, and Sister Thomas had her favorite, a "hot sandwich": an openfaced roast beef sandwich, with mashed potatoes, and with gravy over everything. Grandma ordered a club sandwich and a Pepsi Cola, and then whispered, "Bea, don't tell Al that I *sinned* tonight. I think I need a little pick-me-up." She was being a good sport about eating at the counter. It never seemed to cross her mind that anyone might think it strange she would be there in her expensive black dress—with her black gloves and purse and her hair cupped at her neck in a Lily Daché net.

After the waitress took the order and walked away, Grandma said, "Wasn't she a pretty young woman? I wonder who her parents are? I'll have to ask her."

"Grandma," LaRue said, "you don't know everyone in Salt Lake anymore. It's getting to be a big place."

Grandma, in her usual flamboyant way, waved her hand and said, "You're half right. The town *is* getting big—but I still know everyone. At least everyone who's worth knowing."

Sister Thomas laughed. She liked being out like this; she even liked Grandma's brashness. Sometimes she wished she could be at least a little more like that herself.

"Ah . . . it's so good to get out of the house," Grandma said, too loudly. "I'm so tired of the way we live these days. I hate all these posters telling me to hush my mouth. 'Loose lips,' my foot. What do I know that anyone wants to hear? I'm just tired of the whole business: Save your fat. Save your string. Save your paper. Don't wear out your tires. Don't use too much electricity. Buy bonds. It just never stops. You girls have never had the chance to be young and fancy free."

"I know. And my *young blood* is racing," LaRue said. Grandma didn't know the reference, but Beverly did, and she giggled. LaRue began to tap her finger on the counter and to sing with the radio music playing in the background. It was a crazy Spike Jones version of "Cocktails for Two," with lots of silly whistles and sound effects.

Sister Thomas said, "The headline in the paper tonight said the government is basing all its plans on the belief that the war in Europe will be over by October 31."

"Wouldn't that be wonderful?" Grandma said. "I hope

they're right. But how much longer will we have to fight the Japs?"

That was the question everyone was asking these days.

When the waitress came back with the drinks, Grandma said, "Tell me, young lady, who are your parents?"

"You wouldn't know them. They're not from here."

"Really? Where do they live?"

"In Southern Illinois. That's where I grew up."

"And what brought you here?"

"My husband. He's in the Army. He was stationed at Fort Douglas, but he got sent overseas. I couldn't go with him, so I decided to stay here where it's not hard to find a job."

"Do you like it here, then?"

"Well . . . yes." She sounded hesitant, maybe careful. "I miss home a lot. I guess anyone would."

Sister Thomas thought she was lovely, as Grandma had said. She had a simple quality about her, with pretty color in her cheeks and a sweet smile. She reminded Sister Thomas just a little of Bobbi.

"But are people kind to you?" Grandma asked.

"Most of them are."

Sister Thomas heard the hesitancy again, and so she asked, "Are you made to feel like an outsider?"

"A little. People always ask me what ward I'm in, and when I say I'm not Mormon, they don't know what to say to me."

"Well . . . ," Grandma said, in a huff. "They should welcome you with open arms. You're a *beautiful* girl. Like one of our own."

The waitress laughed just a little and nodded. Everyone but Grandma seemed to catch the irony in the words, but Grandma remained unabashed. "We have to hurry," Sister Thomas finally said. "We want to get to the Centre Theatre as soon as we can."

"I'll move things along," the waitress said, and she left.

As soon as she was gone, Grandma said, "A ward is just a part of town. She doesn't have to take offense."

Sister Thomas looked over at LaRue, and they both smiled. The radio was playing a Glenn Miller song: "Sentimental Journey." Bea found herself tapping her toe to the music, something she didn't remember doing for a long time.

After dinner the four walked to the theater. The movie was certainly as silly as advertised, but Sister Thomas loved the fun of it, the music and the dancing. When it was over and they were all back in the car and driving home, she felt more relaxed than she had in a long time. It was a pleasant evening, and the air coming through the car windows was wonderfully cool.

"I knew I should have gone to the club," LaRue told the others. "That show was as dumb as I thought it would be."

"Oh, hush," Grandma said. "You laughed as much as anyone."

"Not quite," Beverly said. "I laughed the most."

Sister Thomas liked that. Beverly was too serious for her own good most of the time.

"I'll tell you who I like," Grandma said. "That Don Ameche. I've always wanted to kiss a man with a mustache—just to see if it tickles. I kissed my Uncle Henry when I was a girl. He had whiskers and a mustache clear down on his lips. I didn't like that at all. But then, Uncle Henry chewed tobacco, and that's all I could think about when I kissed him. What I want is for old Don Ameche to throw me back, the way he did Carmen Miranda, and really smooch me. Just once before I die."

Beverly screeched with laughter. "I'm going to tell Grandpa on you," she said.

"Ahh, what does he care?" Grandma said. "He kisses me like I'm an old lady. He puckers up like he's got no teeth and gives me a little smack that lasts about half a second. I want one of those big old long ones, good and wet."

"Ugh!" Beverly said.

"Well, what do you know? You've never kissed Don Ameche or anyone else. A little slobber makes it good. And who knows what that mustache might do? It might be like horseradish on a nice cut of roast beef."

Sister Thomas had forgotten she could laugh so hard. She was wiping tears away and thinking how much she needed to get home to the bathroom. She glanced toward the back seat and saw Beverly leaning on LaRue, the two folded up together they were laughing so hard.

"I don't know what you're all laughing about," Grandma said. "There was a day when I could walk down State Street and stop traffic. Old Don Ameche would have begged me for a kiss—and I would have told him, 'Sorry, I can do better.' All the same, I wouldn't mind trying out that little mustache."

By the time the laughter finally quieted down, Grandma was halfway up Twenty-First South, nearing home. Beverly, apparently with kissing still on her mind, said, "In that newsreel we saw, when they showed the soldiers marching in Paris, why were all those French girls kissing our American boys?"

"Paris is finally free," Grandma said. "We kicked the Nazis out. For those girls, that's their way of celebrating—and thanking our boys. French girls are like that anyway—in case you didn't know."

"It sounds like you are, too, Grandma," LaRue said.

"Naw. I just talk."

"Girls in Salt Lake wouldn't start kissing soldiers like that, would we?" Beverly said.

"Well, maybe you ought to, Bev," Grandma told her. "When the war ends, I want you to kiss every soldier you can find. They deserve it, and by darn, so do you—just for getting through all this."

Beverly giggled. "I don't think I'll kiss any soldiers," she said. "Just Wally. And Alex. That'll be enough kissing for me."

The car fell silent, and suddenly, for Sister Thomas, the war was back. She felt the easy mood slip away—in the car, and in herself.

"I wonder what those two boys still have to go through before it's all over," Grandma said.

That, of course, was just what Sister Thomas was wondering.

Bobbi Thomas and Afton Story were at a ward luau in Honolulu. Parties of this kind weren't so common now with the war dragging on and so many food items hard to get, but Brother and Sister Nuanunu had been able to buy a pig from a farmer, and they decided to hold the luau at their house and invite the entire ward.

Bobbi loved the members of her ward, but she had never been able to become part of things as much as she would have liked. She was the one holding back, and not the members, but it just wasn't her way to be quite so affectionate and open as the Hawaiian members were. Soon after Bobbi and Afton arrived, Brother Nuanunu began to coax them to come over and learn to dance the hula.

Bobbi had always loved to dance, but only when she could disappear among a crowd. She never liked to be among the first couples out on the floor. And this, dancing by herself, in front of others—and doing a dance that looked so sensuous—was really uncomfortable to her. But Brother Nuanunu wouldn't take no for an answer. "You have to understand the hula," he kept saying. "You mustn't leave the islands and never learn it."

"Let me watch, and you tell me about it," Bobbi pleaded.

"No, no. You have to do it, not just see it."

Bobbi couldn't understand that, but she had learned that her logic often clashed with that of her Hawaiian friends.

"When you dance the hula, you speak with your hands and your feet, Sister Thomas. It's what we've been doing from the earliest times."

And so Bobbi and Afton, with some other haole members, lined up behind a pretty young woman from the ward, and they tried to imitate her motions. She moved sideways, back and forth, with her knees bent, her hips undulating. Her hands moved constantly as she spoke words to the ukelele music that a brother was playing.

Bobbi felt awkward, but she fell into the rhythm of the dance. She had watched hula dancers many times and had some idea how the dances were supposed to go, but she couldn't forget herself and enter the motion fully the way the Hawaiian girls did. She and Afton laughed as they bumped into each other or got off step. By the time the first dance had ended and another had started, however, Bobbi had begun to think less about the people watching and more about the dance, and she found a surprising satisfaction in the gentle movements. Still, when the second dance ended, she used the opportunity to slip away and sit down.

Afton continued to dance, and Bobbi watched. Hazel Nuanunu came to Bobbi and sat down on a kitchen chair that she had brought outside. Hazel was a large woman with a pleasant, round face and an enormous smile. She was wearing a bright muumuu, full of yellows and oranges and reds, which contrasted beautifully with her rich brown skin. "That's not the real hula," she said. "It doesn't tell the old stories. There shouldn't be this silly music. There should be a chant."

"How did it get changed?"

"I don't know. I think it all comes from picture shows. It's what the haole tourists could understand. But the real hula is a religious dance."

"Someone told me it's all about the myths of the old gods."

"That's right. About Pele and her sisters. About the way Hawaii came to be."

"But you don't believe any of that, do you?"

Hazel didn't answer for a time. And then she only said, "There are many things to believe."

Bobbi wasn't sure how to think about that. She didn't want to think that Hazel accepted other gods—and superstitions.

"It tells us who we are, Sister Thomas. The haoles came a long time ago, and they took almost everything. But we have to keep some of the old ways. If we don't, we lose too much. We lose *us*."

Bobbi told herself she needed to be accepting. "I've studied the Greek myths," she said. "Some of the stories are wonderful, and they teach good lessons. I really find them very interesting."

Hazel smiled. There always seemed something deep and complete in her pleasure, and now she was clearly enjoying some irony she found in Bobbi's words. Bobbi knew that, and it embarrassed her.

"You couldn't give yourself to the dance, could you?" Sister Nuanunu said. "You learned the steps, and the hand movements, but you wouldn't show yourself to the boys the way our girls do."

"It just seems a little too . . . suggestive."

Hazel laughed, her whole face illuminated with some delight she seemed to find in Bobbi's choice of words. "Men and women make babies. It's what life is all about. Didn't your mother tell you those things?"

Bobbi knew she was blushing. And suddenly she felt herself in over her head. Was the hula somehow about *that*? "I thought you said it was religious," she said.

"Having babies *is* religious. Haoles are too embarrassed about things that are part of life. I can never understand that. You're afraid to let yourselves move."

"Yes. I think you're right about that," Bobbi said, and she

laughed at herself. She was wearing a muumuu, which was comfortable, but whenever she went out in public dressed that way, she felt as though she were walking around in her nightgown.

"Haoles. Every time you enjoy yourselves, you stop, look around, and say, 'What if someone sees me having a good time?' Hawaiians aren't like that. We know how to be happy."

"That's really true, Hazel. Sometimes I wish I could let go just a little bit more. But it scares me. It's just not the way I've been raised."

"You think too much. You have to explain everything. You don't know how to listen to your hearts. God doesn't speak to us with words, Bobbi. He touches us. He fills up our chests. If that's God's language, don't you think haoles should learn to understand it?"

It was a stunning perspective, and Bobbi thought it explained so much of the problem she had with her own faith. "That's true," she told Sister Nuanunu. "I do feel the Lord's spirit that way, but I try to put it into words—to explain what I've experienced—and sometimes the words confuse me. Then I lose the feelings."

Hazel took hold of Bobbi's hand, kissed it, and then pressed the palm to her cheek. "It doesn't matter. I love you. You can't help it that you're not Hawaiian." She laughed in her deep, full voice.

On impulse, Bobbi did something out of character. She pulled Hazel's hand to her own lips, kissed it the same way, and said, "Hazel, I love you too. I hope I'll be part Hawaiian before I leave Honolulu."

"Oh, you sweetheart. You're learning."

Bobbi wanted to think so, but she was self-conscious now, and she let go of Hazel's hand.

"Now tell me about your man," Hazel said. "What's happening to Brother Hammond? When will he come back and make pretty babies with you?"

"I don't know, Hazel. Not until the war is over, I guess."

"He's the best looking haole we ever had in our ward. Does he write letters to you?"

"Yes. But the letters are slow getting here."

"That's all right. He loves you. I could see that."

"I think he does, Hazel, but he's careful. He doesn't say much about love. I think he's afraid he'll be killed—or badly wounded—and he doesn't want to make any promises until he comes home safe and sound."

"And what about you? Do you make promises?"

"I've made more than he has."

"And now you worry about him, don't you?"

"Yes."

Hazel crossed her thick arms over her chest, and she nodded, looking serious. "Haoles are the best worriers I know. They think of every reason not to be happy."

Bobbi laughed. There was too much truth in that. "But so many terrible things could happen to him. He's on a ship, in the middle of the fighting, I think. I don't even know exactly where he is."

"Does the worry help you in some way? Does it help him?"

Bobbi smiled and shook her head.

"Does it change anything?"

"No."

"It's a strange thing, this worry. It does no good, and yet you hold on to it so tightly. And now, I see our people learning how to do it. I think it came like the smallpox, from other lands."

"I can't help worrying, Hazel. I want Richard back, and all I can think is that I'll lose him, the way I lost my brother."

"It will be as God chooses. Nothing can change that."

Bobbi thought of Gene's words: "I do believe there's a heaven. So everything will be all right." But she didn't want to give Richard up. How could God want that to happen?

"You have to trust the Lord, my dear. That's what haoles never want to do."

Bobbi thought about that, too. And then she nodded. "You're right, Hazel. It's what *I* need to do. But it's not easy for me."

"It's like the hula. You have to let go a little."

Bobbi looked across the yard at Afton, who was still dancing and was letting herself flow with the music now. She had on a pretty muumuu, all blue and lavender. With her dark hair and suntanned skin, she looked as though she might be Hawaiian.

"Do you see what my boy Samuel is looking at?" Hazel asked.

Sam was Hazel's handsome son, who was a marine. He had been wounded in the Marshall Islands the winter before. Bobbi and Afton had heard his story when he had spoken in sacrament meeting the previous Sunday. He said he had been hit with shrapnel from a mortar shell. A fragment in his chest had collapsed his lung and nearly killed him, but he had called out to the Lord to save him so he could complete his work on the earth, and he had felt strength pour back into him. A hospital ship had taken him to San Diego, where he had spent several months before being discharged. He had come home only a couple of weeks before.

Bobbi had been amazed by Sam's talk. He had sounded like a mainlander, not only in his pronunciation but also in the way he organized his talk. And yet, he was possessed of that powerful faith so many of the islanders had. At the end of his sermon, he described how he had been serving a stake mission when the war had begun, working alongside the full-time elders. He told of administering to a woman, commanding her to arise from her sickbed, and how she had gotten up and cooked him and the other elders a wonderful dinner. He laughed, and the members laughed with him, and it all seemed quite natural to him, this island personality to go with his haole style of speaking.

But the talk had also perplexed Bobbi. She didn't know how much was God's choice and how much depended on man. Had Gene called out for help in his last moments? Why hadn't the help come? Did God really make the decision about each person's time for dying? Or, in Gene's case, had a bullet decided?

After the meeting Bobbi and Afton had spoken with Sam briefly, and then, on the way home, Afton had said, "I wish he wasn't Hawaiian. I think he's the handsomest man I've ever seen."

"You mean . . . except for Richard?" Bobbi asked.

Afton laughed and said, "Except for nobody. He looks like Nephi must have looked. All those muscles and that bronze skin."

Now, here at the luau, Bobbi could see that Sam also liked what he saw in Afton. He was standing near the dancers, watching, but it was clear that his eyes were only on her.

The hula lessons ended soon after that, and some of the men from the ward danced and sang. Brother Nuanunu was in the middle of everything, wearing a flowered shirt like the others, not a native costume. He danced and sang, even shouted at times. Hazel delighted in that. "He's an old thing, but he still looks pretty good. Don't you think?"

"He's a handsome man. Like Sam," Bobbi said.

"Maybe my Sam spent too long on the mainland. Maybe he likes the looks of the haole girls."

Bobbi looked to see what Hazel was noticing. Sam was standing with Afton. They were drinking punch, talking, paying little attention to the men's dance. Bobbi felt a little uncomfortable about that. She hoped Afton wasn't getting into another one of the "situations" she seemed to find herself in sometimes.

After a few more dances the men joked that they were tired

out and needed to eat. The pig, dug into a pit at the back of the yard, had been cooking over coals for a long time. Some of the men began to uncover it, and the sisters brought other dishes outside to start the buffet. Hazel went off to help, and Bobbi joined her. Bobbi hoped Afton would do the same, but Afton lingered where she was, still talking with Sam.

The dinner was good. Bobbi still avoided poi, but she had learned to like some of the other native foods. She especially liked the taste of the pork, cooked in the smoke pit. She also knew the members quite well now, and she took time to talk with some of them. She thought of the ward parties back home. They were nice but never so vibrant with music and dance and animated chatter. She already knew it was this that she would miss someday, back home, and this that she would never experience again.

On the bus on the way back to Pearl Harbor, Afton didn't mention Sam, so Bobbi didn't either. But in their room, Afton seemed entirely too lighthearted, too lifted, to be excited only by the party. Finally, Bobbi said, "I noticed you enjoyed the dinner more than usual. You must be getting used to Hawaiian food. And *Hawaiians.*"

Afton was sitting in a chair with one foot pulled up. She was painting her toenails, something Bobbi had never seen her do before. The lacquer smell of the polish was filling the room. Afton looked up and rolled her eyes. "I liked the pork," she said.

Bobbi was sitting on her bed. She had been reading Richard's last letter over again, but she put the letter aside now and said, "I think the pork liked you, too."

"If you're referring to Sam, he's not pork. He's *prime* beef." Afton giggled.

"Afton, if you let him believe you like him, you could work yourself into an awkward problem, don't you think?"

Afton let her breath blow out. "Don't. Okay? Don't tell me

what I *should* do. You're not my mother, no matter how hard you try to be."

Bobbi was shocked. And hurt. Afton had never said anything like that to her before. But Bobbi knew she had a tendency to instruct Afton too much, even preach to her. She didn't blame Afton for being irritated. "I'm sorry," she said. And yet, she could see trouble ahead, and when the disaster came, Bobbi would be the one who would have to patch Afton back together.

"I'm sorry too," Afton said, after a minute or so. "I didn't mean to sound like that."

"I just thought—"

"I know. I know everything you could say to me. And you're right. But I don't want to think right now. I haven't been this happy in a long time."

"Are you saying you really like him?"

"I don't know, Bobbi. He really is the best-looking guy I've ever seen. I mean *ever*. And when he looks at me I can see in his eyes that he's thinking the same thing about me. I don't want to stop him from looking at me like that, Bobbi. I've waited a long time for someone to see me that way."

"But if he starts thinking—"

"I know. I know. I know."

Bobbi went back to her letter.

It was Afton who finally spoke. "My mother would die on the spot if she'd seen us. And my dad would get his rifle out and run him off."

Bobbi understood, of course. An interracial marriage—or even a flirtation—was shocking to most people back home. And even though it was much more common in the islands, Bobbi was uneasy about the idea. Afton had always been quite vocal against it herself.

"He's just like us," Afton said. "He talks like we do. When I'm around him, I can't think what would be so bad about going out with him. But there's nothing I could ever say or do that would change the way my family feels."

"I know. I understand that. I even know how they feel."

"What do you mean, you 'know how they feel'?"

"Afton, we've talked all about this. When I saw you two together, it gave me a funny feeling—like it wasn't right. You're the one who's told me that yourself."

"So you were sitting over there thinking I was doing something wrong?"

"No. Not exactly. I just . . . I don't know . . . have a strange reaction to it."

"Bobbi, we were only talking. I wouldn't ever marry him. I don't even plan to go out on a date with him."

"Then why do you let him look at you that way?"

"Let's not talk about this."

"Okay. Fine." Bobbi lay down on her side, using an elbow to prop herself up. Once again she looked at her letter.

"What were you and Hazel talking about? Did she say anything about it?"

"She just pointed out the way Sam was looking at you when you were dancing."

"Oh, Bobbi. I've never felt anything like that. I was stiff at first, but I started getting the feel of the dance, and then I saw him watching me and something happened. I started feeling how the hula is supposed to go. Did you see how good I was getting?"

"I sure did."

"What's that supposed to mean?"

Bobbi set her letter down. "Afton, it's a very . . . *enticing* dance."

"Sexy is what you mean, isn't it?"

"Well, it is."

"I don't think so. It's pretty."

"Hazel told me herself. It's supposed to be sexy."

"Oh, it is not. I wasn't doing it like that anyway."

"Maybe your hands were telling a story, Afton, but Sam skipped the plot. He was concentrating on the *action*."

"Just shut up, okay?" Afton said. But she was smiling. And Bobbi could predict that *this* plot was going to thicken before it was over. "What is Richard telling you these days?" Afton asked, obviously to change the subject.

"He's being transferred—or I guess by now he already has been. He's going to an escort carrier, whatever that is. It's called the *Saint Lo*."

"Will that change anything?"

"I don't know. But I don't like what I can read between the lines."

Afton had finished her toenails. She put the little brush back in the bottle and set the bottle on the nightstand by her bed. Then she put both feet on the floor and admired her work. "You're such a worrier, Bobbi. You always see the worst in anything he says."

"But he sounds concerned—like he's expecting to be in danger. He keeps saying he needs to do his duty, no matter what he's called to do. He never talked like that when he was here. It just sounds like he's trying to remind himself—or maybe convince himself—that the war is worth it, if he has to die."

"Oh, Bobbi, don't say that. You shouldn't even let those words come out of your mouth."

Bobbi knew what Afton meant, but she didn't agree. She had denied the possibility of her brothers being killed, and now Gene was gone. Somehow, to Bobbi, it seemed better to tell herself that Richard might die. If she accepted that reality, and then it came about, maybe it wouldn't undo her quite so much as Gene's death had.

"Bobbi, men are dying. I know that. But a whole lot more make it through. My two brothers are still in safe places, and maybe they'll stay that way. Somehow, I just feel like they'll be okay. It's so much better to think that way."

"Until they don't make it. Like Gene."

"Bobbi, I know. I didn't mean. . . ." Clearly, Afton didn't know how to finish her sentence.

Bobbi understood Afton's attitude. But the war had taken Bobbi's beloved little brother, and Richard was not in a safe place. Neither was Wally. Alex had been wounded once and would probably be returning into harm's way. To make it through, she knew she had to admit to all the possible outcomes.

Bobbi also thought Afton should be a little more realistic herself—not only about her brothers but also about Sam.

5

The C-47 transport had taken some minor anti-aircraft fire, but the pilot had stayed his course, and now Alex had made his jump and was floating downward, in daylight, onto the flattest drop zone he had ever seen. When his feet hit the soft ground in a plowed field, he was able to stay up, collapse his chute, and release it. Then he scanned the area. Hundreds of men were descending in white parachutes—like a snowstorm—but there was no enemy fire. From all appearances, the Germans had been taken completely by surprise, just as the Allies had hoped.

The landing was in Holland. The operation was called "Market Garden," and the concept was exciting. Allied airborne troops were to take and hold a narrow corridor—mostly just a road—angling north and east from Belgium through Holland. The British Guards Armored Division planned a quick thrust up that road. If the troops could cross the Lower Rhine at Arnhem, the Allies could skirt the Siegfried Line and make a break into the industrial Ruhr area of Germany, then east to Berlin. It was September 17, 1944, and Alex had first heard of this mission only two days before, but he was now hopeful that the war would be over by Christmas.

"Move out!" Lieutenant Owen was shouting. "Clear the field before the equipment drop." At the edge of the field, a smoke grenade was putting out a dark plume that marked the assembly point for the company. Alex pulled his M-1 loose and looked around for his men. He repeated Owen's command and then ran toward the smoke.

The men gathered quickly. There were none of the usual injured ankles or bruised shoulders. And no one had trouble finding his unit. No drop had ever gone this well, even in training maneuvers.

The 506th Regiment was heading for the little town of Son. The first objective was to take and hold a bridge over the Wilhelmina Canal, just beyond the village. Second Battalion, Alex's unit, would head straight down a little road to the town. First Battalion would march on its left flank, and Third Battalion would follow, in reserve.

Lieutenant Owen told Alex, "I don't expect any trouble between here and Son. The Germans are over on the other side of Eindhoven, way south of here. But we've got to get to Son fast and take that bridge before the Germans get organized."

So E Company set out walking in file along both sides of the road and keeping up a hard pace. Alex felt some pain in his leg, where he had been wounded. Still, he was in decent condition now, and the pace was no big problem for him. In fact, he found it difficult to take this "operation" seriously. The temperature was mild and the sky blue. Cows were grazing in the fields, and crows were flying about, too content to make much noise. This was nothing like the nighttime terror of the D-Day drop.

The soldiers were all laughing and talking. Duncan kept telling the replacement troops, "This ain't right for you guys to get off so easy. We learned the hard way in Normandy."

Alex watched Howie Douglas. He laughed at Duncan's jibes, but he didn't have much to say. He seemed wary, maybe anxious about what lay ahead.

"Let's hold it down," Alex told his men. But he was feeling good himself. If the Germans weren't ready, and the British troops could dash up this road according to plan—through Eindhoven, Son, Veghel, Grave, Nijmegen, Arnhem, and on into Germany—the operation would be over in a few days. The paratroopers would probably be pulled out. If that happened, Alex might be seeing Anna before long. He had managed to get a three-day pass early in September, and he and Anna had gone on another little honeymoon. They had taken a train to Wales and spent two nights in Merthyr Tydfil, not exactly a romantic setting with its slag heaps and coal-dust–darkened buildings, but a quaint town, and the place the Thomas family forebears had emigrated from more than a hundred years before. Alex and Anna hadn't needed a lake or wild-flowers to feel romantic; they had enjoyed every second together.

As the file of soldiers reached Son, Alex could hear the commotion up ahead. What he heard were not bursts of gun-fire but laughter and shouting. D Company had marched into town ahead of E Company, and the civilians had poured into the streets to greet the soldiers and to celebrate. The local men wanted to shake hands with the troops; the women hugged and kissed them. In some of the buildings, from second-floor windows, orange national flags—forbidden by the Nazis—had appeared, and kids were running about in the streets waving flags or yelling their greetings. All that was fine, but Alex became concerned when his men passed a guest house where the proprietor was offering free beer. Duncan was quick to grab a half-pint mug and begin gulping.

"Come on, keep moving," Alex shouted. "We've got to get to that bridge before the Germans do."

Duncan took a last swig and then wiped his mouth with his sleeve. "Hey, I'm ready for the Krauts now. That's what I needed." He handed the glass back, slapped the barkeeper on the back, and moved on. Things had bogged down, however. Too many people were milling about and getting in the way of the soldiers. A priest was even passing out cigars, and many of the men were lighting up.

Lieutenant Owen had to get firm with the men, but it was hard for Alex not to feel like a hero, a liberator. He accepted an apple a woman handed him, and he thanked her. He tucked it into his pocket, however, and kept shouting at his men. Little Earl Sabin had lit up a cigar and was puffing away. He grinned at Alex. "This war stuff ain't so bad," he said.

"That's enough, Private Sabin. Throw that thing away. We've got a mission to achieve."

Delbert Ernst, in his southern dialect, said, "Put it out, Sabin, but don't throw it away. That's a dern good smoke." He was grinning and puffing on his own cigar.

Alex stepped to Ernst and barked at him, "You get rid of that cigar, soldier. Do you hear me? We've got some serious business ahead of us."

"Sure, sure," Ernst said. He set out walking harder, but he was stabbing his cigar against his jacket sleeve, not throwing it away. The men did settle down once they cleared the town, however, and they marched hard and steady.

Then Alex heard the first artillery shell. He hit the ground with the others, but he was watching all the while. A shell, probably from an 88, had struck just left of the road, about a hundred yards ahead. Alex thought First Platoon, or some of the D Company troops, might have taken casualties. By then, machine-gun fire was also clattering from an emplacement straight down the road.

"Let's go," Lieutenant Owen was yelling. "We've got to get to that bridge before the Germans blow it up."

Alex knew a single machine gun could not stop a whole battalion—even with a big gun back there lobbing in shells from beyond the canal. But this was all real now. He had to get his men moving.

First Platoon pushed ahead and took most of the fire. Alex ran forward and waved for his men to come with him, but it was all he could do to keep his squad up and going. The new guys—the young replacements—would dive to the side of the road every time they heard an incoming shell. They still had no sense of which ones were close and which were not.

Alex heard grenades go off, and then the machine-gun fire stopped. At the same time, D Company began to move ahead faster. "We've gotta keep up, men!" Alex told his squad. "Go hard." He ran up the road, keeping low, watching, at the same time hoping that D Company would take the bridge without much resistance.

And then a powerful concussion struck him, knocked him down. The bridge had blown, and the air was full of debris. Alex curled up tight as huge planks and rocks rained down, thumped onto the ground.

It was all over in seconds, and Alex jumped up to see that his men were all right. Nothing was left of the bridge, and a sickening sense of failure hit him. If the battalion had gotten through Son more quickly, or kept moving faster when the shelling had started, the Germans might not have been able to blow up the bridge. Now, somehow, a passage would have to be rebuilt. The problem with the Allied plan was that it depended on speed, and any weak link could bring the whole operation down.

Owen ran back along the road to Alex. "Summers just told me to get to the canal and set up east of where the bridge used to be. Our battalion is supposed to lay down covering fire while 1st Battalion figures out some way to cross."

Alex ran with his men to the canal. The gun had stopped firing, and Alex suspected that the Germans, who had accomplished what they had to do, had now withdrawn. He had Gourley and Pozernac set up their machine gun and fire toward the woods across the canal, but he saw no sign that the Germans were still there.

The command soon came to stop all fire. That meant time to eat, time to wait. And for Alex, it was time to worry. He had no idea what the Germans might be up to, or how many might be in the area. His understanding was that the next target for the regiment was Eindhoven, further south. The site here at Son was firmly held, and engineers could figure out some way to get the bridge rebuilt, but the Germans had to be grouping to stop the advance of the regiment along this crucial road.

Alex also understood the Allied challenge better now. The roadbed was raised a meter or so above the fields on either side. For troops to move along it meant standing out against the horizon and becoming sitting ducks. All the Germans had to do was create a bottleneck at any spot along the narrow corridor and the whole plan would fall apart. The greatest challenge was at Arnhem itself, where the British 1st Airborne Division had to take the well-guarded bridge and hold it until the British tanks arrived. Any delay in the thrust would make their job almost impossible.

Howie was sitting next to Alex. He had eaten a can of fruit cocktail but nothing more. "You'd better get something else in you," Alex told him. "I don't know when we'll be eating again."

"I'm not real hungry," Howie said. His face was pale and dirty, and his field jacket was covered with dust. "What's going to happen next?" he asked.

"I'm not exactly sure. The engineers are using barn doors and anything else they can find to build a makeshift bridge on top of the old pilings. I think we'll be moving across the canal before long, and then I guess we'll make our move toward Eindhoven, which is a few miles down this road."

"We'll be getting into the action down there, won't we?"

"I don't know. But we have to assume we will."

Howie nodded.

"Are you doing all right?"

"Sure."

But Alex saw the change. This was not the boy who had been laughing with Duncan back on the road to Son. He was more than nervous now; he was scared. As things turned out, however, the improvised bridge would allow only a few men to cross at a time. By the time the entire regiment made it over, evening was coming on. It was too late to make an assault. Alex got word from Summers, who was in radio contact with regimental headquarters, that German artillery had stopped the Guards Armored Division south of Eindhoven. That had caused a crucial and dangerous delay, but nothing could be done until morning. Alex got his squad into a barn that night, and they slept in relative comfort. Then, to everyone's surprise, they marched to Eindhoven the next morning with only mild resistance—mostly just sniper fire.

Eindhoven was a large place—a city of more than 100,000—and the mood there was even wilder than at Son. The officers had a struggle on their hands just to keep the men sober and moving. The troops did secure the bridges, however, and the British tanks, having fought off the Germans south of the city, moved in late that day. The Brits promptly set up camp and began brewing tea, which was baffling to Alex and the other Americans. The drive was already a day behind schedule, and an open road lay ahead. Why didn't they keep pushing? But these were not matters that Alex had any say about. Captain Summers commanded his men to move out of town to the east, where they dug in that night and slept in foxholes.

Alex put in a long, restless night, sleeping little and imagining the day that lay ahead. He was almost sure the Germans would try to cut the road before the Guards Armored Division got any farther north. So there would be killing in the morning. When he had dropped into Normandy, he had known the same thing, but only in the abstract. This time he knew what it meant to be shot at—and to shoot.

He kept reminding himself of his resolution. He would follow his training, fulfill his commitment—but he wouldn't think too much. He couldn't go into battle holding anything back. That was a sure way to put his men in danger. But when he

tried to pray about that, tried to ask the Lord to help him fight
with valor, the words seemed wrong to him, and he stopped.
He knew what he had to do, but he couldn't imagine that God
was pleased to see him do it. It was fine to talk about fighting
evil, but when the shooting started, he wasn't facing Hitler; he
was facing young men like himself, and it wasn't easy to get
that out of his head.

Lieutenant Owen showed up at Alex's foxhole long before
first light. "Get the men up and going," Owen told Alex. "We're
marching east to a place called Helmond. The old man wants
our company to widen the corridor on the east side of the
highway and make contact with the enemy."

Alex climbed out of his hole. "Do we have any reconnaissance information?"

"Not much. But it won't be like Eindhoven. The Germans
have some numbers over that way, and by now they have to be
ready to fight."

Howie, who had slept—or tried to—next to Alex in the
same foxhole, climbed out now and stood next to him. He did-
n't say anything, but even in the dark Alex could sense his stiffness.

"Is D Company still leading out?" Alex asked the lieutenant.

"No. This is strictly an E Company operation. First Platoon
will take the point, and we'll be right behind them. But we're
going to have armored support this time. The British have a
squadron of Cromwell tanks they're sending with us."

Alex walked through the area and got his men up, gave
them some idea of what was coming. No field kitchen had
been set up for mess, so the men ate cold rations again, and
before sunrise they were already on the march. Six Cromwell
tanks eventually caught up with the men, and some of the soldiers jumped on and took a ride. The tanks were awkward
machines, and all their clanking and squeaking made Alex nervous. If any Germans were waiting in ambush, they would

certainly have plenty of advance warning that troops were on their way.

The soldiers passed through the little town of Neunen that morning. One of the tank drivers was standing with his head and shoulders out of the hatch. "Say," he shouted to a civilian, "isn't this the village where Vincent Van Gogh was born?" He pronounced it "Van Gog."

"Yes, yes. It's a famous town," the civilian shouted back.

"Who's Van Gog?" Howie asked Alex.

"That's how the English pronounce it. We say Van *Go*. You know, Vincent Van Gogh, the painter."

"I guess I never heard of him," Howie said.

Private Withers, a college man, looked over at Alex, and they both smiled, but Alex said nothing. He doubted that Howie would think much of Van Gogh's paintings anyway.

The troops marched on through town and back into the countryside, and still there was no resistance. Alex was beginning to hope they might get off easy again. But then someone yelled, "Kraut tanks!"

Men scattered and ducked down into the ditches on the sides of the road. The land in that area was flat, but it was divided into fields, with rows of trees and brush along the fence lines. Alex saw the tanks, moving in a file, sneaking out from behind a row of trees, maybe 400 meters ahead. He could see ten or so, and more were still appearing. His company had only the six Cromwells to rely on, and the German tanks looked imposing by comparison. "Those are Tiger tanks," Alex said to anyone near enough to hear. One thing every American soldier knew was that the big German tanks were more powerful, better armored, than anything the Allies had.

"Thomas, look at those trees, off to the south," Campbell yelled. "There's a tank in there. I can see the barrel of its gun."

Alex saw it immediately. He also saw that the Cromwells, which had hesitated, were now moving ahead again. A fence line full of trees and brush was blocking the German tank crew from seeing the British tanks, but in another few seconds that would no longer be the case. Alex ran back along the road and jumped on the first tank. "Stop," he shouted.

The Brit, who was still driving with his hatch open, did stop the big rig. "There's a German tank off to the south," Alex told him. "If you pass this fence line, he'll have you in his sights."

The Englishman smiled at Alex. "Well, if he can't see me, he can't shoot me. But then, if I can't see him, I can't very well shoot him, either, now can I? Hop off now, and I'll have a go at him."

"No! Don't! You won't have a chance."

But the Brit dropped back into his tank and pulled the hatch shut. Alex jumped off. He wished he had time to move his men. He knew the tank was going to draw fire, and the concussion could knock his men senseless. "Stay down!" he screamed to his squad.

The Cromwell groaned and cranked ahead, and its gun barrel swung to the south. Alex ducked down by the road again just as the Cromwell came into full view of the German tank. A resounding explosion rocked the ground. Alex felt the concussion like a blow to the side of his head. He looked up to see that the British tank had been shoved sideways, and flames and smoke were billowing from its side. Another shell from the Panzer rocked it again, and then the hatch popped open. A crewman pulled himself out, then reached back and helped the driver. But the driver was screaming, and Alex saw that his legs had been blown away, only bloody stumps remaining.

Now Alex saw a second tank coming up, about to face the same fate. The driver tried to run past the first tank, but the second tank took a fatal blow in the side as well.

Two more Cromwells moved up. They swung to the north into the field and then east along the road, obviously trying to get into a position to shoot at the German tank that was still hiding in the trees. But the drivers didn't seem to recognize that *dozens* of German tanks were coming toward them from the east. Both tanks were struck rather quickly. One of them did get off a shot at the tank in the trees, but Alex couldn't tell whether the shell had done any damage.

It was all crazy. Four tanks were already destroyed, and Alex could now see a whole phalanx of Tigers on their way. There had to be forty tanks or more. The crews in the two remaining Cromwells had obviously seen the same thing. They held for a brief time and then swung around and headed back toward Neunen. The men were stuck in the middle of a plain with no cover and no armor for support. No one had to be told what big trouble they were in.

"Fall back," Summers shouted. "Back to that next tree line."

Alex looked around for his men. "Let's go!" he yelled.

But now the tanks were firing, and shells were exploding on the road and around it. Shrapnel was flying in all directions, whizzing, whistling. And as the men ran, machine-gun fire began to crack through the air.

Alex pulled Howie away from the road. They angled off through a field toward the next fence. Duncan was with them, at first, but at some point Alex glanced to his left, then twisted and looked back. He couldn't see Duncan, didn't know what had happened to him.

It was a long hard run in heavy boots, with shovels and canteens and other equipment strapped on, pockets loaded, but Alex took no time to shed anything. He spotted a place where the fence was free of brush and trees, and he jumped the rock wall, which was a good three feet high, and then he ducked down. Howie was right with him and made the same jump. Both were gasping as they looked back. The big tanks had broken their single-file formation and had swung out into the fields. They were coming steadily ahead without anything to stop them except the rock fences, which they pushed over without difficulty.

Alex looked up and down the fence. He was trying desperately to spot his men. But dust was flying, filling the air, and everything was chaos. He had no idea how to get anything organized.

"We've gotta get out of here," Howie yelled. He stood up, making a target of himself.

Alex grabbed his arm and pulled him down. "All right, we've got to get back to Neunen. If we get into some houses and barns, we can protect ourselves a little, maybe make a stand. When you start to run this time, don't run straight. Remember what you learned in basic training." Alex took a couple of gasps, still trying to catch his breath. "If I happen to go down, don't stop for me. The medics will take care of that— or the Germans. But no use both of us getting shot."

"All right. Let's go."

Alex saw the terror in Howie's eyes as he took off before Alex could. Howie ran hard, angling back and forth only a little, mostly just getting as far away as fast as he could. Alex was a faster runner, and he could make a few more zigs and zags in his path and still keep up. For a time, it all seemed unnecessary. The two were keeping away from the road, and no one else was nearby. But then bullets began to thump into the plowed ground around them, and suddenly Howie went down.

Alex ignored everything he had told Howie. He dropped on his face and crawled back. "Where are you hit?" he asked.

"I don't know."

"What put you down?"

"I don't know."

Alex rolled Howie on his side, looked him over. "Howie, I don't think you're hit. If we stay here, those tanks will keep coming. We've got to get up and go again."

"I can't."

Alex's nose was not four inches from Howie's, and Alex could see that Howie was in another world, his eyes full of panic. "You've got to!" Alex shouted. He thumped Howie with both hands, hard in the chest, and then he grabbed his jacket and dragged him to his feet. "Now, run!" he screamed.

Howie took off hard again, on a straight line. With maybe thirty feet to go to reach the next fence, Alex heard the thump of bullets again. He picked up his speed, made it to the fence, and cleared it like a hurdler. Howie jumped too, but he hit the top of the fence and rolled over onto the ground. He was breathing hard, maybe crying.

"Howie, we've got to go again." Alex took a big breath. "Catch your breath for thirty seconds, and then we're going to head for that barn up ahead, across this field." It was a barn built of rock, and as a good a place of safety as they were likely to find, Alex thought.

Howie didn't say a word, but he got up when Alex did, and he ran again. And the two made it to the barn. There, they lay on the ground, sucking air, their chests heaving.

Alex got up after a couple of minutes, and he climbed up to the loft, where he looked out over the fields that lay between the barn and the oncoming Germans. The men of his company were strewn in all directions—ducking behind fences, running, and for the most part making it. But Alex saw a couple of men fall, and he saw a shell explode and send four men flying.

He spotted two Americans running across the field in front of the barn. One was still packing his machine gun, and the other was carrying bandoleers of ammo. Alex was amazed they hadn't thrown down their weapons, but he also knew what they were thinking. Somewhere, the troops had to take a stand. They couldn't run forever. And if they took that stand, they would need all the firepower they could come up with.

Then Alex realized who it was: Gourley and Pozernac. He hustled down the ladder and ran outside. "Over here," he screamed. The two changed their angle, charged to the barn, and ran in. Both dropped onto the ground, just as Alex and Howie had done before.

Alex let them breathe, but he grabbed the machine gun and climbed back to the loft. He set it up and aimed it out the opening toward the field. Then he climbed down again. "Howie, get that ammo from Tony," he said. "Carry it to the loft. As soon as you two can climb up that ladder, get ready to lay down some fire across that field. We need a show of strength if we're going to stop those tanks from coming right on through here."

"We need more than a machine gun," Gourley gasped. "We need bazookas, anti-tank guns. We need *tanks*."

"I know. We still have a couple of Cromwells. Maybe more are in reserve. I'm going to make a run to the house just south of here. I saw men going in there. We've got to get mortars firing. We need to make some noise."

Alex made his run, and he found a bunch of scared riflemen, without any weapons except for M-1s. There were eight men, and they were hunkered down in a rock house, all of them still exhausted from the retreat. "Sergeant, those tanks are going to knock this place over," one of the men, a corporal, told Alex. "What can we do with rifle fire? We'd better fall back to Eindhoven, where the regiment is, right now."

"That's way too far. We'd never make it."

The corporal didn't answer. But he looked hopeless.

"Listen. We have to make the Germans think our whole regiment is here. We've got to fire with everything we have. Do you understand that?"

The men nodded, but he saw the look in all their eyes. They thought they were about to die.

"The Germans don't want to drive into a trap and lose a bunch of tanks. They'll check the situation out before they just start mashing their way through. I'm going to move around town until I find some officers. I'll make sure you guys get a mortar team over here, and we have a machine gun next door. So just return fire with your rifles, keep the bullets flying, and we'll build you up as soon as we can."

Alex made a lot more moves around the town. He found
Curtis Bentley and Royce Withers and sent them to the barn.
He also found Lieutenant Owen. The officers were getting
some firepower organized, and the German tanks were staying
back from town for now, firing rounds into the houses but not
pursuing.

Summers was moving about, too, and he found Alex talking to Lieutenant Owen. "Thomas," he said, "I just saw some of
your squad in that house down the street. Get your men
together."

"All right. I've got some of them in a barn on the edge of
town. We've got a machine gun, but we need something we
can use on those tanks."

"I've located a bazooka you can have," Summers said.

"All right. That'll help. We need to get mortars firing, too."

"I know. That's already happening. We've got the two
Cromwells here in town. If I can get any cooperation at all
from these Limeys, I'll move them around a little and hope the
Germans think we've got more than we actually do. But
Thomas, we can't stop that many tanks—not for long. We've
got to hold them up until night. If we can keep them out of
here that long, then we can fall back in the dark and get back
to the regiment. That's our only chance."

"All right. That's what I was thinking too."

Alex ran with Summers to get the bazooka, and he gathered up his men—Campbell and Sabin and Ernst—from the
house down the street. He turned the bazooka over to
Campbell, and then he led the men to the barn, but as they
approached, they saw that one of the Tigers was moving
through the fence beyond the field and crawling toward the
barn. "Campbell, get that thing!" Alex yelled.

Campbell ran around the barn and dropped on his face. A
blue line of fire flashed through the air, and the bazooka shell
slammed the front of the tank, but it hit the angling armor just
under the turret and glanced off. German infantrymen were

moving up alongside the tank, but the machine-gun fire from the barn knocked some of them down and chased others back to the fence. The tank turret turned, and the big barrel suddenly sent a shattering blast through the barn. Alex dropped on his face, felt the panic pumping through him, but he couldn't think what to do.

When the debris settled and he looked up, he saw Campbell, with his bazooka, on a dead run. He was angling toward the side of the tank, and bullets were sending up puffs of dirt around his feet. Another flash burst from the muzzle of the big tank barrel, and again rock and debris from the barn exploded into the air. Alex wondered whether anyone inside was still alive.

Campbell, by then, had dropped down again. He couldn't have been more than a hundred feet from the tank. And this time when he fired, the bazooka shell penetrated the armor, tore a hole in the side, and set off a huge secondary explosion inside. The tank jumped.

When Alex saw that all was quiet at the tank, and saw that Campbell had scrambled up and was running toward the barn, he hurried to the barn himself. The doors were blown off, and part of the wall was gone, but his men were all right. They had all been upstairs, in the loft, and the tank had fired at the main floor.

"All right. Good work," Alex told the men. "Now we need to be ready if another tank comes this way. I think—"

"Sergeant, the tanks are falling back," Pozernac called from the loft. "I can't believe it."

Alex nodded. "Good," he said. "We bluffed them." He looked over at Campbell, who was white with exhaustion, maybe with fear. "Hey, our boy Campbell fights tanks hand-to-hand," Alex yelled. "The rest of us don't have to worry."

"It was our only chance," Campbell said, still breathless. "That bazooka wasn't going to cut through that kind of armor unless I got in close."

Alex nodded. "I know. But most guys would have been running the other way—not *at* a Tiger. You're going to get a medal for that one. I'll see to it."

"I'm alive. That's the only thing I was thinking about. I figured he had us all."

Sabin and Ernst walked into the barn.

Curtis had just climbed down from the loft. He looked at the two men and asked, "Where's Duncan?"

"I don't know," Sabin said. "Hasn't anyone seen him?"

Howie was now climbing down the ladder. When he stepped onto the dirt floor, he said, "Duncan was running next to me, and then he went down." Howie's eyes were set and unblinking, as though the terror was gone now, but a deeper more permanent dread had taken over.

"Don't worry. He's not dead," Campbell said. "No one can kill Duncan."

But Alex didn't believe that. What he hoped was that his wound wasn't too bad, that medics had gotten to him and carried him out. "This might be a good chance to eat something," Alex said. But he wasn't hungry himself. He walked over and sat down next to Howie, who had slumped onto the floor and was leaning against one of the cow stalls. "Are you all right?" Alex asked.

"I don't know. I don't feel like I'm thinking right. I got all confused out there. I couldn't remember anything I learned back at basic." A shaft of light from a crack in the roof, full of little dust particles, streamed across Howie's face, but he wasn't squinting or looking away. His eyes were still fixed.

"You did what you had to do," Alex told him. "And you didn't get hit. Next time, you'll do better." Howie finally looked at Alex, stared at him, and Alex knew what he was thinking. "I'm not saying it ever gets easy. But you learn how to handle it."

"I didn't think we'd make it," Howie said. "I thought they had us."

"Just don't think about it. I told you I'd get you through, and we made it today."

Howie nodded, but Alex knew the boy was in a bad state.

Alex got out some K rations. "Let's eat something," he said. He wanted Howie to start moving ahead and not look back. Alex had only just begun to eat some of the canned meat—Spam—he detested when a shadow appeared at the barn door. Alex grabbed for his rifle, but by then he had heard Duncan's voice. "I've been looking all over for you guys," Duncan said, and he laughed. "You guys didn't get scared off by them little ol' tanks, did you?"

Alex got up and walked to the door. Duncan was grinning, but not with his usual brightness. He looked tired, and something else—maybe a little dazed. "Did you get hit?" Alex asked, and now he saw the hole in the front of Duncan's helmet.

"Look at this," Duncan said. He took his helmet off and showed the burn mark where a bullet has singed his hair and torn the skin in a line right around his head. Then he held up his helmet, and showed that there were two holes, one of them in the back. "It went right around my skull. I guess my head was too hard for the bullet to get through." He tried to laugh. "It went in through the back and out through the front. I was high-tailing it out of there, the same as you guys."

It was too close. Alex felt the air escape from his chest. He took the helmet and looked closer.

"I'm glad you're all right, buddy," Campbell said. He walked over and shook Duncan's hand.

Duncan nodded, and he tried to smile, but he couldn't seem to think of anything to say. He walked away from the door, sat down, and leaned against the part of the rock wall that was still intact. Alex followed and sat down next to him. "It's okay," Alex said.

"I was so scared I almost filled my pants out there," Duncan said. "I thought I was a dead man."

"Yeah, I'll bet," Alex said. They didn't look at each other.

There was a lot to say, but neither one was about to say it.
What Alex could hardly believe was that all his men were still
alive.

"I never thought we'd run like that," Duncan said.
"Paratroopers don't turn and run."

"We didn't have a choice."

"I still didn't think we'd do it."

"I'm just glad you got here," Alex said. "I found out I can
still run hard—if I'm scared enough—but my leg is aching
awfully bad right now."

"Deacon, if that bullet had been a quarter of an inch to the
left, I'd be dead right now."

"I know."

"As far as that goes, we're still in a bad situation here. This
whole operation is in trouble. We might all be dead before it's
over."

"I know that, too."

6

LaRue Thomas hated Sundays. She came home from Sunday School—which she never found interesting—and then had to suffer through the long, boring afternoon until sacrament meeting at seven o'clock. Her father, Alexander Thomas, didn't object to her visiting friends, but the problem was, Mom never knew when he was going to get home from his church meetings, and Dad preferred that everyone—which meant Mom and Beverly and LaRue these days—be home for Sunday dinner. Mom usually tried to have dinner at two, but Dad, who was the stake president, often got tied up in meetings and didn't get home until much later. So LaRue could never really plan anything.

On this particular Sunday afternoon, in October, LaRue had been reading *Pride and Prejudice.* It was assigned reading for her English class. But she was bored with the book, so she wandered downstairs to see what she could find for a snack. What she noticed when she walked through the living room was that Tommy Dorsey's "Your All Time Hit Parade" was on the radio. When she saw that her dad was in his office, with his door open, she called out, "Say, Dad, that program you're listening to isn't very spiritual for the Sabbath, if you ask me."

"Actually, you're right," he said, and he sounded a little

embarrassed. "It came on after the news, but I wasn't really paying any attention. Would you turn it off for me?"

LaRue stepped to her father's door. "That's how it starts,
Dad. You let the devil pay a visit, and the next thing you know,
he's taking up permanent residence."

LaRue didn't get the response she wanted. The truth was,
she was upset with her dad, and she was hoping to get his goat
just a little. "I'm glad to know you understand that," he said, and
he laughed.

"The way I look at it, on the Sabbath you should spend
your entire day reading the scriptures—and *frowning*."

Mom was in the kitchen. LaRue heard her voice through
the door. "That's about enough of that, LaRue," she said.

But LaRue was letting her aggravation build. "If we can visit
the sick on Sundays, I don't see the difference in visiting people
who need company. What would it hurt if I went down to the
USO club for a little while?"

Dad had been dubious about her going to the club, and he
certainly wouldn't let her go in on Sundays. LaRue painted the
picture with lots of red, white, and blue, but President Thomas
accused her of being mostly interested in spending time with
the young soldiers she met there. Some of them were just passing through, and the club was a place for them to kill a little
time between train connections; others were stationed in Utah:
at Fort Douglas, Camp Williams, Hill Field, Camp Kearns, or
one of several supply depots and military hospitals. They came
to the club in the evenings, danced to the jukebox—or sometimes a live band—and drank soft drinks.

It was all very wholesome, according to LaRue. And that
was mostly true. The club was certainly not a bar, but the soldiers sometimes sneaked in their own flasks or hidden bottles,
and some of them came from wild backgrounds. LaRue had
actually volunteered to work around the place: serve dough-
nuts or sandwiches and clean up a little. She was too young to
be a hostess and dance with the soldiers. But the manager

didn't know how old she was, and he had never said anything to her about dancing—especially on nights when not many hostesses showed up.

The supervision was tight, and the young women—many of them University of Utah co-eds—didn't really have to worry about being mistreated. Still, when LaRue was there she always felt she had escaped Utah just a little. She was happy for the chance to experience some of the wartime atmosphere that had changed the nation and was reaching Salt Lake City. There was a freedom, sometimes even looseness, that she found exciting, and she loved the way the boys flirted with her. Maybe LaRue was only fifteen, but she looked older, and she was stunning with her rich, dark hair and hazel eyes, her pretty figure. When she walked through the club, she always turned heads, and she loved having all those eyes on her.

What had upset her particularly today was that her friend Gaye Jennings had gotten permission from her parents to go. And more than that, a certain young man had suggested she come that day. All day LaRue kept thinking how much fun everyone was probably having while she was sitting at home.

President Thomas took a long look at LaRue, and then he said, very simply, "We've been over all this before, honey. You know how I feel about it."

LaRue knew that this tone was her father's idea of being firm but loving, but she found his manner condescending. "When do I get to decide for myself what is spiritual and what isn't? I'm not a little girl anymore."

LaRue saw her father take a long, deep breath. His voice was changed, almost harsh, when he said, "You don't earn your rights by having birthdays, LaRue. You earn them as you show that you can accept responsibility. The truth is, right now, what you are is immature and self-centered. I keep hoping to see some improvement, but it just doesn't come."

The words were a stab, hurtful on purpose, and LaRue reacted. "Thanks, Dad. I'm looking forward to being mature, like you. Then I'll always know exactly what's right and wrong—not only for myself, but for *everyone*."

LaRue knew she had crossed a line. She had never said anything this bitter to her father before. At the moment, however, she didn't care. Mom pushed through the door from the kitchen. "LaRue, I think you'd better go up to your room and cool off."

But Dad said, "Wait a minute. LaRue, I'm sorry."

If he had said "I denounce everything I believe," LaRue couldn't have been more surprised. She turned back toward him, watched his face, tried to see whether he really meant it.

He said, "I didn't mean to sound like that. I don't have all the answers. And before long, you'll be making all your own decisions—no matter what I think. So I do need to trust you."

LaRue was still staring at him. She hardly knew how to react. But inertia seemed to carry her forward.

"So if I decide to skip sacrament meeting and spend the evening down at the club, you'll let me do it?"

"I didn't say that. The *Lord* has told us to attend sacrament meeting. That's not something I thought up."

"But it's still my decision."

"It's also a family rule."

"So it's *not* my decision?"

"Ultimately it is, LaRue. Of course it is."

LaRue had him now, and she wasn't going to miss this chance to call his bluff. "All right. I'm going to take the streetcar into town. I won't be out late, but I won't be back in time for sacrament meeting."

What LaRue now expected was some hedging, but Dad didn't say a word. It was her mother who said, "LaRue, think what you've been taught all your life."

"I've been taught to serve people. And there's no better time to do that than on the Sabbath. Dad always says that being a true Christian is more important than just going to church."

"LaRue, be honest with yourself," Mom said. "Is that why you're going down there—to serve people?"

"That's *exactly* what I do, Mom."

"That's playing with words, LaRue, and you know it. Listen, why don't we all come out in the living room, sit down, and talk this over?"

But Dad said, "That's all right, Bea. It's LaRue's decision, and I want her to do what she *knows* is right."

LaRue could see what was going on. This was Dad's way of making her feel guilty. He expected her to back off. But she wasn't going to let him win that way. She tromped up the stairs to her room and changed her clothes. She put on a pretty, rose-colored dress that Dad hated because the skirt was so short.

LaRue looked over to see Beverly standing in the doorway. "Don't do this, LaRue," she said.

"Leave me alone," LaRue told her.

"You're just trying to make Dad stop you."

"I'm doing what *I* want to do—not what everyone tells me to do."

"You're breaking a commandment."

"Maybe you think so. I don't." She finished buttoning her dress and looked at herself in her bureau mirror. She grabbed a brush and ran it quickly through her hair a few times, and then she applied some dark red lipstick—something else her dad didn't like. She got her coat from the closet, threw it over her arm, and said, "I don't care what you think, Bev. Call me guilty as sin if you want. It's *my* choice, and I'm going to make it."

She hurried down the stairs. "Good-bye," she called as she shut the front door, but she didn't go back and face her parents.

By the time she reached the club, LaRue *was* feeling guilty, but that made her angry. If there was one thing she had learned at the club, it was that Mormons found all kinds of things to fuss about that most people didn't think mattered, and going to church every single Sunday was one of them.

Even so, she was just a little jarred by the sudden change as she walked into the building. The jukebox was blaring, the room full of smoke, and people were laughing and talking loudly. A few couples were on the dance floor, in most cases holding each other much tighter than was ever allowed at church dances. What LaRue also noticed, however, was that her one, clear wish had been granted. *He* was there.

For the past couple of months, a young airman from Hill Field had been coming in regularly. His name was Ned Dimmick, and he was from Newark, New Jersey. He had asked her to dance one night and then teased *her* about her accent. LaRue, in her usual feisty way, had worked him over, pointing out all the defects in his own speech. And he had loved it. "Hey, you're a ball of fire, aren't you?" he had told her. LaRue had licked her thumb, placed it on her hip, and made a sizzling sound.

She had known that she was not only flirting but also giving him entirely the wrong idea about herself. But it was exciting. She liked what she was doing to him. He kept trying to pull her closer as they danced, and she held him off, even teased him about it, but at the same time, she knew how much he wanted to get her into his arms, and she liked that very much. One thing she was careful not to let him know was that she was only fifteen, and when he said something that indicated that he thought she was out of high school, she let the impression stand.

Today, when Ned spotted LaRue, he walked to her immediately. "I was hoping you'd come," he said. "You can't live without me, can you?" He smiled, and LaRue, as always, was impressed with how cute he was. He had dark, curly hair; wonderful walnut-colored eyes; and a bold, confident smile.

"Excuse me. Have I met you before?" LaRue asked.

"Sure. I'm the one you dream about when you go to bed at night."

"I do have a problem with nightmares from time to time."

He waved his hand in a gesture that said, "Don't give me that." Then he took her arm and said, "Come on. Let's dance."

The jukebox was playing "One O'clock Jump," a Benny Goodman number, and Ned began to jitterbug. LaRue felt funny about that, since it *was* the Sabbath, but she danced anyway, and she was good at it. So was Ned. That was one of the things she liked so much about him.

When the dance was over, LaRue told him she had to report to the manager that she was there. "Okay," Ned told her, "but then come over to my table. I want you to meet my friends."

LaRue walked to the little sandwich counter and said hello to her friend Gaye. "I'll come and help you in a minute," she said. "I've got to talk to someone first."

Gaye was the same age as LaRue, but she seemed years younger. She was a big girl, pale, with almost colorless eyes, and she wore no makeup. She leaned across the counter and whispered, "LaRue, you shouldn't be dancing. You know that."

"It doesn't matter. No one cares."

"But when we volunteered, we—"

"It doesn't matter. I'll be back in a minute."

She walked to the table where Ned was sitting with another airman and a young woman in a navy uniform. Ned stood up. "Johnny," he said, "this is the girl I've been telling you about. LaRue. And this is Johnny Bernardi, a friend of mine from home."

Johnny stood up, politely, and said, "Hey, good to know you. But you ain't as good looking as Ned told me." He hesitated and grinned. "You're even betta."

"Hey! Watch who you're looking at!" This was from the girl at the table. LaRue took one look at her and knew she wasn't from Utah. Her hair was curled but cut very short, and there was something a little too brazen in the way she looked at Johnny. She was also holding a cigarette.

Ned and Johnny laughed, and then Johnny said, "LaRue,

this is my girl. She's got her claws dug deep into me, so even if you want me, I ain't available."

"That's right," the girl said. "And don't forget it." Then she looked at LaRue. "I'm Darlene. Nice to meet you."

Ned had pulled a chair out for LaRue, and now she sat down. "Do you want a Coke?" Ned asked.

LaRue's father was very much opposed to Coca-Cola. Normally, LaRue didn't drink it. But rather than ask for something else, she said, "Sure. Thanks."

Ned walked to the counter. LaRue turned to Darlene. "So where are you from?" she asked.

"Cleveland."

"And you're from New Jersey, Johnny?"

"Oh, yeah. Me and Ned are friends from way back. Same neighborhood, schools, everything. We joined the Air Force together, and both got shipped out here to the end of the world." He stumped out his cigarette. He was not as good looking as Ned, shorter and thin, his face too narrow, but he seemed to have as much confidence in himself.

"So don't you like Utah?"

Both Johnny and Darlene laughed. "Sorry. No offense, honey," Darlene said. "But I didn't think a place like this *existed*. Not in the twentieth century."

LaRue had noticed a hint of a smell, and now she picked up just a little slur in Darlene's voice. She realized the three of them had been drinking. She had been fighting back a sense of discomfort from the moment she had left home, but now she felt genuinely ill at ease. But she didn't want to show that. "I guess we're a little old-fashioned in Utah," she said.

"Old-fashioned is one thing," Johnny said, "but people around here don't believe in having fun. I've never met so many sourpusses in my whole life."

LaRue laughed, and the thought crossed her mind that she could tell a few stories about her dad—his worries about short dresses and dancing after midnight on Saturday nights—but she found herself feeling defensive. "You probably have to get to know us a little," she said. "We're not so bad."

There was a sudden awkwardness. "Hey, it doesn't matter to us," Johnny said. "Live and let live, that's what I say."

"If you call that living," Darlene said, and she laughed with a loud sort of chattering sound.

By then Ned had returned, and he looked curious, as though he were trying to pick up on the conversation. LaRue looked up at him. "These two think Utah people are a bunch of sourpusses," she said.

"Hey, Johnny," Ned said, "this girl can dance better than any girl at our high school ever could."

"What else does she do, Ned?" Darlene asked, and she leaned toward LaRue and bumped her shoulder. "Maybe the girls out here only pretend to be so religious and proper."

Ned was clearly embarrassed. He hesitated, couldn't seem to think what to say, and then he took hold of LaRue's hand. "Let's have another dance, what do you say?" he asked.

This set Darlene off in another high-pitched laugh, and LaRue was only too glad to get away from the table. The music was slow and soft, but Ned seemed careful how he held her as they began to dance. "Don't let Darlene get you riled up," Ned said. "She's got a mouth on her, but she doesn't mean anything. She was just kidding around."

"I know."

"I'm glad you're not one of these girls who's—you know—been around. That's the first thing I noticed about you." He stopped and laughed. "No. The first thing I noticed was that you're a *knockout*. But the second thing I liked was that you're a nice girl—not some camp follower or something like that."

"I thought you told me I was a ball of fire."

"Well, you are, in your own way. You're spunky, and you're fun. But you're nice too—nicer than you even know." He had moved just a little closer, and he was looking into her eyes. "LaRue, you're not the kind of girl a guy takes out once—for the kicks. You're the kind a guy wants to keep for himself, for the rest of his life."

LaRue was startled. She pulled back from him. "Oh, you smooth-talking fly boys," she said, and she tried to laugh.

He stopped dancing, but he clung to her. "I'm not selling you a bill of goods, LaRue. I mean it."

The music ended, and they stood looking at each other. But he wanted more from this moment than she could give. She pushed away more assertively this time, and then she took his arm and led him back to the table. There she tried to keep things light. When she finally lifted her Coke to take a drink, she caught the taste of something strange, grimaced, and set it down. This set off a howl of laughter from Johnny and Darlene.

"We added a little *excitement* to your drink, that's all," Darlene said. "Drink that down and you'll find out what you've been missing."

LaRue felt violated. It wasn't that she thought a sip of alcohol had done her any harm; she just didn't like someone tricking her into something like that. Suddenly she wanted out of this situation. "Well, I have to go," she said, trying not to sound upset. "I just ran down for a few minutes—you know, to say hello."

"Hey, no. Don't go," Ned said. "I'll get you another Coke. They were just playing around."

"No. It's not that. I really do have to go." LaRue stood up, and she accepted apologies all around, but she told them she wasn't concerned at all, and she headed for the door. Ned, however, followed her outside.

"I'm really sorry that happened," he said. "I'm glad you don't drink. I think that's good."

"Ned, your friends are right. We are different here."

"Not as much as you think. My whole family goes to church. I went to Mass, on base, before I came down here

today. You'll never see me drunk, either. I take a drink now and
then, but that's all."

"It's not just that. There are all kinds of things."

"Like what? Tell me."

"No. It doesn't matter. I'll probably see you again some
time. Have fun tonight."

She tried to step away, but he had hold of her arm. "Hey,
haven't you been listening to me? I'm trying to tell you something."

"I know. But—"

And then he was pulling her close, kissing her. And she let
it happen. It wasn't because she loved him. It wasn't for any reason that she understood, except that it seemed so childish, so
inexperienced, to fight him off. When he finally backed away
just a little and looked into her eyes, she knew he wanted some
confirmation that she cared about him, but she couldn't grant
him that. She turned quickly away and said, "Ned, I really do
have to go."

She started to walk, and he called after her, "Tell me what
nights you'll be here this week."

"I don't know. I may not be able to come this week."

And she kept going.

It wasn't until LaRue was halfway home that she realized
she still had time to make it to sacrament meeting. She decided
she would go, and let her dad think what he wanted about her
reasons. It was easier to do that than not go. That was not her
big concern right now anyway. She wondered, maybe she
shouldn't go back to the club again. Maybe she should avoid
Ned altogether so she wouldn't have to explain. And yet
another emotion was mixed with her worry. Remembering the
kiss now, she found it thrilling. It was her first real kiss, and she
wanted to tell Gaye all about it. But Gaye would tell her all the
things she already knew: that she was playing with fire. Still,
the alternative—not seeing him anymore—made the winter
ahead seem so bleak.

When LaRue walked into her house, she didn't see her dad in the living room. He had probably headed over to the church a little early. She walked quietly upstairs and began to change her clothes. But she could smell the smoke in her dress now, and she decided to take a bath. She didn't have time to wash her hair, but she wished she could.

She waited until the last minute to go downstairs, and then she walked to church with her mom and sister. Sister Thomas told her, "I'm glad you decided to come back for church. It's the best way to show your father that you can make good decisions."

The best way to show him that he's still the boss, LaRue thought, but the idea didn't matter so much as it had earlier in the day. She actually found herself relieved to see her father look down at her from the stand and nod his approval. If only that were the end of it. But LaRue couldn't hide the fact from herself that she didn't enjoy the meeting, that the speaker seemed entirely too long-winded and pious to her. However much discomfort she had felt at the club, she hardly felt blessed to be "home" in this meeting. As she looked around, she thought many of the others in the congregation were just as bored as she was, and she wondered what value there was in a ritual like this, as though church were a medicine you took, not because you liked it but because it was supposed to be good for you.

But she expressed none of this, and she walked home ahead of her mother and little sister, Mom having gotten herself into a conversation with a couple of the sisters in the ward.

It was maybe an hour later when LaRue was in her room, back to reading *Pride and Prejudice,* that President Thomas knocked softly on her door and then stepped in. "I need to talk to you for a minute," he said.

"Okay." She was sitting on her bed. She placed the open book face down on her lap.

President Thomas took the chair from her desk, turned it around, and sat down. "Needless to say, I was glad to see you at church," he said. "But I know better than to think that solves everything."

LaRue didn't say anything. She wasn't sure what her father meant.

"I've made my share of mistakes as a father," he went on. "The worst ones I made with Wally. And you're an awful lot like him." He gripped his knees and leaned forward a little. "My problem is, I know exactly what I think is best for you, and I just want you to do it."

"Weren't you allowed to do anything on Sundays when you were growing up?"

"LaRue, I hardly know how to answer that. Sunday was Sunday—the Sabbath. I don't remember ever having to decide what I was going to do. We had to take water turns and milk our cows, so there was always some work. I guess, as much as anything, I just felt happy that I had some time to sit around for a while in the middle of the day. That's the only time I ever did that."

"Couldn't I say that going down to the USO is like milking cows—work that has to be done?"

"I don't see it that way, LaRue. But I meant what I said this afternoon. I'm going to put you on your own about that. I'm going to struggle awfully hard if you don't show up to your meetings—or even if I know you're down there in between meetings. But I have to let you decide."

"Well . . . okay. I'll promise to think about all the things you've always taught us. But I'll make my own decisions."

"LaRue, I'm not turning you loose to make *every* decision. We've still got some rules around here. I'm certainly going to have something to say about what time you come in at night, and who you're out with. I'm just saying that I know I have to give you a little more room in certain things. If you can tell yourself, honestly, that what you're doing at that canteen is service, then I'm not going to contradict your judgment."

LaRue almost wished he would tell her not to go to the

USO anymore. Then she wouldn't have to decide for herself. But she would never tell him that.

"LaRue, I hope you'll understand about my being gone so much lately. I preach to the Saints that the family ought to come first, but I'm afraid I put a lot of other things ahead of you and your sister."

"That doesn't bother me."

"I've worked awfully hard lately, out campaigning. And maybe that's a waste of time. There's probably no chance at all of beating Roosevelt—but I feel like I have to try. The thing is, though, when I combine that with my church duties and all the hours I put in at the plant, I know I'm not here very much."

LaRue actually had to fight not to smile. When he was home, he spent his time reading or hiding away in his office, and when he did talk to the girls, he usually said something like, "Have you done your homework yet?" Mom was always easier to be around, and a lot more fun. "That's okay," LaRue told her dad. "I know you have important things to do."

"Well, I'm going to do better. The pressure on us at the plant has let up some, and I plan to cut back on my hours. Maybe we can start going on picnics again, the way we used to—up in Memory Grove or in one of the canyons—or maybe we could take a little trip. We've gotten away from all that with the gas shortages and all the busyness. I'm afraid you and Bev have missed out on a lot of things the other kids got to do— just because of the war."

"What will happen to the plant when the war ends, Dad?"

"Well, it's interesting. I see some good times ahead. People are going to want washing machines and refrigerators—every-thing they can't get right now. We can change over and start producing parts for appliances and cars, or whatever the big companies want. I think people will be flying a lot more, so the airplane parts business may not fall off all that much. On top of all that, the car business should really take off again, so the dealership should do real well."

"So are you going to get rich?"

For the first time, Dad smiled. "We're doing fine, honey. We can keep doing well, too. And your brothers can get in on it when they come home. That way, the money will still be good, but I won't have to do all the work myself."

"What about me and Bev?"

"What do you mean?"

"You said our brothers would work with you. Why can't we do something like that?"

"Uh . . . well . . . I just figure you'll get married, and your husbands will have some kind of work. I guess, if for some reason you didn't marry, and—"

"Lots of married women work these days."

"Sure. But that's only because of the war. After, they'll need to step aside so there's plenty of work for the soldiers coming home. Most of the women will be more than happy to do it, too. It just doesn't work out well to have moms and dads both working."

"Maybe I'll learn your business and open a plant of my own—give you a little competition."

"Well, hon, I'll say this much. You could do it. But that isn't what you'll want at that point in your life. At least I wouldn't think so."

"If you and Alex and Wally are all rich, I want to be rich too."

Dad laughed. "Who knows? Maybe we could bring your husband into the business. There might be enough to go around to everyone in the family. What I would really like to do is get even more involved in politics. And maybe get the boys involved there, too. Some of us need to see what we can do to get this country heading in the right direction after the war."

"Maybe I'll run for Congress."

Dad folded his arms, leaned back, and laughed, and then he said, "Oh, Sis, I can't say the right thing. You young women just don't think the same as women used to."

"Mom has taught me a lot."

"Good. I'm glad I know the source of the trouble."

"Dad, I'm serious though. I want to do things. I don't think men should be the only ones having fun."

LaRue knew exactly what her dad was thinking—that she needed to think about raising children and cooking pot roasts on Sunday afternoons. But he didn't say it, which was a kind of concession on his part. "Well, anyway, our family will have some opportunities if we use them right. It's very important, if we accumulate a little wealth, that we give something back. That's why I want to get involved in the government."

"A girl at East High told me we're now the richest family in Sugar House. She said her father told her that."

"Oh, LaRue, good heavens, no. There are quite a few families who have more money than we do. The last thing in the world we want to do is start putting on airs and acting important. I didn't set out to get rich out of this war; I only wanted to start a business that Alex could use to support a family. All this just happened."

LaRue was surprised. She had told her friend that the Thomases didn't have much money. And she had expected her father to say the same thing.

"Well, anyway, honey, I want you to know I love you. I really do. And I think you'll do the right things—in the long run." He got up, walked over, and sat down next to her on the bed. She had a feeling he wanted to kiss her on the cheek, but he didn't. He merely patted her on the shoulder and then left.

When he was gone, LaRue thought about all he had said. The truth was, she didn't trust him. What he believed was that if he claimed to have faith in her, she would do what he expected her to do. And maybe she would; she didn't know. But she was almost sure that if she pushed the limits, he would rescind everything he had just said. Dad was learning the language that Mom used, but LaRue wasn't at all sure he had changed the way he really felt.

7

Heinrich Stoltz had been allowed to enter the office and sit down, but now he was sitting by himself, waiting. The small oak desk and the shabby furniture were hardly what he had expected, but the American OSS—Office of Strategic Services—was a developing organization, probably not very well financed. The British had been in the spy business much longer. Brother Stoltz had noticed when he spoke with English agents from the SIS—the Secret Intelligence Service—that they seemed to take a dim view of the American attempt to get into operations that the Brits felt they had well in hand.

Ten minutes went by, fifteen, and then a man in a white shirt, with a loosened tie and open collar, finally stepped into the office. He stuck his hand out. "Hello," he said. "Sorry to keep you waiting." He sounded distracted. "I have a hard time keeping up with everything that's going on around here."

Brother Stoltz stood up and shook the man's hand. He said politely, in English, "I appreciate your taking time to meet with me."

"That's fine. What can I do for you?" The American walked around his desk and sat down. He didn't say what his name was.

"I'm a German," Brother Stoltz said. "Perhaps you know that."

"Yes. I do."

"I resisted the Nazis. I took in Jews, hid them. I was discovered, and I had to escape from my country. I crossed into Switzerland with my family, and from there the British helped me contact the French underground, who guided us across the border to France. Later we made our way across France and the Channel, and we live here now. I've been working with the British SIS. I gave them information I thought might be helpful, and now I translate German documents for them. I feel, however, that I can do more. If I had identification papers, I could return to Germany. I have contacts with an underground organization in Berlin—'Uncle Emil' they call themselves. I could enlist them to help with reconnaissance—or I could make observations myself. You must need people who can tell you how effective your bombing raids are, for instance. That is something I could watch and report."

"What makes you think we do such things, Mr. Stoltz?"

"I know a great deal, sir. I know what you have done in France, and I know that you need more operatives in Germany as the fighting moves closer. In my work with the British, all these things have become known to me. It was SIS agents who gave me permission to talk to you."

"If anyone ever did take on such work as you describe, it would be very dangerous, wouldn't you think?"

"Yes. But less so for me, a native German, than it would be for American agents. I know the language, of course, but I also know the people, the customs, the transportation system—everything. I'm much less likely to make a mistake than an American would be."

The man picked up a pencil, held it between his thumb and forefinger, and began to tap it in a steady rhythm against the edge of his desk. "You certainly speak good English," he said after a time.

"My English has improved a great deal since we came here."

Brother Stoltz could get no reading on what the man was thinking. He seemed more an intellectual than a spy. He had that slightly disheveled look of a professor or scientist, his hair rather too long and uncombed, his shirt frayed a little at the wrists. He was still tapping the pencil, steadily; the sound, like a ticking clock, made Brother Stoltz nervous.

"Why would you want to do something like that, Mr. Stoltz?"

"I hate what Hitler is doing to my country. I want to see the war end as soon as possible."

"You're telling me this has nothing to do with your son?" He set the pencil down, leaned forward with his elbows on the desk, and looked into Brother Stoltz's eyes.

Brother Stoltz was stunned. "You know about my son?"

"Of course I do. I don't let just anyone walk into this office. I've talked to the British. They've told me all about you. I know, for instance, that a Gestapo agent tried to rape your daughter, and she sliced his face with a butcher knife. That's what forced you to take sides against the Nazis, Mr. Stoltz. Before that, you went along with Hitler, just like every other German."

"Yes. I suppose you could say that. I disagreed with what the Nazis were doing, but I kept my mouth shut. That's true." Brother Stoltz hated this summary of himself. The matter wasn't quite that simple.

"I also know that you bungled things with a Jewish family you were supposed to be protecting. The Gestapo nabbed them."

Brother Stoltz leaned back and looked at the bare white wall behind the agent. He was offended by the man's bluntness, but he couldn't deny the accusation. "Yes. I made mistakes. You only know this because I admitted everything to SIS agents."

"That's all well and good. But your previous work doesn't

look like the best recommendation for a man who wants to help me." He picked up the pencil and began to tap it again.

"I suppose not." Brother Stoltz could feel this last hope slipping away.

"You also injured a Gestapo agent in Basel, pushed him off a train platform. Every police agency in Germany probably has your picture."

"But they know I left Germany, and they would never expect me to return. They wouldn't be looking for me now."

"Maybe not. But you could still be recognized. Or if you were ever picked up, you would be a dead man."

"I would take that chance. And if I were discovered, it would not damage your work. You have nothing to lose and much to gain, as I see it."

"Mr. Stoltz, here's what bothers me. I think you want to return to Germany to look for your son. If I were to help you get across the border, I'm afraid you would spend all your time searching for this boy. You say we have nothing to lose, but if we go to a lot of work to make papers for you, train you, and get you into Germany—which is *very* difficult—we want to know you're really working for us and not serving your own purposes."

"I could do both. And I don't think you can find many like me. Young men would be noticeable. The police would stop them to determine why they were not in the military. At my age, I wouldn't be watched as closely. What is more, I have contacts that no one else has." Brother Stoltz slid to the front of his chair, sat up straight, and looked the man in the eye. "Above all, I'm willing to do it. If I'm motivated to find my son, at least I *am* motivated."

The man gave the pencil a little toss, and it rattled across the desk. "I'm sure you made all the same arguments with your friends at MI-6. Why didn't England choose to send you in?"

Military Intelligence, Department Six, was another name for the SIS. Brother Stoltz was well aware of both names. "I suppose for the same reasons you have given me. But there is one major difference. The English are not trying to penetrate Germany. From what I know, you are."

"I can't comment on that."

"Of course. But it is what I understand, and it is why I came to you."

The man took a long look at Brother Stoltz, and then he leaned back and looked away. He sat for an uncomfortably long time, looking toward the door, or the wall, hardly focused on anything. Brother Stoltz had no idea what he was thinking. "I suppose you couldn't parachute, could you?" he finally asked.

"I will, if that's what you want me to do."

"What about the injuries to your knee and your shoulder?"

"You know about that, too?"

"Of course I do."

"Well . . . it would be difficult, but not impossible."

For the first time, the agent smiled. "I'll say this much. You're willing to do what it takes."

"Sir, I don't know you. I don't know whether you have children. But what would you do if you had a son in danger? Wouldn't you do anything you could to help him? Maybe my motivation is not quite so simple as yours. But I want to get my son out, and almost as dearly, I want to strike a blow against these appalling Nazis who have destroyed my country. You could never find an American who feels such a passion as I do."

"Passion can get you into trouble."

"It can also sharpen your wits."

The man nodded. And he considered again. "All right. We've talked. But we haven't talked. You can't mention a word of anything that has gone on here to anyone—including your wife and daughter. Not even the boys at MI-6. You seem to think that this is a spy agency, but there's no such thing here. Do you understand that?"

"Of course. Were I to say anything, I know I would lose whatever chance I have with you."

"I need to talk to some people. And I need to think. I don't want to say anything else for now. But I have listened to what you have to say. And I guess I'll admit this much: I am interested."

"Good. Thank you."

"We know where you are. If we decide to pursue this we'll contact you."

Brother Stoltz stood up. He rather hoped the man would at least offer to tell him his name, but he didn't. The two shook hands, and Brother Stoltz left.

The Stoltzes were living in an apartment near the Marylebone BritRail station in London, near Baker Street. Brother Stoltz took the underground to the Baker Street stop, one stop before his, then walked into Regent's Park and sat on a bench for a time. He had told his wife that he had work to do that day in the SIS office. If he returned too quickly, she would wonder why—and of course, he couldn't tell her.

The park was a pleasant place, with its waterways, its ducks and swans, but the rose gardens had been left to go wild, and throughout the park there were long trenches. These had been intended as defenses back in 1940, when a German attack across the channel had seemed imminent. Many of the trenches had caved in now, and some had even been backfilled, but over the years it had been difficult enough to keep London operating without taking time to worry much about filling trenches.

German bomber attacks had ceased in London, but in the past few weeks Hitler had finally unleashed the "secret weapon" he had long been threatening to use. V-2 rockets were striking every day now. Most of them were targeted to hit the docks and heavy industry on the East End, but some had also struck downtown. Recently, one had exploded in the middle of a shopping area in Mayfair, an area near Oxford Street. It had killed a number of people and done considerable damage, but even more, it had served warning that the rockets might strike any part of town, and that no one should sleep too soundly at night.

Brother Stoltz hardly paid attention to the V-2s. He had experienced too much in Berlin during the Allied blanket bombings. Nothing could compare to those attacks—and the fires that followed. These V-2 rockets were no more worrisome than a lightning strike. If they came they came, and he would accept his fate. His concern about Peter was another matter entirely. The Gestapo had his son, and by now the boy could be dead, but as long as Brother Stoltz could find a way, he was going to keep trying to save him. If he was in jail, maybe there was a way to bribe someone—or help Peter pull off an escape.

And so Brother Stoltz sat in the park and considered his options, and in truth, he saw none but this hope with the American OSS. But he had no idea how long he might have to wait before he heard anything, and he wondered whether time might be a factor in saving his son.

Losing Peter at the Swiss border had been the most disheartening experience of his life, and the worry never left him for a moment. He had promised to protect the Rosenbaums—the Jewish family—and he had failed; he had promised to protect his family, and he had gotten Peter into perilous trouble. If he was offered another chance, he didn't want to fail again.

Brother Stoltz waited a couple of hours before he returned to his apartment. When he arrived, he found Anna and his wife sitting at the little wooden kitchen table. Anna had also started translating German documents for the SIS. Many of these were not classified, and in fact, Anna usually saw little value in them, but it was a way to earn some money and help her family pay the rent. Her father brought the material to her, and he gave her help when she needed it. The work was a blessing in more ways than one: besides the income it provided, it had occupied her mind these past few weeks, since Alex had been gone.

Brother Stoltz hung his hat on a peg just inside the kitchen and slipped off his suit coat. Money was very tight, and he never looked at his old coat without feeling embarrassed at how bedraggled it had become. But there was nothing he could do about that.

"What's wrong?" Sister Stoltz asked as he turned toward her.

"Wrong? Nothing is wrong."

"Anna has been gloomy all day, and now you come in looking like a sad little boy."

"What's Anna gloomy about?"

"Never mind for now. Tell me what's bothering you."

"Nothing. I'm fine," Brother Stoltz said. He sat down at the table.

"Mama is the gloomy one," Anna said. "I've been giving her English lessons. And she keeps saying she can't pronounce the words."

"It's true. I can't say this 't-h' sound." She pushed her tongue under her front teeth and blew out an exaggerated, wet sound. Brother Stoltz and Anna laughed, and then so did Sister Stoltz. Then she said, in German, "I'm sorry, but that's the best I can do."

"It's very difficult to learn a language at our age," Brother Stoltz said.

"It's terrible. No one understands me when I try. I told the grocer this morning that I wanted *Rotkohl*." She tried to say it in English—"red cabbage"—and then she laughed at herself. "I can't say 'r' the way they say it here. The man had no idea what I was asking for."

"It's all right. You'll do better in time. I'm not sure they have red cabbage here anyway. I haven't seen it."

"They must have it. How could they not have red cabbage?"

Brother Stoltz was preoccupied. He looked away. "It's hard to say. We eat different things, of course."

"I still hear it in your voice, Heinrich. Something is wrong."

"No. Nothing. I told you that."

"More rockets fell last night on the East End," Anna said. "I heard people talking about it at the market. But the radio still says nothing about it. It's almost like being in Germany. Why don't they tell the truth?"

"I suspect they don't want information to get back to Germany—about where the rockets struck, how much damage they did, all that sort of thing. But Hitler must have observers here. I suspect that sort of information gets back to him no matter what is on the radio."

"If there are spies here, do you think they would try to harm us?" Sister Stoltz asked.

"No, no. We're not worth their trouble now."

"But what if they knew what you do—both of you?"

"We translate, that's all. If we didn't do it, someone else would. We aren't important enough to worry about." He waved his hand in a gesture to show his confidence, but in fact, he was not quite as sure as he pretended. Who knew what a Nazi patriot might do, should the chance offer itself?

"I'm so accustomed to being afraid," Sister Stoltz said. "I don't know how to stop worrying."

"I don't worry for us now," Brother Stoltz told her. "I only worry for Peter. If I could do something to help him, I would do it."

"But there isn't anything for now," Anna said. She patted her father's hand. "I believe he's a prisoner of war—like Alex's brother. But I don't believe anyone would harm him. He's only a boy."

Brother Stoltz told her that was probably true. But he didn't believe it. Peter was not a boy. He would soon be eighteen. In Germany these days, seventeen-year-olds were not boys but soldiers.

"Maybe the war will end soon," Brother Stoltz said, "and I can go search for him."

"Maybe," Anna said, and she shrugged.

"What's this? Don't you think so?"

"She has a new worry," Sister Stoltz said.

"Papa, the news from Holland is not good," Anna said. "I try not to think about it, but I can't help it."

When Alex had made his parachute drop into Holland, he had not been able to tell Anna. But for a few days before his departure, letters from him had stopped arriving, and Anna knew that would happen only if the army wasn't sending his mail. Then the news had come through the newspapers: British and American airborne troops had made a daring move into Holland. The Guards Armored Division was making a head-long drive toward Germany.

For the next day or two, the news had been entirely opti-mistic, and people around London were speculating that the attack could drive a lance into the heart of Germany. Everyone was saying that General "Monty" Montgomery was a genius to have developed such a plan. But then the news had changed. The Germans were fighting back fiercely in many sectors, and the thrust by the armored division had bogged down.

"What was the news today?" Brother Stoltz asked.

"I'm not sure I understand exactly what is happening, but the Germans. . . ." Anna stopped. It was so strange to talk this way, to think of Germans as "them." But her husband was on one side, and therefore Germans *were* the enemy. "German troops have stopped the whole operation. There's been no progress since the first two days."

"The Allies always win in the end," Brother Stoltz said. "Since America came into the war, there has been a steady march toward Germany. This may not go as quickly as they had hoped, but I'm sure it will move ahead."

"Perhaps. But the Allies are nearly surrounded. They're fighting to hold onto one road through Holland."

Brother Stoltz nodded. He wanted to tell Anna something that might help, reassure her in some way, but the Stoltzes had been through too much together. She knew as well as he did what the realities were. He watched her eyes, saw how worried she was. She was not a young woman who fell apart under stress. She didn't complain much, and she certainly didn't vent her emotions. Still, having had such a short time with Alex, the thought of losing him had to be horrifying. Brother Stoltz remembered those early days in his own marriage when life had been difficult in many ways and he and Frieda had relied so totally on each other. How could he have lost that then, and gone on living until now? And yet all over the world young women were becoming widows. He had seen in Germany, and now here in London, so many amputees, men who had lost part of themselves to this war, but what about all the young wives who had lost part of their hearts?

The thought of Anna's pain magnified by the number of people who were suffering as much or more was unthinkable. And no one could blame it on one simple cause or one person. But certainly more than anyone else, Hitler had created this horror. The dissident generals and leaders who had made an attempt on Hitler's life—the men who were closest to Hitler—knew his madness better than anyone and had tried to stop him. They had failed, and many of them had already been executed for their actions. So Hitler's grip on Germany was as tight as ever, and one more chance to end the war had been lost. Brother Stoltz wondered why God hadn't aided those generals. So many lives could have been saved that way.

"What are you thinking, Heinrich? I know you have something on your mind."

"No. Nothing important." He looked at his wife and then looked away quickly. She had to know that he was up to something. What he wanted to tell her was that he wouldn't let Peter die; he would do what he could. But he still wasn't sure he would get his chance.

8

Alex and his squad were crowded into a cellar in the little Dutch village of Veghel. Artillery was pounding the town in a steady rhythm. A Dutch girl, a teenager, and her little brother and sister were huddled together in one corner, and all three of them were crying, sometimes praying. The mother, close by, was holding a terrified baby boy, about a year old, who was crying incessantly in spite of all the comforting the mother could give. The father, in his farmer's overalls and tall rubber boots, sat next to his wife on the dirt floor and stared straight ahead. When the crashing noises came close, he sometimes whispered to his children, calmly, but Alex saw in him a kind of fatalism, his eyes seeming to say, "If it comes, it comes. What can I do?"

E Company had retreated to Eindhoven from Neunen under the cover of night and then had been trucked toward Uden. The attempt to widen the salient—the Allied-held ground—had failed, but the 101st was trying desperately to hang onto the main artery of their operation, the road that soldiers had begun to call "hell's highway." Some of the trucks had made it through Veghel and had probably reached Uden, where a counterattack was expected at any time, but Alex's squad, along with the rest of the platoon, had come under heavy fire. The men had had to jump from their trucks and find cover wherever they could.

Now artillery was zeroed in on the town, and German fighters were making repeated strafing runs. The highway had led to hell itself, it seemed, and Alex wondered whether there was any hope of getting out. He had never heard such a furious, constant cannonade. The house trembled from the concussions, and dirt shook loose from the floor above. The air was so filled with dust that it was hard to breathe.

And all the while the poor little baby, frantic with fear, continued to scream, and the other children sobbed. Alex knew how frightened he was himself; he felt sorry for these kids, who must have been terrified by everything going on around them—including the intrusion of all these rough-looking men. He remembered LaRue and Beverly when they were younger—the way he still thought of them—and wondered how they would have dealt with a war in the streets of Salt Lake City.

Every time a shell hit close, it seemed that the next one would surely take them all. Alex watched Howie, who was sitting next to Alex on the ground with his arms on his knees and his head on his arms. He seemed still, as calm as anyone could be under the circumstances, but Alex could see that he was shaking all over, panting more than breathing, grunting when the shells hit close. Curtis was on the other side of Howie, and clearly he was frightened too, but he seemed to be in better control. He kept glancing at Alex, giving little nods, and a couple of times he patted Howie's back. "We're all right. We'll get through this," Curtis would say.

And then the house took a hit. There was a terrible crash upstairs. Dirt and dust flew, and Alex heard timbers twist and tear, dishes fall. The ceiling wrenched, trembled, but held. The baby screamed with terror and clung to his mother, and the mother, in spite of herself, screamed too. There were a few seconds of confusion as everyone instinctively curled up and waited, but then it was over, and in spite of all the dust in the air, everyone was still alive and safe. For the moment, it didn't seem to matter much what had happened to the house.

Alex had gotten used to the rhythm of the artillery shells, knew about how much time would pass between each little bombardment—the shells always coming three at a time. When the usual interval passed, then doubled, he felt himself breathe a little easier. The airplanes seemed to be gone too. But after a few minutes, reality began to set in. Artillery was for softening up a position. When the artillery stopped, the tanks, with troops, usually followed.

Alex waited five or six minutes and then said, "Okay, men, we have to get out of here. The attack is going to start. We've got to create a perimeter."

"It'll be tanks," Pozernac said, without emotion.

"I know. Let's go."

The men got to their feet and picked up their weapons. Alex walked over to the woman. "I'm sorry," he said. She and her husband nodded. They didn't understand the words, but they seemed to know what he was saying. The woman was still patting the baby, whispering to him. Tears were on her face. The man nodded and said something in Dutch. It sounded much like German, and yet Alex couldn't follow it. What he sensed was that the man was relieving him of blame, saying it couldn't be helped. But Alex knew their circumstances were now becoming clear: their house was blown apart, and the Germans might soon be returning. They had paid dearly, and yet, from all appearances, they had gained nothing.

Upstairs, Alex was glad to see that the house was at least holding together. One wall had caved in and the upper floor was hanging into the kitchen, but maybe there was some way to salvage the place. Alex didn't know, nor did he have time to think about it. As he stepped from the house, out through the hole in the damaged wall, he saw Lieutenant Owen running toward him. "Thomas, take your men and establish a position straight down this street to the west. Get your machine gun in place. Do you still have that bazooka?"

"Yeah. But not much ammo for it."

"Okay. If tanks come at you, you've got to hold your position and not fire too soon. We can't waste the shells. I'll send a 60 millimeter mortar with you, too. We need to put up all the fire we can—and make the Krauts think we're still in good shape."

"All right. We'll do what we can."

Alex led his squad to the edge of town. He found a little orchard there, and he told the men to dig in as fast as they could. He didn't have to tell them twice. All the men pulled their entrenching tools off their belts and began shoveling furiously. The earth was soft, but the water table was high. Alex and Howie dug as deep as they could, all the while glancing across the fields toward a nearby hill and watching for the attack. At about four feet, water began to seep into the bottom of the hole, so they stopped digging.

Alex was surprised not to see tanks by then, or troops. But then the artillery opened up again. Alex and Howie dropped down into the hole. "What's going on?" Howie shouted over the noise. "When's the ground attack coming?"

"The Germans let up long enough to draw us out of the cellars. Now they're hitting us again. It's a smart trick."

"We should have stayed at the house," Howie said. His voice broke a little. Alex thought of his brother Gene, when he was a little kid, the way he would pretend he was mad sometimes when he was really just scared.

"We didn't know. What if they had rolled into town with tanks?"

Howie said nothing more. The two of them sat in the water that was now a couple of inches deep. The rhythm of the artillery returned, the shells pounding in threes again. But now the Germans were changing their aim with each barrage, moving their target to the perimeter, where forward observers must have been directing them. Alex could hear, feel, with each round of shells, that one of the guns was moving its aim closer to the orchard. Before long the shells were crashing in among the trees, jarring the earth. The concussion would send shock waves through the air, sounding in the trees. "Keep your mouth open," he yelled to Howie. "So your ear drums don't pop."

"They're going to get us!" Howie shouted. "They're getting closer. Let's get out of here!"

"No. Just stay in the hole. That's the safest place." But Alex hardly knew whether he believed it. He wanted to jump and run himself.

Howie had curled up in the bottom of the hole, filling much of the space. Alex bent over him, staying as low as he could. He knew that a shell would have to hit them, almost direct, to get them. This soft earth would absorb a shell pretty well. But a direct hit seemed more of a possibility all the time, as the shells hit so close that the ground around them trembled.

After each barrage, Alex could feel Howie, under him, take a deep breath and relax just a little, but as the seconds mounted, he would pull in tight again, getting ready for the next crash. And then it would come: the flash, and an instant later, the booming explosion, and the blast of the concussion, like wind, sucking the air out of the hole. And Howie would gasp, even though Alex knew he was trying hard not to. Alex was feeling the same terror, the silent seconds the worst because of the anticipation, and the explosions always bringing relief for a moment. But he knew something Howie didn't. Alex never admitted it to himself, except at times like this, but he actually expected to die. He prayed every day that he would be allowed to live, but when the fire began, he found that he couldn't pray. The shelling seemed something even God couldn't stop—or at least didn't. And sooner or later the odds had to catch up.

On and on, the crashing continued. Trees were torn from

the soil, dirt pelted down on them, and the blasts vibrated through the ground. Two or three times the concussion was so close it sucked the air from Alex's lungs, left him limp and panting. When the barrage finally stopped, he felt sick to his stomach, exhausted. Howie's words sounded right when he gasped, "I can't go through that anymore, Sergeant. I'd rather just die and get it over with."

Alex was crouching now, looking from their hole toward the trees on the hill beyond the town. "Remember what I told you," he told Howie. "Don't think about it. Just take what comes and do the best you can."

"Do you get used to it?"

"No."

When no tanks appeared after a few minutes, Alex said, "I've got to check on the men. I'll be right back."

He pulled himself out of the foxhole and ran through the orchard. The men in the squad had been sprayed with dirt and broken tree limbs, but no one had taken a hit. What he saw in their faces, however, was the same exhaustion, the same fatalism, he was experiencing. Duncan and Campbell had been through more of this than anyone, and they were together. Duncan smiled, but not with any joy. "Having a nice day?" he asked.

"What do you think they'll do now?" Alex asked.

"They'll check us out. They'll show themselves enough to see how strong we still are. And then they'll hit us with more of the same. They don't have to sacrifice a lot of men to get in here. They can sit back and hammer us. We don't have any artillery to return fire."

"I don't know when we'll get any help, either," Alex said.

"Get ready for a long haul, Deacon." Duncan was still wearing the helmet with the bullet hole. He had pounded in the rough edges, but that was all.

"What do you think happened to the rest of our company—the ones who got through here?"

"They're probably getting shot up in Uden. I wish we were all together. We'd have a lot better chance."

Alex heard the hopelessness in Duncan's voice, but he didn't respond to it. He ran back to his own foxhole. Howie had tried to scoop some of the water out of the hole with his helmet, but he had accomplished little other than to make a muddy mess of his helmet.

In a few minutes Alex heard a Jeep and turned around to see that Owen had stopped and hopped out. Alex waved, and Owen ran to him. He knelt by the foxhole and said, "We've got to expect an attack now."

"I know. We're ready. What's holding them up?"

"I don't know. They may be playing games. They might hit us with more artillery first, but they're running out of daylight hours. If they're coming with tanks, they'll have to do it soon. Did you take casualties in this last round of fire?"

"No. What about the rest of the platoon?"

"We lost some men in a house in town, and two men took a hit in a foxhole. But we've survived pretty well. We just have to keep holding our own."

"Is there any way we could pull out after dark and make it to Uden? We'd be a lot better off if we could get back with the rest of the company."

"We can't leave and let the Jerries cut the road. We have to hold out overnight. We've got tanks coming in the morning, and air support."

"I hope this is worth it. Are the Brits getting through?"

"You mean to Arnhem?"

"Yeah."

"Thomas, I thought you knew. We didn't make it."

"What do you mean?"

Lieutenant Owen held his hand up to shade his eyes, and he scanned the horizon. Then he crouched low again. "I don't know the whole story. From what I've heard, the Limey paratroopers held the bridge for a couple of days, but the armored division got stopped. They couldn't make it to Arnhem, and the paratroopers lost the bridge."

"Then what are we fighting for?"

Owen seemed to have lost some of his mass over the past few days. He looked smaller, less formidable. His field jacket was covered with dirt, his face prickly with dark whiskers. He still had that "big kid" look about him, with the gap between his two front teeth, but his eyes were as empty as the craters in the mud Alex could see all around. "Thomas, we're fighting for our lives," Owen said. "We've taken control of this territory, and now we have to hold it. Maybe reinforcements can push in from Belgium, up this road, and we can eventually make the operation work. But the surprise is over. The quick run into Germany didn't happen. Nothing turned out the way the generals hoped it would."

Alex was taking long breaths by now. He knew that the big brass moved the troops around like pawns on a chessboard, and it wasn't the place of those pawns to make the decisions, or in most cases even to know what was going on. But this whole operation had been sold to the men as a quick end to the war. Now it appeared to have been for nothing, and yet the price, in lives, was far from paid.

"Look, the road is just as important as it ever was. Everyone along this highway is dependent on it staying open. It's our source of supplies. So we have to fight for it as hard as ever. When the attack comes, we have to hold on. There's nowhere to run to anyway. The Germans are all around us."

Alex nodded. He understood. "We'll be all right, sir," he said.

"If they come at us, we can't give an inch. We can't be the weak link."

"Yes, sir."

Owen stood up and walked away. Alex took another good look at the hill, the trees, and then he looked at Howie.

"All this is for nothing?" Howie said.

Alex shrugged. "I guess it was a gamble somebody thought we had to take," he said.

Howie was facing Alex, very close. His eyes were fixed, as though the terror of the artillery attack were still clinging to him. "But think how many guys are dying out here."

"Howie, we can't think about that. Somebody else makes the decisions. What we have to do is hold this perimeter right here in front of us."

Howie nodded, and Alex could see he was trying to accept all this, toughen himself, but all the color was gone from his face, and his lips were pale, almost white.

It wasn't long before the artillery began again, and the two had to hunker down in the foxhole, now four or five inches deep in water. The shelling didn't last very long this time, but when it ended the tanks appeared: four big Tiger Royals. They rolled forward relentlessly.

Alex yelled to his men, "There's nowhere to go. We've got to stop these guys."

Just behind the tanks were troops, moving cautiously, hunched over and making short runs, then dropping down. Alex waited until the tanks were close—maybe two hundred yards—and then he shouted, "Start the machine-gun fire. Duncan, are you ready with that mortar?"

"Yeah."

"Go after that first tank."

In just a few seconds the first mortar shell fired with a thumping sound, and the shell exploded close to the tank. The tank hesitated for a moment but then came forward again. Pozernac was firing his machine-gun by then, tracer bullets flashing through the air, the fire slowing the ground troops but not stopping them. The tanks were separating now, spreading out in a horizontal line. One of them had zeroed in on the orchard and was coming straight at Alex's squad.

"Campbell, are you ready?" Alex shouted

He heard nothing from Campbell. The noise of the

machine gun, and now the rifle fire, was too loud. Alex hoped Campbell was taking aim with that bazooka. But on and on the tank continued, its tracks now audible above the other noise, squeaking, clanking. Alex thought Campbell was holding off until the last moment, to hit the thing at close range.

Or maybe the bazooka was jammed. Nothing was happening, and the tank was almost on top of them.

And then the bazooka fired, with a flash, and the shell crashed against the tank, low and left. It didn't break through the armor, but Campbell, either by luck or good sense, had hit one of the tracks. The big Tiger twisted to the side, only one track still pushing forward. And then the gun began to swing toward the orchard. Alex fired his M-1, pointlessly. He was expecting an 88 shell, from close range.

He saw Campbell, running straight at the tank—as he had before, back at the barn in Neunen. He was not thirty feet away when he finally dropped onto his chest, aimed, and fired the bazooka again. The tank fired at the same moment. The shell blasted through the trees, but when Alex looked up again, he saw that the tank was engulfed in smoke. The bazooka, at close range, had penetrated the armor. Campbell was up and running, returning to his foxhole. As far as Alex could tell, he was all right, and the tank was dead in its tracks.

By then Alex realized that one of the other tanks had changed its angle and was heading toward the orchard. Another 88 shell crashed through the trees and exploded to Alex's right. Shrapnel whistled through the air. He dropped into his hole, in reaction, and waited for a moment. Just as he raised up again, a mortar shell exploded directly in front of the oncoming tank. The tank came to an abrupt stop and then, surprisingly, began backing away. It fired one more time, taking limbs out of the trees and blowing dirt in the air farther to Alex's right.

The tank continued backing for a time, and then it swung around and headed away, toward the distant hill. Alex saw that the other two tanks were doing the same thing, and he took a long breath. What he knew, however, was that Duncan had been right. The Germans had probed a little, had determined what kind of firepower remained in the town, but hadn't wanted to gamble away all their tanks. They could hold the Americans down, keep shelling from a distance, and make a major push when they met less resistance.

As soon as the tanks moved back, the artillery shelling began again. Howie had stayed down through all this, and now he pushed himself lower into the hole. "How long will they keep doing this?" he asked. Alex could tell he was on the edge, close to breaking down.

"I don't know, Howie. But we sent them back. We did what we had to do. We'll get some help in here soon."

Alex hoped Owen was right about the reinforcements. He knew the Germans would be back, probably in the morning. But he was also worried about something else. He didn't know whether anyone had taken a hit from those shells the tanks had fired. So during the next pause, after a round of three shells, he jumped up and ran to the next foxhole. He found Ernst and Sabin all right but looking baffled, dead serious. He crowded into their hole with them, reassured them, waited for the next three rounds, and then ran again. Duncan and Campbell were all right, a little less rattled, but in no mood to kid around.

When Alex ran toward the next hole, he saw before he got there that a shell had hit very close, almost a direct hit. He found his friend Curtis Bentley looking up at him, his face full of pain. He had apparently wrapped his own arm with a bandage, and he was holding onto it, with blood seeping through, dripping from his fingers. Withers was hunched over, folded in on himself. The back of his uniform was soaked with blood. "He's dead," Curtis said, his voice dead, too.

"How bad are you hit?"

"Not bad at all. Some shrapnel cut my arm open, but it didn't break the bone."

Alex jumped into the hole and then pushed Withers's body over to make enough room. "We need to make a run for it after this next round of shells. There's no way to evacuate you, but we've got medics. They can get the bleeding stopped."

"Let's just wait until the shelling stops. I'm not bleeding to death."

"All right." But Alex wondered. Would the Germans keep shelling all night? For the past two hours the sky had been darkening. Alex hoped it would rain, perhaps to drive the Germans inside. Mud would also slow down the tanks if they tried to cross that field again. He kept watching Curtis. His face was pale under the dirt and the stubble of beard, and he was obviously in a lot of pain, even though he wasn't saying so.

A shell exploded in the town somewhere, and that meant two more were coming. Alex and Curtis pulled their heads down and waited. But the next two explosions weren't close. "Let's get Withers out of here," Alex said. He climbed out of the hole, and then Curtis helped as much as he could as Alex dragged the body out on the ground. Then he jumped back in. "Let me tighten that bandage on you," Alex told Curtis.

When they heard the whistle, they ducked low again, waited for the explosions. But none was targeted on the orchard right now. Alex tried to work on the bandage, then got out another one, used it to apply more pressure. "After Withers got hit," Curtis said, "the only thing he said was, 'I hope my mom and dad can deal with this. And my little brother.' He came from a really nice family. He's been telling me all about them."

"Curtis, don't think about that stuff. You just can't."

"I know."

Alex hesitated, and then he said, "Come on. Let's go. Right after this next round. I don't like sitting here."

"You don't need to go with me."

"I don't want you to pass out—and bleed to death."

"Don't worry. I'm okay. I'll be back out here on the line before long. It's not that bad."

"All right."

Curtis waited for the next three explosions, but they didn't come. The shelling had apparently stopped. Curtis waited another ten minutes or so, and then he said, "Okay. This is a good chance. I'll go now."

"All right. I'll check on you when I can."

They took a long look at each other. "Good luck," Curtis finally said, and they both knew what he was thinking. If the Germans overran them tonight, or in the morning, there was no telling who would be left alive.

Alex tossed Withers's rifle out on the ground and then climbed out of the foxhole. Withers was on his side and rather twisted, so Alex turned him onto his back and straightened him out. His helmet had come off, and his glasses were pushed up onto his forehead. Alex pulled the glasses back into place, and for just a moment, he looked at him. With a lock of hair drooping toward his eyes, Withers looked very young, far too young. Alex wanted to say something, maybe a prayer, but he knew he couldn't start something like that. He stood up, looked away for a time, and clenched his jaw tight. He wasn't going to let this get to him. He stabbed Withers's rifle into the ground and hung his helmet over the butt. He hoped someone could come for the body before long and get him out of there.

When Alex walked back to his foxhole, Howie asked, "What happened over there?"

"It's Withers. Curtis got cut up a little, but he's all right."

"Royce is dead?"

"Yeah. Don't talk about it."

"Did he catch some—"

"Howie, listen to me. You can't think about that stuff. We're alive. We'll be okay."

"All right."

The rain was starting. It had been mostly a mist for a time, but now it was turning into drops, pelting down quite steadily. Alex realized he and his men were in for an unthinkably miserable night. They couldn't go back to the houses. They would have to set up outposts and take turns watching and guarding the perimeter. The water in the foxholes would only get deeper, and the night would be cold.

Alex was almost relieved when the bombardment began again. It meant that the tanks weren't coming, at least not yet, and probably not until morning. It also meant that he had something to think about, to fear. It took Withers off his mind.

The Germans continued to concentrate on other sectors, the shells not striking close. That was a strange sort of relief. If the shells weren't hitting here, other men of Easy Company were taking it all the harder. Alex wondered who would be left to fight in the morning.

After a half-hour bombardment, the shells stopped again, and now night was falling. Alex and Howie tried to scoop out more water from their foxhole, but they found the effort pointless, so they sat on their helmets, with their ponchos over their heads. They ate from their cans of rations—their food smelling, tasting like mud—and then they sat in the dark, with the rain making popping sounds as it hit the ponchos. Their feet were in the water, and there was simply nothing to do about that. They didn't want to be out on the ground if the shells started falling again.

At midnight Alex and Howie took a turn on watch, and even though the job was much more dangerous, Alex was rather glad to be out of the foxhole. He didn't believe that the Germans would try to make a night attack, not in all this muck, but it was dangerous to make that assumption. Surprise was the most basic element of warfare, and he had been taught time and again that he should never presume that the most obvious things would happen.

As it turned out, the Germans surprised him in another way. In the middle of the night, when he was back in the

foxhole, sitting up but leaning against the dirt and actually doz-
ing off, the shells started to hit again, and this time the guns
had returned their aim to the orchard, full force. Alex and
Howie didn't worry about the water now. They got low in the
hole and waited as hell opened up around them again. The
shells tore up the trees, spattering mud and broken limbs over
them. Alex was almost sure his squad would take more casualties this time.

Howie was gasping now, holding onto Alex with both
hands. "I can't do this, Thomas," he mumbled between rounds.
"I'm . . . not going to make it."

"Can you make it through the night?"

"I don't know."

"Come on, Howie. You can last out a few more hours."

"Okay, but—"

"This is the worst night I've ever gone through. If you get
through this one, you've caught up with the rest of us."

"But won't we be here tomorrow night?"

A shell struck, loud and wild, ripping trees. Alex waited a
couple of seconds, and then he laughed. "If we're *lucky*, we'll be
here tomorrow night."

But that didn't work for Howie. He couldn't laugh. The kid
was so young, so small. Alex felt like taking him into his arms
and holding him. Instead, he said, "Just hold on. We'll be all
right. I'm going to get you through. Remember? That's what I
promised you."

Howie nodded. "All right," he said. He took a long breath,
as though trying to draw in courage.

When the sun finally began to come up, after what seemed
a dozen nights, not one, Howie ate, and he seemed to be going
about his business, but he was silent, turning inward, probably
telling himself to hold on, to be as much a man as the others.

Alex was glad for that, but he wasn't happy to think what
might be coming. When he heard tanks, his breath caught.
And then he realized that the sound was behind him, and some

big Chieftain tanks—British—were clanking down the cobble-stone street through the town. They kept coming, a dozen of them, and they pushed on into the fields beyond Veghel. As they approached the distant woods, RAF fighters suddenly swooped out of sky, strafing. Bombers followed.

Alex's men all climbed out of their foxholes, and they cheered, Howie as loud as any of them. And when Summers drove up, he had even better news. While the Germans were being held at bay by the Brits, the balance of the platoon was being moved out. Reinforcements were rolling down the road, and they would occupy the town.

So the men boarded trucks and headed for Uden. And along the way they questioned, quietly, whether any of the men from their company who had gone ahead would still be alive. But what they found was that all of them were, that they had taken far less fire than the men at Veghel. Alex watched Howie come back to life a little, but he still saw his wariness, as though he were thinking, as all the men probably were, "What's coming next?"

Bobbi was at Ishi Aoki's house on a Sunday afternoon in late October. She was helping Ishi prepare their dinner while Lily and David were playing outside. "So what's going on between Afton and Sam?" Ishi asked. "They seem to be together an awful lot lately."

"I don't know, Ishi. Afton always says it's just a friendship, but I don't think Sam sees it that way."

"Well, I think Sam's a good man for Afton. I hope she marries him."

Bobbi was straining water from the rice that Ishi had cooked. There were certain subjects that she still found difficult to talk about with Ishi, but she took a chance now. "Ishi, Afton's parents are opposed to people of different races getting married. They don't know about Sam, but Afton's sure they wouldn't approve. Over here, maybe no one would think too much about it, but on the mainland it's different."

"Most people here don't approve either, Bobbi. I heard a sister in the ward—a Hawaiian sister—say she thought Sam was making a mistake, that a marriage like that would never last."

"Do you think maybe it's best if people marry in their own race?"

Ishi didn't answer for some time. She was setting bowls on the kitchen table. "I used to think that way," she finally said. "I thought there were too many differences. Now, I'm not so sure. Maybe we should try harder to get rid of the differences."

"How?"

"I don't know. But there's no reason for people to separate themselves the way they do. We're all brothers and sisters."

Bobbi thought she knew what Ishi was saying, but again she wondered whether she should ask. "Ishi, do you feel like you're not accepted in the ward?"

"I don't know. I can't answer that with a simple yes or no. Most people are very nice to me."

Bobbi decided she wouldn't be nosy. If Ishi wanted to leave it at that, she would let it go.

"Bobbi, you probably think you understand Hawaii by now, but there's more to it than you see on the surface. White people control most of the money, and Hawaiians resent that. And then, lots of Japanese came here at one time. We're more than a third of all the people in Hawaii now. Native Hawaiians aren't so happy about that either."

"But in the Church, everyone gets along well, don't they?"

"Pretty well."

"But not well enough?" Bobbi set the rice on the table.

"Well . . . you see how the members group together, according to their own background. That's not surprising, I guess. And maybe it's not such a bad thing."

"But you must feel left out."

"There just aren't very many AJAs—Americans of Japanese Ancestry, as *we* like to call ourselves—in the Waikiki Ward. That makes us feel a little uncomfortable at times."

"Does the war have something to do with it?"

"Of course, Bobbi." Ishi walked back to the stove, where she stirred the vegetables she was cooking. Bobbi heard the sizzle, noticed the burst of spicy smells. It was strange to think how much she had once disliked the foods she had discovered in the islands. "No one feels quite the same about anyone who is Japanese, no matter where we live. We're the enemy."

"You are not. Brother Hoffer's family came from Germany. That doesn't make him an enemy."

"But that's not how people feel. When they look at me—or my children—I'm sure they see the pilots who dropped bombs on Pearl Harbor. It's going to be that way until this war is over—and probably for a long time afterward."

"But do you notice that kind of attitude even at church?"

"People try harder at church, but they can't help what they feel."

"I just don't understand that, Ishi."

"Bobbi, be honest with yourself. You do understand."

Bobbi was suddenly self-conscious. She thought she knew what Ishi was saying, but she didn't admit anything. "What do you mean?" she asked.

"When you first arrived here, you were uncomfortable around me. I felt that immediately."

"It was just something new to me."

"Your brother is a prisoner of war—and I'm one of those nasty people holding him. Isn't that what you felt?"

"It wasn't quite like that, Ishi. I've just never been around people of different races. My parents are friends with one Japanese family, but I've never known them very well."

"But tell me this. What did you *feel* when you came to dinner here that first time?"

Neither woman was looking at the other now. Bobbi considered for a time, and then she answered honestly. "I felt awkward, I guess," she said.

"Now ask yourself why."

"Ishi, you have to understand, once the war started, I heard nothing but terrible things about the Japanese. The newspapers on the mainland are full of these horrible cartoon drawings, and everyone talks about getting revenge for Pearl Harbor. There's a *lot* of hatred. I don't know whether you know this, but in Salt Lake, Negroes always sit upstairs in our movie theaters—away from the whites—and Japanese and even Chinese were told to sit up there with them. I asked my dad about that, and he told me people of different races would rather stay in their own groups. I said, 'Gee, Dad, I didn't know Japanese and Chinese and Negroes were all the same race.'"

Ishi laughed. "What did he say to that?"

"I don't remember. I was in college and starting to think I knew everything—so he was used to my smarting off to him that way. But the thing is, I was curious about it, and I guess I felt there was something wrong with it, but it wasn't something I'd thought about very much. I've never been acquainted with a Negro in my whole life. We had a few Orientals at my high school, but I didn't know them very well."

"So how did you feel about coming to Hawaii?"

"I don't know. I thought about the palm trees and the beaches. I didn't know how things were here. But on the way over, when I was in San Francisco, I saw this newsreel about the terrible way Japanese soldiers were treating the American prisoners in the Philippines. So when I met you, I didn't blame *you* for that, but I didn't know exactly how to behave either."

"Bobbi, I'm sorry. This isn't like me to bring all this up. I didn't mean to put you on the spot."

"No, that's all right. And I'm not denying that I felt some of those things. But when people get to know each other, all that disappears."

"That's exactly what I would like to do, Bobbi. Get to know more people."

"Then why don't you go to the ward parties?"

"I don't know. I always find an excuse," Ishi said, and she laughed at herself. But then she added, "In church, we leave our cultures behind more easily. At a party, the differences come out. I get restless when the Hawaiians start singing and dancing. I hardly know what to do."

"Sister Nuanunu said the same thing about me. She said haoles don't know how to have fun."

"Haoles do better than AJAs. We can be awfully serious." Ishi brought the vegetables to the table.

"I'll call the kids," Bobbi said.

Ishi put her hand on Bobbi's arm. "Bobbi, let me say something to you." Bobbi was surprised to see Ishi's eyes fill with tears. "I want you to know that with Daniel gone I'm closer to you than *anyone*. I know I don't say things—not the way Afton does—but you're as dear to me as a sister. Not just a sister in the church—but a blood sister. I never know how to tell you that, but it's what I feel."

"I know, Ishi. I feel the same way." Bobbi took Ishi in her arms, patted her back. "We're going through some of the same things. I think we understand each other."

When Ishi stepped back, she said, "You asked me about intermarriage, and I do have to say, I've always been against it. But I'm starting to feel there are things more important than race. You can see why I would feel that way."

Bobbi nodded. "Sure. That's what I'm feeling too."

Bobbi went outside then and called Lily and David in. The four ate together and chatted.

"How are you doing in school?" Bobbi asked Lily.

"I go to school," David said. He was only three, but he always wanted to be part of the conversation.

"You do?" Bobbi asked.

"He means he *will* go to school," Lily said. "When you're a big boy, huh, David?"

"I *am* a big boy." He nodded his head twice, then once more, with exaggerated emphasis.

"But when you're bigger."

"Uh huh."

Bobbi went back to her first question. "Do you like school, Lily?"

"Yes. I'm in the first reading group. I can read fat books. All by myself."

"Maybe after dinner you can read to me."

"I will. I'll read a whole book to you."

"Maybe just part of one," Ishi said, laughing. "We have to go back to church before too much longer."

Lily was eating with chopsticks—something Bobbi was still not very good at. "Sometimes, when we're reading, we have to stop and get under our desks," Lily said.

"Is that for air-raid drill?"

"Yes. In case the Japs come to bomb us."

"Lily!"

Lily was still eating, and she didn't look up. She seemed to know what her mother was about to say. "I'm not a Jap. Steven—the boy who sits next to me—he said I'm a Jap. But I'm not. I'm Japanese American." She finally looked at her mother.

"No one is a Jap, Lily," Ishi said. "Don't use that word."

Lily shook her head. "Someone is. All the kids at school say so. Japs can drop bombs on us if we don't hide under our desks."

Bobbi wanted to say, "Lily, no one will drop bombs on you," but she knew that she couldn't make that promise. She also had no idea how to disconnect a country, a government, from a race of people, and make it clear to Lily that she was not the enemy.

Ishi said, "Lily, we've talked all about this. In war, sometimes people drop bombs. But there are good people who live everywhere."

"I know," Lily said.

Still, Bobbi wondered. How could a child understand that? How could anyone?

After dinner, the children went back outside, where they had a little sandpile to play in. Ishi and Bobbi cleared the table and washed the dishes, and then they sat down in the living room. The Sunday paper was on the coffee table. Bobbi had seen the Honolulu paper that morning, briefly, but now she glanced again at the stories on the front page. The big news was that the battle for the Philippines had begun.

"What's all this going to mean for your brother?" Ishi asked. "Will he be freed now?"

"I don't know. Apparently a lot of the prisoners have already been taken to Japan. Maybe that's where Wally is by now. We haven't heard anything from him for a long time."

"But maybe he's still in the Philippines, and he'll be set free."

"It's possible. And sure, that would be wonderful. I just worry about all the things that could go wrong." Bobbi glanced across the page to an article about the progress of the war in Italy. "Do you know where Daniel is now, Ishi?"

"Not exactly. Somewhere around Bologna, I think. But there's something I haven't told you. I hardly want to think about it."

"What?"

Ishi wiped her eyes and leaned forward, her knees together, her elbows on her knees. "I got a letter from Daniel this week. On Thursday. He said he had been wounded."

"Wounded? How bad is it?"

"I don't know. He told me almost nothing. He said, 'I received a slight wound, but I'm fine now, and I'm returning to my unit.' Those are his exact words. I've read them over and over. But Bobbi, it hurts my heart so much to think about it."

"The wound couldn't be serious, Ishi."

"But a bullet or shrapnel—or something—went into his body, shed his blood, maybe hurt him worse than he's saying. And he tells me nothing—except that he's going back for more. Maybe another inch to the left or right and he would have been dead. Maybe the next bullet will take him. I can hardly stand all this waiting and wondering."

"Ishi, if something happens to Richard, I don't even know how I'll find out."

"Have you had any letters?"

"Not for over a week. And those were a month old."

"He's probably fine, Bobbi."

"Hazel told me not to worry. To accept what God has in store for me. But I can't seem to do that, Ishi. Can you?"

"I'll accept what happens, if it happens. I won't have any choice. But I know I'm going to worry every second until Daniel comes home."

"I've tried not to worry," Bobbi said. "I listened to what Hazel said, and I thought it was right. If I had more faith, I could do it. But I wake up worrying in the night. I get out of bed worrying in the morning. No matter how busy I am all day, it's always there. I should avoid the papers and the radio and just not think about it. But I can't seem to do that. Now Alex is in the fighting again. I don't understand what's happening in Holland, but it doesn't sound good. I think about Anna, in London, all the time. I worry about her, about Alex, about everything."

"It's the same in Italy. There's been snow in the mountains. I read that, and I wonder how Daniel can live in snow, up in the mountains. He's not used to anything like that."

"Oh, Ishi. It's all so awful. When I was younger, I guess I got the idea that if I was good, and prayed, and tried to be faithful, I wouldn't have to go through anything really terrible. But now, since Gene died, it's like my blinders have been taken off—and I feel like I'm fair game for anything. It makes me angry sometimes; it doesn't seem fair, and it makes me mad."

"Who are you mad at?"

"I don't know. No one. It just doesn't seem like life ought to be like that."

"So you think God got his plan a little fouled up?"

Bobbi tried to smile, and she didn't answer, didn't want to say that. But the truth was, what she felt ran much deeper than that. She had worked so hard to accept Gene's death, but it made her furious to think God could stay out of this now. He could bring Richard back to her, safe and sound, if he just chose to.

The two took a long look at each other. Bobbi held on, not wanting to let her emotions get away from her; she knew Ishi was doing the same. It was a relief when David came to the door. "Come and see our castle," he said.

"All right," Bobbi told him, and she got up. "Let's go look," she told Ishi. And so the two walked outside.

Lily and David had used their small pails to stack one mound of sand upon another and create a rather extensive structure that looked very little like any castle Bobbi had ever seen. But she told the kids, "Wow. What a beautiful castle! And you two must be the king and queen."

Lily grinned. "No. I'm the queen. David's a knight. He likes to ride on a horse."

David nodded. And then he galloped away, holding his hands in front of him, as though hanging onto a horse's reins. Bobbi laughed, but what she remembered were her little brothers, Wally and Gene. She had seen them gallop that same way. So many little boys had been knights or cowboys, and now they were being soldiers, all over the world. The thought of it struck Bobbi hard, and without expecting it, she began to cry.

She turned toward Ishi, who seemed to be thinking something similar. Tears were also on her cheeks. Bobbi nodded, and they seemed to understand each other. "Sisters," Bobbi whispered.

After church that evening, Afton invited Bobbi to go for a walk with her and Sam, but Bobbi didn't really believe Afton wanted her along, so she made excuses and then went for her own walk before she caught the bus back to the base. Ishi had warned her not to walk alone. Honolulu had changed since Bobbi had first arrived. So many civilian workers were there now, many of whom seemed to be single men on the loose.

Crime in Hawaii had increased tremendously. Ishi felt that a woman by herself was not really safe, especially after dark.

Bobbi supposed that might be true, but she didn't feel it when she walked the streets. Sometimes she heard catcalls, but no one had ever bothered her beyond that. There was always something so gentle about Hawaiian evenings that made her feel secure. Still, she didn't walk long, or approach the busy parts of town, where men often loitered on Sunday evenings. She caught the bus back to Pearl Harbor, even though she dreaded the long evening alone in her little cubicle of a room.

She spent some time reading that night, but her mind kept wandering to all the things she and Ishi had talked about—her brothers and Richard and Daniel. She lay back on her bed, her book open across her chest, and she wondered, as she often did, what each of them was doing at the moment. She calculated the times in the parts of the world where they were, but it was hard to picture any circumstances that were comfortable or safe. Richard probably had the best chance of being in a port somewhere, or out on the ocean away from the battle, but her heart told her that wasn't the case.

When the door suddenly opened, Bobbi jerked, and then realized she had fallen asleep. She sat up and looked at Afton and then at her watch. "Hey, kid, it's really late," she said.

"I know. And I have to be up early in the morning."

The lights were still on, and Bobbi could see how flushed Afton was. "I think you two are doing a little too much kissing," Bobbi said. "You're glowing just a little too bright for this time of night."

"Oh, Bobbi." Afton sat down on her bed, across from Bobbi. "I don't know what I'm doing. I feel like I'm going crazy."

"You're crazy in love, if you ask me."

Afton looked at the floor. "When I was walking up the stairs just now, I got thinking about something I did when I was a teenager," she said. "I opened a box of chocolates when my parents weren't home. I thought I would take one and stop, but

I ended up eating about half the box. I knew I was getting myself into *huge* trouble, but I just kept eating those stupid things—one at a time. Now I feel like I'm doing the same thing all over again. Why don't I have the brains to stop?"

"I think you're swallowing the whole box this time."

"Shut up." Afton blushed—brighter than before.

"Hey, I'm just telling you the truth."

"You don't have to tell me, Bobbi. I know."

"So what are you going to do?"

Afton dropped backward onto her bed and put her arm across her eyes. "He asked me to marry him," she said.

"Really? What did you tell him?"

"Oh, golly, I don't know. I told him I couldn't, but then he asked me to think about it, so I said I would."

"And then you kissed some more."

"Too much."

"How much?"

Afton popped up. "Bobbi, we're not being bad. Sam never gets out of line that way. He's so sweet, and he treats me like I'm a princess."

"Let me ask you this." Bobbi said. "What if you didn't have to deal with your parents or anyone else? What if this were just a decision between you and Sam? What would you do?"

"Gosh, I'd go find him right now. I'd drive to Laie, wake up the temple president, and say, 'Could you marry us? I don't want to wait until morning.'"

"Afton, we're not talking about how much you like to kiss him. We're talking about life together."

"I know. That's what I'm talking about too. I want to be with him forever. At first I thought we were too different. But we're not. He's smarter and stronger and more faithful than I am. That's the only difference between us."

Afton lay back on the bed again, and Bobbi leaned closer and patted her arm. "I'm sorry; I know how hard this is."

"Maybe we could live here. I love Sam's family, and they

accept me. Here in the islands, people don't seem to mind who marries who."

"That's not entirely true, Afton. The mainlanders—even the ones in the church—might not make you feel all that comfortable at times."

"I could live with that."

"So, is that what you're thinking of doing?"

"Bobbi, to me Hawaii is a foreign country. I love it here, but I want to go *home* someday. If I marry Sam, I could never do that. Maybe my parents would make the best of things once I went ahead and got married, but I don't think they could ever really accept the idea."

Bobbi understood. She thought of her last trip home, when she had felt so close to her family. It was as though, when she walked into her house, she had suddenly remembered who she was. Bobbi would never want to give that up.

"People are changing," Afton said. "I keep thinking that the war will bring people together and race won't matter so much." She stared at the ceiling for a time, and then she added, "But my dad told me not even to date Hawaiians. Sam and I would have beautiful children—I just know it—but I don't think my dad could accept them."

"Maybe not. I don't know. But don't you think, once your father got to know Sam, he would change his mind?"

"That's what I tell myself sometimes. But Arizona and Hawaii are about a million miles from each other. I know how you and I felt when we first came over here."

"That's the point. We've changed."

"Sure. But we've been *here*."

"So what are you going to do?"

"I don't know. But I've got to stop kissing him. I've got to tell him we can't go out anymore. I just have to."

Heinrich Stoltz sat in a car that was parked on a quiet road. It was almost 4:00 in the morning, and the air was cold. The driver, an American, had leaned back and folded his arms over his chest. He seemed a little too well groomed, too educated, for this line of work, but then Brother Stoltz had often seen the same thing in the OSS office in London. A lot of the agents were wealthy Americans from the best families. The man was breathing steadily now, as though asleep, so he surprised Brother Stoltz when he said, "I guess you've been through the whole routine."

"Excuse me?"

"You know your story? You've practiced it with agents?"

"A hundred times, I think."

"Let me give you a piece of advice. You can never be completely prepared. There's always something someone will ask that you never thought would come up. That's why being confident is more important than saying the right thing. You have to halfway believe you're really the guy you're claiming to be."

"You have gone undercover yourself then?"

"No. But I've debriefed a good many men who have, and that's what they always say." The man chuckled. "Of course, I talk to the ones who pull it off. The ones who make a mess of things don't come back."

Brother Stoltz didn't find that nearly as funny as the agent did. The man worked out of the American consulate in Bern. He was OSS, no doubt, but he had never said so, and he certainly didn't admit to such a thing to anyone else in Switzerland. He hadn't even told Brother Stoltz his name.

"It's almost time, isn't it?" Brother Stoltz asked.

"Yes. But the guard hasn't signaled yet."

A Swiss guard had been bribed to let Brother Stoltz cross the border, but the guard worked with a partner. At four the partner was supposed to walk a route along the border to the next station. It was a security check, mostly to guard against Germans escaping into Switzerland. It was rare for anyone to cross in the other direction. The Swiss weren't all that concerned about German citizens fleeing to their country, but they protected their neutrality by cooperating with Germany.

The plan was that as soon as the partner walked away from the station, the guard who had taken the bribe would pull the lantern in the guard station down from its usual perch and set it lower, on a table. Brother Stoltz and the agent had approached without headlights and had stayed well away on a little road that led from Stein, a small Swiss village. They could see the light from the station but little else.

Now it was five minutes after four, and the light hadn't moved. Brother Stoltz was worried that something had gone wrong. He had to get across before daybreak, but then he had to stay out of sight until it was a normal time for people to be moving about. Timing was terribly important.

Then the light moved. "Okay, there you go. Good luck," the American said.

"Thank you." The two shook hands, and Brother Stoltz got out of the car. He took his little suitcase and walked quickly down the dirt road that led to the guard station. The guard had already stepped outside. "Good morning," Brother Stoltz said.

"Are you Alfred Heitz?"

"*Ja. Sicher.*"

"Go quickly. As soon as you are out of the light, make your way into the woods. The German guard station is not far down the hill."

Brother Stoltz knew all of that. He had to get into the woods and avoid the other station. That was not so difficult. The problem was, the Germans had set up listening posts about every hundred meters between their stations. If he moved quietly, he would not be heard, but patrols occasionally walked the border, just as they had along the border of France where Brother Stoltz had crossed the previous spring—when Peter had had to stop and go back.

Brother Stoltz had been carefully schooled. The key was to move slowly, watch and listen, and never get impatient. He could stay in the woods all the way into Germany. At this particular out-of-the-way station, there was usually little activity, and the German guards were often lax. Or so he had been told. That didn't stop his heartbeat from hammering in his ears.

Brother Stoltz nodded to the Swiss guard, walked a few paces forward until he was out of the light, and then stepped off into the trees. It was a cloudy night, with almost no moonlight, and he couldn't use a flashlight. He could tell already that he would have to travel more by touch than by sight. Among all these fir trees, that wasn't easy. The border was downhill, which was always his key in finding his direction, but the slant was subtle in the beginning, and it wasn't long until he was struggling to figure out where he was.

When he became confused, however, he was wise enough to stop, breathe a little and relax, and then look toward the sky. There was a place where the clouds were illuminated by the moon, ever so slightly. He used that hint of light to orient himself, and then he worked his way ahead once again, always feeling for branches and working his way around or under them. As the incline angled more sharply, his job got easier. At the same time, he couldn't walk too fast and make a noise that would be picked up by the electronic listening devices. No noise beyond what the wind might make was allowable, and tonight there was little wind.

So he moved one slow step at a time, and sometimes he stood and listened for a full minute—to keep his breathing soft and to do his own surveillance. What he feared most was that a patrol with a dog might be out there in the darkness somewhere. He remembered all too well what had happened when a dog had caught his and his family's scent when they had crossed into France.

Slowly he worked his way down the hill, and at some point he felt sure he was beyond the listening posts, but he didn't change his technique. He listened, waited, inched ahead while time kept passing. But that was all right. He couldn't be spotted in Singen, the German town below, for quite some time yet. Still, his fear kept pushing him forward. He wanted to be as far beyond the border as possible before he stopped and waited.

Just when he started to feel he had gotten past the worst danger point, he came to a drop-off that he could feel with his foot but couldn't see. He clung to the limb of a fir tree, probed with one leg, and tried to find the ground below. This put a strain on his bad knee, however, and suddenly it gave way. He slipped off the little ledge and tumbled into the darkness. He was still clinging to the limb with one hand, but as it dropped, his hand slipped, and he fell a few feet before hitting the ground. The incline was still steep enough that his feet went out from under him, and he slid down the hill on his backside. As he did, his suitcase thudded against the ground, broke loose from his grasp, and rolled ahead of him.

He wasn't hurt, except for a little pain in his knee, but the noise seemed tremendous in the quiet woods. He sat where he was and listened as long as he could stand to, and then he crawled ahead until he found his suitcase. Again he tried to wait, but fear kept him going. He hoped no one had heard the racket he had made.

When he reached the bottom edge of the woods, he could see the vague outline of the horizon and the town, perhaps a mile away. He would either have to cross some fields or stay in the woods and work his way west to a road. But he couldn't see enough to do that yet. The woods were still the safest place for now—unless a patrol was coming down the hill to find him. But he doubted that. Only a dog could have tracked him, and he hadn't heard the noise a dog and man together would make. He felt fairly certain he had already passed the danger area when he had taken his fall.

So he sat and waited. He told himself the worst was over. But he knew he had to travel the length of Germany, to Berlin, and that meant having his papers checked, perhaps many times. He didn't think the papers themselves were a problem; the OSS had worked with the British MI-6, and they had produced a perfect identification card, along with travel papers. The papers named him Alfred Heitz, and they explained that the company he worked for, as an accountant, had been destroyed by enemy bombs. He was being transferred to another plant, near Berlin, where he would continue to work in the service of his country. Germany had recently announced that all men sixteen to sixty must serve in the military, and so the OSS had also supplied him with papers that showed his medical release from the army. He had supposedly been badly injured in a vehicle accident while serving on the eastern front.

What he was also carrying, sewn into his underwear, was a set of papers that identified him, under another name, as an agent of the SD, the German security police. He would use these papers to pass back into Switzerland when he was ready to escape Germany. He was more of a courier than a spy; he had a mission to complete, and if all went well, he would be out of Germany in a couple of weeks. His family knew that he was doing something for the OSS, and Anna clearly had her suspicions about what that might be, but Brother Stoltz had admitted nothing.

Slowly the darkness abated, and Brother Stoltz began to get a view of the countryside. He had to reach the Singen train station, buy a ticket, and head north, probably through Stuttgart. A larger train station than the one in Singen would have been preferable, since he could disappear among the crowd more easily, but this was an obscure area of the border where the crossing was easier. His toughest test of all, between here and Berlin, and his greatest danger, was getting into town and then making it past his first inspection at the train. Small-town inspectors might not be as cautious and well trained, in most cases, but the ones near the border were likely to be quite vigilant.

When he could see well enough, Brother Stoltz finally began to work his way along the edge of the woods, then down to the road, which he could now see. Once on the road he walked confidently, without hurrying, and he saw no one. He made it to the edge of town and once again breathed more easily. He had studied the map of Singen many times, and he knew exactly how to get to the train station. As he walked along the street, he saw a local policeman, who seemed to eye him rather carefully, but Brother Stoltz tipped his cap to the officer and said, "*Guten Morgen,*" quite naturally. He wondered immediately whether he had made a mistake. He expected the policeman to say, "Heil Hitler" and perhaps stop him, but he only greeted Brother Stoltz with his own "good morning" and said nothing more. That was one test passed—or maybe he had only gotten lucky.

The train station was fairly busy, and that was comforting. Brother Stoltz checked the schedule on the wall and saw that an express train was leaving for Stuttgart at 8:36. A slower train, by way of Ulm and then on to Stuttgart, left in only a few minutes. His impulse was to get a ticket on the slower train and get out of the station right away, but he had to remember that he was on his way to Berlin, and he had to do whatever a traveler would normally do. So he stepped to the ticket window. "I'm traveling to Berlin," he said. "What's the best train to take?"

"Take the express train to Stuttgart," the man said. "You change trains there, but there's another express all the way to Berlin. You'll be there by tomorrow morning."

"Is it much more expensive than a slower train?" Again he told himself to ask the normal questions, to think the way Alfred Heitz might think.

"It costs a few more *Marken*. But it doesn't stop in every little town. A man could go crazy with all that."

"It's good. I'll pay for the express."

That's not really what Brother Stoltz wanted to do. He needed to make contact with the underground in Berlin, but his deepest motivation for being in Germany was to find Peter. He suspected that the boy, if he was being held in a jail, might be in southern Germany. So he wished he could stay in the south for a while, but that would make no sense, considering his travel papers.

So Brother Stoltz bought his ticket. Then he walked to the *Gasthaus* in the train station and bought a breakfast of bread and cheese and marmalade. Again, he waited.

He was sitting at the table about an hour before departure time when a policeman approached. "Heil Hitler," the policeman said, raising his hand rather casually.

"Heil Hitler," Brother Stoltz said, and he also made the salute. But he didn't get up.

"So where are you off to this morning?" the policeman asked.

"Berlin."

"*Ach.* So far. That's a long trip."

"Yes. It will take me all day and all night. But that's not bad when one considers how long it used to take—when you and I

were both a lot younger." He laughed, and so did the policeman.

"I hate to tell you, but you'll never make it that fast. The
tracks will be bombed out somewhere. You can count on it."

"Yes, yes. I know. It's always so these days."

"My name is Grosswald. I don't think I know you. Are you
from Singen?"

This was not friendly chatter. Brother Stoltz had been
warned about this kind of interrogation. The policeman had
spotted someone he didn't know, and he was doing his job.
This offhanded approach could sometimes lead to a mistake,
and then the conversation would take a less affable turn.

"No. I'm not from here. I'm from Donaueschingen, north
of here." Brother Stoltz hoped that would be enough, but he
knew better. The crucial questions were still ahead.

"Oh, is that so? How did you get here from up there so
early in the morning?" Grosswald stretched and yawned, as if
tired himself. He was probably in his fifties, with gray hair and
big, fleshy ears. He seemed harmless, but Brother Stoltz saw
how keen his eyes were, how carefully he was watching.

"I got a ride from a man who makes deliveries here,"
Brother Stoltz said. This was a story Brother Stoltz had worked
out while still in England. Few people had cars available, or
gasoline, and if he answered that he had taken a bus, the
policeman might want proof of that: a ticket or the bus's arrival
time.

"Deliveries? What on earth does he deliver from
Donaueschingen?"

"Vegetables. Mostly cabbage."

"What? He comes for market day?"

"Yes. I suppose that's it. He's not much of a talker, I found
that out. I don't think he likes the early hour himself." Brother
Stoltz laughed again.

"What's the fellow's name, this truck driver?"

This was getting more obvious now, but Brother Stoltz

tried not to let himself seem concerned. "Fleischer. Wilhelm Fleischer."

"I don't remember this man—Fleischer from Donaue-schingen—at our market."

"I have no idea. He may sell his cabbages to someone else here—for shipping perhaps. Maybe to the military, for all I know."

The policeman nodded. He had apparently followed that line to a dead end, but he clearly wasn't backing off, wasn't satisfied. "So what takes you to Berlin?"

"Work. I was an accountant with a ball-bearing factory, but it was bombed beyond repair not long ago. So I'm being transferred to a company up north. It's not what I would choose, but you know how it is. These things happen in wartime."

"What factory are you speaking of? I'm not aware of a ball-bearing factory in Donaueschingen."

Once again Brother Stoltz had his story ready. "No, no. It's not there. It was in Regensburg, in Bavaria. It was bombed—destroyed, actually—on August 17. I suppose it will be back running before much longer, but I'm being shipped up north, where they say I'm needed even more. I merely came to the Black Forest for a little rest—and to visit my sister—before I start work again."

The information about the bombing was accurate—gathered for him by OSS agents—and Grosswald seemed more convinced this time. Brother Stoltz thought he saw the policeman relax a little. Still, he came back with another probe. "I guess it could be worse. You could be called up, if you're not yet sixty, and have to pack a rifle on the eastern front somewhere."

"Actually, I wish I could go back in the army," Brother Stoltz said. "I served in Russia and might still be there if I hadn't been in a bad accident. I was in a truck that was hit by tank fire and went out of control. I was thrown out. I broke my shoulder and my right knee. I had to be discharged. I'll tell you, though, I'd like to go after those filthy Bolsheviks again. They're not human, those people."

"How long ago was this? When were you discharged?"

"Two years ago."

"You have papers to show that, I suppose."

"Of course I do." But he didn't offer to pull them out. He wanted Grosswald to drop the act.

"Let me see them. I'm supposed to check such things, you know. I'm sure you don't mind."

"Not at all." Brother Stoltz pulled his wallet from the inside pocket in his coat. He got out his identity card, his work and travel papers, but he didn't offer them. Instead, he handed over just the military papers Grosswald had asked for.

Grosswald took them, studied them carefully. "So you were a sergeant, I see. You must have served for quite some time."

"I served as a young man, as you see there. And then, in '39, I signed up again. It's what I wanted to do for my country." He laughed. "Besides, it's more exciting than what I do, keeping books."

"But it got a little too exciting when the artillery fire hit your truck."

"Oh, yes. Up until then I was lucky. I never feared much of anything. But that day, I found out. Everyone's day will come if he stays in the army long enough."

Brother Stoltz was growing weary of all this. He was smiling, sounding relaxed, just as he had practiced so many times before, but his life was on the line this time, and he kept wondering how long before a word, a fact, a bad bluff, might give him away.

"You're lucky to be alive and have all your limbs, if you ask me, Herr Heitz."

"Certainly. I couldn't agree more. So many have given their lives. Or a leg. Or an arm. I know that. But my knee is not good at all. It pains me all the time. And my shoulder is bad enough that I can lift nothing heavy."

It was always easiest to sound convincing when he was telling the truth. These, of course, were his injuries, even though they had been sustained in fighting *against* Hitler, not for him. But Grosswald wasn't letting up. "Could I see your other papers?" he said, and he studied the false travel papers, the identity card, the work permit.

After a time he looked up from the papers and said, "What time do you have?"

Brother Stoltz glanced at the clock on the wall. "It's nearing eight. Five minutes before."

"Don't you carry a watch with you?"

"No. Mine stopped working some time ago. How can one get a watch fixed now? The watchmakers are all in the army."

Brother Stoltz knew exactly what this was all about. He had been warned not to take a watch with him. It was easy to check a timepiece and see where the inner movements were from. Even a good fake, from outside Germany, could be discovered by anyone who knew what to look for.

"Would you mind coming with me, Herr Heitz? I want you to talk to someone."

"Surely. What's this about?" Brother Stoltz asked, but Grosswald didn't answer. He walked on ahead.

As they left the Gasthaus and entered the main hall of the station, Brother Stoltz tried to think of everything he had said. Had there been some trap he hadn't noticed? Was there something about his clothes, his dialect, his history, that didn't add up? His impulse was to spin and run for the doors, try to run all the way back to the woods and the border, but he knew that would be the end of him. He had to stay calm.

Grosswald walked to a man who was standing near the entrance to the train platforms. The man was wearing a suit, no uniform to identify him with any particular agency. But he was not a ticket-taker. He was stationed where he could watch people and check the papers of those who were about to board the trains.

"Herr Miller," Grosswald said, "this man plans to board the express train for Stuttgart and Berlin. He tells me he's a patriot, and he shows me his discharge papers from the military, but I have never seen him before, and he tells me he came here with a delivery man from Donaueschingen. He gives me the name of the truck driver but doesn't know where the man takes his cabbages. What concerns me most is that he carries no watch. He says his is broken, and that may be, but when undercover agents cross the border, they never carry anything that can be traced. I wonder if we have such a man here."

Miller was nodding as he heard all this, and he was looking at Brother Stoltz, studying him. "You are a German, am I to understand?" he asked. He took the papers from Grosswald and began to look through them.

"Yes, of course I am."

"But not from *Scwabenland*. I can hear that in your voice immediately."

Brother Stoltz knew to expect this, of course. "No, no. I wasn't born here. I lived in Darmstadt most of my life."

"And what of this cabbage truck? Why don't you know better who the man is you travel with?"

"My sister knew the man, told me he came once a week. So I asked the man for a ride, and he was willing. That's the whole story."

"I know you're a German. That's easy enough to recognize. But Grosswald here, he thinks you're a spy. Maybe you are."

Brother Stoltz shook his head. "I fought for the Fatherland—won the Iron Cross, as you see on my papers. I never thought I would be accused of such a thing. But I guess you two have a job to do, yourselves. I don't take offense."

"What regiment did you fight with, in Russia?"

This was easy. "I was under General von Paulus, in the Sixth Army. The 371st Division, 670th Regiment."

"*Ach.* My goodness. That's interesting. My brother was with that division. That means you fought with General Lattman. He was your commander."

Brother Stoltz took about one full second to make his decision. He had never heard the name Lattman, and yet he was tempted to agree, to satisfy this man who now seemed to be accepting him. But he knew better. He couldn't fall for a trick, if it was one. "No. My commander was General Richard Stempel. He shot himself, committed suicide, during that mess in Stalingrad. It was a very sad thing. I was hurt before the Sixth Army surrendered. I was lucky in that regard. Most of the men in my regiment are dead—or still in captivity. I'm surprised your brother made it back."

The man nodded. "Very good," he said. "If Grosswald here has caught himself a spy, I can only say you're a very good one." He laughed, and so did Brother Stoltz. "I'm sorry. I have to be careful. We're very close to the border here. We can't take chances."

"I understand. I do. Don't worry about it."

Brother Stoltz kept his composure as he walked to the train. But when he sat down, he began to shake. He stayed calm as best he could, prayed silently for continued strength, and told himself to be ready for more of these interrogations. He knew he had been lucky this time. He had come very close to saying the wrong thing.

11

It was early October, and Peter Stoltz was riding on a train through Poland on his way to the Russian front. He had chosen to join the German army; but then, it was hardly a choice since it was the only way he had seen to save his life. The past few months had been harrowing, to say the least.

On the terrible day when Peter had been separated from his family at the Swiss/French border, he had spotted a German guard and his dog. He had realized that the dog would catch his scent, and so he had retreated as fast as he could, back through the woods. And then, when he had heard the gunfire, he had hurried all the way back to the little town of Bure. He didn't know whether his family had been caught, or whether any of them might have been shot. He waited in Bure for a time, hoping for Crow—the guide from the French Resistance—to return. But no one showed up that day, so he had hidden in the forest. He was too old to cry, he was sure, but he had cried anyway, and felt more alone than he had ever imagined he could feel.

The following morning Peter had waited in town again, close to the café where he had first met Crow. But a local policeman had questioned him about his loitering, had become suspicious, and then had tried to arrest him. Peter had surprised the older man by suddenly bolting away. He had run into the woods and stayed off the roads until he had hiked well east of Bure. Eventually, he had taken a chance and hailed a truck that was heading further east, and the driver had given him a ride all the way back to Basel.

Peter had had plenty of time to think, and he knew that his only way to contact Crow, without waiting in Bure, was to get back to the British consulate in Basel. These were the people who had put his father in touch with the underground in the first place. In Basel, however, as he approached the British consulate, he had been stopped by Swiss police. "Is your name Stoltz?" the officer had asked. Peter had not bothered to lie. He thought the Swiss police might jail him, but in the long run he expected help.

Peter never learned the whole story, but he heard enough talk among the police to guess that the Gestapo had raised a huge fuss over the previous incident at the train station. The Stoltz family was considered an enemy of the state in Germany, and a Swiss officer had set them free. Apparently the police department had backed down in the face of such fury and had promised to turn over the Stoltzes this time, should they be apprehended. In any case, Peter was quickly handed over, not to Kellerman but to another agent. Within three hours from the time Peter had been apprehended, he was on a train that was heading back into Germany.

He didn't know where he was going, what he was charged with, or what his fate might be, but it wasn't hard to guess. He would soon be eighteen and would surely be treated as an adult. He and his father had fought with a Gestapo agent, had injured him badly. Peter hoped he would be imprisoned, and that the end of the war would save him, but he feared a death sentence, even had a hard time believing he would receive anything else.

But as the train was leaving Freiburg, near the French border in the southwest corner of Germany, it rolled to a stop, and a conductor hurried into the car and shouted for everyone to get off. Peter had been handcuffed to his seat. The Gestapo agent stood quickly, and for a moment seemed content to leave Peter on the train, but then he pulled a key from his pocket and released him. By then bombs were falling, hitting close. Just as Peter stood up, the train was jarred and thrown sideways as the car just ahead took a direct hit. Peter and the agent were both thrown across the car and slammed into the seats. Peter hit his head, hard. He never lost consciousness, but for a minute or two he was dazed and confused. What he knew, however, was that the Gestapo agent had scrambled off the train and was much more concerned about saving his life than keeping track of Peter.

Peter's escape had been ludicrously easy. Once he overcame his dizziness, he simply jumped off the opposite side of the train, headed into the nearby trees, and kept going. He had no idea how rigorously he would be sought, but he stayed out of towns, slept in the woods for two days, and got as far from Freiburg as he could. The only problem, of course, was that he had to eat. And so he finally walked into a little Black Forest town called Villingen. He had no money and no idea whether local police might be on the watch for him. He didn't dare say that he was hungry—a sure revelation that he was on the run—and he had no explanation for why he wasn't in the military. When he spotted a train station, he decided to go in. He would be less conspicuous there, he thought, but he still had no idea how he could get a meal. When he saw three young men sitting on the wooden benches in the waiting area, he decided he would approach them and seek help. He knew that he might get himself into trouble, but he was getting so hungry he was starting not to care.

He greeted the young men and then asked them where they were going. "Stuggert," one of them said.

"Where?" Peter asked, and all the young men had laughed.

"That's what we say here. It's dialect. You probably call it Stuttgart."

From that, a conversation had begun. The boys were all from Triberg, a small village nearby. They had signed up for the military and were on their way to Stuttgart to be inducted. All three were sixteen and lifelong friends: Hans Rindelsbach, Karl Mohler, and Helmut Schurtz. When one of the boys had asked, "Where are you going?" a story came out of Peter a sentence at a time, even though he hardly knew where it was going: "I've been living on my grandparents' farm, not far from here," he told them. "My parents are in Frankfurt, but they thought I was safer here. I'm going into the army myself. But I've had a big problem come up this morning. I arrived here earlier, and I set my things down. I turned around for hardly a moment, and everything was gone. Someone stole my luggage, my wallet—everything I have."

"You set your wallet down too?" Karl asked.

"Yes. It was foolish, but it was in my hand, and I set it down with my luggage, not thinking."

"Have you reported it to the police?"

"Yes. I've just come back from there. But they're no help at all. They'll watch for the luggage, they say, but I don't think they care very much. I would call my grandparents, but they have no telephone, out on the farm."

Peter was about to explain that he hadn't eaten when Hans asked, "Are you supposed to be in Stuttgart today, the same as us?"

Suddenly, everything was clear. Peter had been praying constantly for an answer to his problem. What he needed, for now, was a safe place to hide. Where could he be more safe than in the German army? Who would look for him there? He saw some frightening implications in the choice, but he didn't have time to weigh all the pros and cons. He merely answered, "Yes," and told himself he could back out at some point if this wasn't the best plan.

"Do you have your ticket?" Hans asked.

"No. I have nothing. I haven't even eaten all day."

Hans was a tightly built young man, small but solid in his chest and shoulders. Strong as he looked, however, he had an innocent, almost childish face. His hair was light as feathers, and seemingly uncontrollable, and freckles were sprinkled over his hands as well as his face. Peter liked him immediately, but he wasn't prepared for what Hans would say. "I've got money, and I won't need it once I join up. I can buy you a ticket."

Peter had noticed the other two, Helmut and Karl, look-ing a little skeptical, as though they hadn't fallen for the story, but Hans not only bought Peter a ticket, he also bought him lunch. And then, on the way to Stuttgart, the two talked at great length. What was strange and terrible, of course, was that Peter had never been able to have a friend, not since he was a child anyway, and now most of what he told Hans had to be lies. He could pull a few truths from his real past, but almost everything he said had to be invented—and remembered—so Peter was purposely vague and incomplete, and he hedged when Hans asked questions that might have pinned him down.

As Peter rode the train to Stuttgart, he tried to think where all this was leading. Maybe the army would have a way to iden-tify him. Certainly the office would have no induction papers—and he didn't know what the recruiters would do about that—but if he could get a new name and could get to a training camp somewhere, he would be safe from the Gestapo. At that point he could consider going on the run again, or pos-sibly even trying to get back into Switzerland or France.

As it had turned out, getting into the army was no chal-lenge. Peter told his story about losing all his possessions in Villingen, and even though the induction center could find no papers in his name, the recruiters were only too happy to take him. Clearly, they had quotas, and they were pleased to see a strong, healthy young man who was ready to join, whatever story he had to tell.

When Peter had first met his three new friends, he had unthinkingly introduced himself with his real first name, and then, when Hans had asked him his last name, on impulse he had chosen Stutz, a name that occurred to him because of its similarity to his real name. At the induction center he worried a little that the name would be too similar to his own and someone would make the connection. But no one paid any attention, and even though the official told him, "You'll have to file for new identity papers," he was supplied with army identification, and no one ever asked him for anything else.

The truth was, Germany, which had been so orderly in the past, was moving toward chaos. There were not enough workers in any of the offices that dealt with such matters, and what Peter saw now was a pretense that didn't hide the despair. Everyone said, constantly, that the war was going to take another turn, that the enemy on both sides would be driven back, that new weapons would turn the tide, that Germany would never stop until it was victorious. But what Peter heard, just under the surface, was a kind of fatalistic acceptance of the disaster that was already upon them. He had managed to sneak into the military because no one cared who he was. Numbers were important, and another boy was free to die if he chose. What difference did it make when so many had died already?

Once Peter had started his training at a camp close to Stuttgart, he was never questioned about his identity, and he felt safe from the Gestapo. What he had done, however, was to step into a boat that was heading for a waterfall, and whatever temporary security the boat provided, he was now too close to the falls to turn back. What Peter learned first was that military training for new recruits had been drastically shortened. The eight weeks in camp were rigorous, but early mornings and hard physical exertion were heavenly compared to the idea of being shipped to one of the fronts. Getting into the army was immensely easier than getting out. The camp was guarded closely, and passes were rare. Peter wasn't sure that he would ever dare to run, but he kept telling himself that if he did so, he would do it after squeezing all the time out of this training period that he could.

And then his training ended, and even with a two-day pass Peter realized that running was suicide. How could he live? Where would he hide? A healthy young man his age would be stopped, checked, and Peter's only identification was his military card. What he didn't have to go with it was any kind of travel papers or any proof of leave, beyond the two days. And so he told himself, "Maybe we won't get into the action right away." Or, "I won't shoot. I'll keep my head down and stay alive." And always, "Maybe the war won't last much longer."

Peter was thankful that another eight weeks of training followed. Many soldiers were being shipped directly to the front, but Peter and his new friends were transferred to a camp in northern Germany, south of Hamburg, where they received weapons training. They learned to fire machine guns, mortars, anti-tank weapons, and anti-aircraft guns. At times it was actually fun for Peter, because he liked Hans so much, and he was meeting so many other young men. It was all just target practice anyway, a kind of game, and Peter refused to think much about the reality that lay before him.

But when the training ended, and he boarded the train for the east, he knew he had passed over the edge of the falls, and the boat was falling onto the rocks below. He was depressed and scared, and homesick for his family. He had no idea what had happened to them. Maybe they had all been caught or killed. Or if they were safe somewhere in France, or even England, he hated to think how sick with worry they must be. He wanted so badly to see them, to let them know he was alive, and then to have his life back. Not since he had been thirteen years old had he been able to use his own name, to be himself, to talk openly. That sort of freedom was so distant now, so unimaginable, that he wondered whether he would ever know who he was.

"Peter, you look worried. What are you thinking?" Hans asked him. Their seats faced each other. Karl and Helmut had been sitting next to them, but they had gotten up to stand in line to wait for a meal in the train's diner car. Peter and Hans had decided to wait until the line was shorter.

"I haven't seen my family for a long time. I've been thinking about them," Peter said, thankful to be honest—even if his truth was actually a distortion.

"I've been thinking about my family too. But no one wants to admit he's homesick—not when he's a soldier."

Peter was only a little older than Hans, but he felt much older. Hans was such a warm-hearted boy, and innocent. Clearly, he *was* homesick. "We'll get by," Peter told him. "We can't cling to our fathers' pantlegs forever."

"No, no. That's right," Hans said. "And I'm not afraid to fight. Don't think that. I'll kill my share of Russians—you wait and see."

"Maybe we won't be in the fight. Maybe we'll be held in reserve for a time."

"I'd rather get in the middle of it, Peter. Why wait around and wonder? I want to show what I can do."

Peter thought he actually heard Hans saying, I want to see for myself what I can do. "Yes. Maybe that would be better," Peter said.

"We have to turn this war around, Peter. It's up to men our age to do it. I hate to think what those *degenerate* Russians will do to our homeland if they cross our borders. They're not human, Peter. They don't care about our culture, our heritage. They'll destroy everything, force their will upon our sisters. It's all unthinkable. I'm happy to die, if that's what it takes to turn them back."

Peter had heard this sort of talk many times. During training the *Unteroffizier* had made negative comments about the British and Americans, especially the cowardly bomber pilots who killed civilians, but he had saved his strongest hatred for the filthy, sub-human Russians. They were madmen without any regard for life, attacking in waves, driving toward Germany. Peter often sensed that his people were no longer fighting for "living room" or for any of the original purposes; they were fighting not to lose, not to suffer the nightmarish fate they could already envision. Maybe their country was being bombed daily, torn up, but at least there was no occupier, no one to disgrace and degrade them.

"Hans," Peter said, "don't you ever think that all these lives are being lost for nothing—that we have no chance to fight a war on so many fronts?"

"No, Peter. I never think that. And you shouldn't say it."

"I'm not *saying* it. I'm just asking the question."

"My Hitler Youth leader talked about all these things. Winning is a matter of will. The longer we keep the battle going, the sooner the Americans and British will give up. They thought they had us on the run, and now look at the Netherlands. We're stopping them there. We'll stop them all along the Siegfried Line, too. They haven't the heart to come into our country and fight us nose to nose. Mark my word, within months the Allies will be pleading for a negotiated peace."

Peter had no doubt that Hans believed every word of this. Even with the steady jiggling and jolting of the train, Hans's eyes held steady. Maybe he was homesick, but he was going to this war at peace with himself. "And what about the Russians?" Peter asked. "Don't they have the heart—and the numbers— to push all the way to Berlin?"

"They haven't the brains, Peter. In Hitler Youth we learned the real secret about the Russians. They only want a full stomach and a female to satisfy their sexual hunger. They don't have our idealism, our commitment to higher purposes. The farther they get from their homes, the more they'll lose their drive. Once we draw them out and slaughter them by the millions, those left alive will run all the way back to Moscow. Herr

Pfefferle, my leader, predicts that the Russians will capitulate in the spring. This war could be over by then."

"It would be nice to think so," Peter said. "But right now, from what I read, we're the ones who are dying."

"Peter, this is not a proper way to talk. Sometimes I wonder at the preparation you've received. Where did you attend Hitler Youth?"

"In Frankfurt. I've heard all the things you're telling me."

"Don't you believe what our loyal leaders teach us?"

"Of course I do." But Peter looked away from Hans's innocent eyes. He hated to think what might be coming for this freckle-faced boy, with all his simple faith. Peter looked out the window at the plowed fields, the leafless trees. He thought of the bitter cold he would face before long.

"I don't think you're as committed as you should be, Peter. In my group, you would have been severely chastised, perhaps even reported. I wonder whether it's your parents who have put these ideas into your head."

"No one has put any ideas into my head. I'm on my way to fight, the same as you. I only said that I hope it turns out as well as you predict."

"It will, Peter. And you must be just as sure of it as I am—the same as Karl and Helmut. Doubt will destroy us more quickly than anything."

"You're right, Hans. I shouldn't ask such questions."

Hans nodded and smiled, seeming satisfied. He glanced over his shoulder, apparently to see how long the food line was now, but the line was not moving fast. Peter noticed the smell of sauerkraut wafting in from the next car. He hoped there was something decent to go with it. Rations were sparse these days. The smell of food was at least a welcome change from the odor of men tightly crowded into the train car—the musty smell of wet wool, all of the men having stood in the rain before they boarded, and the smell of bodies that hadn't been in a shower for several days.

"What does your father do, Peter?" Hans asked. "You've never told me that."

"He works in a government office. He spends his life filling out forms, moving paper."

"Why hasn't he been called up for service now? Is he in ill health?"

"No, no. It's not that. His job *is* important. It only seems dull to me, I suppose."

Hans nodded, and then he leaned back and laughed. "You're so mysterious, Peter. You never tell me anything unless I ask you, and then as little as possible. Why are you so secretive?"

"I'm not. I'm just not the talkative kind. My parents always teased me for being so silent."

"It's not such a bad trait. You're the best fellow I've ever met—except for Karl and Helmut. I'm glad we met you that day."

"I've never had a good friend, Hans. Never in my life. I'm glad I met you, too."

Hans leaned forward and slapped Peter on the knee. "We'll kill us some Popovs together, distinguish ourselves, and then we'll go back and help bring Germany to its rightful place in the world. It's exciting what lies before us. Herr Pfefferle always told us we were the finest generation of Germans ever because we've been raised under our Führer's great influence. There'll be no stopping us in the future."

"That's right," Peter said.

"And here's my promise: We'll *always* be friends." Hans offered his hand and Peter reached out and shook it. He liked this boy so much, and he longed to speak honestly with him, to become his close friend, but the chasm between them was deeper than Hans could ever imagine.

Late that afternoon, the train pulled into a station in a small Polish town, the name of which Peter couldn't pronounce. The troops were commanded to bring their gear and leave the train.

Then they formed up and marched to a camp that was a couple of miles away from the train station. It was not such a bad march, but the garrison bags became heavy along the way. Many of the men in the company were young, like Peter and his friends, and except for some of the smaller boys, they kept up easily. But the older men, some of them in their late fifties, became fatigued and out of breath. No one broke ranks, but Peter heard them gasping for air and pushing themselves to keep going. Training had been rigorous, but it had been short, and the older men hadn't had much time to become as fit as they needed to be.

The men were also dressed in rather makeshift uniforms, not all of them matching. Everyone had a rifle or machine gun of some sort, but ammunition was short, and some of the weapons were badly outdated. The men had been promised many times that they would receive the latest equipment, and better uniforms, but the promises hadn't been honored so far. Peter thought he saw trouble in this, and among other things, he wondered whether adequate winter clothes would be available. He had heard stories about winter fighting the year before and German soldiers lacking warm coats and boots. He had only heard such things on British radio, of course, but he believed it, and he hated to think that he could be heading into a similar situation. He wondered why Hans couldn't look around him and see that this was actually a ragtag unit, made up of children and older men, with inadequate training and weapons.

At the camp the troops were marched to a little parade ground, where they halted and then stood "at rest" until a *Hauptmann*—a captain—walked along their ranks and then stopped before them. "Welcome, my comrades," he said. "We are happy to have you here where you are much needed. You will add strength to our forces as we resist the animalistic Bolsheviks."

He was a powerful-looking man with a bull-like neck. His

uniform, however, appeared worn and faded—and so did his eyes. Peter had the distinct feeling that he was going through the motions, giving the same speech he had given many times before, perhaps not as convinced by his own words as he once had been.

"This is a mere transfer camp. You will not be here long. You will receive additional training each day, but within a week you will be ordered forward. You will board a train again, and you will be carried to the front. I can promise that within a few days you will be shooting Russians, destroying an enemy so hateful and despicable that you will find joy in every life you take. And this is the best news. You will fight with the *Grossdeutschland Panzer Division*—one of the finest, best-trained fighting groups the world has ever produced."

Peter heard a stir around him. Hans and many of the other boys were clearly impressed. But Peter wondered why, if it was such a crack unit, it would take on these ill-trained new recruits.

"The Russians are dogs, not men; they have no honor in them. They would rather cut your throat than take you prisoner, and so you must do the same to them. Offer them no mercy. What you must understand also is that Russian civilians, mongrels that they are, are equally deceitful and dishonorable. Most of them are unwilling to welcome the liberation we offer them, and so they sneak about and snipe at us. You must never trust them, and you need not worry about killing them when the need arises. I wish it were otherwise. Germans are not accustomed to such beastly warfare, but it's what the Russians have forced upon us, and therefore, it's what we give them in return."

Hans was standing next to Peter. "The swine," he whispered. "The filthy dogs."

The captain continued for some time, but the theme was always the same: the Russians had started all the dishonorable behavior, and noble Germans would rather not behave the same way, but war was war, and the Russians had established the rules in this battle. Peter actually wanted to believe that was true, thought maybe it was, because he wanted to trust in the honor of his own people. But he had heard similar descriptions of German behavior on British radio, and in that version it was the Germans who had begun the killing of civilians and refused to take prisoners. Peter didn't know which was true; he only knew that it was a kind of warfare he didn't want to witness, let alone take part in.

When the officers finally marched the troops to their billets, Peter was glad to drop his heavy bag and find a bunk to sit on. The thought crossed his mind that this was the last chance he might have to make a break. But he had no idea how to get back across Poland without being caught.

Hans was fired up from the speech he had just heard. "I can't wait to join with the Great Germany Division," he said. "I hope, within a day or two, to kill my first Russian. Those dogs deserve all the hot lead we can pour into them."

Peter didn't know what to say. He looked away.

"Peter, I think I understand you," Hans said. "You're still sensitive about killing. That's because you're such a kind person. But don't worry. You can do it. We all can."

Peter nodded but again said nothing. All he could think was that he had worked himself into an impossible situation. There was only one answer that he could find within himself. He wouldn't shoot anyone. He would fire his weapon, but not at another man. If he had to choose between his own life and another's, he would accept his fate. It would be better to die than to fight on behalf of the Nazis and then never be able to forgive himself.

1 2

It was still dark, but Wally and the prisoners in his fifty-man group had been up for some time. They were marching toward the coal mine. It was always the worst time in Wally's long day. He was dead tired, and he felt like a sleepwalker, but the worst was knowing that the day would be exactly like every other day. Wally was also suffering from something new. Many of the men, because of the deficiencies in their diet, suffered with boils. Until now Wally had never had the problem, but in the last week three boils had formed on the back of his right thigh. His leg was badly swollen, which made it hard for him to walk. So this morning each step was a strain, but he knew better than to request any special consideration.

When the men reached the mine, a little ceremony began. The Japanese guards and mine officials prayed to the mine gods, and the prisoners, not understanding the words but accustomed to the ritual, would chant and bow along with them. Then an official would call out the name of a supervisor, who would come forward, bow low, and call out his crew. *"Hai!"* each man would respond as his number was shouted, and the crews would form for the day.

On this morning, Wally was teamed with a crew of five prisoners, including Chuck Adair. Lewis Honeywell, a man

Wally could hardly stand to be around, was also assigned to the group.

Honeywell was a sergeant, and he was a buddy of Lieutenant Langston, the American who ran the mess hall. Between the two of them, they seemed willing to do almost anything to please the guards and sell out their fellow prisoners.

The ride down to the third level of the mine was always an ordeal. Wally wrapped his arms around himself to protect against the cold, just as he did every morning. And then, when he got off the train, according to the expected procedure he took off his trousers and worked in his G-string and shirt. He chose also to take off his shoes. He knew that the long walk to the mine would become much harder, especially in winter, if his shoes were not in good shape, so he protected his shoes from wear by working in his bare feet. That often meant standing in cold water all day, but the shoes didn't help much in that regard anyway.

The supervisor allowed the men to take a few minutes to eat their ration of rice, and most of the men smoked half a cigarette, if they had one. The rice was actually the meal allotted them as lunch, but the men had learned from the prisoners who had been around for a time that it was best to get the extra nourishment early. They held up better that way, even though that meant working the long shift without another meal.

Wally had been working in the mine for a few weeks now, and he knew the Japanese words for the tools, for timbers, wedges, and some of the basic operations. Lately he had worked in this same area, where the men were breaking and removing rock in an attempt to find a seam of coal. Operating a jackhammer was almost impossible for Wally right now, with his leg so sore and swollen. Chuck was willing to take all Wally's time on the hammer for him, but Wally still tried to take a short turn when he could.

Wally began by loading rock, broken and loosened the day before, into a train car. Some of the large rocks could be lifted by hand, and then the smaller rubble had to be shoveled. He set about his task, knowing he was in for a miserable day, full of pain. What he hoped was that the boils would finally come to a head, and he could have them lanced that night. But then, that had been his hope for several days, and nothing had changed.

Once Wally got into his work the pain seemed to diminish a little, and the morning moved along, not quickly, but not quite as sluggishly as he had anticipated. When the supervisor let the men break for lunch, they took the time to rest. Most tried to find a dry place where they could curl up and sleep, but Wally was hurting too much for that. He used the time to kill lice. Delousing was a tedious task that the prisoners never stopped working at. Lice tended to hide in the seams of their clothing, and the little creatures were difficult to spot, especially in the dim light of a lantern. But Wally bent back the seams, and he smashed a number of them, enough to feel that one annoyance in his life might be reduced a little.

Keeping his leg still, resting it, also helped with the ache, but pain in his body, like the hunger that never left him, was like a steady background noise that a person tends to forget after a time. Wally waited out the final minutes of the lunch break almost in a trance, as though some impulse for self-preservation wouldn't allow him to accept the full awareness of the long, painful afternoon that lay ahead.

Honeywell had been sleeping, but he sat up before the supervisor called the men back to work. "Hey, men," he said, "we need to push harder this afternoon. If we outwork the other crews, Fujioka said he would let us get out in time to take the first bath."

At the end of the day, the men bathed in a small pool. To get to the bathhouse late was to bathe in water that hundreds of dirty coal miners had already used. There was no way to get clean in such filth, so the men always hoped to be one of the first crews out of the mine.

"Forget it, Honeywell," Chuck said. "These guards promise that to push us harder, and then they make some excuse and we still get out late."

"Yeah, I know. Some of them are like that. But not Fujioka. If he promises something, he comes through."

Wally didn't know Honeywell's whole history, but he had apparently worked on an all-Japanese crew in the Philippines, and he had learned to speak the language fairly well. He was the only prisoner who knew the names of all the guards and supervisors. One of the frequent accusations against him was that he used his connection to the guards—his informing and placating—as a way to get extra rations. Wally had never seen him receive anything additional, but the guy definitely looked healthier than most. Of course, his buddy Langston probably saw to it that he got extra food, too.

"You boys had better listen to Honeywell," a fellow named Clark Johnson said. "He knows *exactly* what he's talking about." Johnson was one of the youngest prisoners, only about twenty-one. He had been a star athlete at his high school, in eastern Colorado, and had done some Golden Glove boxing as a teenager. Wally liked the guy, but his hot temper got him into trouble at times.

"What's that supposed to mean, Johnson?" Honeywell demanded.

"You're very familiar with every Jap backside around here. And you know which ones to kiss."

"What are you talking about? I don't do that." But Honeywell didn't protest all that strongly. Maybe he had no defense. Or maybe he didn't dare stand up to Johnson. Honeywell was a large man himself, a big farm boy from South Carolina, but he wasn't one to take anybody on.

Fujioka had apparently heard the raised voices. He walked down the tunnel and gave a command in Japanese. The men didn't know the words, but they knew the meaning. They got up and trudged to the heap of rocks they were removing. But

Honeywell stood and spoke to the guard in Japanese. Wally had no idea what the conversation was about, but he heard the friendly tone, and he figured Honeywell was doing it on purpose to aggravate the other men, especially Johnson.

Wally, however, was too preoccupied to care. He was going through the agony of getting going again, the pain in his leg excruciating. He didn't really care what kind of stupid games Honeywell was playing.

Shortly after the crew got started, Honeywell called out, "All right, men, Fujioka had to leave for a while, and he put me in charge. He said we would get off early if we can clear this area this afternoon. So let's kick 'er in gear and get it done."

"We can't move that much rock today," Chuck said.

Another man, Dave Jewell, said, "Not a chance, Honeywell. We push that hard today and all he'll do is expect that much tomorrow. It's not worth it."

"You're just lazy, Jewell. Fujioka knows that about you too."

Wally saw Johnson spin toward Honeywell. "Yeah, and who told him?"

"No one has to tell him. He can see it for himself."

"And he talks to *you* about it?"

In the dark, with only the dim lights from the men's lamps, Wally could barely make out Honeywell's face, but he could see the way he was moving. He seemed stiff and unsure, but he was trying to pretend he wasn't intimidated. "Just shut up and get to work," he barked back at Johnson. "I don't want to discipline you."

"*Discipline* me?" Johnson called him a vile name. "Don't you mean *inform* on me?"

"I'm in charge right now, Johnson. I have no choice. If you won't work, then I have to turn you in—or I'm the one who has to pay the price."

Wally wanted no part of this. He decided he'd better get to work. But he saw Johnson step closer to Honeywell. "If you're in charge, let's see you *make* me go to work. I'm thinking I'll sit down and take a nice rest—while that Jap is gone."

"Come on, Clark," Wally said to Johnson, "let's not start fighting with each other. Let's just move what rock we can today and let it go at that."

Honeywell turned and strode toward Wally, stopped close to him. "Lay off that kind of talk, Thomas. Fujioka expects this whole area to be clear before we go home tonight. If you boys refuse to do it, I have no choice but to tell him."

Wally felt the anger swell in him, the disgust. "Honeywell, we'll work hard and steady all day. That's all we *can* do. If we try to push too hard, the way they feed us, it will kill us off."

Chuck walked over and held up his lamp so he could look into Honeywell's face. "Wally's in bad shape," he said. "His whole leg is swollen up. Every step he takes is half killing him. So lay off. Let's start moving some rock."

That might have been the end of it. Honeywell seemed to accept the idea that getting started was better than arguing about it, but Johnson wasn't satisfied. "You work too, big mouth," he said to Honeywell, "or we won't get enough done to satisfy your Jap buddy."

"I'm in charge. The supervisor doesn't haul rock. He sees to it that the crew does."

"Oh, right, Honeybucket—and you call us lazy? I swear, you're the lowest form of life I've ever come across."

The nickname was one the men had hung on Honeywell, and clearly one he hated. He reacted immediately. He rushed at Johnson, but Johnson was ready for him. His left fist lashed out and caught Honeywell in the side of the head, stopped him. And then a crushing right caught him in the eye.

Honeywell collapsed onto the ground and rolled onto his side. For a moment he was still, but then he came up suddenly with a big rock in his hand. "You're a dead man," he bellowed, and he charged at Johnson.

Chuck stepped in the way and met Honeywell like a linebacker. He tackled him and drove him to the ground. Wally heard Honeywell grunt, but then he saw his hand come up with the rock in it. Wally dove and grabbed Honeywell's arm, pinned it to the ground. Chuck grabbed the other arm, sat on Honeywell's chest, and shouted into his face, "We're Americans. We have to stick together—not kill each other."

Honeywell cursed Johnson again, but he didn't move. For a time the three held their positions, all of them breathing hard. Finally Chuck said, "We're going to work now. And you're going to work with us."

"I'm reporting every one of you to Fujioka," Honeywell gasped. "Every one of you. This whole crew is in big trouble. Especially Johnson. He hit me when I was in charge. That's the same as hitting one of the guards."

"That's right," Johnson said, with cold anger. "It's exactly the same thing."

"Shut up," Chuck said. "Both of you. Now listen to me, Honeywell. A lot of men hate you more than the Japs themselves. If you report Johnson—or anyone else—your life isn't safe around here."

"Don't threaten me, Adair, because—"

"I'm not threatening you. I'm not going to be the one to come after you. But listen to me, and ask yourself whether I'm right. If this story gets out—and if other men find out you turned us in—ask yourself whether someone isn't going to get you for it. I've heard men say already they'd like to kill you. Now let go of that rock."

"I'm not afraid of anyone in this camp," Honeywell said, but his voice had lost all its fervor, and he dropped the rock.

"We're going to let you up now," Chuck said. "And what we all need to do is get to work. If we do that, everything will be fine, and if you keep your mouth shut, this whole thing is over."

"I just might kill him right now," Johnson said.

"Clark, lay off that stuff," Wally said.

Wally and Chuck let go of Honeywell's arms. "Let's work," Chuck said. "All of us."

Honeywell walked over and picked up a shovel. "Hey, I have to work now," he said. "You lazy bums won't get enough done if I don't." But that was to save face. Honeywell seemed to know he had no choice.

Wally was relieved. The pain in his leg was worse now, but he had no choice either. He also had to get back to work.

As it turned out, the men did move a great deal of rock that afternoon. They didn't clear the passage entirely, but when Fujioka returned he didn't seem to expect that. Wally had the feeling that the whole idea had been Honeywell's.

Fujioka kept the men until after five in the afternoon. They got to the bathhouse, as usual, when the water already looked muddy from all the men who had been in it. Chuck helped Wally into the pool, and Wally washed as best he could. Then the men dressed and lined up for the long hike back. By now Wally's leg was throbbing, and he cringed every time he put weight on it. But there was nothing to do but keep going.

When the men reached the camp, Wally went straight to the mess hall, ate his rice, and then limped to his barracks. But he had only just lain down when the barracks supervisor appeared. He pronounced Wally's number, and Chuck's, and then motioned for them to follow. Wally struggled to his feet, not daring to defy. And outside he got what he feared. That day's work crew was assembled, all but Honeywell, and three guards beat the men, one at a time.

Wally waited for his turn, tried not to anticipate, not to think or feel. He could deal with this. But the first blow came suddenly and hard, a hammering slam to his chest that knocked him off his feet. Then the guards kicked him in the ribs and abdomen. He was hanging on pretty well until one of the guards kicked him in the back of the leg. The pain was so powerful that it filled up his head. Everything swirled for a few seconds, but he didn't black out entirely. He was thrown into a strange state, as though outside himself, aware but not aware.

When it was all over, and he was lying on his back, he could see the night sky, the stars, and he thought he was rising toward them, maybe dying, and it didn't frighten him at all. There was something restful in the vision, something his body longed for. But his friends came for him and carried him to his mat. He was apparently covered with blood because Don brought in a rag and washed his face. Chuck was somewhere nearby, and men were talking, cursing as they worked on him, too. Wally knew all of that, but he felt very little, only the pervasive pain that was intense and yet distant, as though it couldn't quite reach the inner core of him.

He never really slept that night, and as the hours passed by, the pain began to find its focus, gradually returning to his leg. All the same, he got up in the morning, still dazed but more aware, and he walked to the mine. He and Chuck stayed by each other. They didn't talk, didn't lean on each other, but Wally felt Chuck's presence and knew he couldn't have made the long hike without the help.

It seemed likely that Fujioka would break up the crew, but he didn't. He kept the four battered men. Only Honeywell was gone. As the men pulled themselves from the train, Fujioka screamed at them, demanded that they get to work immediately, without their morning rice. And so, bruised as they were, they began to break more rock, move it. Wally found himself letting out little, uncontrollable gasps with every movement he made, but he didn't let the other men down. He kept pushing himself.

At noon the men lay down, rested, and ate their rice. But this only gave Wally time to stiffen, and the work seemed even harder when he started again. He managed for a few minutes, and then he realized he was about to pass out. He clung to his shovel, leaned on it, and waited for his head to clear. By then

Fujioka was screaming at him. And then Chuck was there. "Are you okay?" he asked Wally.

"I don't know," Wally said. "I almost blacked out. How are you doing?"

"I'm okay." But Wally got a look at his face, saw how swollen and bruised it was.

Fujioka had come closer now. He was shouting, probably cursing. As Wally tried to get his legs under him, he felt them give way, and he sank to his knees. The pain doubled him over. Then he felt hands on his head, and he heard Chuck say, "Walter Thomas, in the name of Jesus Christ, and by the power of the holy priesthood, I command you to arise and be healed."

Wally responded. He got up. "Thank you," he whispered. The pain was still there, in his leg, but not so much in his head, and he found the power to go on.

The day was very hard, but Wally made it through. And he walked back to the camp. He ate, and mercifully he even slept. And when he awoke in the morning, the healing had occurred. He reached down and touched the boils, felt that all three had festered into heads. The pain was not yet over, but it was easier, and that night Wally reported to the medical station, where an American doctor, without any painkiller, lanced the boils. The cutting was excruciating, but once the boils were open, the putrid infection squirted out, and the pain drained away. Wally knew he would be all right now.

Chuck helped Wally walk back to the barracks.

"It's a lot better," Wally told him. "I'll be all right now." And then he took another look at Chuck's bruised face. "How bad did they hurt you?" he asked.

"I've been beaten worse a couple of times. The bad thing is, I lost another tooth. I hardly have any left."

"Honeywell ratted on us to the Japs, didn't he?"

"No question."

A few days later the tenth working day came—the day the prisoners didn't have to go to the mine. It was the only thing to look forward to in the camp. The men, worn down from work and malnutrition, usually spent most of the day sleeping. But late in the afternoon the little Mormon group always got together and held a church service. Chuck and Art always came, and Wally's friend Don Cluff. Several others like Don, not LDS, usually showed up: Eddy Nash and Ray Vernon, old friends, plus a couple of younger guys named Raymond Golson and Joe Fields. Some other Christian groups had formed, but the men who met with the Mormons were guys who liked what they heard at the meetings.

On this particular day Chuck was the assigned teacher. He and Art and Wally took turns leading the discussions. They tried to remember the scriptures as best they could—since not even a Bible was available—and all three wished they had studied more carefully when they were younger so they could explain doctrine more clearly.

The men preferred to gather outside, but it was a cool fall day, so they met in a corner of the mess hall. The place wasn't heated, but it was out of the wind. All of the men sat around one large table. Chuck asked Don to say an opening prayer—something he had become very good at—and then Chuck said, "I've been having a hard time this week. There's something we've talked a lot about, but it seems like the biggest challenge we all have to deal with. That's hatred. The Bible says we should love everyone, even our enemies, and no one here is having an easy time with that, I know. What's worse this time, though, is forgiving someone who isn't supposed to be my enemy but acts like it." He hesitated and looked at the floor. "I think you know who I mean."

Everyone did know, of course. Some of the men nodded.

"I think I understand how a guy gets so hungry or so messed up in his head that he'll do almost anything to get food—or to save himself when he feels like he's dying. I never say too much when I see someone that desperate, because I've been pretty close to it a few times myself. But when a man is in decent health, as good or better than anyone, and he chooses to turn his back on men in his own circumstances, just to get a few advantages—cigarettes, or a little extra food—"

"Or better duty," Eddy said.

"Well, yeah. But you see what I'm saying. How do I forgive someone like that? How can I be a Christian about that? I lost a tooth because of that man this week. And the loss of my teeth has been one of the toughest ordeals for me. Every time my tongue touches that hole in my mouth, I feel hatred in my heart."

Joe Fields was a guy who never hesitated to speak his mind. He looked as emaciated as any of the men, but he kept his spirits up. He was sitting at the end of the table, opposite Chuck. He raised his hand but then spoke before Chuck called on him. "Chuck," he said, "I'm sorry, but I don't think we have to do something even God can't do. And there's no way God likes Honeywell. That guy is about three steps below a cockroach on the food chain." He looked around and grinned, seeming pleased with himself.

Some of the men laughed, and Chuck did too, but then he said, "What if he were your son? Would you love him then?"

"I'll bet his mother can't stand him," someone said, but there was less laughter this time.

Chuck glanced around. "You'd better keep your voice down," he said. No one was near, but Wally knew what he meant. There was no end to the ways that men could get in trouble in this camp. Laughter was always cause for suspicion.

"What Honeywell is, is weak," Art said, in a soft voice. "We're all tempted to be like him. If you ask me, we hate him because we see ourselves in him. He represents what every guy can be, if he lets down just a little."

Wally had been thinking something pretty close to that. "I'll tell you what I've learned from Honeywell," he told the others. He was sitting next to Chuck, both of them occupying a position at the head of the table. "For a long time I've been telling myself there's something wrong with Japs. They aren't like us. But Honeywell shows me that treating people wrong has nothing to do with being Japanese. If Honeywell were guarding a bunch of Japanese POWs, you know how he would treat them. I wonder what a lot of us would do, if all of a sudden the whole situation were turned upside down."

"Okay," Chuck said. "That's what's been on my mind, too. People, when they sink to their lowest level, don't care about anyone. They'll hurt a guy, steal from him, do anything rotten—just to have what they want. But that's not something German or Italian or Japanese. It's something we can all sink to."

"But we can still hate the way these guards treat us. There's nothing right about that," Eddy said. Eddy knew all about tough treatment. He had come very close to dying on the hell ship, and he had taken a severe beating one day because he was late arriving at morning formation. He was a cocky little guy, a sort of bull terrier, but he was also a loyal friend to the men he trusted.

"That's right," Chuck said. "God hates sin. We can too. But if we hate the Japanese, we're sinking to the level of these guards we deal with every day."

There was a long silence. Wally looked around the table. It was a strange sight, all these skeletons trying so hard to think and feel, to cling to their essential humanity. This was their only day of relative freedom, and yet they were gathered here in this corner of the mess hall, and for each the motivation seemed more or less the same. They needed to believe that life had meaning, that this experience didn't have to destroy them.

Joe finally said, "I'm sorry, Chuck, but I can't accept that. I hate these Jap guards with all my heart, and I can't believe God would expect me to feel any different."

Chuck considered that for a time before he said, "I do think God understands what you feel—but nothing I've ever read in the scriptures would convince me that he approves of your hating one of your brothers or sisters on this earth—no matter what that person does."

Some of the men nodded, as did Wally. But faces had been brighter when Joe had spoken. Apparently the justification for hatred had sounded more convincing than the idealism Chuck was expressing.

"Some men have vowed to kill Honeywell," Don said. "I've heard the talk all week."

"So what about that?" Chuck asked.

"Maybe some behavior deserves the death penalty," Vernon said.

"Maybe. But this is no court, not a legal system. We can't start killing each other like a bunch of vigilantes."

"Maybe not," Don said, "and I won't be the one to do it. But if someone gets Honeywell, I won't waste a single second feeling bad about it. I've seen too many good men die to feel bad about him."

"So what are you guys saying?" Chuck asked. "Is God expecting something from us that's just too hard—something we can't do?"

No one wanted to answer, and the silence lasted a long time. The men were all looking at the table—or inside themselves—not at each other. It was Joe who was finally willing to say what he thought. "I know you don't want to hear this, Chuck, but when I look right down to the bottom of my heart, I gotta say, I can't do it. I can't love these Japs, and I sure can't forgive Honeywell for what he did to you guys. Maybe some of you guys can do it, but I can't."

Another silence followed, and Wally saw that Chuck was struggling to think what to say. It was a black and disappointing moment for Wally, worse than the pain he had had to fight. God had touched him, stayed with him through his ordeal, healed him, and that should make a difference now, but even though Wally had said the right things earlier in the discussion, he knew what he felt. Joe was only different in that he had found the nerve to say it out loud.

Wally hated the guards who had beaten him, and he hated Honeywell. He didn't hate all Japanese; he knew better than that. But he hated these distorted creatures who preyed upon the prisoners, and he hated the weakling Americans who took advantage of their own brothers. And what was worse, like Joe, Wally didn't want to give up his hatred. In so many ways, it was still his greatest source of strength. Wally felt the guilt that came with that admission—but it wasn't a strong enough force to overpower his hatred.

13

Anna was still translating documents for the MI-6 office of the British SIS. Gradually she was being trusted with sensitive materials, but to do that she had to go to the office near Grosvenor Square. This was only a short trip on the underground, but it got her out of the house. She needed to be busy, to concentrate on something other than her worries. Everything she heard from Holland was discouraging. Alex's letters, once she finally started receiving them, didn't admit to any personal danger, but Anna knew his situation was precarious. The Allied troops were still clinging to a narrow strip of land from Belgium through the southeast corner of Holland.

Alex said little about any of that, but he did close one of his letters by saying, "Anna, war is worse than anyone can know without experiencing it. It's bad for all the obvious reasons, but what I hate the most is the way it changes me. I'm not myself right now, and I can't be. I get by the best when I don't think too much, but that makes me something less than human. At times I shut my eyes and try to see you, and just feel for a moment the way I do when I'm with you. That's all I cling to now—the idea that I can feel like that again someday."

Anna cried when she read those words. She hated to think what Alex was going through. Just when the two of them should be building a closeness with each other, as newlyweds, they were split apart, each changing, each experiencing things they couldn't share. She feared that the war would create a gap between them that could never be bridged entirely.

What was also distressing was that her father seemed to have vanished. She and her mother had never been allowed to know the reason for his leaving, or even the length of time he would be gone. They only knew he was working with the American OSS in some capacity, and he had promised he would be back "long before Christmas." Anna was almost sure he had returned to Germany, but she never told her mother that. She knew from her work in intelligence that the Americans were sending agents into the country, and she knew how much her father wanted to look for Peter. It would be like him to take any chance to get closer to him. But her father had been gone three weeks now, and Anna and her mother hadn't heard a word from him. He had warned them that he wouldn't be able to write, but the reality of knowing nothing, of having no way to reach him, was more difficult than Anna had realized it would be.

Frieda Stoltz seemed to have her own suspicions about her husband's mission, although she never said so. She was nervous and therefore not easy to be around. She wasn't irritable; she was merely preoccupied and silent. Days with her were tediously long and gloomy, and so it was always better to leave home each day, to be around other people.

But London was frightening these days. V-2 rockets were hitting somewhere in the London area two or three times a day. The V-1 buzzbombs—or "doodlebugs," as most Londoners had called them—had been pilotless aircraft that flew slowly and usually struck only after sirens had sounded. A person could hear a buzzbomb, estimate how close it was likely to strike, and often go about one's business. But the V-2 rockets came any time of the day or night, came suddenly and without sound or warning. And they each packed a far greater punch.

That was not to say that London stopped operating. People continued to go about their lives. During the "little blitz" in the spring, theater attendance had fallen off, but this fall Londoners were queuing up to see Laurence Olivier's performance in *Richard III.* The West End cinemas had remained packed throughout the war, but even in the dangerous East End, the cinemas were full every night. Cricket and soccer matches drew enormous crowds; and on Oxford Street, in spite of shortages and rationed goods, the shoppers still filled the stores. Anna already loved the city and took strength from the persistence of its people. She had seen a similar tenacity in her own people, in Berlin, but the battering had finally been more severe, and Berliners had been forced to make greater adjustments. What Londoners talked about most was the end of the war. They insisted that the day would soon come when all this destruction and fear would end, and they went about surviving this latest horror with amazing stoicism.

Anna and her mother went to church every Sunday. They loved singing the hymns again, remembering the way it felt to take the sacrament, to be joined with a body of believers. They were well accepted for the most part, and yet at times they felt a certain distance between themselves and the other members. Part of it was merely language, but there were layers of feelings that couldn't be peeled away easily. What Anna always sensed was that the kindness she received was a bit self-conscious, as though it required special effort to befriend Germans. That was understandable but not as satisfying as she would have liked.

Anna felt the same gulf between her and most of the other Londoners she met. They heard her accent, of course, and usually wanted to believe that she was Scandinavian or Dutch, not German. People obviously felt a certain unease about her origins. She was an open person, so she didn't hesitate to say that her family had opposed the Nazis, and that always seemed to help. But in a shop or in making a first acquaintance, when she had no opportunity to explain, people would sometimes ask her where she was from, and then, when she answered, they'd seem uncomfortable and awkward.

What Anna knew was that she had left her own land, her own people, probably forever, and that she might never be fully accepted anywhere else. And worse, she was—at least for the present—cut off from the ties she had to the few people who loved her without reservation: her husband, her brother, her father, and even, in some ways, her mother. It was entirely possible that she could lose one or even all of the men in her life, so she wanted to cling to her mother as at least one source of affection, but her mother's own anxiety made that difficult.

So Anna struggled. But she wasn't one to give in to self-pity. She made the best of things, tried to cheer up her mother as best she could, and was friendly at work. Mostly by accident, the Stoltzes had found a flat in a part of London that was rarely threatened by the rockets. She had actually not felt so safe in years, and so, when she went to bed at night, she slept well.

But then one night late in October, Anna was awakened as the concussion of a terrific explosion banged against her building. The house seemed to shift, and she heard the structure creak. She grabbed her blankets, held on, and then realized what had happened. A rocket had landed close, probably between her building and Regent's Park. Within a few seconds she could already see the light of fires through her window.

Anna slipped out of bed and ran to her mother's room. Sister Stoltz was also up but seemingly confused, waiting. "It was close," Anna whispered, and she took her mother in her arms. "But we're all right."

"So many must have died," Sister Stoltz said.

Anna knew that was true, and she was ashamed that her first thought had been only about herself. "We need to help," she said.

"Yes."

Anna tried the light but found that the electricity was out.

So the two dressed in the glow from the fire. Then they hurried downstairs and out into the cool night. They found that a whole block of buildings near Baker Street, one street over from their own, had been demolished. As they hurried closer, they saw nothing but confusion, with people running about, screaming, fire trucks approaching, sirens sounding.

What Anna couldn't see yet was something that she and her mother could do. She knew that very soon the rubble would have to be pulled away, that there might be people to save in the demolished buildings, but fires were still raging, dust and smoke still hanging over the debris.

And then she saw a man inside a mostly destroyed house. He was at a first-floor window. The glass in the window was broken, and he was swinging a stick of some sort, breaking the remaining glass away. A man ran to the burning building, and then two more followed. Anna heard one of them yell, "Climb out. We'll help you down."

But the man inside shouted something that Anna couldn't hear. Then, in a moment, she understood. There was a woman inside, too, and the man was trying to help her out the window. The men on the outside, joined by a fourth now, all reached up, got hold of her arms as she came out head first. It was then that Anna saw that she was an older woman with white hair, that she was dressed in a nightgown.

The woman let the men take her weight and lower her to the pavement below. And then they looked back to the man, who came out the same way. He was obviously the woman's husband, a white-haired man himself. He had pulled on a pair of trousers, but he was barefoot and wearing his striped pajama tops, not a shirt.

"We need to help them," Sister Stoltz said, and she hurried across the street, with Anna following. As she approached, she shouted, in English, "Come. Come with us."

"We must wait, and go back for our things," the woman was saying. "Everything we have is in there."

"No," one of the men was telling her. "The fire must be put out first. You won't be going back in there soon."

"But we need our pictures. All our papers."

"No, no," her husband kept saying. "It's all right. We're alive. We're lucky."

The woman stepped back and looked up at the building. The top floors had collapsed onto each other; flames were shooting up between the splintered timbers and the clinging roof tiles. "Where will we live now? Where will we go?" She asked.

"Come with us. You can get inside, out of the cold," Anna said.

"Who are you?"

"We live close by."

"Yes, love, that's best," her husband said. "Let's get inside where it's warm. In the morning we'll come back and salvage what we can." He began to walk, pulling her along through the scattered rubble on the street. But the woman continued to look back. She had begun to cry.

Anna put her arm around the woman's shoulders, patted her. "It will be all right," she said. "You'll be safe with us."

She and her mother led the couple to their building on the next street, and then inside and up the dark stairway. "We have no electricity," Anna said. "I'm sorry."

"It doesn't matter," the man told her. "It's a place to sit down. To stay warm. You're very kind."

Sister Stoltz managed to get a key into the lock and open the door to their flat. "Here," she said, leading the couple into the dark living room. The light from the fires was enough to provide a silhouette of the furniture. The couple took a seat on the couch.

"Would you like something to drink?" Anna asked. "We have peppermint tea, or—"

"No, no. It isn't necessary," the man said. "You should return to bed. We'll merely sit here and rest. We'll be fine." He had a deep, warm voice. Anna had glimpsed his face earlier, seen his big knob of a nose, his flabby cheeks, but his voice made him seem younger, handsome.

"But I'm happy to make something." It was Anna's only idea; she wanted to help and didn't know how to do it. Sister Stoltz had sat down next to the woman, and now she was putting her arms around her. "I'm sorry," she said in English. "I'm very sorry."

Anna knew that her mother understood as well as anyone what the woman was dealing with—the loss of all she had. And the woman seemed to sense that. She let Sister Stoltz hold her in her arms, and she cried harder than before. She mumbled, "It was so loud, so terrible. I thought the building was coming in on top of us."

"Yes, yes," Sister Stoltz said. "I know." Anna knew that her mother had understood enough words to know what the woman was talking about.

"Thirty-four years we've lived there," the woman said, and she sobbed. She was a little woman, all roundness, but Anna was remembering the eyes she had seen: sharp, like rodent eyes, on the watch.

"It's all right," her husband kept saying. "We weren't even touched."

"But what of the others?" the woman said, pulling away from Sister Stoltz and looking toward her husband. "What's happened to all our neighbors? Poor old Mrs. Grimsley upstairs. And the Browers, that nice young couple. Are they all gone?"

"I don't know, love. I don't know. Maybe they survived somehow."

"Not on the upper floors. Everything was destroyed. How can the Germans do such a thing—send rockets in the night to kill old women and young couples? It's all so wrong."

The woman began to sob again, this time leaning toward her husband, who took her in his arms. For quite some time everyone was silent. Anna was still considering the question: "How could the Germans do such a thing?" The issue was not that simple, she knew, but the question still disturbed her.

Eventually the woman sat up straight, wrapped her arms close around herself, and began to find some control. Her husband found a handkerchief in his trousers pocket and gave it to her. She wiped her eyes and nose, and then Anna heard the resolution in her voice when she said, "I'm sorry to be like this."

"It's all right. We understand," Anna told her.

"Please, tell me your names. You've been so kind to us. You're not English, are you?"

"We're from Germany," Anna said.

"Germany?" the man said, obviously surprised.

"Yes."

Anna feared the worst. During the silence that followed she knew that everyone was recalling what the woman had said.

"Refugees?" the woman asked, her voice more gentle.

"Yes," Anna said.

"Are you Jewish?"

"No. We became enemies of the Gestapo. We had to escape."

"Just you and your mother?"

"No. My father was with us. He's away right now." Anna didn't want to explain any more than she had to—about Peter, or about her father.

"Oh, my. I'm so sorry for what I said." She turned toward Sister Stoltz and patted her hand. "After you were so good to us."

"It's fine," Sister Stoltz said.

"My mother doesn't speak English very well yet. But she understands many things."

"I didn't mean all Germans. I hope you know that."

"We understand," Anna told her.

"You speak very well, dear."

"I'm learning."

"Tell me your names. We're the Dillinghams."

"My name is Anna Thomas," Anna said. "I'm married to an American soldier. My mother's name is Frieda Stoltz."

"And where is *your* husband?"

"In the Netherlands."

"Oh, dear. He must be a paratrooper."

"Yes."

"These are such terrible times."

Anna could hear more sirens outside, see the pulsing orange light of the fires reflecting off the walls. "We had to give up our home and leave everything behind," she said. "So we understand what you feel tonight."

"And you must have lived through *our* bombing raids in Germany."

"We did. We were in Berlin during the worst of the bombing."

"Oh, my. What a war."

Sister Stoltz touched Mrs. Dillingham's shoulder and said, "Stay with us." Then she looked up at Anna and said, in German, "Tell them they can live with us. We have enough room for them."

Anna translated the words, but Mr. Dillingham said, "Oh, no. We won't bother you long. In the morning we'll check to see what arrangements we can make."

"So many have lost their homes," Anna said. "There are no places to go, I think."

"There are temporary shelters. And then, in time, we'll be placed somewhere. I'm sure we can manage. Others are doing all right. We have a daughter in Chelsea. She and her husband have only a small place, but maybe we could manage with them somehow."

"We have room, Mr. Dillingham. You can stay here as long as you have need."

"I don't know, Mrs. Thomas. Maybe for a day or two. And we could pay you something."

"I'm Anna, not Mrs. Thomas. And we want no money."

"Thank you, dear," Mrs. Dillingham said. "Thank you so very much."

The Dillinghams, as it turned out, did stay, and the "day or two" kept stretching. It was the best thing that could have happened for Sister Stoltz. It gave her something to think about, something to do. Her English improved much faster than it had before, and she and Mrs. Dillingham, who knew a little German, carried on some funny conversations, full of motions and pointed fingers, but they seemed to understand each other. Mr. Dillingham, who was retired, was a Civil Patrol volunteer, and he left each day to perform his duties. With Anna gone most days, Sister Stoltz and Mrs. Dillingham—Dorothy—had plenty of hours together.

Mr. Dillingham was able to return to his and his wife's flat after a couple of days, and he brought out most of the things that were valuable to them. Some of their pictures had been damaged by water, but the fire had never reached them. Mr. Dillingham was also able to salvage some other things— dining-room chairs, a chest of drawers, and end tables. The Stoltz's flat, which was sparsely furnished, benefited a good deal from the additions.

On Sunday Anna and Sister Stoltz invited the Dillinghams to go to church with them. They declined, but they were curious about Germans who were Mormons, a church the Dillinghams had always associated with America. And so they kept asking questions, and on the following Sunday they surprised Anna by agreeing to go.

The congregation in the little hall that day, as usual, was a collection of London members along with a good many American and British soldiers and sailors, in uniform. Some of the soldiers were stationed close enough to attend most weeks; others were passing through on their way to the continent or on a weekend pass from a camp in England. The Dillinghams whispered to Anna that they were impressed with the quality of the people, so many seeming well educated, and virtually all of them so friendly. "We English aren't known for our rashness when it comes to making friends," Edward Dillingham whispered.

After the sacrament was passed, President Wakefield introduced the speaker, President Newton, a member of the district presidency. He spoke about Lehi's dream and interpreted the various symbols, including the iron rod. He described the way the world, in war time, was succumbing to temptation, letting those in the spacious building influence them toward sin. It was a good enough talk—although a little harsh on the sinners, Anna thought—but then he said, "The world is currently divided into two great divisions. Good and evil. The Germans have chosen to align themselves with Hitler, who is in league with Satan. We are suffering in many ways, but at least we have the knowledge that whatever our faults and sins, we are standing on the side of right."

Anna didn't exactly disagree with that, and she didn't take offense. But then President Newton said, "There's no question in my mind that the German people will be visited with devastation and destruction. They will suffer for generations to come for the evil they have brought to this world."

Anna saw her mother glance toward her, as though she were uncertain what she had heard, and at the same time Anna felt the tension in the congregation. President Newton didn't know the Stoltzes, and of course all the branch members did.

Anna tried to tell herself that President Newton wasn't calling for revenge on all Germans. He was only speaking the truth, that Hitler had misguided a nation, and now the people of that nation would have to pay. She even knew that many of her country's people had been only too willing to accept Hitler's militarism, and that that was a sin. She simply wondered about President Newton's tone, which sounded so judgmental.

Anna was careful to say "Amen" when the talk ended. She didn't want the members to think she and her mother were offended—even if she was just a little. She wondered what the Dillinghams were thinking.

But then President Wakefield got up, announced the closing hymn and prayer, and said, "May I add one thought to what President Newton has said today. Recently we received a letter from the First Presidency of our Church. The brethren advised all members that when victory in Europe comes—as it certainly will before too much longer—we should not forget that there are faithful Latter-day Saints in many of the countries involved in this war. The presidency warned us not to wound the feelings of our brothers and sisters in defeated lands. We were asked to devote the following Sunday to prayers of thanksgiving, and then to ask the Lord for help in avoiding all wars in the future."

President Wakefield looked down at Anna and her mother. "We are very aware, in this branch, that fine people live in all lands. We see that in the Stoltzes, who came to us from Germany. We love them dearly. It is help and healing that I hope we will offer the German people—all of them—when this war is over."

President Newton nodded and seemed a little shamefaced. When the service ended, he came down to meet Anna and her mother, to tell them he hoped he hadn't offended them. They told him they were not hurt by his words.

After, as the Dillinghams and Anna and her mother waited for the underground train, Edward said, "I must say, I agreed with that gentleman when he spoke about Germany—or at least I would have, if you hadn't been sitting next to me. I liked what your minister said. Not many of us are as Christian as we ought to be these days. You two have done more for us than anyone—and the world would have us believe that you are our enemies."

"Good people are everywhere," Sister Stoltz said. "And bad."

Dorothy hugged her and said, "And ever so many more who are like us—somewhere in between."

14

LaRue was upstairs in her room when she heard her father's voice booming up the stairway. "LaRue, come down here."

She didn't like the sound of this. She was getting ready to go to the USO. At least she hadn't put any lipstick on—yet.

She took her time, partly because she was fixing her hair and it still needed some work, but also because she hated the way her father had demanded that she come downstairs, without so much as asking whether she was busy. By the time she did walk down, she could see that the wait had not pleased him. He was standing at the foot of the stairs, looking stern, his jaw set even tighter than usual, and LaRue wondered what she had done to get him so upset.

"Step back to my office with me, LaRue," he said. "I need to talk to you."

"Sure, Pop," LaRue said. She pretended to slug him on the shoulder. That sort of playfulness sometimes softened President Thomas, but it seemed to have the opposite effect now. He didn't smile back at her. He turned and led the way, striding stiffly.

Inside his office, President Thomas sat down behind his desk. This was the place where he brought people for stake president interviews or for counseling. He rarely used it for family talks. But certainly he had a sense that the place, the desk, added some authority to what he had to say. He used that aura now as he said, "LaRue, I got a telephone call a few minutes ago. Someone warned me that I ought to be looking out for you a little more carefully. I'm very concerned about what I just heard."

"What are you talking about?" LaRue asked, but she knew.

"You make this volunteer work you do at the USO sound like your great sacrifice for the war. But now I find out you have a boyfriend down there—some non-Mormon fellow."

"I don't have a boyfriend, Dad. There's a boy who likes me, but that's all there is to it."

"LaRue, I told you I was going to give you some room to make your own choices—but I didn't think you would abuse your freedom. I thought you would learn from it. The person who just called told me that your behavior is anything but becoming to the daughter of a stake president. From what you've been seen doing in public, I hate to think what else might be going on."

LaRue was suddenly irate. She knew, for one thing, that her friend Gaye had said something to Gaye's mother—and it was the mother who had called. That was the only source for this information. But more than that, it was the accusation that enraged LaRue.

"Dad, I dance with him. And I've let him kiss me goodnight. But that's all. What do you think I do, sneak out in back with him? You have no right to say something like that."

"LaRue, I know how these gentile boys behave. I know what they want from pretty young girls—whether they're nice girls or not. You're too young to be kissing boys, and he's not going to be satisfied with a goodnight kiss forever."

"What do you take me for, Dad? Some little harlot?"

"According to what I just heard, you let him wrap himself all around you when you're dancing."

"Dad, we dance close. That's how everyone dances. I'll bet you danced that way when you were my age."

"No. I didn't. Not like that." President Thomas folded his arms over his chest, across his white shirt and tie. It was his uniform. All LaRue's life, this was almost the only way she had seen him dressed. Most men who wore a white shirt and tie to work seemed to be only too happy to change into sport clothes at home, but her father was always off to a church meeting, or had someone coming over. He never said it, but LaRue knew that even if he went to a high-school football game or stopped off at a grocery store to pick up some eggs for Mom, he felt he had to look like a stake president. Now that shirt and tie—and the desk—only served to remind her that when he called her on the carpet, he always brought the whole church along, and all the extra shame that it evoked.

"Let me ask you this," he said. "Did you lie about your age to start volunteering down there?"

LaRue let out a little sigh of defeat—and disgust. "Not exactly," she said.

"What's that supposed to mean?"

"Girls my age can volunteer. We're just not supposed to dance. I never actually told anyone I was older than I am. They just assumed it."

"When they saw you dancing, I'm sure."

"Yeah. I guess. But I don't see what difference it makes."

"This is one difference. I told you I would trust you. And you abused that trust. Now you've lost it."

"It's interesting, Dad," LaRue said carefully but with acid in her voice, "that you would take a phone call, listen to some busybody, and accept anything you hear. It just shows how little trust you *actually* give me. You granted me a tiny bit of room just so later on you could say, 'See, I knew you couldn't handle it.'"

"LaRue, you just told me you've been kissing some boy

from who-knows-where. You're fifteen years old. What do I need to know that you haven't admitted yourself?"

"Oh, and I guess when you were my age, you never kissed a girl."

All LaRue's life she had known the right buttons to push to get what she wanted from her father. But she saw immediately he wasn't buying this one. He actually smiled, and then he said, "I've watched the way you talk to the young men at church, LaRue. I've watched the way you eye the boys, no matter where we are—and how much you like them to look at you. You wear the shortest skirts you think I'll let you get away with, and you smudge your face with makeup every time you think my back is turned. I don't have to get phone calls. I know just as surely as we're sitting here that you flirt with every boy who walks through the door down at that *canteen*, or whatever it is."

"No, Dad. You're absolutely wrong about that. I only flirt with the good-looking ones. And you need to know, I'm *very* good at it."

It was a whole new approach for LaRue, but she liked it. And she saw that her harpoon had hit its mark. Her father's face was suddenly red. He leaned forward and pointed at her. "You're not going down there anymore. Never again. I've been way too easy on you. I had it in my head that I was too rough on Wally and that I had to ease off on you. But that was exactly the wrong approach. From now on, little girl, consider your wings clipped. No more of this running around you've gotten used to."

"Dad, I'm one of the best volunteers the USO has. Call the manager and ask him if you don't believe me."

"I'll call him and ask him why he's allowing a fifteen-year-old girl to dance with grown men. Then see how pleased he is with you."

LaRue felt everything slipping away, and she couldn't stand it. For the past few months her time at the USO had become the most exciting part of her life. Maybe her dad thought it was wrong to flirt, but that's all she had ever done—except for those few kisses. What she loved was having the attention of all those young men—and Ned's devotion to her. What was so wrong about that?

LaRue stood up. She had watched her dad make these kinds of pronouncements all her life, but she wasn't going to let him get away with it this time—no matter what the other kids in the family had done. "I'm going down there, Dad. I promised to work tonight, and they need me."

"They'll get by. Don't you set one foot outside this house."

She walked to the door. "I told you. I'm going."

Her father stood up, but as he moved toward LaRue, she pulled the door open and stepped out into the dining room. "LaRue, you go up to your room and stay there," he said, his voice almost frantic.

"I *am* going to my room," she said. "I have to put my coat on—and my lipstick."

Mom stepped through the door from the kitchen. "What on earth is going on?" she said.

LaRue was already hurrying into the living room and from there into the front entry and up the stairs to her room. "LaRue," her father called after her, "don't you come down those stairs. You stay in your room."

But LaRue was going to the USO. If he wanted to grab onto her and hold her in the house, fine, but he was going to have to do just that. Or tie her to her bedpost. She wasn't going to stop just because he told her to.

When she reached the top of the stairs, LaRue saw Beverly standing in the hallway outside her bedroom door. "LaRue, don't," she said.

LaRue knew what she meant, of course, but she said, "Don't what?"

"Don't talk to Dad that way. Don't get everyone so upset."

"Baby, you ain't seen nothin' yet," LaRue said, and she tried to laugh. She pushed past Beverly into her own room, where she grabbed her coat. Then she stepped to her dresser, picked up a tube of dark red lipstick and stroked on a wide, exaggerated sweep across both her lips.

What surprised her now, however, was that she was hearing a commotion downstairs. Her parents were talking in raised voices, almost shouting at each other. That hardly seemed possible.

As LaRue banged her way back through her bedroom door, she saw that Beverly was still in the hallway, but now she was crying. "Now look what you've done," Beverly said. "They're *fighting*."

LaRue felt the fear strike her. She didn't want that. Maybe all this was going too far. But sheer inertia carried her past Beverly, down the hall and the stairs. By then she could hear her mother saying, her voice strident, "You haven't learned one thing, Al. You drove Wally out of this house. I'm not going to let you do the same thing to LaRue."

"I'm not driving her out. I'm keeping her home," President Thomas bellowed.

"It's the same thing, and you know it. And why assume the worst about her? You don't know that she's done one thing wrong."

LaRue stopped at the bottom of the stairs. Her father was standing near the front door. Her mother was shaking her stubby finger in his face. Nothing like this had ever happened in the Thomas home before.

"Yes, Bea, that makes perfect sense. Let her get into some *real* trouble, and then try to stop her. I'm shutting the gate before the cow gets loose."

LaRue couldn't resist. "I'm no cow, Dad. I don't wander out just because a gate is open. I can think for myself. And take care of myself, too."

"You *believe* you can, anyway. You have no idea what you're getting yourself into."

"But she's got to find out," Mom said, almost yelled into her husband's face. "We either trust her or we don't. We've either taught her well, or we haven't. She's growing up, and it's time for her to make some decisions for herself."

"She's not grown enough, Bea. She's *fifteen*."

"And who decides when she's grown enough? You didn't even bother to ask me what I think about this."

"I thought I knew what you'd think."

"You don't know that at all. Why couldn't we all sit down together and talk it out? LaRue isn't a bad girl. I *know* she isn't. She's always been willing to listen to reason."

"That's what you told me before, and look what's happened."

"Al, when you *tell* LaRue what to do, she gets her back up. That's how she's been since she was a little girl."

"That's all the more reason she needs to be stopped, Bea. Is that the way you want her to go through life—rebellious and disobedient?"

Sister Thomas was losing some of her strength, some of her anger. She stepped back a little, tucked her hands into the pockets on her flowered apron, and glanced at LaRue. LaRue was feeling more frightened than rebellious at the moment. She didn't want her parents to fight, not for any reason.

"All I'm saying, Al," Sister Thomas said, and now she was trying to control her voice, "is that each child is different. You're never going to stomp on LaRue and get compliance. Maybe some things she's going to have to learn for herself."

President Thomas had his hands on his hips, his big jaw set like a bear trap. He waited a very long time, half a minute perhaps, while everything stood still. LaRue thought maybe it was time to give in, to tell them she would stop going to the USO. But the thought only brought back her fury. She hadn't done anything so wrong as to deserve this—to be stuck home from now on when she loved the USO so much.

"All right, LaRue," President Thomas finally said. "Your mother thinks you have to learn the hard way. Once again, I'm the bad guy because I want to put some controls on you. So you go ahead. You run downtown, and you do whatever it is you do at the USO. And if it turns out to be a disaster, I guess I'm supposed to feel perfectly happy with that."

Suddenly Sister Thomas's voice was full of fire again. "That's not fair! Our whole married life you've been doing this to me." She was holding both her hands up, tightened into fists, as though ready to beat on her husband's chest. "You think you're the only one who knows anything. If I so much as suggest that I have an opinion, you accuse me of challenging your *great* authority."

"Where is all this coming from?" President Thomas asked, sounding honestly surprised. "You've never once said anything like that before."

"That's because you make me coax and scheme just to get my say once in a while. And I'm sick of that. I'm not trying to throw our daughter to the wolves. I've talked to her many times about what she does at the USO, and we've discussed the dangers. Have you ever once done anything but warn her and accuse her?"

LaRue had never seen her father so undone. The color had left his face. Finally, hesitantly, he said, "Bea, this is something you and I ought to talk about alone."

LaRue knew what he meant. Her mother had challenged him in front of his daughters, and that was humiliating to him. But he was also scared—maybe scared he actually was wrong—and surely alarmed that the world as he knew it was tipping on its edge. LaRue sensed that too, that their family would never be the same after this moment.

LaRue also knew what she needed to do. It was the right time to say, "Mom, Dad, let's sit down now. Let's talk about this." But she also sensed her chance to keep what she wanted, and she was almost sure she would lose that in a quiet conversation. So she stepped forward. "I'm going to be late," she said, and she walked past her father, who actually moved out of the way as she passed him. Then she walked to Twenty-First South, where she caught a streetcar downtown. She wondered what was happening at home, but she also felt a new freedom that was rather satisfying.

By the time she reached the USO, however, she was feeling more guilt than she wanted to, and that made her angry. She knew, of course, that she hadn't been as candid as her mother had thought. She had promised to meet Ned tonight. Maybe he even considered that a date. But still, she hadn't done anything wrong with him. That was the accusation that angered her so deeply.

If her father only knew, Ned was as nice as any of the Mormon boys at East High. He wasn't anyone to worry about. Dad had it in his head that any boy who wasn't LDS was some kind of lecher, and that wasn't fair. Ned was sweet, and he was head over heels in love with her, even wanted to marry her. He had stopped swearing when he was around her, and he never drank. Those goodnight kisses were all she had allowed, and he had never pushed for anything else.

When LaRue arrived, a little late, she spotted Ned alone at a table. She was glad for that. She didn't like his friends all that much. She walked over and said hello to him. He stood up and greeted her, but she kept her distance. She didn't want him to show her any affection.

"I've got to check in and see what they want me to do tonight. I'll dance with you after a while. All right?"

"What's wrong?"

"Nothing. I'm fine."

After she checked in and then helped out at the sandwich counter for a while, she did go back and dance with Ned, but again she kept him more distant than usual. After, when they sat down together at his table, he said, "LaRue, I know something is wrong. Just tell me what it is."

"I got in a fight with my dad tonight. He doesn't want me to come here anymore."

"Why not?"

She told him about the phone call, but she left out the things she didn't want Ned to know. He still had no idea how young she was.

"I don't get it," Ned responded. "What's he so upset about?"

"You."

"What's wrong with me?"

"You're not a Mormon. That's the main thing."

LaRue had learned before that Ned wasn't one to fly off the handle. She watched him now, running her words through his head, deciding how he was going to respond. "Is it like Catholics?" he asked. "Do you get excommunicated if you marry me?"

"No. Not exactly." But she was just realizing what he was saying. "Would you get excommunicated if you married me?"

"Yes."

"And you would do that?"

"Yes. I've thought it over. I believe in God, but I don't have to be a Catholic."

"But what would your parents say?"

"Mom would cry and carry on, the same way she did when my big sister married a guy who wasn't Catholic. But I don't know why. She isn't that religious."

"It's not like that in my family."

"I know. But at least you wouldn't get kicked out of your church."

LaRue tried to think what to tell him. He had no idea how different their lives were—or how impossible it would be to fit them together. The truth was, LaRue had never once considered marrying Ned.

"You'd have to be a Mormon to understand," she said. "It's not just going to church. It's . . . everything."

"I kind of know what you mean. I've been around here enough to see how the kids go to church during the week, and you have all these dinners and dances and everything. But I've gotten so I sort of like that. If we got married, we could come back here after the war if you wanted, and I could join your church. Then what would your old man have to complain about?"

"It's not that easy, Ned."

"What isn't? Don't you let people join?"

"Of course we do. It's not that. But you can't just walk in and say, 'Sign me up.' It's not the army."

"I know. You have to take lessons and everything. It's like that when you join the Catholic church. I could do all that."

"It's a big change of life. It's a whole new way of doing things."

"Hey, I haven't had anything to drink for a long time. I could quit smoking, too. What else is there? Coffee, I think."

LaRue didn't want to talk any more about this. She didn't want him to think she was really considering the idea. Sometimes she had thought of having Ned over for a Sunday dinner, just to let him have a home-cooked meal. But she knew what her father would do. He would start asking Ned what college he planned to go to after the war. Ned had graduated from high school, and he wasn't stupid, but he had never spoken of college. He didn't even know what kind of work he wanted to do. The fact was, Ned was a guy who lived one day at a time, which was sort of appealing, but LaRue didn't want someone like that, not in the long run. She wanted someone with more purpose, more future. She knew she was a snob about that, but she wanted nice things; she wanted money.

"Ned, come on," LaRue said. "Let's not get into all that. Let's jitterbug."

So they got up, and they danced. And after the dance LaRue had to leave him again for a while. The rule was only one dance and then change partners, but in fact no one said anything unless a girl started spending too much time with any one boy. Gaye wasn't there tonight, so maybe no one was paying attention, but LaRue thought she ought to be careful. She worked at the counter for a time, and then she danced with some other boys—one a burly fellow from South Dakota who smelled of beer and tromped on her feet and tried hard to pull her close. "Be nice," she said, "or I'll dance on *your* feet for a change."

He laughed, and she took some pride in the fact that she knew how to deal with guys like that.

Later she danced with Ned again, and this time they danced slow and he held her tight. She liked that, but she wondered whether anyone would say anything to Gaye. She was also wondering what was happening at home. It still seemed impossible to believe that her parents could have expressed so much anger. She kept thinking she should go home and have that peace-making talk with both her parents, but she knew that her dad would only be satisfied when she promised to stop coming to the club, and that was something she wasn't going to do. She didn't like MIA, didn't like ward dances or the boys in her ward. None of that was as fun as being here with these boys from all over the country—older guys with some confidence and with interesting backgrounds. The boys her age at high school were such silly little creeps by comparison.

LaRue also knew that she was experiencing things she could never see anywhere else. The major Union Pacific train station in the area was in Ogden, not Salt Lake, so most of the boys she met were stationed nearby, but sometimes troop trains did stop, and the USO filled up with servicemen on their way to battle. A lot of them were brash and vulgar, but it didn't take much to see through all that and discover how homesick and scared they were. She also met servicemen coming home, wounded or burned or debilitated. One night she saw a Marine, a big muscular kid, sitting by himself in a corner, and so she walked over and asked, "Did you want a sandwich or a Coke or something?" The young man had looked up vacantly without answering. So she sat down next to him and asked, "Are you okay?" He nodded but said nothing. It had taken some patience, but LaRue had gradually got him to talk a little. He was from Henderson, Nevada. He was on his way home, and he was ashamed. He had gone to pieces after several months of battle in New Guinea and had spent some weeks in a psychiatric ward in Australia. He hated to face everyone in his hometown. "You just look 'em in the eye," LaRue had told him. "You don't have anything to be ashamed of." She didn't know whether he believed her, whether she had done any good, but she liked the way she had felt about trying to help. She liked feeling part of the war, too, and understanding it a little more. Her father had no idea about any of that—nor would he believe her, probably, if she tried to explain. For some reason he always assumed the worst about her.

When LaRue finally told Ned she was leaving, he walked outside with her. She knew he wanted that kiss she had let him have every time they were together lately. And she wanted it, too. But when they got outside, he seemed a little more eager than usual. He kissed her, but then he clung to her. They were on the street, and it was not as though other soldiers didn't kiss their girls out there, but LaRue was still self-conscious. He kissed her a second time and still wouldn't have let her go if she hadn't pulled away. "LaRue, I'm crazy about you," he said. "I think about you all day. I want you."

He pulled her back to him and kissed her again, and she was suddenly fired by his longing. She kissed him back, more than ever before, not because she wanted to make a deeper commitment, not because she loved him, but merely because she liked what she felt—the excitement, the arousal. And maybe she liked the idea that her father would be shocked if he knew what she was doing. Still, she pulled loose again and stepped away.

She could see that Ned was really excited, and she liked that. But he was also worried about her response. "LaRue, when I say I want you, I mean I want to marry you. I want to—"

"Don't, Ned. I don't want to talk about that."

"LaRue, what do you think this is all about? Do you think I'm just trying to get something off you—and then take off? I want to have you the rest of my life. That's all I think about."

She knew what she ought to do. She ought to tell him to forget all that and then never come back. She ought to tell him how old she really was. But instead she said, "I'll be here on Saturday night." And then she took his hand and let him walk her to the streetcar stop. She even let him kiss her one more time.

15

Bobbi tried to read the Honolulu *Star-Bulletin* every day, and she glanced through the *Stars and Stripes*, the armed forces journal, when she got the chance. She didn't have much time to read either paper thoroughly, but she tried to keep up on the war news. And of course, what she scanned for every day was news of sea battles. Late in October she began to read about a massive navy confrontation with the Japanese in the Leyte Gulf of the Philippines. She felt almost certain that Richard was there, but news reports never listed the names of the ships involved. What she did learn, as days passed, was that a number of American ships had been sunk. She went about her work and did what she had to do, but she felt detached, a little numb, and always she felt that at any moment the bad news might come. But how would she get it? Who would know to tell her? How long before official reports would come out? It was horrifying to think that something might have happened to him and she would know only by his silence.

One evening she came back to her quarters, showered, and then went to the officers' mess for dinner. By the time she returned, Afton had come in. She was sitting in a chair by her bed, a little too stiff, too straight. Bobbi saw immediately that something was wrong. "What's happened?" she asked.

Afton looked away, and she spoke softly. "They brought a sailor into our ward yesterday—from Leyte Gulf. He needed surgery, so he was flown in, and Dr. Saunders operated on him last night. This afternoon he started telling me about his ship going down." Afton finally looked up. "Bobbi, I asked him if he knew anything about the *Saint Lo*. He said that a kamikaze struck it . . . and it sank."

Bobbi sat down on the end of her bed. She looked toward the door, not Afton, and she tried to breathe, but her chest had petrified. She couldn't get enough air.

"Bobbi, he did say there were survivors. He said the ship took some time to go down, and he was sure that a lot of the crew got off."

Bobbi was trying desperately to judge her own feelings. "He survived; he's all right," she told herself first, and she tried to believe it, tried to find a confirmation within herself. But she felt nothing.

"He's probably safe," Afton said. "You'll hear from him soon."

But Afton's words only made Bobbi's futile affirmation seem all the more silly. "You don't know that!" she said, biting off her words. "It's just some stupid thing to say."

"Bobbi, I'm sorry. I don't know what to say."

"If he's dead I don't want to live," Bobbi said. "I can't go through this again."

She was crying, but she didn't want to. She wanted to scream and throw things.

"I'll help you, Bobbi. I'll stick by you. I'll—"

"Shut up! Just shut up! And leave me alone." The absurdity of what Bobbi was doing was clear to herself; she knew that she would have to apologize at some point. But she wanted this rage. Suddenly she stood up, walked out the door, and slammed it hard behind her.

She had no idea where she was going, what she would do now. This is what she had feared every day for a year, what she had prayed about constantly. Suddenly God's indifference struck her like a blow. How could he sit back, impervious, like some spectator, and let this happen? How could she cry to him this long, this hard, only to have him dismiss her with a wave of his royal hand?

As Bobbi left the building, she was expecting to walk, to think, to try to sort out what she was feeling. But her legs had no strength. She walked across the lawn to the place where she and Richard had sat the year before, where they had talked and kissed. She dropped to the grass, curled up on her side, and finally let herself cry. She wished for a passion that would carry her away, that would allow her to howl insanely, to escape reality, but madness wasn't in her. Her mind was already trying to work.

When she finally sat up again, she had begun to discover what she wanted to do. She told herself to assume nothing. For all she knew, most of the men had escaped the ship. She was being childish to jump to conclusions. She had to find out more so she would know what to expect. If he was dead, she would have to find a way to deal with that, but there was no reason, yet, to let him die in her mind. She told herself what Afton had told her, that somehow he had survived. What she needed was some concrete reason to believe it.

What she wanted was to talk to Richard's parents. Maybe they had word; maybe he was safe, and all she needed was to talk to them and they could tell her so. Maybe she didn't need to go through this nightmare.

She got up and walked to the hospital. She was a mess, and she knew it. She tried to straighten her hair a little, brush the grass from her white dress. She dabbed at her eyes with a handkerchief. There was a telephone in the main office at the hospital, one that could be used for long-distance calls. Phoning the mainland was expensive, but Bobbi didn't care what it cost.

So Bobbi sat in the office and acted composed as a young

sailor placed her call to Springville, Utah. She thought of praying as she waited, but the thought brought some of her anger
back. It was too late anyway; what had happened had happened.

The operator in Springville made the connection, and then
the sailor handed the phone to Bobbi. It was only when she
heard several rings without an answer that she remembered
how late it was in Utah—and thought how many people on
the party line she was waking up. It had to be eleven o'clock,
maybe even midnight. Bobbi wasn't even sure what time it was
in Hawaii.

But finally there was an answer. "Yes?" a woman said, her
voice full of trepidation.

"Mrs. Hammond, my name is Bobbi Thomas. I'm calling
from Hawaii. Do you know who I am?"

There was a long pause. "No," Mrs. Hammond finally said.

"I'm from Salt Lake. I'm in the navy. I met Richard at church
over here. Hasn't he ever mentioned me?"

"What's this about?"

Bobbi was crushed. "We . . . uh . . . Richard and I have been
writing to each other. We're . . . friends, I guess. I thought he
would have mentioned me to you." Bobbi didn't want to cry,
didn't want to make a scene, but the tears were coming again,
and her voice was shaking.

"No. Not that I remember." But Mrs. Hammond's voice had
lost its hesitancy. She seemed to understand.

"Sister Hammond, I was just wondering whether you had
heard anything about him."

"We got a telegram. It only said he was missing in action.
That's all." And now Richard's mother was crying. "We heard
on the radio that quite a few got off the ships that went down.
That's the only thing we know."

A thought flashed through Bobbi's head. She had heard the
stories in the hospital: Japanese shooting at lifeboats, sinking
them, or letting men drown rather than picking them up.

"I don't know when we'll hear something more. My husband says that if he made it to land, in a boat or something, he could be taken prisoner."

Bobbi's knees were shaking so wildly that she sat down. Her hope for a quick resolution was gone. Richard could be dead, but she might not find out for a long time, maybe not until the war was over. She knew there was no escaping what her life was going to be now. "Well . . . thanks, Sister Hammond," she said. "I'm sorry I called so late. I forgot . . ." But she was crying too hard to finish her sentence.

"It's all right. I can't sleep. I just lay here and wonder about him, where he is, what's happened. It would almost be easier . . . well, no. I don't want to say that."

Bobbi understood, of course. And for a time, neither spoke. Bobbi knew she needed to hang up, but this woman on the other end of the line was the only person who could possibly comprehend her feelings.

"Listen, dear," Sister Hammond said, "Richard doesn't tell us things. He's always been that way. Don't take it to heart that he didn't mention you."

"He didn't want to make any promises. He was too afraid something might happen."

"Yes, I know. That's the way he thinks. But write to me, send your address, and just as soon as we hear anything, I'll let you know."

"Yes. I will. Can you give me your address?"

"Just send it to Springville. The postmaster knows us. Did you say you're from Salt Lake?"

"Yes. Sugar House. I'm a nurse in the navy."

"Honey, could you tell me in the letter more about yourself? I'd like to . . . get to know you."

"Yes. I'll do that. And I'll come to see you someday."

But those words created a picture in Bobbi's mind: she saw herself sitting in the Hammonds' living room, meeting the people who had been intended as her in-laws. It didn't feel awkward; it only felt dismal, pathetic. Bobbi was sobbing hard again when she said good-bye.

When she put the phone down, the sailor didn't look at her, obviously embarrassed by all he had heard. Bobbi looked away too, thanked him, and left quickly. But now she was lost again. Where was she supposed to go? She still didn't want to see Afton.

So she walked to the front gate of the base, and she caught a bus into Honolulu. Her first thought had been to seek out Ishi, but she wasn't sure that would help either one of them. Ishi was living with the same kind of worry and fear that Bobbi had known this past year.

Bobbi wanted more than anything to be with her mother. She wanted her to hold her and not say anything. She had thought of calling, but she knew a telephone call required too many words, and she didn't want that. And so she was going to find Hazel, who was more like Bobbi's mother than anyone else in the islands. She tried to focus on that and not think, but her mind was still jumping, grabbing for some sort of solace.

The Nuanunus lived close to a bus stop. Bobbi got off and walked to the house. The place was small but usually full of people, and that was one thing Bobbi didn't need right now. When she knocked on the door, Brother Nuanunu came to the door. "Say, Bobbi," he said, "come in. Come in."

Bobbi took off her shoes and stepped inside. It was like Brother Nuanunu to give her a big hug, but he took hold of her shoulders and waited until she looked into his eyes. "What's a matta?" he asked. "You okay?"

"Is Hazel here? I just wanted to talk to her for a minute, if I could."

"Oh, sure. She's out back. She's prob'ly sleeping in her chair out there. But that's okay. She'll be happy to see you."

"Well, maybe if she—"

"No, no. Come on with me."

And so Bobbi walked through the kitchen and out the back

door. The sun was setting outside, clouds in the western sky all orange and bronze. Bobbi could see Hazel, in a bright muumuu, lying back in an easy chair, like a deck chair on a ship. But she wasn't asleep. She looked around and said, "Oh, Bobbi dear, come to me. How good to see you." But as Bobbi came closer, Hazel saw what was in Bobbi's face. "What is it?" she said. "Brother Hammond?" She was working to lift herself out of the chair.

"I'll get you another chair," Brother Nuanunu said. And he hurried back to the house.

Bobbi let Hazel take her into her arms. "His ship went down," she said. "Maybe he's dead."

Hazel gripped her tighter, patted her back. "Oh, sweetheart," she said. "I'm sorry."

But the pity was not what Bobbi had expected, and it stabbed at her. It seemed to say that he was gone already, that Hazel found no hope within herself. Somewhere in the confused logic of the moment, Bobbi had actually thought Hazel would know one way or the other. She was closer to God than anyone Bobbi knew; wouldn't he tell her?

Brother Nuanunu was back with a chair, and Bobbi let herself sink into it. Hazel sat again, facing Bobbi, and she took hold of her hands. Brother Nuanunu knew enough to leave.

"It was a kamikaze," Bobbi told Hazel. "I called Richard's mother, and she said some men got off, but no one knows how many, or what happened to them."

"And now you don't know. And that's the worst."

"I might not ever know what happened to him."

"Can you put it in God's hands? Can you trust him, and wait?"

It was the last thing Bobbi wanted to hear—the very thing she was angry about. "It's not God doing this, Hazel. It's the Japanese. It's *us*. It's Germans and Italians and Englishmen and Australians. We're all killing each other—and what's God supposed to do about that?"

Hazel patted Bobbi on the shoulder. "Yes, I know. We're making a mess of things. But God can protect Brother Hammond, if that's what is best."

"He didn't protect my brother." Bobbi pulled her hands away. She didn't want Hazel's answers. She had only come for her love.

"God knows what's best. That's what we have to accept."

But Bobbi wasn't buying that. There was too much that was random in this war. She had read about two paratroopers who had died in Holland on the same jump her brother had made. They had been floating down, seemingly safe, when one of their own airplanes had been struck by flak and gone down. The falling airplane had struck them in the air, chopped them up in its propellers. Had that been God's plan, to let them die in some freakish accident? Or had God shed tears of pain for his children who had ended their mortality in such a senseless way?

"Hazel, I don't think God is in control of our lives. He doesn't make everything happen."

"I didn't say that, Bobbi. I just said we have to trust him."

"I do trust God. I don't trust man." But that wasn't really true, because in the back of Bobbi's mind was still the idea that God could make this right if he wanted to. He could pluck Richard from the ocean. He could put him in a safe place. He could preserve him for Bobbi. And if he didn't, then why not? Was he unconcerned about such trivial matters?

Hazel took Bobbi's hands again. There were tears in the creases under her eyes, and one tear had made its way down her plump cheek, but she was smiling. "Bobbi, what do you want from God?" she asked.

Bobbi didn't know. She only knew she wanted Richard to come back.

"You need to decide. Do you believe God cares about you or don't you?"

Bobbi knew the correct answer, the one she had learned in

church. But she didn't feel it right now—didn't sense the slightest crack in God's armor. If he didn't choose to save Richard, there wasn't one thing she could do or say that would make a difference.

"Bobbi, you need God. He's the only one who can give you peace at a time like this."

Bobbi was furious and chastened at the same time. She hated what Hazel was saying, and she knew that she was probably right. "Hazel, Richard's dead, isn't he?"

"I don't know."

"If he were alive, he would let his family know."

"The navy said he was missing. That's all you know for sure."

"But missing means dead. Almost always. I've seen it happen to other girls. After a while they get a telegram. Or they hear nothing, and that says the same thing."

"Sometimes the news is good."

"But how do I go on with my life, not knowing? How can I get up every morning and go to the hospital? If I have to deal with death, at least I want to get started."

Bobbi dropped off her chair and onto her knees. She rested her head in Hazel's lap. Hazel stroked her hair, patted her back, and that loosened the emotion in Bobbi again. She was admitting something to herself that had scared her all along. Maybe Richard had had premonitions that he wouldn't make it back, and that's why he had resisted making commitments to her. She had forced herself on him, and she never should have done that.

"It's the war I hate the most," Bobbi eventually managed to say. "I still have two brothers in danger. Who else am I going to lose?"

"Bobbi, that's not the question I asked you. The question is, do you believe God loves you, or don't you? You need to know."

But Bobbi felt nothing from God—no love, no spirit, nothing but abandonment.

She stayed with Hazel for a time after that, but there was nothing more to say. And the reality was, Bobbi knew she had no choices. When morning came, she would have to get up and go to the hospital, the same as she did other days. She had to start summoning the power at least to do that.

She also knew that Afton would be worried about her, and she did need to start thinking of someone besides herself. So Bobbi left Hazel, and she took the bus back to the base. When she stepped into her room, she found Afton there, looking tired and worried. And so she took Afton into her arms and whispered, "I'm sorry."

"It's okay. I would have acted a lot worse."

"I feel like I'm never going to have anyone now," Bobbi said. "It seems like that's always what's been meant for me." She was crying again, and she didn't want to. She pulled away and walked to her bed, lay down.

"Bobbi, that's what I was saying not long ago. But at least now I know that a man can love me. Something will work out for you, too."

"If I were you, Afton, I would hold on to Sam. I wouldn't let anyone else make that decision." She looked up at Afton, who was sitting primly, her hands in her lap, her dark hair and eyes so pretty.

"I don't know, Bobbi. I wish I had stayed home. I wish I had found someone back there. Then I wouldn't have to make a choice like this."

"Maybe so, Afton. I don't know. But I'm glad you're here right now. I don't know what I'd do without you—even if I didn't act like it earlier."

"We'll have to get through this together."

Bobbi rolled over onto her back. She looked at the cheap light fixture, the one Afton had cracked one night when she threw a pillow, trying to chase a gecko off their ceiling. For just a moment Bobbi sensed some value in all this, in the experience itself. She knew that to pass through a time, any time, had some inherent value. But she only felt that for a moment, and then the logic carried her thoughts forward. This next experience, the one that lay ahead, was surely also of value, no matter how awful it looked. But she didn't want to admit that, or at least didn't want to face it.

"I have to go to work in the morning," Bobbi said. "I have to get up at five o'clock and get myself ready. I have to walk to the hospital and work my shift."

"Maybe that's good. It will keep your mind busy."

"And not thinking so much about myself, I guess."

"Well, yes."

"But Afton, I feel like I'm not in here—like my body is empty. I don't want to do anything. I hardly had the strength to walk back from the bus."

"Bobbi, have you made up your mind that he's . . . you know . . . gone?"

"No. But I wish I could. That would be easier."

"But that's not right. Maybe I was silly to say that he's alive. But it's just as wrong to say that he's dead."

"When Wally was taken prisoner, there were lots of reasons to think he was probably still alive. But mostly I just felt that he was. And my mom was certain of it. But this time I don't feel anything like that. I just feel all empty inside."

"It's because of Gene. It's because of all the things we see here. But Bobbi, lots of MIAs turn out to be alive. In the first few days after a ship sinks, the navy doesn't know much, but they have to say something to the families."

Bobbi nodded. She knew Afton was right. Hope wasn't wrong, even if it seemed to hurt so much more than hopelessness. But when she tried it, tested it a little in her head—and in her chest—it didn't work. What she felt was a sense of terrible loss, and that seemed to mean he was dead.

16

Alex and the men in his company were occupying a stretch of lowland between the Lower Rhine and the Waal River, not far from Arnhem in Holland. The Germans were dug in across the Lower Rhine to the north, and also in the lowlands to the west, but the truth was, Americans were clinging to land that no longer had much meaning. The American and British forces had overreached, and they had failed. British paratroopers had held the bridge at Arnhem for a few days, but in the end they were decimated. Ten thousand had made the drop; just over two thousand got out. Many were now held captive by the Germans, and many were also dead.

Alex and his squad were dug in near the dikes along the river. This was land that was actually below sea level, and dikes twenty feet high had been built to hold back floods when the river ran high. The 506th—a single regiment—was occupying an area that had previously been held by an entire British division. Troops were spread thin, and patrols, especially at night, had to move along the perimeter to guard against sneak attacks through the many breaks in the MLR—the Main Line of Resistance. Across the river the German troops had their own nation at their backs, with ready supplies, and so they could keep up a steady barrage of 88- and 105-millimeter artillery

fire. From an area south of the Americans, British artillery regiments returned the fire, but the Germans were on higher
ground and were better supplied. Fire was not constant, but it
was frequent, with no particular pattern. So the men spent
most of their time in foxholes and trenches, just as troops in
the first world war had done.

The fall rains had begun, and the lives of all the soldiers
were made tedious and difficult by the ubiquitous mud. The
men slept in mud, wore it, trudged through it to get to slit-
trench latrines, and ended up eating it with their rations, however hard they tried not to. It took continual work to keep their
weapons functional. Supply trucks spun in to their axles.
Artillery was sometimes impossible to move. And for Alex the
worst was that he was *never* clean or dry. The rains came and
went, but the mud never dried out, and there was nothing—
not a towel or even a rag—that was dry enough to wipe his
hands on. There was no tent, no shower, no respite from the
constant misery, except of course, that several times a day
artillery shells would crash among the foxholes, and then the
mud didn't matter.

Supplies were coming from the Brits, and so that meant
bully beef, which Alex hated. Even worse was the ox-tail soup
that seemed only a mass of grease with floating bones. Alex's
only joy was receiving letters, but that was a sporadic, unpredictable occurrence, and writing a letter in a mud-filled foxhole
required all the effort he could muster.

In quieter times the men scavenged the countryside for
stray milk cows they could relieve of their burden. Or they
searched for abandoned German rations, which all in all, the
Americans liked better than the British stuff. But the soldiers
also raided empty houses, and they looted anything they could
find of value: jewelry, clocks, watches, cameras, money, and
always, all the liquor they could find. Alex often remembered
the way the Dutch had welcomed the troops as saviors. He
wondered how these same people would feel when they

returned to their farms and found them ransacked, not by the enemy but by their heroes.

When Alex heard the men speak of the vicious Germans and all their depredations, he would think of the German brothers and sisters in the Church he had known. By contrast, he wondered at the men around him, who used war as an excuse to forget all the values they had been raised with. And yet the normal rules of civilization hardly seemed to matter now, and it was hard to work up much indignation. There was a coarseness, more unfeeling than sinister, that seemed to fill everyone's soul. Part of the problem was that every guy out there was beginning to feel that the odds were against him. After all, shells landed close by every day, and men kept dying. How bright did a soldier have to be to recognize that his day was probably coming?

But Alex didn't tell Anna that. In one letter, written on a day in early November when the rain had let up, he told her:

Sometimes I feel like a drowning man, pulled under by the power of so much ugliness. I hardly think about the enemy anymore. There are guns across the river, and there are mines for a man to step on, if he wanders into the wrong place, but it's the weapons themselves that seem the threat, along with the absence of everything clean and good. I try to remember what we're fighting for—freedom, and all those other abstractions—but the mud I live in is much more real.

Still, don't worry about me. I'm resilient. I promise I'll be myself again someday. And however far away you seem to me right now, you are no abstraction. You are the only real thing in my life. I'm glad we got married. I'm glad we had a little time together. It's remembering that, and looking forward to having it again, that keeps me going.

A few days later Alex got several letters from Anna. In one of them she said:

I worry about you every moment, Alex. When I wake up in the night, I wonder if you are warm. I wonder if you can sleep. If I could take half the hard things for myself, half the cold and half the sadness, I would do it. I stay busy here, and I sleep in a warm bed. So I am fine. But nothing feels the way it should. I can't breathe the way I want, not eat or laugh or work. I need you to make everything right. I am well, but everything for me is waiting, not living.

I'm sorry. I won't be so negative. What if I didn't have you to wait for? What would my life mean then? I am very blessed, and I promise not to complain.

After reading the letters, Alex pulled his picture of Anna from his wallet. He studied her face. So often, especially in the dark that filled so much of his life now, he tried to envision Anna, fill his head with her, but there were times when he couldn't do it, and the harder he tried, the more vague her image became. So he took some extra seconds to imprint her face in his mind, but as he put the picture away he tried quite purposefully *not* to think of her. He was on the edge—after reading her letters—of feeling too much.

A few days after that, Alex's squad got pulled off the MLR. They went into reserve, which meant they were able to live and sleep in a barn near the farmhouse that Captain Summers was using as his company command post. Alex and his men were finally away from the shelling and the night patrols, and even though all that would return soon, soldiers had a way of living in the present. They were able to wash themselves and their clothes, scrape the mud from their equipment, and clean their weapons. And they could sleep a few nights on cots, without the constant fear of artillery or enemy attacks. It was luxury almost too wonderful to imagine.

Then one morning, before five o'clock, Captain Summers rushed into the barn and shouted, "Get up! Everybody out. The Krauts have broken through!"

Alex was on his feet immediately, automatically. He grabbed for his rifle and shouted to his men to get moving. In only a few minutes they were all running for the command post nearby. There another reserve squad, from a different company, was also gathering. "We've got trouble up at the dikes,"

Summers told the men, forcefully but with no panic. "One of our patrols ran into a German unit—probably a company. We've got to get up there and see what's happening. I'm going to go hard. Stay with me."

Captain Summers moved out, and the men followed in single file. The trouble was, neither squad was at full strength. Having lost Withers, Alex only had nine men, counting himself, and in the dark Alex thought he saw about the same number under Sergeant Pearce, the other squad leader. The two squads could be facing a *much* bigger unit. Alex knew this was only a patrol, which would make contact and then call in help, but he wasn't sure how much help was available in the sector.

Summers double-timed most of the distance—a kilometer or so—but he slowed as he drew near the dike. Then he turned and whispered, "Sergeants, hold your men here for a couple of minutes. I'm going to take a look."

The high earthen dike sloped outward from the wide crest. Summers clambered up to the top. "Stay down," Thomas whispered to his men, and they hunkered down in the soggy field.

Summers wasn't gone long. When he climbed down, he said, "Sergeant Thomas, leave a couple of your men here to watch our rear. The rest of us are going to cross over this dike. There's a ditch on the other side, and we can use it to get to the road up ahead. It's just a little road that leads on a right angle from the dike to a ferry dock on the river, but that's where the Germans were spotted—on the other side of that road."

Alex, in a hushed voice, said, "Sabin, stay put. Ernst, move up this side of the dike a little to the west, and then wait. Keep an eye out. Don't start shooting, but if you spot enemy coming in behind us, get to us quick."

Alex hated to leave these two young guys by themselves, but he hated even more to march them into the teeth of a battle, if that's what was coming. He had thought, briefly, of leaving Howie, but he preferred to keep him close by.

"Let's go," Summers said, and the men followed him over the top of the dike. Once on the north side, he told them, "We need to locate the Germans before first light. We've got to move fast—but silent—so watch your step."

Alex had noticed the sky, to the east, brightening just a little. He knew they didn't have a lot of time. The men moved quickly through the trench, which was maybe three feet deep—not deep enough to cover their movement once the sun came up.

Summers stopped and listened several times, and eventually he whispered, "The road is maybe two hundred meters up ahead. I'm going to go forward and scout the situation. Stay here."

Alex and the others knelt in the ditch, which was muddy but not full of water. Alex felt the tension, the eerie presence of the enemy very near. He breathed quietly, listened, and hoped that Summers didn't get himself into trouble.

Summers was gone only ten or twelve minutes, but it seemed three times that long. When he approached again, his voice sounded tense. "There's a machine gun emplacement on the dike, overlooking the road. I think it's a big MG 42, and I counted seven riflemen alongside it. There's enough light to see a good silhouette. We need to get up there and take them by surprise. Hurry. The light is coming on fast now. But don't stumble and make a noise."

He was off, moving quickly and quietly through the ditch. Alex and the other men hustled to keep up. As they got closer, Summers slowed and crouched even lower. When he finally stopped, Alex figured they were less than a hundred meters away from the machine gun.

Summers slipped back to the men. He whispered something to Campbell, who began to set up his 60-millimeter mortar. When Summers reached Alex, he whispered, "Take the third rifleman from the left. Can you see him?"

"Yes."

"When I fire, you fire too—and don't miss him."

He then moved to Howie and asked him to shoot the fourth man.

"All right," Howie whispered. But Alex heard the tension in his voice.

Alex got himself into a good position, with his elbows resting on solid ground, and took aim. He knew that Campbell would fire the mortar at the machine-gun position at the same time the others tried to take out the riflemen, and Pozernac would open up with his machine gun. What he didn't know was how many other Germans were out there in the dark.

Seconds continued to tick by, and Alex watched his target. The third soldier was a dark lump with the dim sunrise behind him, but Alex could see the outline of his distinctive "square" helmet. Alex tried to breathe evenly and keep his sights steady, but his heart was pounding in his ears.

When Summers fired, Alex squeezed his trigger and the dark lump jerked and then dropped over. At the same time, a whole volley of gun fire sounded around him, and all the German riflemen dropped. Alex also saw machine-gun tracer bullets flying high. Just as the bullets dropped into range, a huge explosion tore everything up. The mortar had been right on target, and the German machine gun was gone.

Alex could hardly believe how accurately his men had hit their targets, but small-arms fire—bursts from German machine pistols—began to pop in the night from the other side of the road. "All right, fall back. Quick!" Summers yelled.

The men took off back down the ditch, running hard. When they reached a ditch that angled off, parallel to the road but a couple of hundred meters away, Summers called out, "Turn here. Spread out along this ditch."

Alex turned into the new ditch and ran hard. He let the men in front of him get far enough ahead to spread out, and then he called to the men behind him, "Take a position. Don't bunch up."

A moment later Sergeant Pearce called out the same order to his men. Alex had just dropped down to take his own position when he glanced back and saw a flash of light. He saw Pearce catch the full brunt of an explosion and get thrown backward. Alex knew immediately that a rifle grenade had hit him, but he wasn't sure where it had come from. A quick volley of fire followed, however, and someone called out, "They were in a culvert, at the road. We put two of them down. One fell back."

The men stayed down after that, and Alex wondered whether an attack might come at any moment. Maybe they had stirred up a hornet's nest. He could hear Summers talking on the radio, calling for reinforcement troops and machine guns, but Alex didn't know how long it might take for more troops to move in.

In a few minutes Summers sneaked along the ditch to Alex. "Thomas," he said, "Pearce took some shrapnel in the chest—through the lungs. He's still breathing, but he's not going to make it."

Alex nodded, and then he said, "We're in a bad spot here, Captain."

"I know. We had to take that machine gun out while we had the chance. But I'm not sure what we've got to deal with now. The Jerries have a better position than we do, behind that raised road. If we give them any time, they can head north, get some men over the road, and outflank us on the right. Or they might just come straight at us."

"It they take us, what would stop them from crossing the dike and heading straight down that road to the battalion CP?"

"Nothing. If we let them get that far, they could overrun this whole sector. The way I see it, just as soon as those reinforcements get up here, we've got to attack. We've got to stop the Krauts right where they are and drive them back across the river."

"How bad are we going to be outnumbered?"

"I don't know. But if they come at us and catch us falling back across this muddy field, we won't have a chance."

"That's right."

"All right. As soon as we get those troops up here—and let's hope it doesn't take long—tell your men to be ready. We're going to attack."

Summers slipped away, and Alex continued to crouch in the ditch. He scanned the horizon, looking for any movement.

"Did he say something about attacking?" Howie asked, and Alex heard the panic in his voice.

"We've got more troops coming up to help us," Alex said. "We'll be all right." But he didn't believe it. He figured they were heading into a mess.

It was maybe twenty minutes before the reinforcements arrived, but it was fully daylight by then. There were fifteen men or so, with a Sergeant Scott. Sabin and Ernst had come along with them, and they rejoined Alex's squad.

Summers pulled the squad leaders together. "Okay," he said, "we're going to go straight at that road. That's the last thing the Krauts expect. Thomas, you take the left flank; Scott, the right. I'll take Pearce's men straight up the middle. I'll have machine guns between our columns, and they'll lay down cover fire until we reach the road. Once we do, they'll stop firing and move up with us. So tell your men to fix bayonets, and when you see me move out, we'll all go together."

"Bayonets?" Sergeant Scott asked. Alex heard the alarm in his voice.

"We might as well have them ready," Summers said. "It may come to that."

Alex felt the adrenaline set his heart pounding. He didn't ask himself whether this was a good place to die or whether it was worth it; he merely let the scene play out in his mind, and death seemed the most likely end to all this. He went back to his men, described the plan, and in the same tone Summers had used said, "Fix your bayonets."

He saw the foreboding in their eyes, but he offered them no comfort. They wouldn't have believed him anyway.

When the machine-gun fire began, Summers was the first soldier up and running. Alex took off hard at the same time. He slogged through the damp earth, moving slower than he wanted to. At any second he expected mortars or gunfire, and he wanted to get across the open field.

Summers outdistanced everyone, even though Alex was pushing to keep up. Alex was still twenty meters behind when he saw Summers jump onto the road and begin to fire his carbine. Alex made the leap a few seconds later, and he immediately saw a huge number of Germans on the other side—at least a hundred—massed tightly together and face down, forced to the ground by the cover fire from the machine guns.

But they were rising now, as though in slow motion. They were wearing heavy winter coats, and they made big, slow targets. Some were twisting to run, to escape the fire that Summers and Alex, and soon the others, were spraying at them.

Some stood and aimed, and others ducked away, but they were falling . . . falling . . . riddled by the heavy fire. And then all were running, slowed by the heavy coats and the muddy earth. More and more were falling. Alex didn't aim at anyone but kept spraying bullets into the moving mass. Alongside him, he heard men laughing, exulting, shouting their pleasure.

The fire continued for some time as the Germans continued to retreat. Summers called out, "Get that radio up here."

Alex saw what Summers had noticed. The surviving Germans were joining another group—probably another company—that had already crossed the dike farther to the west. This second group was pouring back over the dike and retreating toward the river. Summers got hold of the radio and barked out orders for artillery fire. Within a minute or so the first explosions began to strike among the escaping Germans, who were moving through the high weeds and marshes, scrambling onto another road, and then running north toward the river.

In a few more minutes Summers got back on the radio and shouted above the noise that he wanted more reinforcements. Alex knew why. Summers was not satisfied to leave that many Germans alive. He wanted to chase them down.

For the present, however, Alex's men had time to drop down, to breathe. Alex walked along and checked with them. Earl Sabin had taken a bullet in the thigh. He was sitting down, cutting his pants away. He was grunting, puffing, but refusing to complain. Duncan walked over and looked, and then he laughed. "Some guys get all the luck," he said. "I've been hoping for a nice, clean wound like that this whole war."

But Sabin didn't laugh. He was staring at his own blood.

As it turned out, four Americans had been wounded, but only Pearce had died. Eleven Germans were soon discovered hiding in some weeds and were taken prisoner. Maybe fifty or so were on the ground, many of them dead. Some of the men moved among them, looking for souvenirs, Lüger pistols, or binoculars. "They're SS troops," someone yelled. "We ought to shoot the ones who are still alive."

Alex walked close enough to look at one of the bodies. He could see that the young man's uniform, under his coat, was black, and on his collar was the double lightning-bolt SS symbol. No troops were hated more than the *Waffen SS*, since they were considered true Nazis, not just drafted soldiers. But Alex looked at the face of the boy: square jawed, clean cut, handsome. Hanging from his side was a *brotbeutel*, a cloth bag that German soldiers used to carry slices of military hard black bread. Alex thought about serving the sacrament in Frankfurt— breaking that black bread into morsels to symbolize the body of Christ.

Some of the wounded Germans were pleading for help now. Alex walked toward one, but Summers called to him, "Don't get involved in that. I've got medics coming up."

Alex knew what Summers was thinking: A soldier had no business dressing wounds. It was the wrong way to be thinking when the action was about to start again. Alex walked back to Summers. "You did the right thing," he said. "If they had come across the road before we did, we would all be dead now."

"I know. They were just getting ready to attack, too. We caught them all bunched up. We got lucky."

"Are you going after them?"

"Yeah. Just as soon as those other men get up here. I've got a platoon on the way. But we've got to hurry. I want to catch them trying to cross the river. Keep your men ready."

So Alex gathered his men together and told them to take a drink of water, and smoke if they wanted to, but not to worry about trying to eat anything. Alex saw the grim look in their faces when they realized they would be making another attack. Howie looked dazed.

When the reinforcements moved in, Summers had the new soldiers share their ammo. This backup platoon was not at full strength, but altogether there were now about sixty troops. Summers told the machine-gun teams to start a base of fire again, and then he had the men, half in each group, begin to leapfrog up the road, covering for each other as they charged. They moved up a few hundred meters and had maybe a couple of hundred more to go to reach the river. But just as they reached the point where a little grove of trees provided some cover, Alex heard the whine of an artillery shell.

"Hit it!" he screamed. He shoved Howie off the road and then jumped off after him. He heard the explosion just a second later, heard the shrapnel whirl over him as he lay on the ground. And then chaos opened up as explosions rained in on the men—mortars as well as artillery. Small-arms fire began, and Alex knew a counterattack was underway. He grasped his steel helmet and held on for a moment, but he knew he had to get his men out. "Fall back," he shouted. "Now!"

Alex knew the only chance the men had was to get all the

way back to the dike, and over, and that was a long run. He jumped up and took off, still screaming at his men to come with him. The artillery fire seemed zeroed in close to the dike. The last hundred yards were chaos. Explosions were everywhere, with mud spattering and shrapnel buzzing in all directions. Men were falling too; Alex saw that, expected to go down any time himself, but he reached the dike, scrambled up and over it, with Howie still close by.

As they reached the other side, they dropped to their knees, thankful for the cover. Alex kept watching the road. Duncan got over the dike, and Curtis, and then Ernst. Alex hoped the others weren't down. But he and Howie had caught their breaths for only a couple of minutes when artillery shells began to land on their side, and Alex realized they weren't out of danger yet.

"We've got to go again," Alex shouted to his men.

Curtis was the first to take off. Just as Alex jumped up, he saw Curtis drop. Alex dove to the ground and crawled to him, then rolled him over. He saw blood smeared all across Curtis's face, but he also saw the cut. Shrapnel had torn Curtis's earlobe, creased his neck, but it wasn't deep. "You're okay, Curtis," Alex shouted. "You're okay. Let's go."

Curtis nodded and then pulled himself up. He and Alex ran hard again, Howie with them, until they reached another of the ditches that crisscrossed the fields. They jumped in, lay in the mud, and drew in all the air they could get. "We're all right now," Alex told Howie. "We're out of their range."

But Howie was huddled up, rolled into himself, and he was shaking uncontrollably.

"Howie, are you okay?" Alex asked him.

"No, I'm . . . I don't know. I'm . . ." He was crying. Alex put his arm around his back, held on to him.

"Don't worry about it. You did fine," Alex told him.

Later that day Summers admitted that he had made a mistake. "The Germans were heading back to their ferries. We should have let them go. We didn't have enough men. I just didn't count on the artillery power they had backing them up."

Alex knew why Summers felt so bad. Half the sixty men who had attacked toward the river had come back wounded. None had died, but a lot of them had been torn up with shrapnel, some of them badly. Alex was relieved that he had only lost Sabin who, by now, was probably realizing how lucky he was.

What Alex did worry about was Howie. He was silent that night, and he hardly said a word for a few days after. When Alex would ask him how he was doing, he would say he was okay, but he didn't look well.

Within a few more days Alex's squad was put back on the line, back into their foxholes. Rain was still falling off and on, so life was as miserable as ever, and the men knew they could probably expect further attacks from across the river.

The days were full of mud and cold again, bad food, tedium, and fear. At night Alex sometimes led patrols. Every second he was moving about, he expected another firefight. The fact that it didn't come never made him feel that it wouldn't. And the artillery fire continued, night and day. Each time it opened up, Alex could see that it was breaking Howie down, one deafening explosion at a time, shaking the will out of him.

One afternoon, after a barrage of shelling, Howie said, "Sergeant Thomas, I can't stand much more of this. Sometimes I hope the next shell gets me, and this whole mess will finally end."

"Hey, don't wish that. If it gets you, it gets me."

Howie was leaning against the end of the foxhole with his knees pulled up close, his arms around his legs. He didn't smile. He looked thin and pale, and his uniform was caked with mud. He was hardly the same kid who had joined the unit back in Aldbourne.

"Look, Howie," Alex said, "you're doing all right. Maybe you're scared, but you're doing your job."

Howie took a long breath and let his eyes go shut. "That ain't true, Sergeant," he said. "I don't shoot."

"What?"

"I don't shoot at no one. I've never pulled my trigger."

"You shot at that guy up on the dike, didn't you? The one Summers told you to shoot."

"No."

"You must have. He went down."

"Someone else got him. Maybe Summers. Maybe he knew I wouldn't shoot." Howie was gripping his knees tighter, his arms were shaking. "I told myself to do it. And I aimed right at the guy. But I didn't fire. I just shut my eyes and waited for all the noise to be over with."

"Look, Howie, I read somewhere that after battles, the army has checked, and only about half the men have fired their weapons. You're not the only guy out there with that problem."

"Maybe so. But guys like us get other guys killed."

Alex believed that, but he didn't want to put too much pressure on Howie. "Hey, it's not natural to want to kill. No one wants to do it."

"But I've *got* to do it. I know I do."

"Sure. We all have to lay down some fire at times. It's not very often that we aim right at someone, like we did at that machine-gun crew."

"I didn't shoot at those Germans that were all bunched up together by that road either. Pozernac and Gourley were laughing and yelling, having a good old time. But it was like shooting ducks on a pond. It made me sick."

Alex wished there were a way to send this kid home. "Howie, how did you end up in the Airborne, of all places?"

"I know what you're saying. I don't belong here."

"No. I'm just—"

"It's stupid, what happened. I didn't have to go into the service at all." Howie crossed his arms and tucked his hands, in woolen mittens, under his arms. "When I was coming up for the draft, I got a job with the railroad. That was one of them war-effort jobs that could keep you out of the service. At first I liked that, but then all the guys I knew were signing up, and they started telling me I was a coward."

That was something Alex could understand. He had felt some of that kind of pressure himself.

"So I was thinking about joining the navy. But I was at a dance on a Saturday night, and this paratrooper from the 101st was home on leave. He walked into this little dancehall we have back home, and he had his pants stuck down in his boots and that Screaming Eagle patch on his shoulder. I watched how all the girls looked at him." Howie shook his head. "I guess I just wanted to be a big shot like that."

"Was it one particular girl you wanted to impress?"

"Yeah. I guess it was." Howie nodded several times, and then his eyes drifted away. "But that was stupid. This girl's old man owned about half the town. And me, I lived in this run-down little old rented house on the wrong side of the tracks. My mom worked mostly as a waitress after my old man ran out on us. This girl kind of liked me, in a way, but nothing was going to come of it."

"So did she ever see you in your paratrooper uniform?"

Howie shook his head. "Nope. I had a seven-day leave when I finished jump school, but I couldn't afford the bus ride home. I wanted to go back, even if I only had a day, and just walk into that dance hall one time. But I never got the chance."

"That's all right. When you go back, you'll be a war hero."

"Yeah, sure. A war hero who didn't dare shoot his rifle."

"You'll shoot it."

Howie nodded, resolutely. "You're right about that. I don't care if I get shot next time; I'm pulling the trigger. I ain't going home knowing I never fired a bullet."

"Okay. But don't do anything stupid. All right?"

"Sure." He sat for a time. And then he said, softer than before, "I can take the bullets. It's just those big guns, the way they pound the dirt and everything, and suck all the air away. I always think I'll deal with it next time, but when the noise starts, I feel like I'm going crazy."

"We all feel that way, Howie. Every one of us."

"You guys don't show it much."

"Everyone has his own way of hanging on. Most guys just don't admit what they're feeling."

Howie shrugged. "All I know is, I gotta shoot next time."

"Don't worry. You will."

But Alex saw more irony in that than he wanted to. Since the day of this last battle, Alex had been trying hard not to see those Germans, huddled together, falling, splotches of blood soaking through their wool coats. He found himself wishing now that he, like Howie, had not been able to shoot.

17

One morning, at the entrance to the mine, Wally was surprised to be called out by a supervisor he hadn't seen before. The man seemed less menacing than most, older, and in fact, rather gentlemanly. He was a civilian, not a soldier. He gave Wally a little bow and said something in Japanese that had the ring of politeness.

"Sonbu San," the man said, and he touched his own chest.

Never before had Wally seen a guard or supervisor introduce himself to a prisoner. "Go-ju ichi," Wally said, stating the shortened number he was known by, and he nodded in response.

But the man shook his head, pointed to Wally, and then pointed to himself again. "Sonbu San," he repeated.

Wally understood. "Thomas San," he said. Again the man bowed. And this time Wally bowed too.

As Wally walked to the train, he glanced at the other men on the crew—four besides Wally—and he could tell that all of them were wondering what was going on. The cold train ride was longer than usual. By the time the men got off the train, Wally could see they were in a section of the mine that hadn't been worked for a long time, apparently never by prisoners.

Sonbu San stood before the men and pointed into the

depths of the mineshaft. "Rocks. Fall down," he said, and he motioned with his hand. Certainly Wally understood what he meant by that. The shaft had collapsed at some point and had been abandoned. "We dig," Sonbu added.

Wally thought the crew would mine for coal. As it turned out, however, they were working to extract some conveyor machinery that had been buried by the cave-in. What the men could see as they peered down the shaft was that there were no timbers, and the ceiling was high. Wally knew that extracting the machinery would be a delicate, dangerous operation.

Wally was certainly not surprised that mine officials would put prisoners' lives in danger for the sake of salvaging equipment. But the Japanese had to be getting desperate if they were willing to send a nice old man down into such danger. Wally had to hope that was a good sign, that the country was running out of resources to fight with. The POWs all liked to watch for such indications and then convince each other that the war was coming to an end.

All the same, life was difficult enough without working a collapsed shaft. There was some comfort in the idea that Sonbu San seemed to know what he was doing, but as Wally followed the man into the dark, he was still frightened.

What he learned over the next few days was that Sonbu was much smarter and more experienced than most of the supervisors. There was no way to timber this section of the mine. The ceiling, after the collapse, was too high. But Sonbu knew where to work and how to remove the fallen rock without disturbing weak areas. Still, there was no way to prevent the crumbling tunnel from letting rock fall at times—and that meant death was always just an instant away if a man were in the wrong place when a boulder crashed to the floor. After a couple of days, the other men on the crew were so frightened that they worked tentatively. And after work each day, they complained that they didn't want to go back. Finally Sonbu released the others from the crew, but Wally said he would return. He was afraid, the same as the others, but he trusted Sonbu, and the man's kindness was something he had never experienced from a supervisor before.

After the two had worked alone for a few days, Sonbu noticed that Wally had nothing to eat at lunchtime. And so the old man gave Wally some of his own rice, which was richly laced with meat and vegetables. After that he brought extra food every day and shared it with Wally. The nourishment was wonderful, and Wally felt stronger than he had in months. "*Arigato*," he always told Sonbu San. He wished he knew something more to tell him.

One day as they were eating together, Sonbu pointed to Wally. "Fam-i-ry?" he asked.

At first Wally didn't recognize the word. And then he realized, and he nodded. "Three sisters," he said, holding up three fingers.

Sonbu smiled. "Yes," he said, nodding to show he understood.

"Two brothers."

"Ah," Sonbu said, but then his face clouded. "Soldiers?" he asked.

Wally nodded.

Sonbu nodded too, and then he got up and walked to where he had folded and set aside his clothes that morning. Like Wally, he only wore a G-string in the mine, although he did keep his shirt on. He took from his jacket what appeared to be a billfold. He opened it and removed a photograph, which he brought to Wally.

Wally held his lamp so he could see better. There was Sonbu, looking serious and proper but appearing much younger than he did now. Next to him was a woman in a kimono—a pretty young woman with a pleasant smile. They were surrounded by three sons and a daughter, the daughter perhaps eighteen, and the sons all younger. It was a beautiful family. Wally nodded to Sonbu. "Very nice," he said, and he was touched by Sonbu's gentle act, this openness.

When Sonbu took the picture back, he held it close to the light and pointed to the oldest son. "Dead," he said. Then he pointed to the second one. "Dead," he said again.

Wally was stunned. He saw the pain in Sonbu's face. He pointed to the youngest boy. "Soldier?" he asked.

"*Hai,*" Sonbu said. Wally read the fear in the man's face, and automatically, he wondered whether his own brothers were safe. He was kept alive, more than anything, by the desire to see his family again, and he hated even to address the possibility that something might have happened to his brothers.

After that day Wally felt a change between him and Sonbu. They couldn't say much to each other, but they respected each other for their work, for facing danger together perhaps, and mostly for the bit of humanity they had shared with each other. It was strange to think that the supervisors he had known were probably children from some nice family like Sonbu's.

One thing gradually became clear to Wally: the managers who roamed the mine and checked on all the work crews did not come into the shaft where he and Sonbu worked. They probably worried little about Sonbu's skills, and no doubt they feared the danger. What that meant was that Sonbu seemed to feel no urgency to work terribly hard. One afternoon he sat down for a rest, and then he motioned for Wally to do the same. Sonbu was soon sound asleep. Wally was too nervous to sleep that first day, but he rested and waited, and the following day, when Sonbu took another nap, Wally lay back and drifted off himself. After that it was their daily ritual late in the work day to sleep an hour or two.

At dinner one night Chuck noticed the change in Wally. "You're looking stronger lately," Chuck said. "You have some color in your face, too."

Wally laughed, but he was hesitant to admit what was happening. He didn't want to create jealousies with his friends, but above all, he didn't want the word to get out and for Sonbu to get into trouble. But he took a chance with Chuck. The two of them were alone, and they were two of the last in the mess hall. "Don't tell anyone," he said, "but Sonbu San brings me extra rice every day. Good rice, with vegetables and meat. And we take a nap every afternoon."

Chuck looked astounded. "What do you mean? He just lets you lay down and go to sleep?"

"We both do. No one ever comes down there to check us."

"No wonder you're looking good," Chuck said.

"I know. I keep wondering, maybe I'm as bad as Honeywell—getting in good with the Japs."

"No. This is different. The guy is giving you a gift. There's nothing wrong with accepting it."

"I'd bring some rice back to you if there were any way to do it."

"Oh, hey, don't worry about it. Any of us would take some extra food if we got the chance. You don't have to apologize."

"Yeah, I know, but I've been eating my full portion in the morning, too. I'll start splitting some of that with you. I should have been doing that all along. It just felt so good to have something close to three meals a day."

"You don't need to—"

"No. I'm going to. You fed me your own food when I was dying. I'll always be in your debt for that."

"I'll tell you what you can do. When we get home, you can use some of your back pay to buy me some false teeth. Then I can eat something besides rice."

"I hope it's in '45, Chuck. It seems like it has to be. We're wearing out. Men are starting to die again."

"I know. This work is grinding everyone down." He leaned forward and put his elbows on the table. Wally could see the bones in his forearms, his wrists. Chuck had been such a powerful young man in high school, such a great athlete, and now he looked fifty years old. "The worst thing of all is never having *anything* to look forward to," he said.

"Cabanatuan was better than this," Wally said, "and look how much we wanted to get out of there."

"Maybe the Philippines are free by now. Maybe, if we'd stayed, we'd be liberated."

"Yeah. Or maybe we'd be dead," Wally said.

Chuck looked up at Wally. "They still might kill us here—when the end comes."

Wally nodded. The terrible irony of all this drudgery was that it might be for nothing. "I wonder if Alan West stayed in the Philippines. Maybe he's out now. Maybe he's home."

"I hope so. I hope some of the guys are home by now."

Wally still thought about Alan often. He was one of the men, like Chuck, who had kept him alive. "Do you think the guards back in the Philippines really would kill the prisoners—rather than let them be liberated?"

"That's what they always said. But . . . who knows?"

Wally glanced around the almost empty mess hall to see that no one was close, and then he whispered, "Sonbu San showed me a picture of his family. Two of his sons have been killed in the war. When he showed me, I thought he was going to cry."

"I've never heard of a supervisor doing something like that."

"He treats me like a regular guy—like one man to another. When I saw those sons—nice looking boys—I really felt sorry for him."

"I wish I was down there with you. I'd like that."

"Chuck, most of the time we're like oxen. We plod back and forth to the mine, we wash in that filthy pool, we eat a little rice, and then we sleep again. When Sonbu showed me that picture, it was like a shock went through my system. I felt like a human being."

Suddenly a guard was shouting, demanding that the

stragglers in the mess hall move out. One guard was coming toward the table.

Wally got up and picked up his rice bowl. He was heading for the kitchen, where he would wash it out and put it away. But suddenly he felt a powerful blow in the middle of his back, and he was knocked to the floor. He hit hard on his shoulder and rolled onto his back to see what had happened. A guard was already kicking at him, striking him hard in the side, the ribs. "Get up! Get up!" the guard was shouting. "No sitting. Get out!"

Chuck grabbed Wally, pulled him up. Wally was desperately trying to get his breath, get his legs under him, before the guard attacked again. But there was no surprise in any of this. Sometimes the guards would allow the prisoners to stay in the mess hall as long as they chose, but a sudden show of force, however unnecessary, was always a possibility.

Wally, still gasping for breath, clung to Chuck and made his way to his barracks. Chuck helped him onto his mat, where Wally curled up and hoped for the pain to subside.

Most of the men were already asleep, but Ray Vernon had awakened when Chuck and Wally had come into the room. "What happened?" he asked.

"Flat Face knocked him down and kicked him—because we sat too long in the mess hall."

Ray called him a filthy name. Wally didn't use that kind of language, not out loud, but he grabbed onto Ray's words, savored the hatred in them. He wished he could, just once, have a chance to strike back. Then he would like to see whether one of these guards could knock him around that way.

* * *

In Hawaii, Bobbi was keeping up the best way she knew how. She went through her schedule because it was required of her, but she didn't feel part of the here and now. She had cried a great deal when she heard that Richard was missing in action, but since then she had made up her mind to keep under

control, to deal with the problem with some courage and some
of that pioneer stoicism her father always spoke of. The only
trouble was, she wasn't trudging forward with a song in her
heart. She was sometimes angry, sometimes resentful, but
mostly just disheartened and hopeless—no matter how hard
she tried to tell herself she wasn't going to give up.

The nurses knew what Bobbi was going through, and they
didn't try to console her. Everyone knew that an MIA usually
turned into a KIA—"killed in action"—so there was little that
anyone could say to reassure her. Besides, Bobbi was all business right now, and her expression seemed to say, "Don't try to
tell me that everything is going to be all right."

Afton clearly had no idea what to do. She didn't laugh and
joke, as she had always done, and she avoided questions. Bobbi
felt the tension between the two of them, but she couldn't help
what she was feeling. It was probably just as well that Afton
was spending most of her off-duty hours with Sam. Bobbi knew
that Afton was still struggling to make a decision, but the truth
was, Bobbi felt more jealousy than sympathy. Afton had what
Bobbi wanted—and no courage to take it. Bobbi hated herself
for resenting that, but she did all the same.

Bobbi knew she had to get herself together and stop acting
this way, but nothing she tried seemed to work. When she
attempted to believe that Richard was alive, her emotions only
came alive, and her sadness deepened as she admitted what she
really believed. When she told herself to accept reality and
deal with it, she felt the loss so deeply that she could hardly
get out of bed. What she found most helpful was a sort of cyn-
icism. She told herself that life was miserable, that her own des-
tiny was never to have what she wanted, and that she should
expect nothing good from the future. She knew there was self-
pity in that attitude, but there was also anger and bitterness,
and they filled her with a tough kind of spitefulness that provided a bit of perverse pleasure.

Bobbi had recently received a letter from David Stinson,

the man she had fallen in love with back when she was in college. The letter was full of David's usual irreverence and wit, but there was a new undertone. He was in the military himself now, and of all things, he had joined the marines. Bobbi just couldn't imagine him carrying a rifle, taking orders from some young officer, adhering to all the military rules. He joked about that, and he joked a little about Richard, whom Bobbi had mentioned in her last letter to David. "What is it about this guy you like?" he asked, and then he had added, quite seriously it seemed:

Bobbi, I'm not sure that I didn't make a mistake when I told you that we were wrong for each other. Some things that mattered then don't seem important now. I've never felt for anyone what I felt for you, and now, facing some harsh new realities, I wonder whether I threw away my best chance for happiness. I suppose you are in love—although you didn't quite admit to that—and I'm out of the running. But if that's not so, maybe it would be possible for us to think, once again—if this stupid war ever ends—about a future together. Or maybe you don't want to do that. If not, I understand of course. I suppose I just want you to add that to your considerations, as you decide about this Richard fellow and as I go off to do what I have to do. Who knows? Maybe I'll find God in a foxhole—that's supposed to happen, you know—and I can become religious enough for you.

Bobbi couldn't help but think that if Richard didn't come back, maybe David really was an alternative. But the truth was, she couldn't picture that happening now. She had given her heart over, and it felt wrong to turn back to David after that. What bothered her most, however, was the question David had posed. What was it she liked about Richard? The longer he was gone, the less clear she was about what had happened between them. Did she even know him? What if he did get back? Would she get acquainted, for real, and then realize that they weren't right for each other either? Maybe no one was right for her.

It was all so confusing and disturbing. She longed for

Richard, spent every waking hour in fear that he was dead, and at the same time, couldn't even remember why she loved him, or maybe, deep down, *whether* she did. She knew that in her state of mind she was looking about and spotting closed doors down every hallway of her life. But she had always been a realist, and she didn't want to invent happy endings that just weren't there.

One afternoon she was working in the burn unit, feeling distant and uninvolved, when a sailor, a young man with his face bandaged, said, "Hey, nurse, I know my face is covered, but I'm not invisible."

Bobbi stopped and looked at him. She could see in his eyes that he was smiling. "I'm sorry," she said. "Tell me your name."

"Paul Farrell. And in case you're wondering, I'm very good-looking. Or at least I was the last time I looked."

Bobbi wondered what he would look like after the bandages came off. She hoped he would still feel all right about himself. At least he seemed to have some self-confidence, which would probably get him through some hard times. She also suspected, however, that this was the beginning of a flirtation, and she didn't need that right now. "Nice to meet you," she said, but she didn't tell him her own name. "I'm glad you're feeling so well."

She was about to step away when he said, "Hey, my ship was going down. I thought I was going with it. The way I look at it, a few burns might scar me up a little, but at least I'm alive—and heading home."

"You were on a ship that sank?"

"Yup."

"Where?"

"In the Leyte Gulf, off the Philippines."

"Not the *Saint Lo?*"

"No. The *Johnston.* A destroyer. But the *Saint Lo* was part of the same task force. It went down the same day we did. Why? Did you know someone on the *Saint Lo?*"

"Yes."

"Did he make it?"

"I don't know."

Bobbi watched the man's eyes for some reaction. He was lying on his back, flat. His face was completely covered, with only holes for his eyes and nose and mouth. His arms were bandaged too, and he lay motionless. It was hard to know what he might be thinking. "Is that a bad sign—that I haven't heard anything?"

"It's hard to say." He sounded hesitant.

Bobbi stepped a little closer to his bed. She didn't want the men in the ward to hear this. Some of the nurses had talked about Richard, and the word had spread among the patients. They were nice about it, but they asked her every day what she had heard, and she hated answering. "How did you get off?" she asked. "In a life raft?"

"No. I got thrown into the water. That's what happened to most of the men on the ships that went down. I had a life jacket on, but I was in the water for two days."

"Two *days*."

"And two *very* long nights."

"Who picked you up?"

"The navy sent out LCIs—you know, landing craft—to look for us. Most of us were in really bad shape after that long in the water, and a lot didn't make it."

"Do you know anything about the *Saint Lo*—how many got off, or anything like that?"

"No. But I know that a lot of their survivors were in the water for two nights, the same as us. They got picked up around the same time."

"Once you got picked up, did someone let your family know?"

"Sure. But not real fast. There were a lot of men—and every situation was a little different."

"What would it mean if someone's family hasn't heard anything by now?"

Those eyes were still looking out from the bandages, but they weren't meeting Bobbi's now. "It could mean all kinds of things. He could have been picked up by the Japs, I guess."

"Would the Japanese pick them up—or shoot them?"

"It's hard to say. I do know that some men said the Japanese sailors left them in the water but threw cans of food to them."

Bobbi had tried to consider every possibility, and now she couldn't resist; she wanted to ask the questions that had plagued her. "What about sharks?"

"That *was* a problem for those in the water, like me. There were a lot of sharks around, and sometimes they did attack. A guy I knew got killed that way."

She nodded. "Can you think of any other way he could be alive, without his family getting word?"

"Really, I'm not sure. You ought to ask someone who—"

"It's okay. But if I haven't heard anything by now, that probably means he didn't make it, wouldn't you say?" Bobbi's voice had gotten louder, even though she hadn't intended for that to happen. By now the room was silent, and she knew everyone was listening. She turned and looked at the men in the other beds. "Isn't that true?" she asked. "Won't someone at least tell me that?"

A sailor at the other end of the room, an older fellow who had been in the ward a long time with burns over most of his body, finally said, "Bobbi, you know that's true. The longer you don't hear, the worse it probably is. But no one can say for sure. Sometimes the Japs do take prisoners, especially if the men made it to land. He could be a prisoner in the Philippines."

"Thanks," Bobbi said, but her voice had lost all its power. "I needed someone to be honest with me."

And she left the ward. All the rest of the day she told herself it was settled. He was dead, and so that was what she had to deal with. She would assume that Richard was gone—not fret, not whine, not feel sorry for herself. She wasn't the first person to lose a brother and a boyfriend in this war. She had no right to expect anything better.

But that night, in her room, after Afton had gone out for the evening, Bobbi's anger returned. And when it did, she finally told God what she thought. "It isn't fair!" she shouted. She knew people who were better off because of this war. She knew so many families that hadn't had to send a single son. But she didn't say all that; she said what lay closer to her heart: "I ask and I ask and I ask, and you don't answer. If you're going to say no, just say it! I'll deal with that. But don't just sit back and *ignore* me!"

She tried to calm herself, tried to tell herself that she had no right to talk to God that way. But still no answer came. She felt no comfort, no strength, nothing spiritual—not even a reprimand. She wished God would strike her down for her insolence, punish her. At least that would be something. But there was nothing, and she couldn't cry. "Fine!" she told God. "I can be as tough as you. If you don't care, I don't either."

The next morning she told Lieutenant Karras that she wanted to volunteer for a hospital ship. The lieutenant had announced recently that the navy was looking for nurses willing to serve on those ships, and the only thing Bobbi wanted right now was for her life to change in some way. She didn't want to be in Hawaii, where everything reminded her of Richard.

Berlin was a devastated city. Much of the central part of town was in ruins. Walls of buildings stood like shadows of a grand past. Heinrich Stoltz was not truly a Berliner; he had only lived there during the time of his exile, and he had seen much of this destruction before he left. Still, returning now, he brought with him the memories of what the city had once been. What it had become, this wasteland, was to him a symbol of what Hitler had brought to the German people. And it wasn't just here. All across the nation Brother Stoltz had seen the havoc and destruction. When he considered the sorrow represented in all the bombed-out buildings—the homes and shops, the museums and churches—the magnitude of the tragedy was overwhelming.

Brother Stoltz sat on a bench in the Tiergarten. The park was full of craters and trenches, military equipment and debris, and yet lovely white swans still swam in the nearby pond. It was as though, in their serenity, they refused to be bothered by all the noise and fury they had surely experienced. Brother Stoltz was sitting on the same bench where he had sat the year before, but he hardly felt himself to be the same man.

His contact, the man he called Georg, approached and

nodded, and then sat down on the bench—at the opposite end. "Nice day we're having. No?" he asked.

It was actually a rather gray day, and quite cold, but Brother Stoltz said, "Yes. Compared to many."

"Any day is pretty when no bombs are falling," Georg said. He was slowly scanning the area. There were people here and there in the park, but not many, and no one seemed to be paying any attention to the two of them.

"How is Uncle Emil surviving?" Brother Stoltz asked.

"Not so bad," Georg said. "But we have lost a few more people since you were here. One would think the Gestapo would ease up now, with the war going badly for Germany. But the ones who have stayed true to the party are fanatics. They search harder than ever."

"What do the common people feel? Do they think the war is lost?"

"People worry about getting food, more than anything, and keeping a roof over their heads. Some speak of Hitler's secret weapons. They claim the rockets will turn the tide—and jet airplanes—but even as they say it, I see in their eyes that they know better."

"What keeps them going then? How do the factories keep putting out arms?"

Georg was a little man with a bushy mustache and dark bags under his eyes. He was dressed in a heavy black coat, wool, with a gray scarf wrapped around his neck and a fedora hat perched low and level on his head so it touched the tops of his ears. He looked sad when he said, "I wonder myself. It's force of habit, to some degree—and maybe hatred. However much the people may doubt the Nazis now, they hate the bombers more. What I hear people admit—intelligent people who whisper to me cautiously—is that they hope for a truce and a new treaty with the Allies. The worst fear of all is that the Russians will pour over our borders. Everyone knows how dearly we'll pay if that happens."

"Are you afraid?"

Georg shoved his hands into his overcoat pockets.
"Certainly. When Berlin is overrun, no enemy soldier will know
what I've done for the Jews. You and I remember those bitter
years after the first world war. I hate to think what our people
will suffer for another decade now—maybe longer."

The two sat and watched the gentle motion of the swans.
Leaves were drifting down from the tall sycamore trees, big
leaves like parachutes, settling on the grass and the water.
Brother Stoltz felt the sadness again, the immeasurable sorrow.
Everything he loved about Germany had been stolen from him,
even Germany itself. "I have an envelope for you," he finally
said. "It's from the American intelligence agency. I'm here pri-
marily as a courier for them."

"Take it out and set it on the bench between us. When I
leave, I'll pick it up."

And so Brother Stoltz pulled the envelope out from under
his coat and set it on the bench.

But Georg didn't leave. "When the Nazis began to take
away Jews, I knew it was wrong," he said. "And so I took action.
But I'm not a traitor to my country. I don't know what the
Americans want from me, but I won't help them bomb my city."

"They sent me because I knew how to make contact with
your organization. They want to communicate with any underground or resistance movement. If all those in Germany who
oppose the Nazis could work in concert, the war could possibly be brought to a quick end."

"You saw what came of the great anti-Nazi movement.
Stauffenberg and the others who tried to kill Hitler only ended
up getting themselves killed—or thrown into prison. Since
then the oppression by the Gestapo and the SS has only gotten
worse."

"I know that. But the Allies are at your borders now—and
the Russians aren't far away. A quick end to the war could save
hundreds of thousands of lives—German lives."

"What on earth could we do? We have no way to get to Hitler."

"You can help to pinpoint bombing raids—to make certain that armaments are destroyed, crucial railroad crossings are struck, airplanes are knocked out on the ground."

"I told you. I won't help England and America bomb my people."

"Georg, I love Germany, but I had to make a decision. Was I willing to do what I could to make certain Hitler lost his war—and the real Germany could return someday?"

"I only want to do one thing—protect a few innocent people."

"It's not that simple. If Allied bombers can strike more accurately and then learn, quickly, whether their air raids have been effective, this will also save lives. If fuel and vital parts for airplanes and tanks and trucks can be destroyed, Hitler will have to give up—or his generals will overthrow him."

"We're told here that it's the Allies who refuse to consider a truce."

"That's true. Only an unconditional surrender will be considered. So there's no hope for a separate peace with the Allies. The only way to keep the Russians from taking Berlin is for Hitler to end the war."

"I understand all this." Georg looked out across the pond, and his voice was softer when he said, "I'll look to see what's in this envelope, and I'll consider what the Americans want to know. But I cannot promise to answer any of their questions."

Brother Stoltz knew there was no point in pushing the issue, at least not yet. "Could I meet you here again tomorrow? If you have answers, you could give them to me."

"Yes. But we must choose another place. It's never good to follow a pattern."

And so they arranged a meeting for the next day, this time in another part of the vast Tiergarten. But before they parted, Brother Stoltz said, "When my family escaped the country, my son didn't make it out with us. He turned back, and I now know that he was caught by the Gestapo. Is there a way to know whether he's alive, or to find out where he is?"

"I do have contacts who might be able to learn something. I can't say for certain. Tell me his name and his birth date. I'll see what I can do."

And so Brother Stoltz gave him the information, and then he walked away. He spent the rest of the day moving about the city, trying to get some sense of the morale of the people, and to locate certain arms factories. What he found didn't surprise him. People were continuing with a sense of dogged determination that was deeply German—and he loved them for that. The factories he had known before were functioning and productive, even though they had been bombed a number of times.

As evening came on, Brother Stoltz found himself drawn to the building where he and his family had twice hidden themselves. Somehow it seemed only natural that Peter would go there, as the place in Germany where he had found momentary safety when he was being chased. What Brother Stoltz found, however, was that the block had finally been cleared. The rubble was gone, and so were the basements, all pushed in now. But he stood on the street and looked out across the flattened neighborhood. He thought of those frightening days in the dark, and what came upon him was regret for the life he had given Peter. The boy had been running since he was a child. He had been such a wonderful child, but he had never experienced the casual growing-up years he deserved.

Brother Stoltz stayed at a little hotel outside the city that night. He showed his travel papers, and the man at the desk accepted them, but he said, "Too bad they would send you here now. There must be safer places."

"I'm not so concerned about my own safety. I want to do my part for my country," Brother Stoltz said.

The older man looked up from the ledger, where Brother

Stoltz had signed his assumed name. But he didn't react. It was as though he knew better than to pay attention to such empty words. He handed Brother Stoltz a key to his room on the third floor.

The following afternoon Brother Stoltz met Georg again. They met on a path and pretended to be friends, merely stopping to chat. Georg had the envelope inside a newspaper, and he passed it to Brother Stoltz, who hid it in his coat. "I told them some things," Georg said. "But not everything they wanted to know."

"I understand."

"Still . . . I gave them information that I didn't think I would ever share with an enemy. And if it does help end the war a little more quickly, I won't regret it."

"Yes. That will be our hope. But Georg, the Allies need information on a regular basis. They need to find out, after a bombing raid, whether they have knocked out the intended target. They need to track troop movements and arms shipments. I won't be here long, but I'm hoping to set up a network of people who can observe such things and then get information out. We have radios now that beam a narrow wave to airplanes overhead—ones that carry a special receiver. There's almost no chance of detection. I was hoping your people could help—and perhaps recruit others to assist us in other places."

Georg looked at the ground, and his voice was a mere whisper when he said. "I don't know. I can talk to people. There are some who may think we should do this. It's difficult to say."

"All right. That's all I ask. I'll be in touch with you again— in our usual way."

"No. Use a new code name. Don't call me for a time, and when you do, refer to yourself as Franz Wolf."

"Yes. I'll remember that." Brother Stoltz hesitated, and then he added, "Georg, were you able to learn anything about my son?"

"Yes. A little. The Gestapo is looking for him. They have printed a description, and all agents are to watch for him."

"Was this recent?"

"It is a current bulletin."

"Then he's not in jail?"

"I only know what I've just told you. He seems to be on the run, and the Gestapo wants to find him."

"Then he must have escaped. I know they had him at one time."

"It must be so."

The two men stood facing each other. They both knew they should not linger. But Brother Stoltz wanted desperately to get a lead, to have some idea where to look. "How can I find him?" he asked Georg.

"I have no idea. But I have thought about this. A young man his age—healthy and strong—cannot walk the streets of any city, any village, in this country. He would be stopped and checked for his papers. If he could show that he was in the military, and on leave, he would be all right. But otherwise, he would be arrested."

"Maybe someone is hiding him. It's what he's had to do before."

"Perhaps. Maybe he found someone. But the only safe thing for a boy on the run would be to sign up with the military. Few questions are asked these days when someone is willing to serve."

"I don't think Peter would join the German army. That's the last thing he would want to do."

"That may be true. You know him better than I do. But it's the best place to hide. Recruiters are the only people these days who are perfectly willing to accept any explanation for lost papers—so long as they can fill their quotas of new recruits."

That did make sense to Brother Stoltz, but he still doubted

that Peter would take that step. It was an idea, however—something to begin with.

"Thank you, Georg," Brother Stoltz said, and he shook the man's hand.

Georg breathed, and steam escaped his mouth in a little puff. "I wish I could do more," he said. "What will you do with my information? I don't want it traced back to me."

"I'm to make contact with a radio dispatcher. I will give the papers to him. And he will destroy them once he has passed on the information."

"Then you should get out, if you have a way," Georg said. "There is almost no way to trace your son. You would be better off now to wait until the war is over—and then begin your search. It sounds as though he's managing for himself for now."

"Perhaps you're right," Brother Stoltz said. He shook Georg's hand. "Good luck to you," he said. "And may God bless you."

Georg made a quick bow as he shook hands, and he clicked his heels in the traditional German manner. Brother Stoltz knew what it had cost this man, so deeply German, to hand over this envelope.

Brother Stoltz thought he would accept Georg's advice. He would carefully go about his business—and not take chances by seeking Peter. But that night in bed, as he struggled to sleep, his body aching from the broken bones he had suffered at the hands of the Gestapo, he was sickened by the idea of giving up. He began to consider a plan, a means at least to discover whether Peter really was in the German army.

On the following morning, Brother Stoltz walked into an office of the German military that was housed not far from where he had once worked in downtown Berlin. He knew he was taking a great chance to be seen in the area, but he felt he had to make this much effort before he stopped searching. He understood the operation of German bureaucracy, and he felt

certain that he could bluff his way through the system and get
to the files he wanted to see.

He stepped to the counter in the records office, and he
showed his identification card, the one that placed him in the
Sicherheits Dienst—the secret police. "Excuse me," he said, "but
can you help me? I am Officer Wetzel. I am trying to track
down a traitor—a soldier who left his military company without permission."

A woman behind the counter, sitting at a desk, looked up
from some papers and took her glasses off. She seemed tired,
uninterested. She was middle-aged, with graying hair, but her
eyes made her seem elderly. She got up slowly and walked to
the counter, and then she glanced at the identification. "How
can I help you?"

"I simply want to check some records."

The woman seemed ready to ask another question, and
then she nodded. "It doesn't matter to me," she said. "What do
you want to see?"

"Recruiting records for August and September, perhaps
October, of this year."

"For what city?"

"Let me start with records from southern Germany."

"Can't you be more specific than that? There are dozens of
record books."

"I'm sorry. I can only guess that he might have joined in a
southern city."

She didn't look pleased. "I'll have to look around a little.
Those are still new records to us. We can't keep up here, with
so little help. We make permanent records, in time, but I doubt
that's the case yet for August and September names."

"I understand. I'll do the search myself." Brother Stoltz
found himself sounding a little too kind, not as commanding as
he thought he should be. But he did feel sorry for the over-
worked woman.

"We have no space," the woman said. "The building was

bombed last summer, and now we're all pushed together in these offices. You'll have to come to the records room. There's not even a place to sit down in there."

"I'll manage," Brother Stoltz said, sounding a little more curt this time.

He walked to a back room with the woman. Many of the records were in ledger books, on shelves, but others were stacked about, or still in boxes. The woman searched them out and kept bringing them to him. Brother Stoltz stood in a corner, near a window, where the light was decent, and he read the many names. The sad part was, he had no idea what he was looking for. He thought of the pseudonyms Peter had used when the Stoltzes were hiding, but he doubted he would revert to those. He wondered whether Peter wouldn't want to keep his first name, or whether he wouldn't choose to use his own birth date—but he didn't know.

An hour went by, and Brother Stoltz saw names that might have had some vague connection to their family, but he saw nothing that stood out as a sure thing. What he was beginning to accept was that this was the fruitless chase he had assumed it might be. And then, looking in the Stuttgart ledgers, he saw the name *Peter Stutz*. His eyes stopped, of course, and he looked more carefully. And then he saw the clue that convinced him this was the right name. The birth date was not Peter's. He had chosen a year that made him younger than he really was— which made sense. But the day and month were Anna's. It would only make sense that he would choose a birthday he would be able to remember easily.

So Brother Stoltz walked back to the outer office. "I think I've found the name I'm looking for," he told the woman. "Is there a way to determine what unit this person is serving with?"

"Not here. Down the hall." She directed Brother Stoltz to another office.

Brother Stoltz had assumed his role rather well by now, he thought, and he seemed to have the woman's confidence. He wasn't worried all that much as he approached the new office. But here a man checked his identity card more carefully. And then he said, "What is it you want?" as though he doubted the SD had any business looking into his files.

The man appeared healthy enough, and yet he was here and not out fighting somewhere, so Brother Stoltz guessed that he might have been wounded. He said, "I'm sorry. It's my job. I was hurt last year at the Eastern front. They told me they didn't want me in the army anymore, and they gave me this duty, doing work for the SD. I know I can be a bother to men like you who have business to take care of."

The man looked surprised. He was a thin man with little hair even for eyebrows. His dark eyes seemed piercing, sitting in the pale wasteland of his face. "Yes. I took a bullet myself, near Kiev. Otherwise, this is the last job in the world I would be doing. What is it you need?" He sounded more at ease now.

"I have the name of a recruit." He held out a slip of paper with Peter's name, birth date, and service number on it. "He's reported now as absent without leave. But I think, in fact, he may be missing in action. Is there any way to know his unit, and where it's fighting now?"

The man took the slip of paper from Brother Stoltz and said, "But why wouldn't you know this? Who reported him missing?"

"Who knows? It's the usual sort of foul-up. They ask me to check out these things, and half the time they give me no information."

The man shook his head, some of the annoyance returning to his face. "Let me look. But I may not be able to tell you very much." He walked from the room. He was gone for quite some time, and while he was gone, Brother Stoltz had time to become nervous. He was wearing an overcoat still, and holding his hat in his hand. He found himself pacing back and forth.

When the official returned, he announced, "The boy is

with the Grossdeutschland Division. Seventeenth Battalion. They were fighting, when last known, near Lublin, in Poland."

"What do you mean, 'When last known'?" Brother Stoltz asked.

"Oh, *mein Herr,* you must know, all is in chaos in that sector. Our men are retreating, holding on, then falling back again. It's a terrible mess."

"Is there no way to find out exactly where they are?"

"What difference does it make to you? Whether he's on the run from his own battalion, or from the Russians, he took off from someplace other than where they are now."

"Yes. But I would like to have some idea of where he could be—or where I could look for him."

"You would go *look* for him?"

"No. Of course not. Not myself. I'm merely . . ." But Brother Stoltz knew he had to be careful. He was forgetting his role.

"If I were you, I'd send someone to check his home. He's just a young boy. That's where he might run to."

"Yes, yes. That will be done."

"Why didn't you search there first?"

"I'm only just beginning to . . . look into this."

"It's crazy. They give you no more information than his name and service number? What fool sent you out on such a search? I've never heard of such a thing. This is all handled by military police, in my experience. They stop boys on the street, check their identity cards. There's none of this searching around in records, trying to trace them back to their unit."

"Yes, it seemed . . . inefficient to me, too." Brother Stoltz knew it was time to get out. He was only creating suspicion now, but he had a lead and no way to follow it. "Is there an office here somewhere that keeps closer track of troop movements? Is there a way to locate this boy's unit more precisely?"

The man stared at Brother Stoltz for several seconds before he said, "This doesn't make sense to me. You want to know things that shouldn't matter to you. I don't like the sound of this."

"It's only . . . oh, my, never mind. I'll do as you say. I'll let the police know, in the little village where he lives. They can be on the watch for him."

"This all makes me nervous. I've never heard of anyone being taken on by the SD the way you describe. That's not how these people work. I wonder why you want this information."

"Nothing to be nervous about. I won't bother you anymore." Brother Stoltz turned to walk away.

"Wait a moment. Tell me your name again."

"Heitz," Brother Stoltz said. "Alfred Heitz." But as the words left his lips, he realized what he had done. He had used the pseudonym he had been using the past few days since entering Germany, but not Wetzel—the name on the identification card. That was his second identity, the one he was planning to use mainly for his escape from Germany.

"What?" the man said. "Let me see your identification again."

"It's no matter. Thank you for your time. I'll manage things from here." He was moving away, edging toward the door.

"No. Wait a moment. Come back here."

The man was coming out from behind his desk as Brother Stoltz glanced back the last time. He kept right on walking, quickly, but trying not to seem on the run.

The man burst from the office. "Stop right there!" he called.

"No, thank you. You've done enough." Brother Stoltz waved and smiled and kept going. In a few more seconds he was out the door. But he glanced back, and he saw the man step back into his office, surely to make a phone call.

Brother Stoltz hurried down the street to the subway station on the corner. But he hadn't realized that the station had been struck by a bomb and was closed. He glanced around frantically, and then, when he looked back toward the office building, he saw that the man he had dealt with there had walked outside. He was waving to Brother Stoltz, calling him back. Brother Stoltz walked around the corner and then began to run.

Heinrich Stoltz ran halfway down the block, crossed a street, and cut through an alley. But rubble from a bombed building obstructed the alley at the other end. By the time he saw that, he was well into the trap. Now he had to retrace his steps and go back to the street. He ran again, turned another corner, and looked back to see a car coming down the street. There were few vehicles on the streets these days, and Brother Stoltz knew this couldn't be good news. He slowed to a walk. He was passing another area where there was nothing but hollow, gutted structures, but as he reached the door to the next operating building, he turned and walked in and then hurried down the hallway to the first office he saw.

Brother Stoltz was frantic, but he was trying to keep himself under control. When he stepped inside the office, he could see that this was another bureau of some kind. "I was hoping to see your supervisor," he told a woman, a secretary, who was sitting at a small desk. He had to gamble that she would do things the way most secretaries did.

"Yes. And who should I say wants to see him?"

"Siegfried Schultz," he said, using the name of an old friend of his.

"Does he know what this is about?"

"Oh, certainly."

"Just sit down a moment. He has someone else in his office right now." She was a pleasant-looking young woman, with big round eyes, and she smiled in such a friendly way that Brother Stoltz felt ashamed to have lied to her. But things were working out as he had hoped. He wanted to stay in the office for now. He feared that the people in the car would follow him inside.

After only a few minutes a man came out of the main office, and the secretary got up and walked inside. When she came out, she said, "He'll see you now, Herr Schultz. But you'll have to tell him what it's about."

Brother Stoltz stood up and was about to tell her never mind, when she walked into a back office. He stepped to the office door and then noticed a black coat hanging on a hall tree. His own coat and hat were brown. He quickly pulled his coat off, hung it up, along with his hat, and then grabbed the black one. As he put it on, he could tell immediately that it was all wrong for him—too long and too tight. He pulled it off and merely draped it over his arm. Then he stepped outside the office and walked calmly toward the front doors. He was almost to the entrance when he realized what he had done. He had left his SD identification card in the brown coat. He stopped, tried to think. Did he dare to go back?

But just then a man in a leather coat pushed his way through the door. The man—surely a Gestapo agent—took a hard look at him, and Brother Stoltz said, "*Guten Tag, mein Herr.*"

The agent nodded in his direction and seemed ready to pass on by, but then he stopped and said, "Didn't you just enter this building a few minutes ago?"

"No. I've been here for quite some time."

"You didn't have a hat on?"

"No. I'm sorry." Brother Stoltz smiled and tried to walk away.

"Wait just a moment. What were you doing here? Do you work here?"

"No. I had some business in an office in this building. I work down the street."

"Were you in the military records office just a short time ago?"

"No."

The man eyed him carefully. His prominent forehead gave him something of a Neanderthal look, but his eyes, appearing almost black under his heavy eyebrows, were intent and clear. "What were you doing here?"

"Just the usual bureaucratic nonsense. My boss sent me down to check on a trivial matter."

"What trivial matter?" The agent stepped closer and hunched his shoulders, seeming more diabolic than before.

"It was really just one of those . . ." Brother Stoltz stepped back a little so that he was partway through the door, but he still had hold of it. " . . . complicated record-keeping issues. It's not easy to explain."

"What's your name? Step back in here and show me your identification papers."

"Schultz is my name," Brother Stoltz said, "but I'll have to be going now." He took another step back.

"I told you. Come inside. Immediately."

"No."

As the agent stepped forward, Brother Stoltz drove the door into him. Some of the force of the big door was absorbed by the man's knee, but it struck him in the face too, cracked it hard. The man went down.

Brother Stoltz took off running, directly across the street. He glanced back to see no one coming yet, and he rushed into the first building he came to. He hurried on through, found a back door, and went out. He was in an alley. What he found when he came out of the alley was a whole street that had been demolished by bombs. He was suddenly standing in a wilderness of rubble where he would stand out like a tree on an open plain. But it was too late to go back, so he ran the length of the street and then turned toward a street filled with apartment houses, mostly intact. By now the agent might be up and looking for him. Other agents would be called in. Brother Stoltz knew he couldn't be seen on the streets, certainly not running.

And then he saw a bus coming his way. It stopped at the corner he had just passed, and he ran back to it. This was providence, he had to believe. Transportation in Berlin was sporadic these days, with few taxis and unpredictable bus schedules. But now, when he needed it, a bus had come. He stepped on, paid the driver, and then moved to the back, where he hunched down. He watched the windows, saw nothing, and began to feel better as he moved steadily away from the central part of Berlin.

But he was in an enormous predicament, and he knew it. He had assaulted a government agent, probably from the Gestapo. He knew all too well what a manhunt that would set off. All that was bad enough, but now his means of escaping Germany was lost. The SD identification card had been his ticket into Switzerland.

He kept taking deep breaths, and he searched his mind for answers. He could try to contact Georg, eventually, but for now he needed to get out of Berlin. And he had to get away from the city quickly, before a search closed his escape routes.

For the first time he began to pay attention to where the bus was taking him. He was moving away from the main *Bahnhof*, the Potsdamer Station, but there were other stations. The problem was, a person couldn't leave Berlin without a special permit. He knew that it was sometimes possible to use commuter trains or streetcars to get outside the city boundaries, and then to catch a train from a smaller town. He got up and walked quickly to the front of the bus. "Excuse me," he said to the driver, a woman. "I want to catch a streetcar to Neustadt. Where can I do that?"

The bus driver didn't bother to look back. She said, "I'll show you. It's only a few more stops from here."

So Brother Stoltz waited and watched as the bus continued south, and then, when the woman said, "Here you are," he got off. But he had to wait much longer than he wanted to—at least twenty minutes—before the streetcar came. It was a long, slow ride to Neustadt, and by the time he got there, he wondered what he might face inside the station. Agents might have been alerted at all the little train stations. Still, he couldn't think what else to do.

So Brother Stoltz tried to act confident again. He was still carrying the black coat, since he knew that no man would travel without an overcoat this time of year. But he was without luggage, which would make him conspicuous. He had to hope that security was not as tight as it would be at a major *Bahnhof*.

In the main hall of the station, Brother Stoltz checked the big board and decided that a train leaving for Munich was his best bet. It was scheduled to leave in just a few minutes. But he knew he had a problem. He would have to use his identity, and the travel papers only justified his travel *to* Berlin. If someone checked him closely, he would have no explanation for why he was returning south. Still, it was his only chance, so he walked to the ticket booth, made his purchase, and headed for the train. At the gate was a railroad employee, a ticket taker, but just beyond him was an officer, perhaps a local policeman. "Could I see your papers?" he asked.

Brother Stoltz handed over his identity card and the travel papers. He asked immediately, "What can we expect today? Any delays on this line?"

The policeman swore. He was a dull-looking man with a flattened nose and squinted eyes. "One can always expect delays these days," he said. "You know how it is."

"Yes, but the raids haven't been so bad lately. I think maybe we have the British on the run with our rockets. That's something new for them."

The whole idea was to keep the man talking and not paying too much attention to the papers, but the officer was taking a look at the identification card when he said, "That's right, you know. We may have a few more weapons to throw at them before long. That's what I hear."

"Yes, and they have it coming, after all they've done here, with their damnable raids on civilians. They have no shame." Brother Stoltz knew this was a favorite complaint, something most Berliners would gladly talk about.

"It's more than a shame. It's something we have to make them pay for," the policeman said.

"You have it right. Exactly right. And what of this—"

But now the policeman was handing back the papers, pushing gently against his arm. "Go on through. Your train is about to leave. And there are others waiting."

"Oh, I'm sorry." Brother Stoltz took back the documents. The man had looked at the travel papers but clearly hadn't read the destination. And so Brother Stoltz took a deep breath and walked on to the train, where he took a seat and hoped that the train would depart on time. He knew his problems were far from ended. Once his false SD identity card was discovered in his abandoned coat, and that might have happened by now, the Gestapo would know he was a spy. If his true identity was somehow recognized, his previous crimes would also be known. That would only heighten the intensity of the search.

Minutes were ticking by, and the train was still not moving. The departure time had come and gone. Brother Stoltz kept hoping that the train would begin to move.

Then he saw two men in leather overcoats. They had reached the entrance to the platform, and they were talking with the policeman. At the same time, the train finally bumped and started to roll. It was easing along slowly when Brother Stoltz saw the agents running toward the train. They were not boarding yet but moving faster than the train and looking through the windows. The policeman was with them. And they would soon reach his car. If they spotted him, he knew he was finished.

Brother Stoltz stood up and walked quickly to the end of the car and then out the door and onto the little platform between cars. By then the train was picking up speed, but he jumped anyway, on the opposite side from the agents, where there was no platform. He landed on another line of tracks, and when he hit, his momentum carried him forward and threw him down on the railroad ties. He tried to catch himself with his hand but felt a shock of pain as his wrist took his weight and twisted under him. Still, he jumped up and then climbed onto the platform on the opposite side from where he had seen the agents. He straightened himself then, and he walked res-olutely—trying not to call attention to himself—back toward the main hall of the station.

As he reached the gate, he looked back. The train was gone, and he saw no sign of the agents. He guessed they had boarded the train. What he did see was the local policeman walking back toward the gate where he had been stationed before. Brother Stoltz ducked out the next gate, and he didn't think the man had seen him, but as he walked into the main hall, he saw two more men in leather coats. They were stand-ing near the main doors of the little station, and they were looking about.

Brother Stoltz turned quickly away, and he walked into a *Gasthaus* inside the station. He sat at a table, lowered his head, and tried to think what to do. His wrist was throbbing with pain, but he couldn't worry about that now. In his hurry he had left the black coat on the train. The agents would probably dis-cover that—and perhaps guess that he had gotten off before they had gotten on. But how soon could they get back? Did they have some means to notify the agents who were in the main hall?

Maybe he should try to get out of this station, but what then? He still needed to get away from Berlin. He looked up at the train schedule on the wall of the restaurant. A train was leaving in about twelve minutes, for Leipzig. The gate was a good choice—at the opposite end of the building from the gate he had used before. Brother Stoltz tried to think how he could get past the policeman there.

He looked toward the door to the restaurant, alert to the possibility of someone coming to look for him. What he also noticed was a conductor's coat and hat hanging on a hook near the door. He acted instantly, without much of a plan. He stood up just as a waitress was approaching his table. "Oh, never mind," he said. "I suppose I'm out of time." He walked to the door and then glanced back. The waitress had turned away, and no one else was looking his direction. He grabbed the coat and hat and stepped quickly outside. He plopped the hat on his head, threw on the coat, and, in spite of the pain it caused to his wrist, buttoned the coat as he walked. He hoped the wrist wasn't broken. He had no idea how he could get medical help.

Brother Stoltz walked quickly, but he tried not to let his panic show. He didn't have the right sort of tie, nor the proper uniform trousers, so he had no idea whether he could pass himself off this way, but Germany had become used to makeshift uniforms, with so many shortages.

He walked, rather casually, to the gate where the train to Leipzig was leaving, and there he tipped his hat to the ticket taker. The man looked confused, obviously not recognizing him.

"I'm a last-minute replacement," he said. "The regular man got sick, so they called me in. I'm new on the job."

The man nodded, not seeming to care.

Brother Stoltz stepped quickly on past and hurried to the train. But it wasn't leaving for a few more minutes, and the one thing he couldn't do now was let himself be spotted by a real conductor. He stepped into a car and waited, standing up. And he chatted briefly with a passenger. When the man offered to show him his tickets, he said, "I'll check all that when the train starts. I need to go on forward for now," and he walked into another car.

Again he waited, and the minutes seemed to pass like hours. He knew he would have to dump his disguise at some point, but then he would be without a ticket. He had no idea how he could manage that. He was far from out of danger, and he was wearing down. The tightness in his chest kept him from breathing normally. Pain was spreading into his shoulders. He wondered whether he might be having a heart attack.

But then the train started moving. He held his spot in the nearly empty car. Three men up front were chatting with each other, and they didn't seem to be paying any attention to what· he was doing, so he decided not to change anything until he had to.

Perhaps ten minutes passed before the men began to glance around at him, as if they were curious why he wasn't doing anything. Brother Stoltz didn't look at them straight on. He stalled a little longer, and then he finally did walk forward. "Could I see your tickets?" he asked.

The men each in turn handed over the tickets, and Brother Stoltz chatted with them. "This is not bad weather for November, now is it?" he said.

One of the men said, "I spent last winter on the Russian front. This feels like summer to me."

Brother Stoltz nodded and smiled. "I'm certain that's true," he said. He glanced ahead, through the window on the car door, and he saw that in the car ahead of him, the real conductor had just stepped in. "*Danke Schön*," he said. "*Gute Reise.*" Then he turned and walked back through the car and out the door. He knew what the men would tell the conductor when he arrived in the car, and he didn't know what would happen then. Would the conductor drop what he was doing and come looking for him?

Brother Stoltz walked through all the cars—four of them—

and then took a seat in the last. He would ride as far as he could and get away from the city. When the conductor showed up, he would have to bluff him as best he could.

But the conductor didn't show up right away, and that seemed a good sign. At least he hadn't become so concerned as to make a quick search. When the man did finally show up in the car ahead, Brother Stoltz got a better look. He was rather a frail-looking man, older. If nothing else, Brother Stoltz could overpower him rather than allow himself to be detained.

But when the conductor came into the car, he looked sharp and aware, not like a man who could be gotten over easily. He cut off his ticket taking and walked directly to the back of the car. "What's going on here?" he said.

"I'm off duty. I'm heading home."

"You had no business checking tickets. What were you doing that for?"

"I started doing it before I even thought—out of habit. I've hardly slept lately. I'm not thinking straight."

The man took a long look at Brother Stoltz, who averted his own eyes. It was a weak story, and he knew it. "Let me see your papers," the conductor said. "Do you have your railroad pass?"

"No. Not with me."

"You have no right to ride this train without a pass—no more than anyone else. You know that as well as anyone."

"I know. But we were bombed out last week. Everything is such a mess with me right now. I must get a new pass, and—"

"Bombed out where?"

Brother Stoltz knew there had been few raids lately, and he didn't know how to answer. He had dug himself one more hole, and he was beginning to lose concentration, even the will to keep this up. "I don't mean last week," he said. "It was two or three weeks ago, or maybe—"

"I want you off this train. I don't think you're a conductor. What are those trousers and shoes you're wearing?"

"I'm new actually. I—"

"I don't know where you got that coat, but I think you're jumping on for a free ride."

"No, no. I wouldn't do that."

"We're stopping in five minutes, in Luckenwalde. I want you off this train—either that or I'll turn you in."

"It's all right. I'll get off."

"I should turn you in anyway."

"I'll get off. I don't want trouble. I should have known better than to travel without my pass."

The conductor gave him a skeptical look, but then he turned and walked back to the front of the car, and he began again to check tickets. When the train stopped at Luckenwalde, Brother Stoltz got off. He looked back and forth along the platform, saw no one, and so he pulled off the coat and hat. He stuffed them both into a garbage can as he walked into the station. Then he bought himself a ticket for Leipzig.

He had a long wait, since another train wasn't coming for almost two hours, but no one in this little station seemed to pay attention to him, and this time no one was checking papers. He made it to Leipzig very late that evening. He was temporarily safe, but he was also trapped. He didn't dare try to board another train in a big station like this—not without proper travel papers—so his thought was that he would have to find someplace to hide away in Leipzig for a time. But as he was leaving the station, he saw three trucks lined up outside. They had apparently been loading some sort of cargo off a train. Brother Stoltz took a chance and asked one of the drivers where he was going and whether he could catch a ride. The man was heading south to Stuttgart, and then on to Karlsruhe. "That would help me," he told the driver. "I'm trying to get to Freiburg."

"We're not supposed to carry people," the man said.

"I know," Brother Stoltz said. "But here's my problem. Someone stole my luggage, and now I have no travel papers. I can't buy a railway ticket. I can file for all my papers again, but by then I'll miss my brother's funeral—in Freiburg."

The man shrugged. "But if I get caught, it could be my job."

"Yes. I understand," Brother Stoltz told him, and he turned to walk away.

But the man called him back. "It's all right," he said. "No one is likely to find out. Go ahead and get in."

So Brother Stoltz got his ride, and it was just what he wanted. He was getting back to the south, close to the French border, and not so terribly far from Switzerland. If the Americans crossed the Siegfried line, in the south, the way might be open to escape Germany. Or if he could get help through Georg or through his OSS contacts, and get new papers, maybe he could cross into Switzerland. Karlsruhe was a big enough city to get lost in, but it was out of the way, far away from Berlin. So he felt good as the truck rolled down the *Autobahn* that night—and relieved that the driver was not a talkative, questioning man. But slowly the reality was setting in. He had done nothing to help his son, had accomplished little for the OSS, and his chances of survival were improved— but not good.

2 0

Wally's time with Sonbu San had been rejuvenating. The extra food, the rest, had rebuilt his strength, and the positive response he felt toward an "enemy" was a blessing to Wally's emotions—even if it didn't change the way he felt about the guards. Perhaps the war wouldn't end in 1945, but if he could get his strength back and find more peace within himself, he could outlast whatever came—and then return home a better person. After that he would try never to think of the guards again, and the hatred wouldn't have to be a problem. What he didn't want to do was plague himself with guilt about it now. Chuck was right about hatred, of course, but some problems took time to overcome, and now was not the time to deal with this one.

Or at least that's what he told himself. But at another level, he knew he was clinging to the hatred, needing it. It was a kind of pleasure, the one part of himself he could hold onto in the face of such brutal treatment. He could look at the guards and let them see his disdain, his abhorrence of them. Maybe Chuck would say that was the wrong attitude to take, but if it was, it was an attitude that helped Wally stay alive, and he was not ready to give it up.

Wally had received nothing from his parents since the

package they had sent him for Christmas almost a year before, so he had no sense of what was happening to his family, but he believed his father would be satisfied with some of the changes he had made in himself. Maybe he wasn't all he should be, but he would have the rest of his life to grow into that kind of person.

So Wally was feeling quite good, but it was easy to feel better, more confident, when he was receiving an extra meal each day and getting extra sleep. Unfortunately, all that came to an end. After a few weeks Wally and Sonbu San finally removed the buried equipment from the mineshaft. On the following morning Wally was called to another crew. On the way into the mine that day, Wally asked one of the men, a fellow named Hernandez from New Mexico, what to expect from his new supervisor.

"He's got a bad temper," Hernandez told him. "His name is Kiku, but we call him 'the kicker.' When he gets mad, he'll haul off and kick you. And I mean, he really lets you have it."

"What kind of work are we doing, anyway?" Wally asked.

"Timbering. And the guy is good at it. I never worry about the shaft caving in once we get the timbers up. He does things right. But you'd better hop to with whatever he wants. The man has no patience at all."

Wally felt the loss of what he had had with Sonbu. When he reached the shaft where the crew had been working, he quickly ate his day's ration of rice from his *bento* box, and he knew that was the last he would eat again until the end of the workday. He also knew he would be working harder and longer. He hadn't realized until that moment how difficult it was going to be to go back to a regular schedule. The idea that this drudgery could still continue for years was depressing. For almost three years he had told himself not to hope, not to expect things to get easier, but the weeks with Sonbu had softened him just enough to make this return to normal seem almost too much to deal with.

Still, he went to work. The kicker certainly did push hard, but he worked hard himself, something most of the supervisors didn't do. He got up and wedged in the timbers himself, made sure they were placed correctly. His crew carried the timbers and cut them, but he could work wonders with a little handsaw and hatchet in fitting the logs to the shape of the shaft walls. In the course of the day, Kiku began to rely on Wally to work next to him, help support the timber as he worked on it, and then hand up the needed wedges.

Wally didn't mind that because the work required some thought. He had to watch and be ready, and he had to recognize what Kiku was saying. The morning passed rather quickly as a result, and Wally began to think that things were not going to be as bad as he had feared. But then, just before the midday dinner break, Wally apparently misunderstood Kiku's command. Wally handed him a wedge, and Kiku threw it back at him. The wedge missed Wally, but the man had thrown it hard enough that it certainly would have done some damage had it hit him. Wally was astonished. The man continued to scream and point, and Wally apparently got the right wedge the next time, but now he realized what he was up against.

During the break Kiku left. Wally wanted to catch a little nap after the hard morning, but he sat down next to Hernandez and said, "I see what you mean about that guy's temper."

"No, you don't. Not yet," Hernandez told him. "That was nothing." Hernandez was a marine, and a tough guy. He had managed to keep a little more muscle on his body than most of the men. What he was losing was his hair. He wasn't going bald in a pattern, the way men usually do, but all his hair had thinned out and grayed, so that he looked unhealthy, like someone diseased.

"What's wrong with the guy?" Wally asked.

"I think he's under pressure from his bosses. But he's worked me over three different times. I mean really beat me up. And I never gave him a reason. When this war ends, I've promised myself I'm not going home until I find the guy, and I'm going to kick him until he pleads for mercy."

"Naw. You won't do that."

"What makes you think so?"

"Just because you won't want to stay and look for him. If we ever get out of here, we'll just go."

Hernandez had picked up a little rock. He was fiddling with it, rolling it from one hand to the other, but now, suddenly, he gave it a toss into the darkness. It struck a wall and then rattled onto the mine shaft floor. "We're going to live with this the rest of our lives, Thomas. The health problems. The attitudes we've picked up. You can't go through something like this and just walk away from it."

"Maybe. But that's what I'm going to try to do."

"Well, sure. But I need to get some revenge on some of these guys—especially Kiku. Right now, that's the main thing that keeps me getting up in the morning—knowing I'm going to pay him back someday."

"You wouldn't kill him, would you?"

"I don't know. I've thought a lot of times that if I could kill him and get away with it—hide his body or something—I would do it. I don't think I'd ever regret it, either."

"You might, Hernandez. Once we get out of all this, you might not want that on your mind."

"I'd take my chances."

"You know Lewis Honeywell, don't you?"

"Who doesn't?"

"He reported me to the Japs once. He got me beat up, really bad. I think a guy like that is worse than these supervisors."

"Hey, I don't argue that."

"When I see him, he always gives me a grin. Sometimes I think I could kill him right on the spot. But I'm trying to let it go. I don't want to think about things like that."

"Maybe I'll kill him for you," Hernandez said. He lay back and shut his eyes.

Wally did the same, but he didn't go to sleep. He tried to picture the day that Hernandez had spoken of—when the prisoners were liberated. What would happen then? How soon would he get home after that? What would life be like when he could eat what he wanted, do what he wanted? It was nice to think of working with his brothers perhaps, going into business the way they had talked about: all of them home from the war, all stronger for their experiences and closer to each other. What he didn't want to be was bitter, plagued with hate all his life.

He finally drifted off for a few minutes, and then Kiku was back, shouting to the men, getting them going.

The afternoon was hard. Wally wasn't used to pushing himself so long. By late in the day he was exhausted. When a timber had to be pulled down and cut shorter, Kiku's patience was gone. He was shouting every request, and twice he had not only told Wally what to do but then had shoved him in the direction he wanted him to go.

As Kiku got ready to reset the modified timber, he had the men set one end of a log against the wall, on a fairly steep angle, and hold it steady while he stood on it and placed the timber against the ceiling of the shaft. This was something he had obviously done many times before, and he was adept at it. But now the re-cut timber was slightly too short, and Kiku was furious. He shouted a Japanese word Wally didn't understand. Wally looked up, unsure what to do. Kiku gestured with his hatchet, apparently pointing to something on the floor.

Wally looked down and spotted a wedge, and he assumed that's what Kiku wanted. So he grabbed it, stepped close, and then reached up with it. As he did, Kiku suddenly lashed out with his foot and kicked Wally in the face. Wally spun away, grabbed his cheekbone, and knelt to the ground. And then, suddenly, he lost control. He came up in a rage, his mind on fire. He took a step back toward Kiku, and he reached for that boot that had struck him. He fully intended to jerk Kiku off that log and kill him. But in that instant, as he was reaching, his better judgment took over. His hand stopped, halfway to the boot.

As Wally stopped himself, he looked up, and he saw the terror in Kiku's eyes. The man was in a vulnerable spot, balanced as he was. Wally could have given one hard tug on his foot and put him on his back on the floor of the mine, perhaps with his head cracked open.

Wally stood with his hand still suspended in the air. Kiku seemed frozen. The two stared at each other, reading one another's thoughts. Wally knew already that he was in trouble. He thought of going ahead with his intention, since he had revealed it anyway, and the mere gesture might have already put his life in jeopardy. But he told himself he couldn't do that. He didn't know whether he was frightened to do it or unwilling to take a life. Either way, it wasn't something he could do. But his heart was pounding in his ears. He knew he had come within a few inches of killing a man, or at least making the attempt.

Kiku climbed down, and now Wally expected his punishment. If Kiku didn't beat Wally, he would probably go for help—to make certain Wally had no chance to fight back, or that others of the crew wouldn't help him. But instead of approaching Wally, he walked to his tools, which were spread out in front of his tool box. He picked up the wedge he wanted, and he held it up. Then he spoke in Japanese, perhaps instructing Wally, or maybe explaining his anger. There was no telling. But he did seem to be making peace.

It was a strange moment. Kiku gave his little speech, and then he climbed back onto the log and went back to work. Hernandez looked at Wally and nodded, as if to say, "You just got away with one."

The next day Kiku called Wally's number again, and during

the shift he didn't curse as much, didn't kick at all. Wally didn't want to admit it to himself, but he liked the fear he had apparently created in the man. He felt more power than he had known throughout this ordeal, since the day he had first been knocked down and searched by the soldiers who had taken him prisoner, back in the Philippines. He had some of his pride back, and he savored the feeling. If it was sinful pride, it was far too satisfying to let go.

* * *

President Thomas enjoyed the General Authorities who came to his quarterly stake conferences. He loved having them in his home for dinner between the morning and afternoon sessions. He was especially pleased this time, because his friend J. Reuben Clark, first counselor in the First Presidency, was visiting. The two were active in the Republican Party together. President Clark didn't campaign or even make public statements on partisan politics, but he and President Thomas had talked several times that fall about the need to elect Thomas Dewey and remove President Franklin D. Roosevelt, who—in their view—was guiding the country toward socialism. As it turned out, however, Utah had not only voted overwhelmingly for FDR, but the voters had elected *all* Democrats to state offices once again. Herbert Maw had faced a tough test from J. Bracken Lee, but after days of counting and recounting, Maw, a Democrat, had come out on top, and Elbert Thomas, another Democrat, had been re-elected to the Senate. This was really the first time President Clark and President Thomas had had the chance to commiserate with each other. "What we have is a one-party state," President Thomas complained. "And I just don't think anything good ever comes from that."

But Bea Thomas had obviously heard enough. "Now you two, don't get started again," she said. "I voted for Roosevelt— as you well know—and I think I did the right thing. Plenty of the Brethren agree with me too. So if you want to criticize the president, do it on your own time. I didn't cook this dinner so I could sit and listen to a couple of hard losers."

President Clark was a big, meaty man. When he began to laugh, he set the dishes on the table rattling. "I can see how much authority you have around this house, Al," he said. "About like I've always had in mine. Now that Lute's gone, my daughters tell me what to do."

"Well, Luacine was always a little gentler than I am," Bea said. She glanced at President Thomas, and he knew what she was thinking. The two of them had had some serious talks lately, and he had realized some things about himself that he had never suspected before. He had promised to make some adjustments, too, but it wasn't easy for him.

"You only knew one side of her," President Clark said. "When she got her back up, I always knew it. That's when I had to be a *real* diplomat."

President Thomas knew enough about Sister Clark to know there was some truth in that. Luacine had died in August, and President Clark had suffered from the loss. But he wasn't one to say much that sounded like self-pity. He was a man who liked to laugh, and he could be tender at times, but in public, he rarely spoke about his personal life.

"Well . . . I respect my husband's authority," Bea said. "I always do exactly what he tells me—whenever he's right."

Everyone laughed again, but it was LaRue who flashed her pretty smile and said, "President Clark, I think you can see that the women in this house aren't afraid to think for themselves."

President Thomas didn't mind Bea spouting off a little— mostly in fun—but he was not pleased at all that LaRue, at her age, would speak so arrogantly to such an important man. President Thomas had agreed with his wife to be more patient with LaRue, but of all his children, she was turning out to be the greatest test of his self-control.

President Clark chuckled and said, "Well, that's as it should be. There's nothing wrong with women—even little girls—

thinking for themselves." He winked at LaRue. He ate some of his potatoes and cut off a rather large piece of roast, which he chewed up quickly. Then he said, seriously, "Bea, tell me about your family. Have you managed to deal all right with your loss? Al tells me that he does all right with it, but I'm wondering what you're feeling."

"Al always thinks about everything from a religious point of view. He looks at the eternities and tells himself that he's only lost Gene for an instant in time. I hear him say that, and I think, 'Then why does it feel so long?' Some days I just want my boy back, and that's all I can think about."

"What about the young woman? Wasn't Gene engaged?"

"Not exactly. But they had an understanding. So it's been very hard for her. She's started dating a little, but there aren't many boys her age around right now, and she hasn't met any-one she's interested in. She works for us, and I'm not so sure that's the best for her anymore. She probably needs to break away from us and forget about the life she *thought* she was going to have."

Beverly had been sitting quietly all this time, eating little, dabbing a bit at her potatoes. It was easy to forget she was there. But now she said, "I don't want Millie to marry anyone else. I want her to marry Gene—in heaven."

President Thomas saw a softness come into President Clark's face. Beverly was sitting next to him at the dining-room table. He touched her arm with his big hand. "I'm sure you do feel that way," he said. "But be a sister to her, no matter what she decides to do."

"I will," Beverly said, her voice little more than a whisper. She had put on a white apron to protect her pretty green church dress. It looked like a pinafore, and it made her look younger than she actually was.

President Clark continued to pat her arm, but he looked back toward President Thomas, and then at Bea. "Everywhere I turn, I meet young widows, or girls like this Millie—ones who were waiting for a boy who isn't coming back now. It breaks my heart. It's one of the horrors of this war—the loss of all this priesthood, boys who might have stayed home and been good fathers and Church leaders."

"How's your daughter doing?" Bea asked.

"Louise? Well, not bad. She's certainly a blessing to me. I don't know what I would do without her. But I'm certain that mortality looks very long to her right now. She misses Mervyn, of course."

Mervyn Bennion, Louise's young husband, had been killed in the attack on Pearl Harbor. Louise now lived with President Clark in his house on D Street in the Salt Lake "avenues."

"How can anyone ever measure the damage this war has done?" Bea asked.

Everyone knew that President Clark had taken a stand against the American involvement in the war. He had spoken out against it openly and publicly. Even after the Japanese had attacked Pearl Harbor—and his own son-in-law had been lost—he had continued to argue that peaceable negotiations were possible.

"I've read estimates that fifty million people in the world have already died," President Clark said. "But that doesn't start to measure what we've lost."

"But could we have avoided it?"

"I don't know, Bea. I still believe we could have stayed out of it. But my dear friend David McKay disagrees with me, and so does most everyone else. What I keep asking myself is whether the world is ever going to learn to deal with problems in some other way. I've devoted my life to the idea that nations ought to be able to negotiate and not resort to combat."

"How can you negotiate with Hitler?" LaRue asked, and there was a tone of challenge in her voice that once again embarrassed President Thomas.

President Clark was silent for a time. Finally he said, "I'll just say this, LaRue. Hitler has more to answer for than anyone else in this whole mess. But in a war of this scope, no one's hands are completely clean."

"I don't see what—"

"LaRue, that's enough," President Thomas said.

But President Clark gave his head a little shake, the flesh under his chin quivering as he did. "It's all right," he said. He looked across the table at LaRue. "Every nation involved in this war is killing civilians, and doing it on purpose. The Allies are bombing German cities into oblivion, killing vast numbers of people. I'm ashamed of that."

LaRue nodded, seeming impressed by the solemnity of President Clark's words. It was President Thomas who said, "But Hitler was the one who started killing civilians."

"For me, that doesn't change a thing," President Clark said. "Nothing is more brutal than war, but there's also nothing more brutalizing. We've given up some of our national honor by stooping to such behavior. We've lost our sense of morality, and no one even seems to notice. I hear nothing but praise and enthusiasm for what we're doing. I just don't understand it."

Everyone was silent for a few seconds, and President Clark seemed to sense the awkwardness. "I'm sorry," he said. "I'm only speaking for myself. It's not something any of you have to agree with."

President Thomas said, "Let me ask you this, President. I got a long letter from our son Alex this fall. He talked about some of the things you and I both told him before he joined the army. What I hear in his letters is that he's disappointed with himself. He told me he felt he was doing all right as a soldier, but he felt very little of the Spirit of God within him. I haven't known what to tell him. What would you say?"

For a time it seemed as though President Clark hadn't heard. He was a vigorous eater, and he had begun to eat again. He was now going after the slices of roast on his plate, the potatoes and gravy. After a time, however, he put his knife and fork down, and he said, "Al, I think we asked too much of him.

I know I told him to try to keep the Spirit, but I don't blame him if he finds it difficult. Killing—or trying to kill—*ought* to bother him. Alex knows the German people, knows he's shooting at young men he'd rather teach the gospel to, sit next to in church. I'm glad he takes no joy in it."

"But what's the war going to do to him?"

"I don't know. I don't know what we're going to get back when this war is over. These boys will never be the same, that's certain. And I'm afraid that some of them will be lost entirely. I didn't mean to put pressure on him. I only wanted him to keep in touch with the Lord as best he could—and come home with his testimony."

"I'll tell him that when I write him next time."

"Yes. Please. Do that."

President Clark went back to eating, and he accepted seconds when they were passed to him. But then, for no apparent reason, he began to laugh. "Bea," he said, "I'm going to mention politics again—just this once." He waited until Sister Thomas smiled and nodded. "I want Al to run for public office— Congress, I'd say. He and I don't agree about this war—not entirely—but we do agree about most everything else. He's highly thought of in this valley. Plus, he's got some money now, which helps. I want to see the day when he's not building weapons. Another tragedy of this war is that we've taken on too many defense plants—and now our state economy is going to rely too much on waging more wars."

"I think I'd rather see my sons become the politicians," President Thomas said. "At least in any big way. The state legislature is about as far as I would ever think of going."

"You always forget your daughters," LaRue asked. "I told you I might want to run for office. Except I'm a Democrat, like Mom. And I think Alex is, too."

"I'm not a Democrat," Bea said. "I'm not anything."

President Clark smiled. He had tucked his napkin into his shirt collar. He pulled it out and wiped his mouth. "I don't care whether it's Al or his sons—*or daughters.*" He grinned. "I'm just saying that good people have to stand up for what's right. We've lost our moral bearings during this war, and we need to get them back."

"Can government do that?" Sister Thomas asked.

"Now, Bea, that's a profound question." He shook a finger at her, playfully. "Government is certainly trying to do too much already, but I'm saying we need leaders who stand for something. And I'll tell you one more thing—now that I've turned this dinner table into a pulpit—we Church members have got to get back on track. The latest statistics show that twelve percent—*twelve percent*—of the elders in the Church are attending priesthood meeting. The Aaronic Priesthood attendance is only thirty-two percent."

"Isn't some of that caused by boys being shipped off to where they can't go to church?" President Thomas asked.

"Of course. But you see what I'm saying. Bea asked how we can measure the damage of the war, and I'm saying we've lost our direction. We're devoting ourselves to the wrong things. And we've let far too much corruption into our lives. We need to be out preaching the gospel again, not devoting our sacrament meetings to the glories of war—which is exactly what I hear these days."

"I hate to see all these non-Mormon soldiers coming in here, and so many defense workers moving in," President Thomas said. "I think that's where a lot of the trouble comes from." He glanced at LaRue.

"Well, sure. But we like to place too much of the blame on that. We're doing just fine, growing our own corruption."

President Thomas glanced at the big clock in the corner of the room. "President, we're running out of time," he said. "And we do need to eat just a small piece of sponge cake—since Bea found enough sugar to make it for us—and some of her canned peaches."

"Now that's the sort of corruption I can accept," President

Clark said, and he laughed in a huge burst, setting the dishes clattering again.

Bea asked Beverly to help her, and the two headed for the kitchen. President Clark looked at President Thomas. "I do have one other thing I wanted to ask you," he said.

"Sure."

"A young Japanese fellow—Brother Nakashima—talked to me this morning, before the meeting started. He was wondering what I could do for his brother. He said you've tried to help, and you've never gotten anywhere."

"That's exactly right. Ike—his brother—is certainly no spy. He simply made the mistake of visiting his family in California at the wrong time. But I've never been able to get anyone to budge an inch. I hear that some of the interned Japanese are starting to be released. But so far, Ike and his wife are still being held."

"Why didn't he go into the service? That's one way to get out of those camps."

"He volunteered, but they wouldn't take him. He broke his leg when he was a kid, and it never healed just right. One leg is a little shorter than the other."

"You mean to say he was willing to serve in the military, and they keep him stuck in that camp anyway?"

"Yes. And he's got a little daughter now, too. He got married since he was put in the camp."

"Well, that's a shame. There's no need for that. I'll see what I can do about it."

Sister Thomas and Beverly soon returned with the cake and fruit. President Clark and President Thomas ate quickly, and then they got up to leave. President Clark thanked Bea and then turned back toward the table, where LaRue and Beverly were still sitting. "Girls," he said, "I hope I haven't said the wrong things here today." He stepped back toward the table, and he put his hand on LaRue's shoulder. "I love America. I truly do. And I love these young men who are fighting for our country. I know how you must feel about your brothers: one lost, one in a prison camp, and one in battle. That's a terrible price for your family to pay." He hesitated and cleared his throat. "All I want you to know is that war is the greatest evil Satan has invented to corrupt our hearts and souls. We should honor our soldiers, but we should never honor war."

President Thomas felt the words deeply, and he wondered about himself. He had made a great deal of money making parts for weapons, and he had always claimed his patriotism as his ultimate motive for what he was doing. But he had also been a little uneasy about his own justification at times. Now he wondered what he could do to be certain that his accumulating wealth accomplished something good.

2 1

The navy hospital at Pearl Harbor had never been busier, the wards filled and overfilled; even hallways were congested with hospital beds. With intense fighting going on in the Philippines, and the Pacific war being fought on so many other fronts, every hospital ship and military hospital was packed. The Japanese were resorting to desperate means now, sending waves of kamikaze pilots to commit suicide by crashing their airplanes into the decks of American ships. Such methods weren't turning the tide. Tokyo and other major Japanese cities were being destroyed in American bombing raids, and General Douglas MacArthur had, according to his promise, returned to the Philippines. But still, the kamikazes were killing or injuring thousands of sailors.

Bobbi hated the human suffering she saw at the hospital, but she preferred being busy. She worked long shifts and took few days off even though she often experienced the sensation that she didn't exist in the present, that her body was going about its work while her mind and heart were not engaged. So much time had passed now, and Bobbi had accepted the truth: Richard couldn't possibly be alive. She wasn't going to cry the rest of her life; she would do what she had to do, and maybe someday she would be happy again. But she wasn't dealing with this death the way she had tried to deal with her brother's. She was only surviving it.

She could think of nothing to say to herself that helped, nor did she really want to. The occasional aphorisms and bits of advice she got from others bothered her more than helped her, and for the present, her family heritage gave her more pain than comfort. Mormons, she finally understood, didn't have patience with mourning. They got up and got going, like her great-great—and just-a-little-too-great—grandfather, who had worked on his blessed bridge after only one day of grief. She had once admired the man for that; now she wondered whether he had a soul.

Everyone at church knew about "her loss," and one thing about Hawaiian members, they said what was on their minds. So everyone had to tell her how sorry they were about Brother Hammond. And then they would tell her how strong and brave she was to continue her work at the hospital. At times she wanted to shout, "I'm not brave and strong; I'm angry." But even that wasn't true. She didn't feel angry; she felt dead. She knew that a tiny corner of her was still trying to believe that Richard had survived somehow, but that was the very cause of her numbness. She had to fight off hope because that was the one impulse that enlivened her, and when she came alive, the hurt was so much worse.

Faith had the same effect on her. When she asked the Lord to help her, she had to imagine herself feeling good again, strong again, full of spirit. And that meant passing through all the pain it would take to get there. It required crying and regretting and missing; it required a whole person. And so she said her prayers almost by rote, or at least by routine, and she said nothing that mattered very much to her. And she didn't cry.

Lately she had been testing her mind with another idea. Maybe she and Richard had been wrong for each other anyway. Maybe it "wasn't meant to be." Maybe she should think about David Stinson, after all. But none of that worked. She was still in love with Richard, and she knew it. She had no idea why her feelings ran so deep, given the short time she had shared with him, but those were her feelings, and having him "gone"—the word people used now—didn't change the commitment she felt.

One evening Bobbi was alone in her room. Afton had been out with Sam, but she came home earlier than usual. Bobbi saw immediately, when Afton walked into the room, that she had been crying. Whatever it was this time, Bobbi didn't want to hear it. But Afton never suffered alone; she had to disclose every thought or worry that came into her head. Bobbi was weary of Afton and her little tragedies, which she had to analyze—out loud—so constantly.

Tonight, however, Afton threw herself onto her bed and began to cry, audibly. Bobbi let her do it. She wasn't going to ask. It took a while for Afton to realize she was getting no response, but she finally rolled over on her side, and with her dark hair falling across her face, she said, "Bobbi, I finally did it. I broke up with Sam."

"That's good," Bobbi said. "You've been telling me for weeks now that's what you had to do." She picked up a towel and walked to her door. "I'm going to take a shower," she said, and she stepped out.

As the door shut, Bobbi heard Afton mumble something, probably about Bobbi's lack of compassion. But Bobbi had been through these breakups before. They never lasted long.

The truth was, Bobbi had already showered after work, but she broke all the rules about conserving water and stood in the shower for a long time. And when she returned, she pulled her robe tight around her and used the towel over her hair to cover much of her face. She wanted to hide from Afton, just get into bed somehow without saying a word, and go to sleep. More than anything, she loved sleep.

But Afton was ready for her. She had stopped crying, and

she was sitting up. She seemed to have her ideas organized now. "Bobbi, I don't know what else I could do," she began. "Golly, he just forced me to make a decision. Before, it was always, 'Don't stop seeing me. Anything but that.' But now he wants to know, 'Once and for all,' as he says, whether I'm going to marry him or not."

"That's what we all want to know."

"What?"

"I don't blame him, Afton. You've played him along for months. You told me from the beginning you would never marry him. Why didn't you just break it off a long time ago and forget it?"

"That's what I just said, Bobbi. He always begged me to keep seeing him."

"Well, enough is enough. Tell him you have royal blue Arizonan blood, and you won't mix with the inferior brown stuff running through his veins."

"Bobbi!"

"Isn't that it? You're too good for him? Isn't that what you've been telling me since the first day you met him?"

"No. I've never said that. I've said my parents don't think people of different races should marry each other."

"So which race do they consider better? Yours or his?"

"Neither. You know that," Afton said. She looked away from Bobbi's gaze.

Bobbi stepped closer and leaned over Afton. She could hardly believe how much anger she was feeling. "Honest, Afton?" Bobbi swung her arm dramatically, making a cross over her chest. "Cross your heart and hope to die?"

"Bobbi, I don't feel that way. I—"

"Afton, I don't want to hear any more about this. You just said it's over. I assume—even though you've said that a few times before—that you mean it. I've certainly heard all your reasons. So cry softly and I'll try to get some sleep."

Bobbi rubbed her towel through her hair. She had had it

cut shorter than ever lately, and she wasn't going to fuss with it now. She discarded the towel and marched to her chest of drawers, where she grabbed her nightgown. Then she took off her robe and threw it onto a chair. She slipped on the night-gown as quickly as she could, ran a brush through her hair a few times, and got into bed. Then she reached and turned her lamp off, leaving her side of the room dark. She turned away from Afton, who was still sitting on her bed.

"I don't know you anymore, Bobbi," Afton said.

Bobbi didn't let the words in. She knew, of course, what Afton was saying, but she wasn't going to respond, not even internally.

"I know you're going through a terrible time," Afton continued, "and I'm sorry. But I never thought you'd change like this."

Clearly, Afton wanted Bobbi to ask about that. But Bobbi wasn't going to take the bait. She wasn't a high school girl any-more, just dying to know what Afton *really* thought of her—even if Afton was destined never to grow up.

"I don't judge you at all. I don't know how I would behave if I were in your shoes," Afton said softly. "I guess I'd probably go all to pieces. But I never thought you would turn bitter. Gee, you've always been so sweet and kind and understanding."

"Afton, that's enough. Just stop now before you find out what bitter really sounds like."

"I'm sorry. I didn't mean it that way, Bobbi." And she did the last thing Bobbi wanted. She came to Bobbi's bed, sat down by her, and put her hand on Bobbi's shoulder. "I know you can't help what you're feeling right now, but Bobbi, I'm so worried about you. I don't want you to let this ruin your whole life."

Bobby rolled over quickly. "My life *is* ruined," she said. "So spare me your pity."

"No, it's not, Bobbi. You just have to—"

"I don't have to do anything." Bobbi sat up and grabbed hold of Afton's arm. She stared directly into her eyes. "But I'll tell you this: If I'd found someone like Sam—a decent, good man who loved me the way he loves you—I wouldn't be telling him, 'Daddy thinks your skin is too brown.' I'd be telling my daddy to straighten out *his* thinking."

"Bobbi, I want to do that, but I can't."

"Why not? Because you're sixteen years old—and always will be?"

Afton looked shocked. But she didn't respond to the accusation. "Bobbi, I can't lose my family," she said.

"Hey, buck up. You just told me that's what I should do. I've lost the man who was going to be my husband and give me children. But that's just the breaks. Life goes on. Right?" She lay down again and turned her back to Afton.

"No, Bobbi. I wasn't saying that. I just love you, and I don't want to see you hurt so much. I'd do anything to help you, if I just knew how."

Bobbi didn't want to give in. She was searching for something else to say, something biting and defensive, but then Afton lay down next to her and put her arm around her waist. "I love you, Bobbi," she whispered. "I'm so sorry this happened to you."

Something in Afton's honesty—in the use of the past tense—seemed to force the last breath of hope from Bobbi's chest, and she thought, "He really is dead." Until now it was something she had actually tried to believe—as an antidote to hope and emotion. But it was suddenly a reality, and everything broke loose inside Bobbi. She began to sob, and after a time she took hold of Afton's hand. "I'm sorry," she tried to say. "I'm sorry."

"Bobbi, I know. You're just hurting so bad you can't stand it."

"Why, Afton? Why couldn't I keep him? What would it have hurt for God to step in—just this one time—and let me have him for a while?"

"I don't know, Bobbi. I don't understand—"

"Why did anyone have to think up all this death and stupidity in the first place?"

"Oh, Bobbi, I don't know."

Bobbi had tried to fight off all these questions so often in the past few weeks, but they always came back. Now she let them take over, fill up her head: Where was God? Why didn't he care?

Afton, for once, had the good sense not to say anything. And she cried too.

"I'm sorry, Afton. Your situation is hard too. I had no right to say it wasn't."

"But I think you're right, Bobbi. If I love Sam, I need to stand up to my family, not to Sam. Maybe I can do it."

"Afton, I don't know what's right for you. I'm just so angry that you have someone to love—and I don't. I wanted Richard back so bad. I only had those few days with him."

"It's so unfair, Bobbi."

But Afton's words didn't sound right. Bobbi wanted to grab onto them, wanted to curse the universe, but she heard the self-pity in the accusation, and she hated her own weakness. In a world so full of pain, why should she expect to be spared?

Bobbi stopped crying. She suddenly saw herself—recognized her own self-centeredness and visualized the way she had been treating people. She thought of Millie, who had lost Gene, and now she was making the best of things. Why should Bobbi think she was different from millions of other women in the world who were having to do the same thing? Everyone was sharing in this misery, and Bobbi had been walking around angry, as though she were the only one. She was embarrassed and, gradually, ashamed. "I need to pray," she whispered to Afton.

So Afton left her alone, walked down the hall, and took her own shower. And Bobbi poured out her feelings to the Lord. "I'm sorry for my anger," she told him. "I accept things as they are. But Father, please comfort me. Please let me feel thy love."

And then the comfort came, the love. It was like warm water in a bath, filling in around her, touching her, soothing her skin, reaching to her center. She didn't know why things happened the way they did, but she trusted that God did, and she finally felt able to accept.

She cried for a long time, and that actually felt good, the life coming back into her. However sad she was, at least she felt a sense of self returning, not the distance, the numbness, she had been living with.

Bobbi was not surprised when some of her discouragement, even some of her anger, returned again the next day. She knew enough about herself to understand that just because she felt the Lord's Spirit one day, that didn't mean she would never have to work to feel it again. And she knew that to get an insight was not to hold it every second, forever. But she had something to go back to now. She had found some things she could say to herself that helped. And what she kept saying was, "I'll be all right. I do know God loves me. I'll learn the things there are to learn from this experience." And she kept reminding herself: "So many others are doing this. I can do it too."

One of the things Bobbi did was start to mend some fences. She went to see Ishi, whom she had avoided lately. Ishi was always worried about Daniel, but he was still all right, and Bobbi had been resentful of that—whether she admitted it or not.

And so Bobbi told her what she had been feeling, acknowledged her jealousy.

Ishi nodded gently, spoke quietly. "Oh, Bobbi," she said, "I've done the same thing. So many of my friends have husbands who didn't go to war. I see them with their men, their children, all having a nice time, and I wonder why I have to raise my children alone while my husband is off on the other side of the world."

"That must be so hard, Ishi."

"But here's what I know about life, Bobbi. I'm not an old

lady, but I've seen enough already to know that sooner or later everyone has to go through something—some kind of pain or suffering. And I think that's how it's supposed to be. It doesn't even out exactly, but we all have to pass through our own tests, and if we make it through, we're better for it."

"*If* we make it through."

"Well, yes. Some give up. Some think only of themselves and harbor their resentment."

"I'm going to try to do better now."

"You've done fine. The only thing you've done wrong is not come to see me enough. The kids and I miss you."

So Bobbi stayed for dinner, and she played with the children. She enjoyed that, but when she left and boarded her bus back to Pearl Harbor, she searched inside herself for happiness and found very little evidence of it. She couldn't help but think she might never have her own children now, and she had to struggle to keep that thought from driving her back toward self-pity.

Two days later Bobbi actually got a day off. For a couple of weeks she had worked long hours every single day. But finally, on a Monday, her scheduled day off didn't fall through, and she was able to get some extra sleep and take the bus into Honolulu. She had some Christmas shopping she wanted to do, and then she needed to send presents to her family. She was very late now, and she knew the package wouldn't make it in time, but she finally had the heart to bother with something of that sort.

Bobbi had told her parents about Richard's ship being sunk, but she hadn't gone into much detail about her own attachment to him. She had tried not to sound distraught, but her mother had read between the lines enough to send a sensitive letter, which at the time, Bobbi had not really appreciated the way she knew she should have. Now she felt she needed to get a decent letter in the mail. So she bought some new stationery, and on the bus she started her letter. She tried to be more open about her feelings, which she knew was the right thing to do, but it also seemed to open the wound again. By the time she got back to her room, she was having a hard time. Still, she went to her desk immediately. She knew she had to finish the letter before she lost her will. But as she sat down, she noticed something on the floor, and she looked back to see what it was.

Then she realized it was a telegram. Someone had pushed it under her door. She hurried over and picked it up, and she saw that it was addressed to her, not Afton.

Bobbi's breath stopped. The universe seemed to hesitate, hold. Possibilities were firing through her consciousness. She tried desperately to think of something positive that someone would let her know in a telegram. But that was not what telegrams meant these days. Alex could be dead. Or Wally.

Wally could have been freed, in the Philippines. That was possible.

But behind all this was the likely truth: it was word about Richard. His parents had promised to let her know. In spite of everything she had told herself today, she still felt the terror of hearing this final word.

She was holding the telegram, still unopened, when she knelt down by her bed. "Father, I don't want to go back to where I was," she said. "Please give me the power to deal with this. Hold me in thine arms while I open this letter."

Again she felt the warmth, the comfort, the confidence that she could accept. She shut her eyes for a moment and felt her thanks without using words. Her hands trembled as she opened the envelope. And her eyes filled with tears before she ever began to read.

But what she read stunned her: "Richard is safe. In a hospital in Guam. He will write you soon."

It was impossible. Bobbi's mind could not accept this. She had thought of everything else. She plunged her face into her bedspread and sobbed. And then she read it again and continued to cry. "Thank you. I'm sorry. I'm sorry," she kept repeating. "Oh, thank you."

When Bobbi could finally think, she had a hundred questions. Why Guam? Why hadn't he been able to let her know sooner? Why was he in a hospital? How badly was he hurt? But all that didn't matter. He was alive.

Bobbi held this joy to herself for a time while she sat and cried, enjoyed the wholeness, her gratitude. Then she started over on her letter and told her parents what she had just learned. Afterward, she walked to the hospital and found Afton.

Afton squealed with delight, sounding fully like a sixteen-year-old again, but she was genuinely happy for Bobbi, and Bobbi did appreciate that. But Bobbi didn't feel like squealing; she was feeling too deeply blessed. And she didn't want to gloat over her good news in a place where so many people had so much to deal with.

"Maybe one good thing came out of this," Afton said. "What you said that night made me look at everything a little different. I'm thinking really serious that I might marry Sam."

Bobbi smiled. "Seriously that you *might?*"

"Well, that's a big change for me. Before, I always said I knew I couldn't."

Bobbi wasn't in any mood to give advice, but the advice was in her heart. When you find someone who loves you that much, keep him. That's what she was going to do. She wished more than anything that she could talk to Richard, go to him and help him, nurse him through whatever pain he had. And then she wished there were a way to get out of the navy so she could take him home to Utah, where they could start building something together. She knew Richard enough to love him, but she wanted to discover all there was to understand about him. He had been dead, and now he was alive. She knew she had received a gift, and she wasn't going to take it lightly.

2 2

Peter was lying on the ground, pressed against a rock wall. His body was convulsing as he tried to get enough air into his lungs to bring himself back to life. He had made a long, desperate run, pushed himself harder than he ever had before, and he expected any moment to be caught by the mortar fire that was crashing in the field around him.

This was a place to catch his breath, but it was not a safe place. There *were* no safe places. For more than a month now, he had been frightened every waking moment. He had slept only when he was so exhausted he could do nothing else—and then only in short snatches.

He was in eastern Poland, but for an entire month he had been in retreat with his company—or when the chaos was too great, in hordes or in bunches or even by himself. Time and again he and his fellow soldiers had been stopped, organized, and commanded to hold the line at all costs, never to give another inch of ground, and each time masses of howling Russian troops, with their incessant, rattling tanks, had spilled toward his Grossdeutschland Division, and the Germans had fallen back, losing lives by the thousands as they ran. The wounded and mutilated tried to escape by fleeing with civilian refugees, who filled every road in Poland, or they caught trains when they could, but there was little help for these casualties and almost no medicine. Peter had seen men lying on the ground, their wounds gangrenous, their stench disgusting. One man had pled with him, "Can't you do something for me? Kill me, if nothing else."

Peter had kept going. He didn't want to kill the man, and there was nothing else he could do except wait there with him as the Russians pushed forward, and that only meant that both of them would die.

Peter hardly knew any longer who he had been before he had arrived on the Russian front. He knew that he had vowed not to kill anyone. But he had killed almost immediately. In his first battle, he had crouched in a trench, terrified by the noise of the attacking army, their artillery fire, their tanks. He had no intention to fire his rifle. But the Russians, screaming and shouting, had charged. They ran straight at Peter's trench, and when *Hauptmann* Albrecht had shouted *"Feurer frei!"* Peter had waited. But a huge man had bolted toward him, his face full of fury, his yellow teeth bared, and Peter had pulled the trigger. The man had fallen in front of him and then had lain on the ground groaning. For several minutes—the worst minutes of Peter's life—he had listened to the air sucking through the hole in the man's chest, heard the blood gurgle in his throat, and finally heard him choke on the blood and die.

Soon after, Peter had jumped from the trench and run, had caught up with his friend Hans, who had abandoned the trench before him, both of them defying the order to hold their position and not retreat. Machine-gun fire had sprayed around them, even taken a chunk from the heel of Peter's boot, but they had made it to a village and to a barn, where they had found the remnant of their company. Twenty men of the company had died that day, *Hauptmann* Albrecht told them. What he hadn't done was reprimand them for running. He had fallen back himself, even though he had told them before that they must hold the line or be shot for treason.

Peter and Hans had lost Helmut in the confusion, but they found him in the barn. They were happy for the reunion, though Helmut looked dazed. "They killed Karl," he said. "We were running. A mortar, or something, hit right next to him. It tore him to pieces. His insides were smeared all over the ground."

Hans sat down on the ground, leaned against the wall of the barn, and cried. There were veterans in the barn, older men who had seen it all, men who had been through four or five, even six years, of battle. They didn't say a word to Hans, didn't begrudge him his emotion. Instead, they sat and stared, their eyes full of a weariness that ran too deep to call exhaustion. Peter had never seen such haunted faces. The men complained about the food, the cold, the lack of equipment and ammunition, but there was no passion in anything they said. One man, maybe forty-five or so, told Peter, "I don't care whether I die. I can't remember why I ever wanted to live." But still, he had run when he had faced death.

Peter found himself a spot in the barn away from Hans and Helmut, who needed to talk about the friend they had lost. Peter had something else on his mind. Now that he had time, and quiet, he was tormented by the groans of the Russian he had killed. He didn't know what to tell himself. In another second, the Russian would have killed Peter. Wasn't that reason enough to fire his rifle? But was he a murderer now? Back in Basel—what seemed years ago now—he had pushed a Gestapo agent off a train platform, hurt him badly. But Peter had lived with that by telling himself that he was defending his family, fighting the Nazis. What was he doing now, fighting *for* the Nazis?

And yet, horrified as he was by what he had done, what he had seen and heard, he didn't feel the regret he thought he should. He couldn't bring himself to play the hypocrite and ask God for forgiveness.

After a time, Hans came to him, sat down next to him. "I

killed two of those stinking Bolsheviks today," he said. "Tomorrow I hope to kill a hundred. They're going to pay for what they did to Karl."

Peter didn't say anything. He could hear the truth in Hans's voice. Hans was still a freckle-faced child from a Black Forest village, and he had shown it by running for his life, by crying for his friend. Now he was trying to make up for his disgrace.

"They're not human, those Russians," Hans said. "If they overrun us, they won't give us any mercy. They shoot their prisoners and then mutilate their bodies. If they're hungry enough, they'll even eat the men they kill."

Peter didn't know whether he believed any of that. It was what the veteran soldiers claimed. On his march to the front, Peter had seen German soldiers drive civilians out of their homes into the cold—just to have a place to sleep for the night. He had seen them eat everything in the house and let the family starve—or die from the cold. Sometimes, too, they had shot civilians for no apparent reason. "Filthy partisans," they would say, and offer that alone as their justification.

But Peter did understand what Hans was saying and feeling. Peter did hate the Russians. He had been at the front forty-eight hours, and already he felt the deepest hatred of his life. He couldn't explain it, but he had felt it as the Russians had fired the first volleys of artillery shells into the German trenches, and then as they had come over the horizon, early in the morning, their tanks clanking and their riflemen hunched and charging forward. These men wanted to kill Peter, and if they managed to do it, they wouldn't stop to ask themselves whether they were sorry.

Worse than that, they *were* going to kill him sooner or later. That was already clear to Peter. And he hated them for it now. He didn't care whether that made sense; he only knew what he felt.

That night *Leutnant* Schuldt had come to the barn. He told the men that the company would fall back a little in the morning, but then they would draw the line at a river—some river the name of which Peter could no longer remember. They would make their stand and hold—or they would die. Once the Russians were stopped, reinforcements would arrive, and then, probably in the spring, the Germans would rise up and push the Russians back. "These animals fight like barbarians, but they don't have our will. I've seen it before. Once we break through, they'll run like scared rabbits all the way back to Moscow. We will never be forgotten for what we do in the next few days. Our children and grandchildren will sing our praises forever."

So the men had dug in and prepared to make their stand. Then the tanks had come again, the artillery, the throng of infantrymen, the smoke and dust and the smell of explosives in the air, and once again the lines had broken and the Germans were the ones running like rabbits. Peter had tripped as he ran, and he had felt a bullet buzz over his head. The fall had saved his life. That night he tried to thank God, but he didn't feel it. He had fired his weapon plenty that day. And maybe he had killed again. He didn't know. He only knew he would fire the next time the Russians came after him.

Eventually the Grossdeutschland Division had been reassembled at Lodz, in central Poland. Half of Peter's company was wearing the heavy Russian jackets they had pulled off dead soldiers, and all of them were suffering from fatigue and undernourishment. But for two days they rested, and they were issued somewhat better uniforms. Replacement troops joined them there, too, and Peter was astounded by what he saw. He had thought the men who had entered the army with him were surprisingly old or young, but some of these soldiers were men in their sixties, with wrinkled faces and bent backs. The rest were little boys. The oldest of them were sixteen, and some who said they were fourteen looked younger. They looked frightened, like any child away from home the first time, but when they had the chance, they would laugh and roughhouse like kids on a camping trip.

In Lodz the men of the division heard great speeches. The Russians must never reach their homeland, never enter Berlin. If that were to happen, the division would be "covered with shame." Here a "definitive rampart" would be established. The progress of the Bolsheviks would be stopped entirely. It was what the veterans had heard before, many times, they said.

At the end of the last speech, delivered by the camp commander, a major, the infantry soldiers did not react. They waited, silent, to be dismissed. Finally, an officer shouted, "Heil Hitler!" and the men did repeat the cry. But there was no spirit in it. And after, Peter heard the soldiers mumbling about winter. For these men, most of whom had lived through Russian winters before, the cold was as much an enemy as were the Russians. They did almost anything, while in Lodz, to secure enough warm clothes, and they told the newcomers to do the same. They talked in almost reverent tones about the viciousness of the winter, the misery of surviving out in the open.

The experienced soldiers expected the worst. One, a gruff old trooper named Kitzmann, had returned from a hospital in Frankfurt am Oder, in eastern Germany. In the place where he'd once had an ear was only a patch of delicate pink skin now, but Peter had already seen so many men with gouges and scars that he hardly paid attention. The men wanted to know from Kitzmann what was happening at home. He sat on his bunk and stared at the men. "Frankfurt is gray," he said, "like the color of dead trees. There are a few walls sticking up, all black and burned. Nothing else. The people live in trenches, like infantry."

One of the men in the company was from Frankfurt am Oder, a man named Heidinger. He pushed his way forward and demanded of Kitzmann that he tell the truth, not exaggerate. It was the same reaction Peter and his friends had received when they had described the other Frankfurt—Frankfurt am Main—

and the other big cities of Germany. The veterans didn't want to believe that they had fought for years to save their country, and meanwhile it had been destroyed behind their backs. Heidinger's wife and children were in Frankfurt am Oder. Was he fighting now for nothing at all, perhaps no family to go back to?

Peter heard one man whisper to another, "The war is lost. What are we doing here?"

"We still have to stop the Russians," the other soldier said. "They'll destroy all of Germany, scorch the earth."

"What earth? It sounds like everything is gone already."

The next morning the men had mounted trucks and made a cold trip north to a region near the Gulf of Riga on the Baltic Sea in Latvia. But all the speeches came to nothing. Almost immediately the troops were thrown back again, and every day seemed to bring further retreats.

After a few days Peter no longer knew where he was, Latvia or Lithuania. Today, once more, he had made a wild dash to save his life, and now he was catching his breath behind this wall, and the Russians were pushing forward again.

But they didn't come immediately. They were resolute these days, in no great hurry. And so the men in Peter's company, or what was left of it, gradually assembled. Someone drove a sidecar to headquarters and brought back a load of withered and mostly rotten potatoes, with a few cold sausages. Peter ate everything he could get his hands on, caring little about the taste. It was terrible food, but more and better than anything he had had in days. He was about to lie back and rest when someone shouted, "Ivan!"

Peter had hoped it would be morning before the Russians attacked, but they were apparently coming now, and he didn't think he could run again. He hurried to the wall as the men of his company spread out. A sentry had obviously spotted foot soldiers, but no one knew how large a unit might be out there.

Ten minutes passed, and finally the *Leutnant* told some

men—six of them—to go over the wall and make contact. Peter was relieved that he wasn't one of those chosen to go. He had already been on many patrols of that kind, and there was nothing more frightening.

But he also hated this wait. When the bullets and the artillery started, the noise and chaos were unnerving, but the time just before, when the madness was about to break loose, was the worst. Each time Peter knew without saying it to himself that he might finally be among the unlucky ones. After every battle there were men down, often screaming with pain, some of them dying slowly and miserably. And every time, Peter wondered why others had been hit and he had survived. But then he would wonder about the next battle. When would his turn finally come?

Now he peered over the wall, felt his breath coming in brief gasps, listened, watched. In the beginning his greatest fear had always been that he would die without ever again seeing his parents and Anna. Now, however, he feared that he *would* see them, that they would find out what he had become. He was sure they wouldn't want him back now that he had changed.

At least reality was simple for Peter. Behind him was another nameless village, and in front of him, in a valley filled with farms and groves of trees, were soldiers in hiding, waiting to make another push. He was a German *Landser*—an infantry-man—and the men who cared about him were at his side. The men who hated him were beyond the wall. That was how life was now.

Before long the patrol returned. Peter heard the men report to *Leutnant* Schuldt. "They're everywhere down there," a young *Gefreiter*—a private—said. "It must be a whole regiment."

Peter knew that might be an exaggeration, but it probably did mean they were facing a thousand, maybe two or three thousand Russian soldiers. The Germans couldn't have more than three hundred men left—the remains of several companies. They were scattered along the perimeter of this village, with no chance to stop such a force.

In a few minutes *Hauptmann* Albrecht, crouched and running, approached the men at the wall. "We're not giving an inch," he said. "We've got a good position, and we're holding right here. Let's show the Reds that we're not going to back away this time."

It was insane. Even the *Hauptmann* didn't sound convinced. He was merely saying what he had been told to say. When he moved on down the line, Hans slipped over next to Peter. "We have no chance," he said. It was the first time Hans had admitted that anything his leaders did or said was questionable. "It's not supposed to be like this."

"What's not?"

"In Hitler Youth they told us the Russians were stupid as cows. We could slaughter them at will."

"They're bulls, not cows," Peter said. And what he knew was that he had acquired a certain kind of respect for the Russians. Their incessant charges were brave beyond belief.

"They may be bulls, but they're stupid," Hans said. "That's why they charge into us the way they do. Sooner or later we'll kill so many of them, they'll have to stop."

"No they won't. We're the ones who can't hold out."

"It's still a great thing to die for the Fatherland," Hans said.

Peter said nothing. For some reason the Russians were holding off again, as they seemed to do when a battle was near.

He and Hans stood next to each other, their rifles ready, and then, finally, they sat down and leaned against the wall. They didn't talk.

When dusk came, Peter concluded that the Russians had decided to wait until morning. He was relieved, and he was tired enough to sleep—in spite of everything. But the night was cold, and even though Peter rolled up in a blanket and huddled close to Hans and Helmut, he slept only in short spells.

Toward morning a steady rain began to fall, but Peter didn't dare put on his rain poncho, which would make movement more cumbersome should he need to run. The rain gradually soaked into his coat, adding weight, intensifying his shaking. His legs ached now, his whole body, from the running the day before and from some illness he had been fighting off for days.

And then, as the clouds became slightly illuminated, Peter heard the first rumblings in the valley, and he knew the terror was about to begin again. He felt the movement in the ground first—the vibrations the tanks and armored halftracks made—and then he heard the clanking, the reverberation, the pounding of the engines.

Peter knew that his company had no full-blown anti-tank weapons. It had small *Panzerfausts*, like the American bazookas, that could, at short range, destroy a tank, but there were only three of these, each with six shells. Even with perfect results, only eighteen tanks could be knocked out. And there were certainly many more than eighteen coming.

And then the word spread through the men. They were withdrawing after all, in spite of what the *Hauptmann* had said the night before. *Leutnant* Schuldt crept up to Peter. "We're pulling our artillery back first," he told him. "You six men right here along the wall, stay for now. Hold off the charge as long as you can. Two other patrols will do the same. You're all riflemen, so I'm putting you in charge. Keep the men here as long as possible. Do everything you can to slow the attack. If you knock out a few tanks, the Russians will stop. Once they do, join the rest of us, as fast as you can make it."

Hans and Helmut were in Peter's patrol. The other three were young too, all boys who had come to the front with Peter. One of them, a boy named Rietenbach, was assigned to carry the *Panzerfaust*.

As the main body of the company pulled back, Peter stared into the dark valley. He thought at times that he heard infantry, close, and he felt the hair on his neck stand up. But he was resigned this time. What he knew was that he had been sacrificed, that he and his friends had been left behind to die.

When he heard a shout, he looked to his left, and in the dim light saw a *Feldwebel*—a sergeant—named Wedemeier. He was waving for the patrol to move into a little depression a hundred meters or so to the east. There was a farm there, and a few outbuildings. Peter saw no advantage to moving over, but he was happy to let someone else make the decision. "Follow me," he told his men, and they ran for the new position.

He ran hard and then jumped over some downed trees. Behind these he began to dig frantically with his entrenching tool. "Dig in. Fast!" he yelled, and almost at the same time, the artillery opened up. The fire was directed at the position the boys had just left behind. Huge explosions sent the earth flying, shattered the wall, crushed the houses in the village just beyond. It was a hellish sight and sound, the air seeming to shudder around them even at this distance. And Peter knew that if he and his men had stayed three minutes longer, they would have been in the middle of it. He thought of God, but he knew better than to assume too much. The threat was only a few paces away now.

Peter and Hans were still together, digging a hole for the two of them. They dug wildly, with hands and shovels, and all the while the big guns never stopped. Peter glanced to see that the village was almost gone, leveled in only a few minutes, and now debris and dust were filling the half-light of dawn. He realized at the same time that the rain had turned to snow, that gentle flakes were drifting down into the chaos.

Another few minutes passed, and the light continued to increase. And then, as though by a trick of magic, ten tanks suddenly appeared, pushing up a road toward the village. One of the three patrols was guarding that road, and the tanks were coming straight at those six men, not far from Peter's patrol.

It was like watching an execution, seeing the tanks roll toward the little patrol, and Peter saw it as though in slow motion. Every second seemed to be the last, and yet the seconds kept ticking, and finally, with the first tank not more than twenty meters away, one of the soldiers fired the *Panzerfaust* directly into the armored front apron of the tank. There was an explosion of metal and rivets, and the tank clanked to a stop. And then a second explosion from within blew the insides out of the tank, surely killing the tank crew. But the other tanks came forward like living things, working their way around the carcass of the first tank, angling for the men, who were crouched by the road. Another explosion tore up the side of the second tank, but the third was coming around the opposite side. It continued straight at the Germans, and they finally lost their nerve. They jumped up and ran for a wooded area behind them, but the tank tracked ever closer and then riddled them with machine-gun fire. All six fell.

Peter watched all this with a cerebral kind of revulsion, but he felt almost no emotion. It was something he had seen many times in the past few weeks. The tanks rolled on by, continued up the road. Peter thought of commanding a charge, laying down his life—and that of his friends—to stop another tank or two. But tanks were everywhere, and some were veering toward the farm where his patrol was dug in.

Wedemeier's men had dug in at the front of the farm, and they had apparently been spotted. Four tanks crawled toward them. "They're dead," Hans whispered.

Wedemeier fired his anti-tank gun, and it ripped through one of the tanks. Another tank was now angling more toward Peter and his group, passing Wedemeier's patrol. Wedemeier turned and fired at it—and missed. The big tank kept coming, and Rietenbach raised up and fired, but the shell struck on an angle and glanced off the armor. Now the tank driver knew the position of Peter's men, and he drove directly at them, the crew firing machine guns. Peter curled up in the shallow hole next to Hans. The tank crashed directly over them, but the tree trunks kept the weight of the tracks from reaching into the hole. Twice the tank backed up, then moved forward, the driver obviously hoping to grind the boys into the earth. The noise, the wild shaking of the ground, the breaking of the trees—all of it was paralyzing. It seemed impossible to survive. But the logs held up enough, and the tank backed off. The driver seemed to think that he had smashed them. His tank twisted and moved away.

"Are you all right, Hans?" Peter asked.

"*Ja*," Hans gasped, but he had hold of Peter's coat, and he was shaking wildly.

By then another of the big T-34 tanks had driven over some men in Wedemeier's patrol, and Peter heard their screams. One man managed to get up and run, but a machine gun knocked him down immediately. Maybe the men in Peter's patrol were dead too. He had no way of knowing.

Peter raised his head enough to see that the tanks were staying nearby, turning their turrets, checking for anyone alive. He ducked his head again, but he knew this couldn't last. Infantry always came in soon after the tank attack. How could he and Hans survive the onslaught? He thought of running for the woods, but he knew what would happen. And so, more dazed than wise, he stayed where he was.

"Shoot me," Hans whispered.

"What do you mean?"

"You heard me. Shoot me. I don't want them to kill me. You do it."

"No."

"You're afraid. You don't want to be here alone."

Peter knew that was true. The two lay there, waiting, expecting the end at any second. On and on, the sound of the tanks continued, and Peter couldn't imagine what was happening. And then, from behind them, he heard a vehicle of some sort. He and Hans were surrounded. Peter didn't know whether he was pretending to be dead, or whether, in fact, he couldn't have moved had he tried. But time kept passing, and nothing happened. And then he was startled by a voice.

"Are you alive?" someone asked.

Peter looked up, unbelieving. "Yes, yes. What's happening?"

"The tanks are moving off. The whole Russian regiment has turned to the west. Some of our troops must have attacked them from the flank."

Peter sat up, pushed some of the dirt off him. But he still couldn't believe it.

"Come on. Get on the truck," the soldier said. "Is anyone else alive?" And now the others in Peter's group stood up: Helmut and the other three. And two from Wedemeier's patrol. Eight of the eighteen had actually survived.

Peter was too scared, too spent, to feel happy. He got up, and he pulled Hans up after him. They staggered to the truck and climbed on. Neither said a word to the other, and when the men on the truck asked what they had been doing, they didn't answer. Peter had already died, in his mind, and he could hardly accept the idea that he was alive again. But he didn't exult in this reprieve. Death was still waiting.

For Alex and the men of E Company, the war was now monot-
ony broken by intervals of terror. The men were still in
Holland, still dug in near the Lower Rhine, but it was
November, and the weather was turning colder all the time.
The soldiers dug their foxholes with split-level bottoms so the
water would run to the lower level and could be dredged out.
The ground never dried, however, so the men had to drop ponchos or tree limbs into the mud and then curl up and sleep as
best they could. But the dampness in Alex's clothes made sleep
almost impossible. After fitful nights that offered little rest, he
would awake to an empty day, with nothing to do but wait
again. From time to time he led a patrol toward the river, but
there was little action now. The Germans, too, had become
content to sit and wait.

The *Wehrmacht* possessed the higher ground, however, and
they could observe the Americans. They would lull the troops
into expecting nothing and then send in a barrage of artillery
fire. If the shells caught a man out in the open, the flying shrapnel would slice him up, so it wasn't wise to stray too far from a
foxhole.

Alex heard rumors about a pullout, and he couldn't imagine that paratroopers would be left like this—dug in like

infantrymen all winter—but days kept passing and nothing changed. At times the numbness that came from the cold and the wet and the mud filled his head so completely that it was difficult to care about anything, even to remember why he had to be careful to preserve his life.

Alex was still buddying up with Howie. Duncan and Ernst were dug in together. Ernst was rough around the edges, much like the young Duncan who had shown up at training camp in 1942. So he and Duncan had a natural affinity—especially since both were Southern boys—even though Duncan had changed so much. Pozernac and Gourley remained close buddies too, even though they sometimes got on each other's nerves. Campbell was alone for now and seemed to like it that way. Curtis had taken a young replacement under his wing. The kid, Irv Johnston, was only eighteen, from the hills of West Virginia. He was a muscular boy with a subtle smile and odd but handsome eyes, the color of pea soup. His strong accent made him seem something of a hick, but he was smart, and he had a difficult time accepting the strange way the army did its business.

One day, when the rain had let up a little and the sun was actually filtering through a layer of thin clouds, Alex walked over to Curtis and Johnston's foxhole. "How are you guys doing?" he asked. The two of them were out of the hole, sitting on a log. They had kept a little fire going, and they were trying to heat up a pan of water for tea with their lunch. Not many of the men liked tea, but it was what they got with their English ration boxes.

"We're having us a great ol' time, Sergeant Thomas," Johnston said. "Sort of a picnic, I guess you'd call it."

"Yeah," Curtis said, "I think, after the war, I'll come here every year for vacation—and camp out."

"You want some tea?" Johnston asked Alex.

"No, thanks."

"He doesn't drink coffee or tea," Curtis said. "He's a Mormon."

"What's wrong with coffee?" Johnston asked. "My pa would never make it through a day without a big ol' pot of coffee—blacker than crude oil."

Alex crouched next to the men and tried to get as close to the little fire as he could. "It's not really good for your body," was all he said.

"I can see where you wouldn't want to harm your body," Johnston said. "After a nice night in a wet foxhole, and sitting down here where an 88 could drop on your head at any second, you sure wouldn't want to take a chance on a cup of tea."

Alex smiled. "I would like a little hot water," he said. "Just to get something warm inside me."

"Are you really that strict in your religion, Sergeant?" Johnston asked.

"He was a missionary," Curtis answered for Alex.

Johnston asked, "Are you like a Jew who won't eat anything that's not kosher?"

Alex tried to think how to answer that. He had gotten out his mess kit and removed the cup. Curtis poured him some hot water. "We don't have a lot of health rules, if that's what you mean. I don't smoke or drink, and I don't use coffee or tea. Otherwise, I eat pretty much like anyone else."

"Yeah, but I'm just wondering how a guy can be a million miles from home—without his preacher nowhere around—and worry about a cup of tea."

"I don't think about it that way," Alex said. "I just don't drink it. It's not like I have to make a new decision every time someone offers me a cup."

"Alex isn't like anyone I know," Curtis said. "Religion isn't a list of rights and wrongs to him. It's who he is."

Alex looked away. "You make me out to be a whole lot better than I am, Curtis," he said. "I wish that were true, but it's not."

Curtis laughed. "He's humble, too," he said.

But Johnston asked, "Why do you say that, Sergeant?"

Alex didn't want to get into this. He merely said, "I don't use a lot of hard language, and I don't go out and get drunk—so the men get certain ideas about me. But religion runs a lot deeper than that."

"It's the deeper stuff I'm talking about," Curtis said. "When the shooting starts, I'd rather have Thomas next to me than anyone I know."

Alex glanced at Johnston, and he knew they had picked up on the same irony. Johnston shrugged. "I guess I never put good soldiering and religion together," he said. "In fact, I've always put 'em pretty far apart."

Curtis did try to explain. He praised Alex for his concern for the men, his willingness to put his own life on the line, for his righteous indignation toward the Nazis. Alex hardly listened. He told himself that he needed to pray, needed to think about his spiritual life, but he knew he couldn't do it—knew he feared to do it. He was hiding from the Spirit, not seeking it, but he knew no other way to keep doing what he had to do.

"War makes me religious," a voice said. It was Duncan, who had come up behind Alex and had apparently heard what Curtis was saying. "Combat leads me to prayer and loose bowels every time." The men all laughed.

"I get sick," Curtis said. "I want to heave my guts up, just before it all starts."

Duncan walked around the men and crouched in front of the fire, almost on top of it. "I can tell you about Deacon," he said. "He's mild-mannered Clark Kent. And then he grabs his weapon and turns into Superman."

"If I'm Superman, how come we haven't won a battle since we jumped into this country?"

"I don't know the answer to that," Duncan said. "But we've sure gotten our pants kicked. And there was a time when I didn't think that was possible."

"The Germans had the tanks, the better positions," Johnston said. "This whole plan was stupid. It never had a chance of working." He swore and spat into the flames.

"I'll tell you something else," Duncan said. "Everyone underestimated the Germans. They ain't giving up near so easy as Montgomery and some of them generals thought. We'll have to slug our way through the Siegfried Line and then take one town at a time. This war ain't anywhere close to being over."

Alex had been thinking the same thing lately in spite of all the optimism he had felt when he'd first made the parachute drop.

"Even if we do get things cleaned up here next year," Johnston said, "the war in Japan is going to be a whole lot worse. We're looking at a long ol' haul over there, and that's where they'll send us. Every one of us airborne boys will get dropped into that place, and the casualty rate is going to be higher than anything we've seen so far."

Duncan nodded. "That might be right," he said. "But we've taken a pretty good beating already. I was talking to the XO the other day. He told me E Company dropped in here with 154 officers and men. We're down to right around a hundred now—and we've got some replacements. We've taken something like 120 casualties since we landed in Normandy. And that's not counting guys like me. I've been hit a couple of times but never left the line."

"You're talking an eighty percent casualty rate," Johnston said.

"If you ask me, the odds don't look good," Duncan said. "You feel like sooner or later . . . your time has to come. I don't even get scared of dying anymore—and I'd love to get one of them million-dollar wounds—but I don't want to get all tore up and be limping around the rest of my life—or eating through a straw. You know what I mean?"

"We all know what you mean," Alex said. He moved a little closer to the fire and sipped at his hot water. But he didn't want to think this way. He had promised Anna he would make it back, and he could never forget that commitment to her.

When Alex walked back to Howie, he found him sitting on the edge of the foxhole. It struck Alex how much weight the kid had lost, how haggard he looked. He seemed less fearful lately, but he had become increasingly quiet.

"Are you doing all right?" Alex asked.

"Sure."

"You haven't been eating much, have you?"

Howie looked up. He seemed, for a moment, not to understand the question, but then he said, "Enough, I guess."

Alex sat down next to him. "Howie, I think they'll pull us out of here before too much longer."

"I'll believe that when I see it."

"Well . . . me, too. But it doesn't make a lot of sense to leave paratroopers sitting in holes."

"Like Irv always says, don't look for anything the army does to make too much sense."

"I gotta hand it to you, Howie, you've stayed with this thing. You're getting to be a vet."

"I told you before, I'm going to do what I have to do from now on."

"And then go back home when it's over and impress all those girls in Boise. Right?"

Howie turned and looked at Alex. He seemed curious, or maybe surprised. "No, Sergeant. It ain't nothing like that. I just want to be able to live with myself."

"Yeah," Alex said. "I know what you mean."

"In one of those letters I got yesterday, my mom said that girl I used to like got married. So there ain't nothing to that anymore."

"So are you feeling bad about that?"

"I don't know. How would I know? I don't ever feel good. Do you?"

"No. Not really."

"War ain't nothing like it is in all those picture shows I saw back home."

"Did you think it would be?"

"I guess I did. A little."

"Look, Howie, you're getting tough. You'll get through this, and you'll go home and get a good job, marry some girl, and have a nice family, and someday you'll look back on all this and say, 'That was the making of me. I did a hard job, did it like a man.'"

Howie looked into the bottom of the foxhole, seemingly lost in thought for a long time. When he looked up, he said, "Sergeant Thomas, I've never had much of anything in my life. Me and mom and my sisters learned how to get by, and that's what I'm trying to do here. But I don't want to look back on this when it's over. Not at all. I want to forget everything about it."

Alex saw something simple, childlike, in Howie's eyes, and he thought again, as he often did, of Gene. It struck Alex how wrong it was to pull boys out of high school, out of childhood really, and send them into all this. "Howie," Alex said, "the worst thing about war is that it turns everything upside down. It's the very best people who just aren't suited to be here."

"Well . . . I'm gettin' suited. I ain't going to be no sissy anymore. I was a little too young when I got here, maybe, but I'm going to be a man from now on. All the same, that still don't mean I'm going to look back on this and say how swell it was."

Alex nodded. He knew the feeling. He decided to dig some paper out of his pack and write to Anna. In his letter he told her that little had changed, but that he was relatively safe for now. He told her it was cold and wet, but he didn't try to give her much idea about the boredom and the misery of it all. He closed his letter by saying:

Anna, it's hard sometimes to stay human out here. I don't know how to explain that to you, but maybe you can imagine what I'm feeling. Every day I tell myself this won't last forever, but in a way, it already has. Still, you keep me in touch, through your letters, with all the things that really matter. You are an angel to me, and you're too good even to imagine the hell I live in. Someday I'll bring you down from the heavens and let you be a person, but for now, let me just worship you. I have to believe that heaven really exists, that it's waiting at the end of this nightmare, and for me, you are its loveliest resident. I would defile you now, should I approach you in my muddy boots, but I cling to the belief that I can be worthy to be with you again someday.

And then, on November 24, some portion of heaven came to Alex and his men. They were pulled off the line. Canadian replacement troops moved in, and E Company, with all the other paratroopers, was trucked back along Hell's Highway, the road so many men of the 101st and 82nd Divisions had given up their lives to take. Some of the men made cynical comments about the waste, but most were too happy to get out of Holland to think much about the past.

The cold penetrated through the canvas cover of the troop truck, and the men complained, but even the grousing had a rather good-humored tone to it. They were getting out of the mud; that was the important thing. Rumor had it that they would spend the winter in France, in a camp away from the action, and that they wouldn't make another drop until spring.

The men were relieved, and when they arrived at Camp Mourmelon, where they took hot showers and received clean uniforms—then slept on a cot in a warm barracks—they all talked as though they couldn't have had it better. But they were changed men, and everyone seemed to sense it. What they knew now was that they could be beaten. There was no other way to look at it: Market Garden had been a disaster. Thousands of men had lost their lives, and thousands more had been wounded—and the goal had never been achieved. General Montgomery claimed that ninety percent of their goals had been reached. The men read that in the *Stars and Stripes,* and they laughed and shook their heads. That was like throwing a dart at a target and watching it drop to the floor—

ninety percent of the way there. The only goal that had been important was a surprise drive into the heart of Germany, the breaching of the Rhine—the early end of the war. That had not happened, and the soldiers who had been there no longer trusted the army decision-making process the way they had after D-Day.

But most of the men were not philosophers. They had done what was asked of them, and they had survived. Now they were clean and warm, and the months of winter stretched before them as a long season of bliss. They were the lucky stiffs now who didn't have to sit out the winter in Holland. Besides that, passes were available to Reims, where the men could drink and fight with the men of 82nd Airborne, and better yet, to Paris, where everything most soldiers dreamed about was available.

Alex certainly enjoyed the increased comfort and the prospect of being out of harm's way, but the training now seemed tedious, and none of the other activities in camp enticed him. The men played a lot of poker, and they played some baseball and football when the weather was good. Some men tried to recruit him to play in a football game that was being organized. The "Champagne Bowl," they called it, a big New Year's Day game. But Alex didn't want to play. He used his wounded leg as an excuse, but the truth was, he had no desire to bang around on a football field. What he wanted was to negotiate a pass for a week or two at Christmastime so he could cross the Channel and have a little time with Anna.

Somewhere along the line, the mail for the regiment had lost its way. Alex knew that his letters had probably been sent to Holland and now had to find their way to France, but as each new day passed without word from Anna, he felt as though his lifeline had been cut.

Alex didn't worry about passes for Reims or Paris, but he kept trying to get something worked out for a trip to England. Finally, however, Captain Summers told him that it wasn't likely to happen. He might as well take a couple of days in Paris and settle for that. There was no time for Anna to join him there, and after his disappointment, Alex hardly cared about going. But it was better than staying in camp every day, and so he and Curtis, Howie, and Duncan got their passes on the same weekend, and they took the train to Paris together.

It was a strange combination of men, but Duncan actually spent all day Saturday wandering through tourist sights with the others: the Louvre, the Eiffel Tower, Notre Dame, and Napoleon's Tomb. When evening came he had had enough. He wandered off to Place Pigalle—"Pig Alley," the men called it—with some other men from the 101st. And yet, he returned to the hotel surprisingly early, and he hadn't even been in a fight. "There's something wrong with me," he told Alex. "These stupid kids, drinking and getting wild—they make me nervous. Every time I start to let go a little, I think some German is sneaking up behind me. I don't even like to be drunk anymore. It scares me."

On Sunday Alex located a Mormon branch that met in some rented rooms. He took his friends with him, and they went to sacrament meeting that afternoon. There were more American and British soldiers in the congregation than French families, but the language of the meeting was French. Still, the branch president gave a short talk in English, and he spoke about living by faith in a world that was struggling to keep hope alive. Alex liked having his friends there to hear the simple testimony, the carefully prepared words. "God certainly hates this war," the branch president said, "but he can be with you, giving you strength, even at the worst moments of your life. Even in war."

Afterward, in the train car on the way back to Mourmelon, Curtis told Alex, "I like your church. I liked the music, and I liked those people gathering together to keep each other going—no matter what's going on in the world."

Duncan smiled. "My mama won't believe it if I write her

and say, 'I went to Paris and went to church.' He roared with enjoyment. "Of course, I won't mention what kind of church it was. She thinks Mormons are devil's children."

"Hey, we baptize people underwater, just like you do," Alex said. "Just tell her it was a Baptist church."

"Well . . . maybe. But it might not be a good idea to tell her at all. I wouldn't want her to have a heart attack—from the shock."

Alex laughed and said, "I don't know, Duncan. You might want to get her used to the new you. By the time you get home, you're going to be a serious man."

"Maybe so," Duncan said. He seemed to know that was actually true. He sat for a time, jiggling to the motion of the train, looking out the window into the dark. "What *do* Mormons believe?" he finally asked. "It sounded a lot like what I used to hear in my church—back when I was a kid."

Alex confirmed that, that Mormons believed a lot of the same things Baptists did, but then he told about the plan of salvation, as Latter-day Saints preached it, and about eternal progress. "We think life is all about getting better, becoming more like God. And the way we see it, that goes on forever. Heaven isn't a place to sit and rest; it's a place to keep growing and learning."

Curtis was the one who found that most interesting, and he kept asking questions. He and Alex had talked about Joseph Smith and the Book of Mormon before, but they talked about all that in more detail now.

What Alex longed to do was to bear testimony, to speak with the power he remembered from his mission. But he only explained; he didn't testify. And then, when the conversation quieted, he looked out the window, trying to see outside. In the dark he saw only his reflection in the glass. There was a shallowness in the image, a seeming two-dimensionality, and that seemed all too fitting. But he didn't know what he could do about it.

LaRue was surprised when she came home from school one day in November and smelled baking bread. She found her mother in the kitchen. "What are you doing at home?" she asked as she stepped through the kitchen door.

"I just thought everyone would like a decent dinner for a change," Bea Thomas said. "So I told your dad I was going to leave a little early."

"It doesn't seem like it's as busy at the plant anymore."

"It's not. We have plenty of work for the moment, but we're not up against those constant rush orders we used to get."

"What's going to happen when the war ends?"

Mom was peeking into the oven, checking her bread. She turned around, lifted her apron, and used it to clean her hands. "We'll be fine. In some ways it'll be nice. I probably should be home more."

"Won't you miss all the excitement?"

"Well, yes. I do like being in the middle of things down there. It's the first time in my life that anyone has asked my opinion about much of anything. Now I'm supposed to know *everything.*"

LaRue walked over to the kitchen table and sat down. "Is that just bread, or did you make hot rolls, too?"

Sister Thomas smiled. "Rolls, too. If you'll wait a few minutes, you can have one while they're still hot."

LaRue felt some nostalgia come over her, and it saddened her. She had loved to be in the kitchen when she was a kid, chatting with her mother, supposedly helping her, eating "shoe-fly pie" or the oatmeal-and-raisin cookies Mom would make. It seemed such a long time since she had felt that close to her mother.

"I don't want to stay home all my life," LaRue said. "I'm thinking I'd like to run my own business."

"Then you'd better bring that C in English up to an A before the end of the term."

"What difference does that make?"

"Oh, LaRue, I've never been able to convince you that one thing leads to another. You need good grades—a good education—to do the kinds of things you're always talking about."

LaRue really doubted that the businessmen she knew had had good grades in school all the time. But Mom was always going to say things like that, and LaRue was in no mood to argue with her.

Sister Thomas walked over and sat down across the table from her. "Honey," she said, "I came home to fix a nice dinner, but I also came home to talk to you."

Just then Beverly pushed the door open and looked in. "Is that bread I smell?" she asked, her eyes wide.

Sister Thomas laughed. "What is it with you two? You act like I never bake anymore."

"You don't," LaRue said.

But Beverly, always nicer, said, "You haven't for a while."

"I'll have some rolls out before long," Sister Thomas said, "but run along for a few minutes. I need to talk to your sister."

Beverly seemed just a little too quick to nod and then to leave, as though she were saying, "I understand. LaRue needs some talking to." That bothered LaRue. Was she the family worry these days? Did everyone, even Beverly, think she had turned into a problem child?

As soon as Beverly was gone, Sister Thomas reached over and took hold of LaRue's hand. "Honey," she said, "I'm worried about you."

"You sound like dad," LaRue said, and she pulled her hand back.

Sister Thomas took some time to react to that. LaRue could tell she was being careful, and that bothered her, too. "You know what I said to your dad when he tried to stop you from going to the club that day. But I hope you didn't misunderstand what I was telling him. I believe when someone is your age, that you have the right to make a lot of your own decisions. But I also believe that trust is something you earn, not something that comes automatically."

"I thought a person was innocent until proven guilty," LaRue said. "Dad assumes I'm doing something bad—with no reason. That shows what he thinks of me."

Sister Thomas shifted in her chair, gripped her fingers together in her lap. She was clearly nervous. "Honey, your dad and I aren't as dumb as you might think. We know the kinds of things that go on in this world. And we know that someone who's inexperienced can get in a difficult situation and make a mistake very easily."

"What mistakes have I made?"

"I'm not saying you've made any. I'm saying that some situations are hard to handle."

"Mom, I know exactly what's going on here. You stood up to Dad for once in your life, and you almost knocked his socks off. But as soon as I left this house that night, I'll bet he got you under his thumb again. Now you're just telling me what he's told you to say."

LaRue was shocked by what she saw. Mom's face hardened. Her finger poked toward LaRue. "You have no right to say that to me, LaRue. You've always been convinced that the world makes its orbit right around your head—and any time it doesn't seem to do that, you get put out. What I'm saying to you is what I want to say. I'm not under any *instructions* from your father."

LaRue was irate. She was so tired of the same old accusations. It was what Dad always said about her, that she was somehow more self-centered than other people. LaRue stood up and said, with ice in her voice, "My whole life I've watched you back down to Dad and let him have his way about everything. I know how things work around here. So don't tell me he didn't ask you to talk to me."

LaRue saw instantly that she was right. She saw her mother's indignation disappear, saw her eyes disengage. LaRue had her little victory, so she turned to make her proud exit. But she already felt something else—the loss that had come with the victory. And when her mother said, "Don't go, LaRue," she did stop and turn around.

"LaRue, I wish I'd never said those things to your dad with you and Beverly there. It's not that I didn't mean them, but I was mad, and I know I gave you the wrong impression in some ways."

"I don't agree, Mom. Dad had it coming."

"Just listen to me for a minute, okay? I need to say some things to you, and I want to get it right this time."

LaRue sat down again. She was actually touched by her mother's tone of voice, and she felt her own anger fade.

"First," Mom said, "your father is the head of our home. He has that stewardship, and he has the priesthood. I honor that, and I honor him. I want you to understand that. I lost my temper that day, so I exaggerated some things, but I do think it's important for a righteous father to lead his home."

"Why can't a father and a mother lead together?"

"Actually, that's exactly what they should do, and you heard what I said that day. I think that your dad sometimes reacts before he thinks, and before he talks to me. He has fault in that, as far as I'm concerned, but so do I. And I want you to know that since that day, he and I have had some long talks. I think we've worked some things out that we should have dealt with long ago. As you say, I usually let him get away with making decisions without me. But I don't think he'll do that in the future."

"Mom, he's like a bulldozer. He may claim he's going to change, but he can't do it."

Sister Thomas took a breath. LaRue could see she didn't like that. But she didn't say so. She got up and walked to the oven, opened the door, and peeked inside. Then she turned and tucked her hands into the pockets of her faded blue housedress, under her apron. "LaRue," she said, "all I can tell you is that we're both going to try to do some things a little differently. That's what marriage is all about—working out differences, adjusting to new circumstances."

"If I ever get married, my husband is going to know he's got his hands full," LaRue said, and she finally smiled.

"No doubt. Your generation is going to be more like that, I'm sure. But don't think that will solve every problem. It will also create some new ones."

LaRue didn't know about that. But she did know that she would never be a "silent partner" in a marriage.

"Honey, you still don't understand that I'm just as worried about you as your father is. And maybe I have more reason. I think I know you better."

So here it was again: LaRue and all her problems.

"I know you can make mistakes at a church dance, or out on the front porch, as far as that goes—but I think you're in an element down at the USO that is dangerous. And even though you think you understand those dangers, I'm not sure you do."

"Come on, Mom. I'm not a child."

"LaRue, please. Listen for a minute. If we're going to trust you, we can also give you some warnings. If you think you can kiss this young man you've met down there without building

up his expectations for other things, you simply don't understand the ledge you're standing on."

"Mom, I've told Ned what my standards are. He understands that. He knows I won't drink, and that I won't let him
start fooling around—if you know what I mean."

"Yes, LaRue, I do happen to know what you mean—
although you may think that impossible."

LaRue saw some color come into her mother's face and felt
some heat in her own. She glanced away at the kitchen window, over the sink. The sun was setting already. Even with "war
time"—the daylight saving time that was in force for the duration—sunset came very early this time of year. The valley was
very smoky today, with so many coal stoves going, and the sky
was full of a dirty red glare.

"Ned wants to be serious. But I don't. I've told him that."
LaRue felt a sudden impulse to admit a little more, to chat with
her mother more intimately.

"What do you mean, 'serious'?"

"Well, I think he'd like me to marry him someday."

"Does he know how old you are?"

"Not exactly."

"LaRue!"

Suddenly LaRue felt her defenses rise up again. "It doesn't
matter. He thinks I'm a little older than I am, but he also knows
I don't want to talk about marriage."

"Have you told him you wouldn't marry out of the
Church?"

"Yes. We talked about that. He says he wants to join."

"Without knowing anything about it?" Mom walked back
to the table and sat down again. As she did, the light reflected
off her face, and LaRue saw a little smear of flour along her
cheekbone. It suddenly struck LaRue how planned this all
was—the baked bread, the early arrival home, even the little
speech. It was irritating, however well meant.

"Mom, that's not the point," LaRue said. "I'm not going to

marry him. I'm just saying that he likes me that much, and I've told him what my standards are. So there's nothing to worry about."

"But if you're kissing, LaRue, other things can start to happen."

"Mom! What kind of girl do you think I am?"

"A normal one. And he's a normal young man. Things can get out of control if you let them. What I think you should do is break up with this boy. And the truth is, I think you should stay away from the USO."

"Here we go again."

"LaRue, *listen* to me. I didn't tell you to stop going. I told you I think that would be best. I would hope you would see what all this is doing to you. You hardly ever go to Mutual anymore. You spend most of your time with older girls and all those soldiers at the club. It's just not the best atmosphere for you."

"You don't know the rules down there, Mom. They don't let anything wild go on."

"LaRue, you're trying to grow up too fast, and that isn't healthy. I'm getting frustrated, and I don't want to, but I see you drifting away from the things you've learned in this family, and it scares me. I'm not trying to run your life, but I'm asking you to make your own decision to do the right things."

"Mom, the only difference between you and Dad is that he comes straight out with what he has to say, and you try to beat around the bush."

LaRue knew that wasn't fair, not entirely, but what she felt from her mother was what she felt from her father: mistrust. And once again, someone was trying to take away the most exciting thing in her life.

"LaRue, what would you do if you saw your own child doing things you thought were dangerous? Wouldn't you try to warn her?"

"I guess so. But I've been warned plenty. And I'm tired of it.

I've never done anything wrong. And then I come home and all I hear is that I'm some little tramp. Maybe I'll do some of those things you accuse me of—just to give you something to *really* worry about."

This time LaRue got up and walked out, and when her mother called after her to come back, she kept on going. She headed upstairs to her room. She did some of her homework—half-heartedly—and ignored the rest. She liked the good dinner that night, but she didn't say so. In fact, she said nothing, and when she got up from the table, she announced to her mother that she was going to the club, and she left.

That night she danced with Ned, or talked with him, most of the evening. She had actually been planning to break up with him soon, since he always wanted to talk about marriage, and she didn't want that, but tonight she took some pleasure in toying with him. She liked the idea that she could entice him by letting him hold her close during a dance, even by kissing his ear, but that she could suddenly change the mood—move away, tease him, get him laughing—and keep things under control. All this was her choice, and she enjoyed knowing that. She liked feeling grown up and skillful with a boy so much older.

"What's going on?" he asked her finally, after a dance.

"What do you mean?"

"You've been playing games with me all night. I don't like that."

"What games?" She stepped a little closer and adjusted his uniform tie, straightening it a little, but then running her fingers along his neck and behind his ear.

"Those games," he said. He laughed, reached around her, and pulled her against him.

She gave him a little peck on the cheek, and then she said, "Come on. Let's dance." A fast number—"One O'Clock Jump"—had started to play on the jukebox. She stood up and took his hand, leading him onto the dance floor. Around them, couples were starting to dance, and with the blaring music, it wasn't easy to hear.

Ned shook his head with some frustration, but he was still smiling. She loved the way she was keeping him off balance. He leaned toward her and said, "I've got a surprise for you."

"What?"

"I borrowed a car from a friend of mine. And I have plenty of gas. I'm going to give you a ride home tonight—the first time I've ever been able to do that."

LaRue felt some of her confidence disappear. She wasn't sure she wanted that. And yet she hated that her mother's warnings were setting off alarms. There was nothing wrong with riding home with him. And so she said, "Let's go now. You can take me for a ride."

"Have you ever been to Gravity Hill?" he asked.

"Sure."

"You *have?*"

She pulled him off the dance floor, away from all the movement and noise. "I've only been up there with my family," she said. "My brothers used to get my Dad to stop up there."

"Is it really true? Does the car roll uphill?"

"My dad says it doesn't; it just looks like it. But Dad thinks he knows everything."

"Well, let's try it out for ourselves." He winked.

"Neddy, boy, now what do you have in mind? I was talking about a science experiment."

"Yeah, that's what I was talking about too."

What they both knew, of course, was that Gravity Hill, actually a road just past the Capitol Building on Capitol Hill, was famous as a place for teenagers to park.

"I know what you want," LaRue said. She touched his chin with her finger. "You want to park up there and neck. And I don't do that."

"I know. You've told me lots of times."

"Well, don't forget it."

But as they left the club, the same kind of joking continued, and LaRue knew that Ned would make some sort of
attempt. She could handle it; she wasn't worried about that.
Still, she felt a little nervous—and maybe excited, too. What
she liked, though, was that when she got into the car, she felt
more grown up than she ever had in her life. She was wearing a
brown skirt and tan sweater—an outfit that Bobbi had left
behind in her closet. LaRue had taken a long look at herself
before she had left the house. She thought she looked like a
college girl—very sophisticated—and she knew she looked
pretty.

"What kind of a car is this?" she asked, without the slightest
interest but at a loss for something to say.

"It's a Plymouth. It's kind of a wreck, but it got me here
from Hill Field." LaRue noticed a little strain in his voice, as
though he were nervous himself.

He drove to Capitol Hill, and LaRue showed him where
the road was. Halfway along the hill, he stopped the car, put
the gearshift in neutral, and took his foot off the brake. There
was enough moonlight to see the rim of the little canyon in silhouette, but most of the illusion was lost. When the car started
to roll, Ned said, "It doesn't feel like uphill to me."

"You have to come in the day so you can see it right."

The car was rolling slowly forward, and Ned let it angle off
to the side of the road. Then he stopped the car and set the
emergency brake.

"No, no, Ned. Don't get anything in your head. We're leaving now."

"Give me one kiss first."

"No. I don't think so."

"You always kiss me goodnight."

"Drive me home. I'll kiss you goodnight when we're there."

"You won't want to kiss me out in front of your house.
You'll be too afraid someone will see you." He was smiling, and

he looked handsome, with his easy smile and the firm, clean lines of his jaw, half in silhouette, in the moonlight.

What he had said was actually true. Besides, LaRue wanted just a little of this. She wanted to kiss him. She knew that lots of kids came up here to kiss—Mormon kids, whether her Mom knew it or not—and it wasn't such a huge thing to worry about.

She didn't slide toward him, but when he shifted toward her, she didn't stop him, and when he turned her face to his, with his hand on her chin, she did let him kiss her. And after the kiss, he held her, kissed her on the neck, and ran his hand down her back and along her side. She felt chills from his touch, and when he kissed her again, she didn't stop him this time either. She told herself, *Just this much and then no more,* but she put more of herself into this kiss, reaching her arms around him. When his hand moved across the front of her, touching her waist, she pushed his hand away, but she liked the tingling excitement of it, and when his hand came back and they were kissing the third time, she didn't push it away. When he moved his hand under her sweater, on her skin, she liked that even better. He wasn't touching her anywhere that was wrong, she told herself. And they would stop in just a moment.

But his fingers were working back and forth across her skin, each stroke moving higher. And LaRue was feeling something wildly exciting that she didn't know she was capable of. She was about to say stop when he pushed his hand farther up her sweater, but still she was kissing him, harder than ever, and he was pushing his body against her, gradually pushing his weight over on top of her.

And suddenly she panicked. "No!" she said, and she thrust her hands against his chest, jolting him away.

"I'm sorry, LaRue. I'm sorry. I thought you liked it. I thought that's what you wanted."

"Just take me home."

"All right. But I wasn't trying to force anything. You acted like you wanted something to happen."

She *had* wanted something to happen. Even in her horror now, she still wanted it. She had never felt so removed from her own body, so full of conflict. "I'm sorry, too. I shouldn't have let you think that. I need to go home now."

And so he started the car, then drove all the way out State Street to Twenty-First South. Along the way, he kept telling her that he hadn't meant to compromise her standards. He would never do that again.

But LaRue knew the truth: he had been perfectly willing to let her go back on her own word. He had left all the choice up to her and would never have stopped until she made him stop. She was sure of that, and it made her angry.

When LaRue walked into the house, she saw her mother sitting in the living room by herself, listening to "Kraft Music Hall" on the radio and embroidering. Dad was probably at the stake center doing interviews or holding a meeting. "You're home early," Mom said, trying to sound neutral but clearly still self-conscious about their earlier conversation.

"Just a little," LaRue said, and she headed for the stairs.

"Was there some reason for that?"

"For what?" LaRue knew what she meant, but she didn't like this kind of interrogation.

"Coming home early."

"I just thought I'd better get home." And then she thought of the right half-truth: "I still have a little homework to do." If she had said, "And I'm going to do it," that would have been an out-and-out lie.

"Well, that's good. That shows some wisdom. Although I think it would be better if you had taken care of that earlier, when you weren't so tired. You can always learn better when you're not all worn out."

LaRue couldn't believe it. There was never any end to this. Dad would have said, "I want you to get that done before you leave this house and go down to that *canteen*." Mom was only saying the same thing in more measured words. Either way, they were both saying, "You don't know what you're doing, do you, LaRue?"

LaRue was all the way up the stairs before her anger boiled over. She dropped onto her bed, and she struggled not to cry. She pounded her fist into her pillow, and then she picked the pillow up and screamed into it. She was so furious with her mother. She knew exactly what Mom would be saying right now if she knew what had just happened. *I told you, didn't I? You really aren't old enough to take care of yourself.*

But she was. She just hadn't done it. She would never be so stupid again. She had learned her lesson now.

She lay back on her bed when the anger had passed, and she felt a nervous, buzzing sense inside her, a confusion and excitement she didn't know what to do with. She thought of the things that had happened, went over it all, slowly, and the fact was, she had liked it all so very much.

Suddenly she was ashamed. "I'm sorry, Father," she said, in her own little version of a prayer. It crossed her mind to tell the Lord that she would break up with Ned, that she would stop going to the USO. But she couldn't bring herself to go that far. Instead, she closed her eyes and began a real prayer. She promised not to get into a car with Ned again, not to let him touch her like that.

When she opened her eyes, she stared at the ceiling, focused for no reason on a little crack in the ceiling plaster. She didn't feel relieved of the guilt; she even knew that she was clinging to things that weren't good for her. But she didn't want her parents to be right, or think they were. She had been thinking lately that she ought to stop going to the USO one of these days. She knew she had to stop cutting herself off from her high-school friends. If she was going to be popular at school, she had to be more involved. There was one particular boy, Reed Porter, who had been paying attention to her lately, and she really did hope he would ask her out. But she wasn't going to quit the USO yet—and let her parents win. She would do it when she was ready, and in the meantime, she would prove to herself—and to Ned—that she wasn't dumb enough to make a "mistake" with him.

She shut her eyes again and rolled over on her side. She had begun to cry. What she really wanted to do was go downstairs and tell her mother that she was sorry, tell her that she loved her, and then talk, the way they used to do. She missed her mom so much sometimes. She didn't know when life had become so complicated, what had forced such a distance between her and her parents. She couldn't tell her mother what had happened. She was too ashamed to do that. But she wondered, was that what growing up meant? Feeling so alone all the time?

2 5

Heinrich Stoltz was in Karlsruhe, near the French border. There was no obvious way to get across the wide Rhine, and he knew that if he decided to escape Germany, he might have to wait until the Allies crossed into Germany and occupied the area. That meant he could get caught in the action—the bombing raids that might come first and the artillery barrage as troops approached—but it still might be his best hope of getting out.

He took a room in a little boarding house, identified himself by the name of Heinrich Stutz, perhaps for the same reasons Peter had chosen the name but also to feel some connection to his son. He had the one full set of identification papers, but the name on them was known to officials now, and he would have to be very careful about using them. Fortunately, the older woman at the boarding house listened to his story—that he was a veteran who had been injured in Russia and that his family had been lost in a bombing raid in Hamburg—and she believed it all. She didn't ask to see any papers. It was illegal to move without registering a departure and then registering again in the new city, so he was highly vulnerable if officials became aware of his having arrived in

town. Brother Stoltz knew he was going to need a lot of luck—
or guidance—if he was going to survive.

Another problem was that he could run short of money if
he was forced to stay very long, so after a few days of hiding
in his room to make sure his path was cold, he looked about
the city for work. He found a baker, a man named Franz
Kieffer, who said he was desperate for help but couldn't find
any with all the men off to war. "I've been discharged myself,"
Brother Stoltz told the man. "I hurt my shoulder in an accident,
near Stalingrad. But I'm well enough now to do some lifting—
as long as it's nothing terribly heavy."

"Can you lift a sack of flour?" Kieffer asked.

"That I can do. But can you buy one?" Brother Stoltz asked.

"Sometimes," the baker said, and he laughed. He seemed
to like Brother Stoltz. "That's good then, Herr Stutz. Can you
get yourself out of bed and make it here by four o'clock each
morning?"

"Oh, yes. I don't sleep very well anyway."

"That's my curse, too," Kieffer said. "But I'm an old man.
That's how it is with people my age." Then he stuck out his
hand. "Call me Franz," he said.

"And you call me Heinrich." Brother Stoltz waited. Would
Franz ask for his papers? But the man didn't seem suspicious,
didn't even seem to think of checking his identity. So Brother
Stoltz had gotten lucky again—or blessed—and he felt some
comfort in that.

What evolved over the next couple of weeks was a strange
sort of peace for Brother Stoltz. He longed to be with his wife
and daughter, and he knew they would worry about him, but
at least there was comfort in the simple life he had found. He
arose in the night and went into the warm, lighted bakery,
where he carried out his specific assignments, mixing the various types of dough, kneading it, folding it into proper-sized
lumps for bread or rolls. He and Franz talked at times, but
Franz was not a gabby man; he spoke mostly about the work,

the bread. They talked about the war, of course, but only to guess what might be coming, not to discuss the politics.

Once the sun was up and the bread was ready, Brother Stoltz put in a few hours out front in the store. The neighborhood women would come in, present their ration cards, and ask for a loaf of dark rye, or of *"weiss Brot,"* and Brother Stoltz would chat with them a little, choose a nice loaf, and stick it into the bags or nets that the women would bring with them. Then he would collect the ration cards and the change that the women parceled out so carefully.

He knew that many families were living almost entirely on bread, and it seemed a sacred thing to him to provide it—or at least be part of providing it. What he saw in these good people was what he remembered of the Germany of his younger days. The customers were reserved people, hard working and decent. It was difficult to imagine that any of them had ever screamed their support for Hitler. Almost no one greeted him with Nazi salutes or with "Heil Hitler." In fact, many had returned to their familiar religious greeting, *"Grüss Gott."*

Brother Stoltz liked these good mothers, felt glad in his heart that he had come back to Germany to see this. He knew that the sins of the Nazis had to come back on the heads of all Germans, to some degree, but he also knew that these people who got up early, walked or bicycled to the store, and spent their few pfennige for a good loaf of bread were not killers, not haters. He liked the look of the women on these December mornings, in their heavy wool coats and their mufflers bundled around their red cheeks. They were so much like his mother, who had worked hard for his family, labored on their farm next to her husband, and made certain that he and his brother and two sisters got to church every Sunday.

So many of the women were widows, and so many others were home with their children while their husbands were away at war. They were doing their best to keep going in the midst of air raids and food shortages. Sometimes the younger women came with small children, and they demanded proper behavior from these little ones, speaking to them strictly, the way Brother Stoltz's mother had done. It was charming to see, the little children with their rosy faces and lively eyes, not understanding about war, not seeming disheartened by it all. They were the best of Germany—the part that would survive when the war ended, Brother Stoltz told himself.

One morning a young woman came into the store after the morning rush had ended. She had her little boy with her. She was a pale little thing herself, and thin, but her son was full of life. He paced back and forth before the glass display case and looked at the bread. The mother finally told the boy, "Stay still, Reinert." The child did stop pacing, but he continued to look into the case, as though wishing for something better than the bread that was there.

"I wish we had some pastries or something sweet," Brother Stoltz told her. "But you know how things are. We can only bake bread these days."

"He's never eaten a pastry or *Kuchen*. He doesn't even know what they are."

Brother Stoltz was struck by the sadness of it, and again he thought of his own childhood when his house had been full of the smells of his mother's baking. His family had been poor, but they had always eaten well. "Is your husband a soldier?" Brother Stoltz asked.

"My husband was killed in action last winter," the young woman said. "In Russia."

Brother Stoltz nodded. He looked down at the little boy. "I have a son on the eastern front," he said softly. "It seems only a few days ago that he was like this one."

She glanced down at her son, then stepped a little closer to him and touched his hair. He could guess what she was thinking.

"There's too much of this," Brother Stoltz said. "So many widows. So many children without fathers."

The woman looked him straight on for only a second or two, and then she looked down again. "He's only known war in his life," she said. "He doesn't even cry when the air raids come. We go down in the basement and play together. He's never had things, either, so he has no idea how much we do without."

The boy was so lovely, with his big eyes, brown like his mother's, full of curiosity. "I'm four," he said, smiling.

"And such a big boy," Brother Stoltz said, smiling back at him. Then he told the mother, "Things will be better in time."

"I suppose. But not quickly."

Clearly they understood each other. Neither was claiming, as Germans sometimes still did, that the war would be reversed and Germany would still win. What they both knew was that the Allies would occupy this territory before too much longer, and a bad time would follow—like those awful years after World War I. But even that was better than things continuing this way, with bombs dropping and the men gone, all in danger.

"Maybe Reinert won't have to go to war," the mother said. "Maybe there won't be more wars."

"I hope that's right," Brother Stoltz said.

When the woman left, he could only think of his own little boy, who was probably in danger somewhere—if he was alive. He would have given anything to have Peter next to him, like little Reinert, to be able to stroke his hair, to comfort him.

There was a branch of the Mormon church still carrying on in Karlsruhe. Brother Stoltz found it on his second Sunday in town. He was careful not to let his landlady know where he was going, and he used his false name with the members, but he was happy to be able to attend church. In London he had enjoyed the meetings, but here, with his own language, his own people, he was more at home. The branch was sizeable, too, although many couldn't make it every Sunday. Usually there were fifty or so, and the branch president, President

Griebel, was an impressive man. He was a good speaker and a warm man who kept track of his scattered flock.

Brother Stoltz loved the meetings, the friendship before and after, and the faith that was expressed in all the sermons. It struck him as strange, sometimes, how easily faith came to him now. He had always doubted, instinctively, but these years of depending on God had made faith a practical matter, something he needed, something that worked. He rarely argued with the things he heard in church now, even when much of what people said seemed simplistic to him. It didn't matter. It was their own expression of faith, their own experience, and he accepted the spirit of it.

On the second Sunday he attended, the branch president asked "Brother Stutz" to stay after sacrament meeting, and then he sat down with him in one of the rented rooms. "I merely wanted to get to know you," he said. "Tell me where you're from."

President Griebel was a white-haired man, probably in his sixties. He had a rather gaunt look about him, with thin cheeks and hardly any flesh on his neck or arms. But his wonderful voice, rich and gentle, was fatherly, and it bespoke his kindness. Brother Stoltz knew he would have to trust this man. He couldn't tell him the lies he had had to invent to protect himself. "My name isn't really Stutz," he said. "But it's better that I not tell you my real name. If I do, and someone comes looking for me, you will be better off not to know."

"My goodness," President Griebel said. "I wonder what this is all about."

"It's best only to tell you this: I am a member of the Church—an elder. I've served in a branch presidency before. I'm a member in good standing, too. My problems are with the government—the Nazis—but I am guilty of nothing that would put my membership in question."

The president nodded. "I believe you," he said. "And I don't need to know anything else. I understand how things can be these days."

What he didn't say was what he thought of the Nazis himself. Very few Germans, even fellow members of the Church, dared to say exactly what they thought. Even when people expressed their enthusiasm or commitment to the Führer, it was never easy to be certain that they weren't posturing, perhaps even protecting themselves.

"Let me ask you this," President Griebel said. "Would you be willing to teach a class in Sunday School—a small group of young people? There are both girls and boys, all between twelve and sixteen. Most Sundays we have four or five, sometimes more."

"I would love to do that. But one day, suddenly, I could be gone, without ever saying a word to you."

"One day, suddenly, we could all be gone. That's the nature of war. And mortality."

"No. I mean, I might have to leave."

"I know what you mean. But my point is still the same. Nothing is certain for anyone right now. If the Allies cross the river and push through Karlsruhe, I have no idea what will happen to us."

"Yes, yes. I understand. But I have family—a wife and daughter—outside of Germany. If I can find a way to get back to them, I will go. I also have a son in danger. If I can work out some way to reach him, that could also take me away."

"Also outside Germany?" President Griebel asked.

"I can't tell you more than that. It's not fair to you to do so."

"That's fine."

"Let me ask you this, President Griebel. Does the Church have any way to contact other members, outside our country? In America—or anywhere?"

"Not that I know of. Not anymore. Early in the war, before America was part of it, we could reach Church leaders sometimes through certain contacts, but those were all forced out when America joined the Allies."

"How do you keep the branch functioning without any guidance from Church leaders?"

"I do have a district president. But I don't see him often. Mostly, we just do the best we can. Before the war, we relied a good deal on the missionaries to give our sermons and teach classes. Sometimes, now, the members—especially newer ones—get away from the doctrine and teach their own ideas. I do what I can about that, but it isn't always easy."

It was what Brother Stoltz suspected. "I promise not to teach the young people my own ideas—but I should warn you, I'm a fairly new member myself, and during the war, I've rarely been able to attend church. Do we have any lesson manuals I can use?"

"Not really. Sister Wood left certain lesson books long ago, when she and President Wood had to leave so suddenly, but we've used those over and over, and our children know them by heart. It's better now to study the scriptures with them—choose the things you want them to learn, and teach those from the Bible and Book of Mormon."

"President Griebel, I have no Book of Mormon. Is there any way to get one?"

"It's very difficult. I can lend you one for now."

Brother Stoltz was touched by such a generous loan. He had longed so much in the past two weeks to be able to use more of his time for study. He had been reading a Bible he had borrowed at the boarding house—reading it more carefully than ever before in his life, but he had wanted so much to have a Book of Mormon.

For the next couple of weeks Brother Stoltz got up each morning and walked through the cold but snowless streets to the bakery. He spent his morning with the bread, with Franz, and then with the good people who came to the bakery. After, he returned to his small room and slept for an hour or two, and then he spent his time with his Bible and the borrowed Book of Mormon. It was a life without the things he wanted, and yet oddly, it was very full. He liked the young people in his Sunday School class, and he found them surprisingly open and inquisitive.

The class was made up of girls and younger boys. Most boys fifteen and older were in the military now. On the surface the class members seemed as lively as any young people, but they had grown up knowing war most of their lives, knowing the sound of bombs, knowing brothers and fathers and neighbors who had died, knowing their own vulnerability. At times they expressed bitterness about all they had been through, but more than any young people Brother Stoltz had ever known, they were curious to know what life meant, and what lay ahead in the next life.

Brother Stoltz felt a need to be well prepared, to bring these young people the best he had to offer, and they seemed to recognize that in him. After the first class, a girl of thirteen or so, Ursula Glissmeyer, stayed after, thanked him, and then said, "There's something I've wondered, Brother Stutz. My brother was killed in Italy a long time ago. I was so little that I don't remember him very well. Everyone says I'll have a chance to know him in the next life, but sometimes I talk to him now—so he'll know me, even if I don't know him. Do you think he can hear me?"

"I don't know, Ursula," Brother Stoltz said. "Maybe someone knows, but I'm not very experienced in the Church. I would think that he does hear you, though, or at least somehow knows about his family on earth. It seems the best way for families to stay close during the time they are separated."

"I think so too," she said. "And it helps me to talk to him."

"I have a son who is away from me. And I can't talk to him. I don't even know for sure where he is. So I know how you feel."

"Talk to him. Maybe he'll know what you say—like my brother."

It was a simple idea, and not one he would have thought of himself, but there was something right about it, and Ursula's faith made it seem possible. That night Brother Stoltz prayed, asked that Peter might know his thoughts, and then he told Peter, out loud, how much he loved and missed him, how much he was praying for his safety. He told him about his mother and sister, about Anna marrying Elder Thomas, about his own attempts to find Peter. And then he said, "Peter, don't lose hope. You may have been pulled into circumstances you wouldn't have chosen, but don't give up. Your mother and sister and I love you, and we want you back. I'll find you if there's any way I can do that."

When Brother Stoltz had finished, he was no longer comfortable with hiding this way. He felt that he needed to make another effort to find Peter. But to do that he needed new papers, and the only person he knew who could help with that was Georg. And so he talked to Franz, told him he needed to be away for a few days, and he did the only thing he knew to do, even though he was sticking his head into the jaws of a lion. He took a train back to Berlin.

He had no choice but to use his first identity and his travel papers, justifying a move to Berlin. The dates on those travel papers would be hard to explain, should someone look closely. He only hoped that his simple dress and his skill at bluffing would get him through if someone questioned him. If someone happened to recognize the name, perhaps from some list of fugitives, nothing would save him.

But no one checked his papers carefully, perhaps because the greatest threats to the trains were the frequent raids on the tracks, and even on the trains themselves. He was held up for a long time outside Frankfurt. He had to wait several hours, and he was told that a crew was working on damage to the tracks ahead. But eventually, he was able to get going again, and he made it to the familiar old train station, not terribly far from where he and his family had once lived. The destruction he saw in Frankfurt, however, was shocking. He wondered what had happened to all the people he had known there, his old neighbors, his friends in the Church. But there was no time to find out. He changed trains and traveled to Hamburg and then on to Berlin. Once there, he telephoned Georg and used code language to make an appointment. The next day he met Georg in the Tiergarten, where they had met before.

It was a cold day, but the sun was bright. "I thought you were gone," Georg said, when he stood next to Brother Stoltz by the pond.

"I was," Brother Stoltz said. And then he told about his mistakes and his flight to Karlsruhe.

"You should have stayed there," Georg told him. "You had found some safety."

"I know. But I need new papers. I'll never really be safe until I have them. I wondered if you could help."

"We can do that. But I fear that you still want to search for your son. That's what this is all about. No?"

"Perhaps. I don't know what to do, but I can't bear the idea of giving up."

Brother Stoltz watched an innocent white swan as it turned gently and headed to deeper waters. He thought of Peter, who was smart, but Peter's natural tendency was to be forthright, not to live a lie. Maybe, in his own innocence, he would trust someone and not see the danger.

"I can get you papers," Georg said. "But don't be a fool. There's nothing you can do."

"How long will it take to get the papers?"

"That's never certain. Go back to the bakery. Stay with your work there. I have contacts in Karlsruhe. I can get the papers to you through my friends."

"All right. But I don't dare take the train. I have no papers that explain my traveling in that direction."

"I can help you there, too. I can get you a ride. Call me in the morning, and I'll have something arranged."

"Is there a way to create papers that would get me out of Germany?"

"No. You're too well known. You're putting me and my people in great danger just being here, contacting me. Wait out the war now."

"Georg, what if we were to blow up train tracks and power stations? Couldn't we shorten the war that way?"

"Maybe. I don't know. There are a few people doing that, I think. But the Gestapo has become more brutal than ever. They'll kill a man just for suspicion. They don't have to have proof. If that's what you think you have to do, do it. But you're not likely to survive—and how will that help your son?"

Brother Stoltz felt the cold. He tucked his hands into his coat pockets. He looked about, wondered whether anyone was watching.

"Do you know where I can contact people who are resisting?"

"Yes."

"Are any near Karlsruhe?"

"Somewhat. Most are in the Ruhr, north of Karlsruhe."

"Tell me how to contact them."

Georg hesitated, ran his fingers over his cheek and across his bushy mustache. Finally he said, "I can give you a name and address. You must learn them, not write them down. I warn you, however, that you are entering into great danger to have anything to do with these people. We have helped them with false papers at times, but that is my only contact with them."

"Please. I want the name and address."

"I don't have the address in my head. I'll have to see you once again. But now I must go," Georg said.

The two separated, and Brother Stoltz strolled on through the park. At least, once he got the new identity papers, he could contact the OSS agent he had been scheduled to meet with before everything had gone wrong. He could possibly convince the organization to let his wife and daughter know that he was alive. That would take one great worry off his mind. But his frustration had finally struck him full force. Peter was probably not so terribly far away, perhaps in need of help, and there wasn't one thing he, as his father, could think to do.

He stopped and looked across the park again, making certain he wasn't being followed. And he took a final look at the swan, now drifting in the placid water. He shut his eyes and said, "Don't give up, Peter. If I can find a way to help you, I will. But for now, stay strong. I love you. Your mother and Anna, they love you too."

Chapter 26

It had been a long time since LaRue had shared much of anything with Beverly, but when LaRue finally got the call she had
been waiting for, she knew she had to tell someone, and
Beverly was the only one home. She ran up the stairs and burst
into Beverly's room. "Guess what?" she squealed.

Beverly was reading. She was always reading these days.
She had a few friends in the ward and at school, but she spent
most of her time alone with a book in her hands. She often
curled up downstairs on the couch, near the radio, when Dad
wasn't around, but today she was lying on her bed. She twisted
around to look at LaRue, but she didn't ask; she only waited.

"That was *him*," LaRue said. "He asked me to the Christmas
dance."

Beverly sat up. "Really? How did you get him to do it?"

LaRue, of course, knew exactly what Beverly meant, but
she pretended not to. "What do you mean, how did I 'get him
to do it'? The boy has a mind of his own, doesn't he?"

"Not once *you* start to work on him."

LaRue believed that was exactly right, and she smiled with
satisfaction, but she didn't make that claim. She walked over
and sat down next to Beverly on the bed. "But I didn't think he
was going to do it. He waited until the last minute. It doesn't

give me much time to work on Dad—and get myself a new dress."

She laughed at herself because what she knew was that she could pull that one off too. Dad wasn't the tightwad he had once been, but he still had to be handled just right. He would claim that he and Mom had already spent way too much for Christmas, and then he would start his old tune about Christmas being too commercialized "these days." But LaRue saw the angle to play, immediately. Reed Porter was not only president of the junior class; his father was a bishop in President Thomas's stake. He was just the sort of boy Dad would want LaRue to be going with. She could play that trump card all the way to the prettiest dress in town.

"He's the best-looking guy in the whole school," LaRue said.

"How come you always say you don't like the boys at school?"

"I don't like the ones my age. They're all *infantile*. But Reed's not like that. He's sort of serious. He's seventeen, and he looks even older than that. But he's shy. I had his face almost burning up this week, just from teasing him."

"Is that how you do it—by teasing him?"

"Do what?"

"You know what I'm talking about. You told me you wanted him to ask you to the dance, and then, all of a sudden, he does. How do you know how to do that?"

LaRue got up and walked to Beverly's dresser, and she looked into the mirror. She leaned close to it and checked to see what was happening with the pimple next to her nose that was finally drying up. She didn't get lots of pimples, the way some kids did—but she hated to get any at all. She washed her face with Woodbury's Facial Soap every day, and she used Armand's Cleansing Cream before she went to bed at night. "I don't know what I do," she said. "If I like a boy, I just talk to him. You have to let a boy know you like him. Boys never seem to think of anything by themselves—until you plant a few ideas."

"What do you say to them? I wouldn't know one thing to say."

LaRue turned around and sat on the chair by the dresser. "I don't know. I told Reed he was conceited because he's such a big sports star."

"Is he conceited?"

"No. He's sweet as pie. He was about the best player on the football team, and he's only a junior, and now he's playing basketball. But if you compliment him, he always says, 'So and so is better than I am,' and things like that."

"So what did he say when you told him he was conceited?" Beverly was clearly enjoying this. Her skin was pale normally, but her face had brightened with color now. LaRue felt bad that she didn't talk to Beverly more often; it seemed to mean so much to her.

"I don't remember what he said—something about trying to do his best for the team. You know how boys talk."

"No. Not really."

"Well, you should. You read those lovey-dovey romance stories night and day."

"No, I don't." She held her book out. It was a library book; that's all LaRue could see. "I read mostly books about horses."

"A girl and her horse. And the boy she meets."

"Sometimes." Now Beverly was really blushing. She looked away for a moment and then asked, "Did you say anything to him about the dance—that you wanted to go or anything like that?"

"Oh, Bev, no. Are you crazy? You can't come straight out with something like that. I told him that all the girls liked him. He wouldn't admit that either, but I told him unless a girl was really, really cute, she didn't have a chance with him. He was almost dying, he was so embarrassed."

"Didn't that make him mad at you?"

"No. He just tried to act like it did. And then . . ." LaRue hesitated for effect, and she winked at Beverly. "And then he told me . . ."

"What?"

"Well . . . after I said that about having to be really cute, he said, 'I guess you know you're the cutest girl in the whole sophomore class. I've heard lots of guys say that.'"

"Really?"

LaRue was embarrassed to have told the story, but she was also triumphant. Reed Porter was the boy all her friends talked about, the boy she had targeted, and now she was going to the dance with him.

"What about Ned?" Beverly asked.

"What about him?"

"Don't you like him anymore?"

"Sure I do. But he's mostly just a friend."

"Are you still going to dance with him at the canteen?"

"Sure. What difference does that make?"

"Do you want two boyfriends at the same time?"

"No. Of course not. I want ten . . . or maybe twenty."

Beverly giggled, and LaRue liked that. But the truth was, she did feel the need to break things off with Ned. He had been a gentleman since that one night, but he was still pressing her to be serious about him, and LaRue didn't want that. This new attachment was going to make a breakup a lot easier. LaRue was even thinking that she wouldn't go to the USO anymore. Rumors had spread to the high school, and some girls had asked her whether she had a boyfriend at the canteen. She wondered what else people might be saying about her. She didn't want the boys at the high school to start telling tales or to think she was getting wild.

"What kind of dress do you want?" Beverly asked.

Beverly was wearing an ancient thing herself, a green cotton school dress, faded and limp, with puffy little sleeves. It made her look even younger than she was. LaRue wouldn't have been seen in anything so worn out. "I don't know what I want," LaRue said. "I need to look around. Maybe you can go with me."

This was a major concession for LaRue. She had gotten so she didn't like her sister tagging along, saying "little girl" things in front of the salesladies, but she also felt sorry for Beverly, and in this moment of victory, she could be generous.

"I think you should get red velvet. That's perfect for Christmas."

"Red velvet is for little girls. It's what we always used to get when we were kids."

"I know. I loved those dresses. Remember that year we both got new red dresses and new winter coats?"

"Sure. But that was a long time ago."

"That was the year Wally took us down to W. T. Grant's, and we bought that funny tie for Dad—the one with the ducks painted on it."

"He still wears it, too," LaRue said. "I've thought about dipping it in gravy some time, just so he'll throw the old thing away."

"Wally was funny that day, wasn't he?"

LaRue nodded. It hurt to think of that Christmas. Wally had made everything so fun. "He took us to Walgreen's for strawberry sodas. Remember that?"

"Yeah, I do. He caught me looking in the mirror at myself—and he teased me about it. But I remember what he said. He told me, 'Come on, Bev, you're just as beautiful now as you were a minute ago. You don't have to keep looking.' I still think about that sometimes."

And LaRue understood. Not many people told Beverly that she was beautiful. "I wonder if he's still like that," LaRue said. "I wonder if he still laughs and jokes around."

Beverly gripped her book close to her, wrapped both arms around it. "I saw some prisoners of war in a newsreel at the Marlo last Saturday. They got out of prison in the Philippines.

But they were skin and bones and sick looking. Do you think Wally is like that?"

"I don't know. But Dad says he's probably not there anymore. He thinks the Japs took him to Japan."

"I know."

"Maybe it's better there."

Beverly nodded. And then she asked softly, "Do you remember that time Wally and Gene played Fox and Geese with us? We were up in the fields by the prison."

"We did that lots of times."

"I only remember once. Wally got me down and was going to wash my face with snow. And then Gene threw snowballs at him to make him stop."

"That's how Gene always was."

"Do you still miss him?"

"Sure." LaRue looked down at Beverly. Her shoes were off, but she was wearing white anklets, folded down. One had slipped down onto her heel. LaRue pulled it up for her and tugged it straight.

"He was funny, too. And nicer than Wally. He didn't tease so much."

"It seems like he was the nicest boy ever," LaRue said. "But maybe that's just the way I want to remember him."

"No. It's true. He was." But LaRue didn't want to talk about that—not now, on a day when she was so happy. She tried to think how to change the subject. Before she did, however, Beverly said, "Sometimes, I hope I can go a whole day without thinking about him. But I never can."

"It's all right to think about him. We *should* think about him."

But now tears were in Beverly's eyes. "Not when it always makes me cry."

"Don't, okay? Let's go down and see if the paper has come. I want to look at the Christmas ads." Then she laughed. "Here's what you do, Bev. Wait until I talk Dad into a new dress and then look pouty and say, 'LaRue always gets everything she wants.' Dad'll buy you a new dress too. If you can make him feel guilty, you can get him every time."

"I don't need a new dress. I'm not going anywhere."

"Oh, Bev. I've got a lot to teach you. There's no such thing as 'I don't need a new dress.' That's the greatest truth a girl can learn."

Beverly giggled, but LaRue had her doubts about her little sister. She never would learn how to get what she wanted, no matter how hard LaRue tried to teach her.

On Friday afternoon LaRue and Beverly took the streetcar to town. They spent a few minutes in J. C. Penney's, just so LaRue could say she had looked there, and then she shopped at ZCMI and Auerbach's. She tried on almost everything and finally put a dress on layaway at each store. The one at Auerbach's was a fancy party dress, and way too expensive—$24.99—but she figured that would make the one at ZCMI for twenty not seem so bad. It was white, with a long skirt, but sleeveless and rather low cut. She knew her dad would throw a fit if he saw it that way, but it came with a black crepe bolero jacket, with long organdy sleeves. It was like a dress LaRue had seen Greer Garson wear in a movie. Mom could come with her on Saturday and make the purchase, and then she could be the one to explain to her father that dresses didn't come cheap these days.

Everything was falling into place for LaRue. She had made up her mind to take the final step. She would break up with Ned that night and possibly even tell the manager of the USO that she couldn't volunteer any longer. It was what she knew she had to do, even wanted to do now, but she also knew how pleased Dad would be when she told him—before she mentioned the price of the dress.

The truth was, giving up Ned was not that difficult. He was good-looking—though not so cute as Reed—but he was not very fun to be around anymore. He was way too serious, and lately he kept talking about the war and about all the boys who were going to be killed before Japan could be taken. He kept saying that he would be transferred before too much longer, and he wondered whether he would ever make it back. It seemed like every guy these days liked to say those kinds of things. It was their way to get some pity from the girls back home—maybe even get some "cooperation" from them. She didn't like it.

She arrived at the canteen that night before Ned did. When he did show up, he seemed serious again, not at all the way he had been when she had first met him. During their first dance, he told her, "LaRue, I need to talk to you about something tonight." When she didn't respond, he said, "I got word this week. I'm leaving."

"When?"

"Next week, on Thursday. I don't know why they have to move me right before Christmas."

"Where are you going?"

"They didn't tell me. But it will be somewhere in the Pacific—probably at an air base on some island."

"That shouldn't be too dangerous, should it?"

"It depends. When the Japs attack an island, the first thing they bomb is always the airfield."

That was probably true, but LaRue could tell he wanted her to think he was about to die, when he was probably headed for some out-of-the-way base, far from the action.

"You don't look all that broken up," Ned said.

LaRue didn't answer. She didn't want to be manipulated that way. What did he want her to say?

Ned was sullen after that, which only annoyed LaRue. But she was relieved to know she could break up with him now without having to say anything. She could let him ship out, write him a letter or two, and then stop. That would be the end of it. She could still tell her father that things were over, and if she told him she had decided to stop going to the USO, he would be thrilled. The best thing was, Reed had been talking to her at school every day, all week; and around East High, the two of them were already an "item." Two different girls had told her that Reed was telling his friends that he "had it bad" for LaRue Thomas. He was emerging as the star of the basketball team, just the way he had been on the football team, and in a basketball uniform, he was much more visible. There were girls at the school—juniors and seniors—who were so jealous of LaRue they could hardly stand it. Or at least, that was the other rumor LaRue was hearing.

LaRue spent a good deal of the evening at the sandwich bar—longer than she probably had to—but she wanted to avoid the scene that Ned was obviously pushing her toward. Gaye was working at the counter too, and at one point she told LaRue, "Everywhere you go, you've got the cutest boys after you."

But LaRue took the chance to make sure the right word got back to East High. "I don't care about these boys at the USO. Reed Porter is the kind of boy I want to go with. I'm thinking about quitting down here."

"Really?" Gaye said. "It's about the funnest thing I do."

"It used to be for me, too. But I'm losing interest."

Gaye was not exactly unattractive, but she was a big-boned girl, built too much like a man. The servicemen flirted with her, but the boys at the high school hardly noticed her. LaRue could see why she would want to keep coming. But the important thing was, she did talk, and she would certainly tell her friends what LaRue had said.

As the evening wore on, Ned seemed increasingly tense, and finally he said, "LaRue, let's get out of here. I need to talk to you."

"I can't leave. I promised to stay until Patsy gets here. She's coming in late tonight."

"What's going on, LaRue? Is this the brushoff?"

"What are you talking about?"

"Come here," he said, and he took her hand. He pulled her to the distant end of the room, away from the blaring jukebox and the dancing. There were people sitting at the tables, but he led her to a corner table where they were as far from people as they were going to get. He pulled out a chair for her, and then he sat down next to her and took her hand. "LaRue, I'm going out of my mind tonight. I'm on my way to the war, and I feel like you don't even care."

"I don't know what you want me to say, Ned. It's too bad, but I think you'll be safe—probably just about as safe as you are here."

"You don't know that." He looked away, across the room. "It Had to Be You" was playing—with Dick Haymes singing— and Ned seemed to listen for a time. "That's not the point," he finally said. "I thought you'd feel bad I was leaving."

"I do, Ned. But you always did want to make things serious, and I've told you before, I don't want to do that."

"I want to marry you, LaRue. So yeah, I guess that's pretty serious."

LaRue didn't say anything. She let him hold her hand, even move his other arm around her. She could see now that she wasn't going to get out of this situation easily after all.

"LaRue, you've never told me you love me. But the way you've kissed me, the way you've looked at me sometimes, I had to think that you do."

Again LaRue didn't answer. There was something so weak about the way Ned was doing this. She wished he would just demand an answer, and then she would give it to him.

"Here's what I'm thinking: I know you aren't ready to get married right now. I wish you were, but I also know it's hard to get married and then see your husband leave immediately. But what if we got engaged? We could make a promise to each other, and then . . . no, wait a minute . . . I'm doing this wrong. Let me say it this way: LaRue, will you marry me? Will you accept an engagement ring, and then marry me when I get back?"

"No, Ned. You know I won't do that."

"Can't we at least reach some kind of understanding?"

"Ned, I'm still in high school. I'm not ready to think about marriage."

"High school?"

"Ned, I'm only a sophomore in high school. I'm only fifteen."

"What are you talking about? I thought you were eighteen."

"I never told you that. It's just the idea you got."

Ned pulled his chair away—around the circular table—so he could look into her face. "Fifteen?"

"Yes."

He struck the table and swore. "What's going on here, LaRue? I've been talking to you about marriage for a couple of months. Why didn't you say something?"

LaRue shrugged. And for the first time, she felt ashamed. He was handsome in his khaki Army Air Force uniform, and he looked so crushed. She could hardly believe she had the power to hurt someone that much.

"I don't believe this." Ned sat silent for a long time. LaRue hoped he would tell her off; she had that much coming. And it would finally end everything. But Ned took hold of her hand again and said, "It doesn't matter. We can work this out. Once I get out of the service, you'll be old enough to get married. And I still want to marry you."

"Ned, listen to me. I liked dancing with you and everything—having a boyfriend—but it never was serious with me."

"That isn't true. I know the way you kissed me. That wasn't any little girl stuff."

LaRue was embarrassed about that. She knew that she had liked the kissing more than she had ever liked Ned, but she couldn't tell him that.

"Guys do stuff like that," Ned said. "Get hot and bothered,

and go after a girl, without really caring about her. But girls aren't like that. At least nice girls aren't. And I know you're a nice girl."

LaRue felt the stab, even though he hadn't meant it. She sat and looked at him, asked herself what she did feel—about him, and about herself. "I do like you, Ned. I mean, I had a crush on you, and—"

"A crush?"

"Yes. But now there's a boy at school I like. I'll probably like a lot of boys before I think about getting married. I want to go to college and things like that."

Ned was staring at her, and she didn't like the accusation in his eyes. She looked toward the dance floor. The smoke in the room, the smell of the place, bothered her tonight. She didn't know why she had liked it so much. Couples were dancing slowly, holding each other close, and over the clinking of glasses, the talk and the laughter, LaRue heard the plaintive lyrics: *What'll I do when you are far away? And I am blue; what'll I do?* She suddenly felt sorry for Ned.

"I don't understand any of this," he said.

"Ned, you just took everything too seriously. I didn't want it to be like that."

"No. I don't buy that. You kept telling me how religious your family is, and about your high standards. I believed that."

"What do you mean? You're the one who tried to do things. I wouldn't let you."

He shook his head slowly back and forth. "You did enough to get your thrills."

"I liked you kissing me, Ned, but I didn't think you would make so much out of it."

"You're a little tramp. Do you know that? You were the one in this for the fun. I was *serious*. I fell in love with you, head over heels."

"I'm not a tramp. What did I do?"

"If you were religious, you wouldn't toy around with a person like that. You knew what I was feeling for you."

LaRue looked down at the table.

"The first time you saw I was getting serious about you, why didn't you say, 'Ned, I'm only fifteen'? Why did you play me along like that? That's not what a decent person does. If I'd been chasing some skirt—some little chippy who knows what's up—I wouldn't have got caught off guard. But I took you for what you said you were: a nice Mormon girl—too nice to tell lies."

"Ned, I'm sorry. I didn't know what to do."

"Yes you did. All you had to do was tell me the truth. Isn't that what you're supposed to believe in?"

"But I liked you. And I wanted you to keep liking me."

"LaRue, there's something wrong with you. All you keep talking about is yourself. Now you've got some high school boy after you, so that's it for me. I could never do anything like that to you."

She glanced up at him and saw that he was really hurting. Tears spilled onto his cheeks. "I love you, LaRue. I'm crazy about you. I can't believe you did this."

For the first time, she saw what he was seeing. He was going off to some island somewhere, and now he had nothing to look forward to, no one back home to hang onto. She was suddenly filled with guilt. "I'm sorry, Ned," she told him. "I didn't know it would end up like this. But you're right about me. I'm not a nice girl."

His response was to reach out and take hold of her shoulders. "Let's start from scratch," he said. "Let's be honest with each other. I think you do care for me. That's the only way I can think about this."

LaRue stood up. Now she was crying. "Ned, I'd better just go. Let's not make this worse." She patted him on the shoulder. "I hope everything goes okay for you. I really mean that."

A fast, loud number had begun to play: "G. I. Jive." The

noise was mounting. Ned stood up and grabbed LaRue, pulled her to him. "Don't go. Please. I feel like I'm being pushed off a cliff."

"I know. But I don't want to make things worse. That's not fair to you."

"Dance with me. Let's just—"

"No, Ned. I've got to go. I'm really, really sorry for what I did to you."

"Can I write to you?"

"If you want to."

"I want to. Will you be here next week, before I leave? The last time I can come down is on Tuesday."

"I don't know."

"Please. I don't want to leave without seeing you again."

"All right."

"LaRue, when the war is over, I'm coming back here. You'll be older, and maybe you'll feel different about things. Will you at least think about me—and write back? Maybe something could still work out between us."

For the first time, LaRue actually considered that possibility. "I'll be here next Tuesday," she said. "And I will write to you. But don't make too much of it, okay? I don't want to lead you on anymore."

"That's good. That's what I want." And then he kissed her. LaRue had no idea whether she felt any love for him, but this kiss seemed something new, something between the two of them, not just something for her. And she was very clear about one thing: he was a better person than she was.

She walked away, left the USO without telling her boss she was going, and she cried most of the way home. She found her parents in the living room, so she stepped in and said, "Dad, I decided tonight that I won't be going to the USO anymore. After next Tuesday, I'm going to quit."

"What brought this on?" he asked. He had his reading

glasses on and was looking at some kind of papers, probably something from work. He sounded a little skeptical.

"I don't know. I guess I'm just tired of the whole thing."

"Did something happen?" Mom asked from across the room.

But LaRue didn't want to go into that. She just wanted a truce with her parents. "No," she said.

"Then why have you been crying?"

LaRue couldn't help it. The tears came again.

"Honey, what's going on? Is it about this young man you've been seeing down there?"

"Not exactly." LaRue needed to think, to sort things out, but she didn't want to talk with her parents right now. And so she headed for the stairs.

"Honey," Mom called out. "Did you find a dress today?"

LaRue stopped on the stairs. She was surprised by her own reaction. "Mom, I don't need a new dress," she said. "I can wear one of the ones I have."

27

Alex could hardly believe his good fortune. Captain Summers had managed to pull some strings with division brass, and he had arranged for Alex a ten-day pass for Christmas, starting December 21. Alex would cross the Channel and spend Christmas day and another few days with Anna. It was all he lived for now. He imagined from morning until night what it would be like to hold her in his arms, to share Christmas dinner, to bask in the civilized, kindly atmosphere. Away from the army there was another world, another life; it seemed only fantasy at times now, but he would rediscover it, and the experience would recharge his will so he could get through whatever lay ahead.

When he returned to France, conditions would not be bad for a few months. All the talk was that the airborne units wouldn't drop again until infantry troops made it through the Rhine and the Siegfried lines. No one knew how much longer Germany could hold out after that, but the men were all telling each other that German soldiers would spend their last effort at the borders. The war, at least in Europe, would end quickly after that. The men would probably have to make a drop into Japan, eventually, and that looked like a grim experience, but Alex didn't want to look that far ahead. He wanted his time with Anna; he wanted to feel alive and whole again, and then he would deal with the rest.

On Sunday evening, December 17, he had not been in bed long but was sound asleep when he heard someone tromp into the barracks. "Wake up, men. I've got something to tell you."

It was Lieutenant Wells, the new company commander. Since pulling back to Camp Mourmelon, Captain Summers had been promoted to battalion executive officer, the officer who made the actual decisions in the field. Summers was the most highly regarded officer in the battalion, so he was a popular choice, but Lieutenant Wells was a big disappointment to the men in E Company. He had transferred in from another company, and this was his first command. He talked big, but the men who had known him as a platoon leader said he was indecisive, even skittish, when the pressure was on.

"The Germans have started a big counteroffensive up in the Ardennes Forest in Belgium," Wells announced.

Alex sat up. He was still half asleep and was trying to let the words register in his mind.

"We're going in with the 82nd, but this won't be a drop. Trucks will haul us up there in the morning. So get some sleep but roll out early and get ready to go. All leaves are canceled. Everybody's going."

Alex dropped back onto his bunk. His first reaction was to tell himself this couldn't happen; it was too terrible. He tried to think whether he couldn't talk to someone, maybe Summers, and . . . but he knew it wouldn't work.

Wells hadn't turned the light on. Somewhere in the dark someone said, "What time are we pulling out?"

"I can't say for sure. Be ready by 0800."

"What about ammo? Where do we get that?"

"There's none here," Wells said. "If you brought anything out of Holland, take it with you. Otherwise, we'll have to be supplied somewhere along the line. We don't have winter uniforms, either. Take your trench coats and anything else you have to keep warm."

There were other questions, but Wells had no answers, and he soon left. As the door to the barracks closed, one man swore bitterly, and then curses filled the air. Someone said, "No ammo. No winter clothes. If there's a way to make of mess of things, the army will find it every time."

Alex had the strange sensation he was sinking—falling into darkness. But it had always seemed too good to be true, this chance to see Anna. He felt a kind of inevitability in the arrival of more evil, more suffering, and suddenly he was gripped with resentment. It seemed so obvious that sooner or later he was going to die in one of these battles, and he would never see Anna again in this life. After his escape from all the misery in Holland, he had allowed himself to begin to hope, but now he knew that had been a terrible mistake.

Alex heard the other men, but he didn't curse, didn't say anything. He lay on his bunk, stiff and awake, but in a kind of protective daze. And he stayed that way all night. Very early he used a flashlight and wrote Anna a letter:

I'm sorry. You know how much I wanted to be with you. But I think Hitler is making a huge mistake to come out from behind the Siegfried Line. We'll stop this offensive, and the Nazis will be finished. I know this is hard for both of us, but one more time we'll just have to make the best of things. I love you, Anna. Keep praying for me.

The letter did express his opinion, or at least what he wanted to believe, but it didn't represent what he felt. He couldn't tell her that he was numb, that his heart seemed to have stopped pumping. He had been hoping every day that his mail from Anna would catch up to him, but now he was pulling out without so much as a letter.

When others began to stir, Alex got up and packed. But as usual, the army asked its soldiers to "hurry up and wait." The first trucks didn't arrive until 0900, and it wasn't until nearly

1200 that Easy Company finally got underway. Some men complained the whole time, but most had grown quiet. The hope of an easy winter was lost now, along with Christmas in a fairly pleasant camp. Clearly, more men were going to die— maybe before the day was over. Alex felt the dread, of course, the tightness in his chest he had known before each battle, but he didn't calculate his odds of surviving one more time. He was moving into that other self, the one he had resorted to in Holland, the one that didn't think or feel.

"How bad do you think it's going to be up there?" Howie asked him. The two were standing behind the deuce-and-a-half truck, getting ready to board.

"I don't know," Alex said. "But it doesn't do any good to worry about it. We'll know before long."

"Everyone kept saying we were going to be here all winter."

"I know. But forget that now."

"Are you going to get me through this one, too?" Howie laughed, but there was strain in his voice. Clearly, he wanted to hear the promise again, the reassurance Alex had always given him.

"I told you—just stick with me. You'll be okay."

"I'm going to be a better soldier this time, Sergeant."

"I know you will." And Alex did believe it. Howie obviously had more confidence, more trust in himself this time. What Alex hoped was that the boy was hard enough now. In all this cold, he could easily break down again.

When the company finally got under way, the troops were packed tight into the backs of the trucks, and there were no seats, no protection from the bouncing and jostling. Before long the men were also chilled through. The driver of Alex's truck was one of the Negroes from the Red Ball Express, and he was a skilled driver, but he pushed hard, and he made very few rest stops.

"The way these truck drivers are pushing it," Duncan said,

"they must need us up there fast. I've got a feeling this ain't going to be no picnic."

"The army is moving something like 60,000 men up there," Campbell told him. "The drivers probably have to go back and make another run."

Campbell was sitting next to Alex, but the two were crowded so close together that they shifted back and forth, bouncing, as though they were conjoined twins. Duncan was on the other side of Campbell. "I don't see why Hitler had to pick Christmas, of all times," Duncan said. "The dirty . . ." Duncan stopped. He was swearing less these days, especially around Alex.

"Hey, that's the whole point. He figures the German boys have more will than we do."

Alex thought of the Germans he knew, how much they loved Christmas, but he didn't say that.

Howie was pressed against Alex, on his other side. He leaned forward, looked around Alex, and said, "The Krauts have this all planned. They'll have plenty of winter gear. We're not going into this thing ready, the way they are."

"That's exactly right," Duncan said. "They've got that smokeless gun powder, too. I hate it when they have cover and they can snipe at you—and you can't spot 'em."

"We'll be all right," Campbell said. "It's not all that cold. In Minnesota, we have days colder than this in September."

"Hey, what about me?" Duncan asked. "This time of year in Georgia, we sit on our front porches and listen to the birds sing."

"I'd hate that," Howie said. "At home, we don't figure it's even Christmas if we don't have snow."

"Same here," Campbell said. "We always go out and cut our own Christmas tree. My grandpa has a farm, and up in the hills, along one side of his land, he's got a big stand of pine trees. Me and my brother and my little sisters, we'd always hike in there on snowshoes. Then we'd pick out any tree we liked. No store-bought trees for us."

"Is your brother in the service?" Howie asked.

"Yeah. The navy. But he's got a nice, soft office job in San Diego."

"How old are your sisters?"

"I don't know. They're all teenagers. Eighteen, I guess, and probably sixteen and thirteen—something like that. But don't get interested. They're all too pretty for a dogface like you."

Howie laughed. "Yeah. I gotta admit, the girls never did line up just to get a look at me."

Actually, Howie was fairly good-looking. If he hadn't gone out much, that was probably because of his shyness. What Alex was glad to see was that he was talking, not turning inside himself.

"Well, I'll tell you what, Idaho. When the war is over, you borrow your dad's car—if you're old enough to drive by then—and you take a trip to Minneapolis. I'll let you take a look at three of the prettiest girls in Minnesota. Maybe one of them will even take you dancing."

"It's a deal. I'd let you dance with my sisters, but they're both married. I'll tell you what, though. We've got a couple of cows better looking than ol' Elsie, the Borden cow, and you can dance all you want with either one of them."

"Well . . . that's a tempting offer, but there's one more girl back home—as pretty as my sisters. If she's still there when I get home, I think I'll spend the rest of my Minnesota winters with her." He grinned. "Boy oh boy, that sure would be nice right now."

The men laughed, but no one made any crude remarks, and even the banter gradually stopped. Alex thought of what was coming, the days in the open, the battles ahead. He was sure everyone was thinking the same thing: Christmas, and now this.

As the day continued, Alex saw nothing to encourage him.

When the truck stopped late in the afternoon and the men piled out, they were on a country highway, and in the distance, the sound of heavy artillery fire was rolling, echoing across the hills. "Okay, men," Lieutenant Owen hollered. "We're hoofing it from here on in. We're heading to a place called Bastogne. It's a crossroads for the roads in this area, and the generals say we have to hold it. You squad leaders, lead out. Spread out a little and stay on the sides of the road. We could catch some fire now, so be ready to hit the dirt."

"Where's the ammo?" someone yelled.

"I still don't know. Maybe in town they'll have a supply dump."

This was unbelievable. The artillery was not that far off. The men were heading into battle, some with a clip or two of M-1 ammo, others with nothing.

As the men hiked the two or three kilometers to town, they saw no sign of enemy troops, but they began to see American soldiers, infantry troops from the First Army, heading in the opposite direction. Alex was surprised to see men retreating, not regrouping, but even more, he was shocked by the look of the soldiers. Most of them seemed dazed and frightened. Some had thrown away their rifles and ammo, even their coats. Apparently, at some point, they'd had to run for their lives.

When an older-looking man, a sergeant, walked past, Alex stepped out of line and stopped him. "What's going on?" he asked.

"You're walking straight into hell," the sergeant said. "The Krauts threw everything at us. I didn't think they *had* that many tanks. Whole divisions, heavily armored, are pouring in from everywhere. We lost most of our company. I don't even know where my company commander is. Dead, I'd guess."

The sergeant was already starting to walk away, obviously hesitant to be slowed down.

"Could I have those grenades?" Alex asked.

"Sure." The sergeant stopped long enough to hand them

over, and then he said, "Take these too," and handed Alex two M-1 clips. Then he was gone.

All along the line, the same thing was happening. The retreating soldiers were warning the 101st troops about the massive force they would be facing, and the paratroopers were asking for ammo and then walking with grim expectation into the combat that they could hear up ahead. When they reached Bastogne, they found a town of shops and little hotels, built mostly along one long strip of highway. By then the men were almost frantic about the shortage of ammunition, but they found no ammo dump in the city, and the direction came down the line to continue on through town and north, along the road toward Foy. Supplies would come.

Alex made sure everyone in his squad had at least one ammo clip for his rifle, but he had a machine-gun crew without a machine gun and a mortar team without a tube or any mortar rounds. In the dusk ahead, the blaze of exploding shells was lighting up the low-hanging clouds. He just hoped his men could get dug in somewhere, and supplied, before the action came closer.

The steady march had kept the men fairly warm, but the wind was picking up now, and the air was extremely cold. What Alex knew was that a frigid night was coming on. The men had no winter boots or galoshes, no long underwear. Almost everyone had a coat and a blanket, but they would have little protection should it snow that night.

Finally a truck came down the road from the north, driving hard. When it reached the first of the men, it slowed and then stopped between the columns. A lieutenant jumped down from the driver's seat and shouted, "This truck is full of ammo and weapons. It's not enough, but it will get you started. Don't everyone crowd around. You squad leaders come up and get what you need for your squads."

The sergeants hurried to the truck, and everyone grabbed for all he could get. Alex made sure he got a machine gun and a mortar tube. He made several trips, and he brought back a couple of cases of M-1 ammo and a case of hand grenades. The men grabbed all they could, but they were more than happy to share. They wanted ammunition, but they also wanted the guys next to them to have some too.

The troops fell back into columns and continued their march toward the tiny village of Foy, which lay in a valley to the northeast of Bastogne. As the village came into view, Alex could see only a few houses silhouetted against the false twilight created by the explosions not far away. First Battalion had arrived ahead of Second and had marched on through Foy. Those troops were clearly in the action now, taking heavy fire.

When word came down the line to halt, Alex was not at all sure what was going on, but eventually Owen met with Wells and then walked back to the platoon. "First Battalion is trying to get to a place called Noville," he told his squad leaders. "Third is supposed to move on past us and march into Foy. Our battalion will head into those woods and dig in. This road will be our left flank, and the railroad line beyond the woods will be our right.

"Where's our platoon going to be?" one of the men asked.

"We'll create a line along the edge of these woods," Owen said. "Our outposts will be in that field, just outside the tree line. No matter what the Jerries throw at us, we have to hold that perimeter. We can't let them into Bastogne."

That sounded clear enough, but once the platoon marched to the woods, Alex was unsure about where each squad was to locate. Finally the platoon leaders worked it out, since Wells seemed to disappear. But that worried Alex. If the units weren't placed just right, there could be gaps in the line, and the Germans could send patrols in to penetrate.

But he placed the men as best he could, and then, in the dark, they dug two-man fox holes at least deep enough to sleep in that night. The men knew all too well that they could be moved again in the morning, and they were tired. On the other hand, they also knew that artillery fire could open up at any time, and that was enough incentive to dig a decent hole.

Alex and Howie dug in together again and then put in a terrible night. They were exhausted from the long, hard day, but the cold was so penetrating, and the apprehension so unnerving, that neither got much sleep. And then in the morning, true to everyone's expectation, the squad had to move again—and dig new foxholes. The platoon took a position a couple of hundred yards to the east, looking down a long, sloping field toward Foy. They set up outpost stations—what the men called OPs—in the field, just as they had the night before, and dug in deep this time on a line just two or three meters inside the edge of the woods. Alex saw the danger in those pine trees. He walked along, stopping at each foxhole, telling the men, "If we take any fire, the shells are going to break up these trees and send limbs and splinters and shrapnel flying everywhere. I'd cover up your holes some way. Find logs if you can. Or cut yourselves some pine boughs."

When he stopped to talk to Duncan and Curtis, Duncan said, "You don't have to tell me, Thomas. I'm working on it. I scrounged a piece of canvas, and I'm going to hold that down with logs. I want to keep more than tree limbs out. I figure we'll have some snow one of these days, too."

"Where in the world did you get canvas?" Alex asked him.

"Never mind. In this man's army, it's not what you know, it's who you know."

"Or what you can steal," Alex said, and he laughed. Then he crouched down closer to Duncan. "I'm worried about these three young boys we picked up," he said. "This could be a baptism of fire." In Mourmelon, just a couple of days before pulling out, three kids, all just seventeen or eighteen, had arrived, straight from training camp.

"They were scared spitless last night," Duncan said. Then he grinned. "About half as scared as me and ol' Curtis. We know what to be scared of."

"Do you know their names?"

Duncan looked away and gave his head a little shake.

"Look," Alex said, "I know how you feel. But get to know them. Help me look out for them."

"I know their names," Curtis said. "Buckley's the big, tall kid from Washington State. Ling's from California, and Davis—I can't remember—somewhere in the Midwest."

"Illinois," Alex told him.

"Irv Johnston has already fallen in with those guys," Curtis said. "They're his age. He'll help 'em. We all will."

"Yeah. I will too," Duncan said. But then he asked, "What's that one kid. A Jap?"

"That's Ling. He's Chinese."

"Hey, as long as he can shoot a rifle—and will shoot at Krauts—he could be colored for all I care."

Alex felt himself tense, but he only said, "Dunc, from what I hear, the army might start putting colored soldiers in with regular units now."

Curtis was as southern as Duncan, but Alex knew that his attitude was quite different. "Won't there be Negro regiments anymore?" he asked.

"I think so. But I've heard that some of the regular infantry divisions will get colored replacements. There was something about it in *Stars and Stripes*."

"Don't worry," Duncan said. "They won't ever put any of those boys in the Screaming Eagles. There's not one of 'em that would jump out of an airplane."

"Duncan, the colored units have fought well."

Duncan finally seemed to notice that Alex was bothered by what he was saying. "Hey," he said, "I've lived around coloreds all my life—more than you have. And I just told you, those boys can fight right next to me, as long as they can shoot." He grinned. "When it comes to digging in with one, though, I think I'll let you do that."

Alex didn't laugh. He merely said, "Anyway, I had a chance

to talk with Ling when he got to camp. He's as American as apple pie. He played halfback on his high-school football team in Bakersfield."

"No complaints here. The only thing I wish is that we had back all the guys we started with."

And of course, Alex felt that way too. There was a tendency at this point not to want new friends. Replacements hadn't learned the tricks of surviving, and no one wanted to be close to someone who was only going to get himself killed.

"Does anyone know what's happening up ahead?" Duncan asked. "I've never heard so much shelling."

"The only thing I know," Alex said, "is that First Battalion took it on the chin last night. They're falling back now, going into reserve. Someone told me they've lost about a third of their men already, and no one is moving up to take their place. We're looking right down on the front line—there in Foy, where the Third Battalion is. I have no idea why the Germans haven't hit us here yet. They seem to be zeroed in on both sides of us."

"They'll be sending stuff in here before long," Duncan said. He spat on the ground and cursed.

Alex had no doubt Duncan was right. "Well, anyway, get that hole the way you want it, and then help me make sure these other guys have some decent cover."

"I ain't giving nobody our canvas," Duncan said. He reached up suddenly and gave Alex a push on the knee. In his crouched position, Alex fell backward and landed on his backside. But he jumped up quickly and kicked a little dirt in Duncan's foxhole—which brought a loud protest—and walked away.

After Alex had checked with all the men, he went back to his own foxhole and helped Howie get it finished. Howie had cut some branches for cover. That helped keep a little warmth in, but they both found themselves painfully cold that night. Alex slept a little more than the night before, simply because he was so tired, but he was awake and miserable much of the time. Daytime was always easier, when he could think like a soldier, keep himself busy. But at night his mind wanted to cross the Channel, envision what he had missed by losing his pass. He tried not to do that, fought the thoughts, but the images still came.

Alex and Howie took a two-hour turn at the outpost, which was a scary experience, but even worse were the hours when the new guys were out there. Buckley and Ling were teamed up, and that worried Alex. It was easy to get nervous and make a mistake—shoot your own men as they approached to take the watch or miss movements by the Germans.

As the cold intensified toward morning, Alex began shivering so uncontrollably that he felt as though he were convulsing. But there was nothing he could do about it. He had no other clothes, and a fire would signal to the Germans the position of the troops—and attract artillery fire.

"Are you awake?" Howie asked.

"Sure."

"I've never been so cold in my life."

"I know," Alex said. "But we should get some winter gear soon—maybe today."

"I need to get out of here and just move around. That would warm me up more than anything."

"You can't start walking around. One of our own guys might blow your head off."

"Then what can we do?"

"We'll just wait it out. Once it gets light, we'll try to get hold of some more blankets or clothes or something."

"I'm not sure if my feet are froze or not. I can't feel 'em anymore." Alex could hear in his voice how discouraged he was becoming again.

"We'll have to get our shoes off today and rub our feet—for circulation. We could all get frostbitten if we're not careful."

"Yeah, that's just what I need, to take my shoes off." Howie laughed, and Alex knew that was his way of showing Alex that he was all right, that he was going to work to keep his spirits up.

It seemed as though the sun would never rise, the night lasting forever this time of year. Alex heard other men stirring eventually, complaining. As the sun began to lighten the clouds a little, he moved out among the foxholes. The men in his squad were eating K rations and asking whether they couldn't build a small fire. He had to tell them no and had to tell them, as he had told Howie, that he would do what he could that day to find some relief before night came again.

But there was no relief—no supplies—and the day never warmed much. It was damp and misty, with low clouds hanging in the valleys. The sound of battle was all about them, northward beyond Foy, and on both sides. The men knew they were lucky not to be in the heat of battle, but the heat of anything sounded good compared to the overpowering cold.

In the afternoon, Lieutenant Wells called the officers and NCOs back to a headquarters tent that was set up in a clearing on the south side of the woods. When Alex got there, he saw his friend Captain Summers, who looked as confident as ever. Summers told the men, "We were able to get a few medical supplies this morning but not enough. And there's nothing available in the way of underwear or blankets or galoshes. Make sure the men take care of their feet."

"What's going on?" one of the sergeants asked. "Why can't headquarters get supplies in here?"

"The Germans have cut off the road we came in on. We're encircled. There may be some kind of a supply drop, sooner or later, but not with this cloud cover."

"We're *surrounded?*"

"Yeah. I'm afraid so."

"How bad is it?" Alex asked. "Can't someone break through?"

"The word is, we're outnumbered something like ten or

twelve to one. But we've got position, and we're getting dug in. We have an artillery unit to help us, too, so we're better off than usual—for paratroopers." Summers laughed. "When I sent Harper into town for that medicine, some supply officer told him, 'The Krauts have us surrounded, the poor suckers. We've got 'em right where we want 'em.'"

But no one else laughed, and Alex knew Summers was trying to put a good face on things. The 101st did have some artillery help, but the supply of ammunition was inadequate, and it was hard to know how much food headquarters had, beyond what the men had carried in. In the long run, the lack of clothes and supplies might turn out to be as big an enemy as the Germans.

"This isn't as bad as it looks," Summers said, obviously sensing what the men were thinking. "The Germans are out there moving around. They make better targets than we do. All we have to do for now is hold our position and not take any chances. The Krauts are cold too, and many of them have been at this for lots of years. The rest are young kids and old men. I'm not so sure their commitment to this thing runs very deep."

But Alex wasn't buying that. The Germans had supposedly been on the run in Holland, and yet they had turned and fought with fury.

2 8

Alex walked back to his squad. He had to tell the men that no supplies would come that day, that everyone should improve their foxholes and get by the best they could. He heard lots of complaints, of course, but he tried not to join in. He almost wished the action would pick up in their sector, just to take the men's attention off their own misery.

But the daylight passed away quickly, and the long night began again. Alex and Howie huddled together. They had stacked more pine boughs over their foxhole, but that didn't seem to help. Alex shivered until his muscles ached, and Howie, who had become so thin, was worse. Alex could tell from the way he was panting at times, making little grunting sounds, that he was at his limit. But he didn't complain, didn't speak at all.

Alex finally said, "Are you all right?"

Howie hesitated, then said, quickly and simply, "I'll make it."

The sun never seemed to rise that morning. Eventually there was enough light, however, to see that thick clouds were hanging over the hills, and then the snow began to fall. It was a fleecy, dry snow—easier to deal with than if it had been wet and soaking—but it kept coming all day. By the time it finally let up, late in the afternoon, a foot had fallen. The valley was beautiful: the little town of Foy, the scattered woodlands, the fields and fences—everything was white and pure and peaceful. Even the sounds of artillery fire were muffled by the snow.

Alex looked out across the scene, wondered how the world could look so lovely at a time like this. He kept stamping his feet and moving back and forth, trying to keep his blood flowing. He moved among his men, reminding them to rub their feet, to keep them dry. The men all carried an extra pair of socks. They had learned in Holland to change every day, and to dry their wet socks inside their shirts, against their bodies. Wet feet were one sure guarantee of misery.

Another night passed with the men sleeping little, dealing with the cold as best they could but miserable and getting more vocal about it all the time.

The next day was warmer, with some sun, and that seemed to help a little. Then, when the men saw American airplanes, saw parachutes, they knew supplies were being dropped, and everyone's spirits brightened. Late in the day, however, word came that food and ammunition had been dropped but no blankets, no winter gear. That was hard enough to take, but everyone also knew what was coming: the clear skies would mean a colder night.

No one said it, but Alex knew as well as anyone that the surrounded 101st Division was in deep trouble. The supply drop would help. The American troops could come a little closer to matching the artillery fire they were receiving, and certainly the soldiers needed bullets for their rifles. But the Germans were attacking from every direction, with far superior numbers. The 506th Battalion had been lucky so far to be sitting in a quiet sector, but that couldn't last much longer.

Late that afternoon, Alex watched a German unit with his field glasses—tanks and riflemen—moving along a road. The men were wearing heavy coats and winter boots, all white for camouflage. With that kind of gear, they were certainly getting more sleep, and their morale had to be better. Alex's men were not breaking down, not yet, but they were suffering, and they were already tired. A few more days like this, and the Germans would stand a good chance of making a breakthrough, somewhere, and then chaos could follow. There was no telling whether that was likely to happen, but one thing was certain: before this was over, a lot of men were going to die.

When night came this time, the temperature dropped quickly. There was nothing for the men to do but huddle together and stay in their foxholes. Late in the night Alex could feel the cold penetrating to the core of his body. He passed beyond shivering and drifted into a numbness, a feeling of warmth that was both relieving and terrifying. Somewhere in his brain was buried the knowledge that this was dangerous, the first stage of hypothermia. Part of him didn't want to fight it, but an alarm also seemed to go off, and he forced himself awake. Then he awakened Howie, whose breathing had become shallow and raspy. "Howie, Howie," he shouted in the boy's ear, and he shook him by the shoulders.

"Don't," was all that Howie mumbled.

"Wake up! You've got to stay awake—or you'll freeze to death."

"Don't."

But Howie was waking up. "Listen to me," Alex said. "I've got to go out for a few minutes. I've got to wake the men up, make sure they aren't freezing. While I'm gone, keep your body moving—do some pushups. We've got to get our blood moving."

Alex couldn't see Howie's face. But he could hear him breathing better. And finally he said, "Okay."

"Are you going to do some pushups?"

"Yeah."

"All right. I'll be right back."

"Won't they shoot you out there?"

"I'll warn them I'm coming. I've got to do it, or someone might freeze."

Alex was surprised at how unwilling his body was to get going. The stiffness had rendered his limbs almost useless. It was all he could do to pull himself from the foxhole, but he struggled out into the snow, onto his chest, and got himself up. Then he moved about, waking the men, making sure they were still alive. Everyone was in bad shape, but they were all able to answer him. He told them to move around as much as they could but to stay in their holes. Then he went back to his own.

"Howie, I'm coming in," he said, and he dropped in at the end of the rectangular hole. "How're you doing?"

"I did some pushups." He sounded like a little boy telling his dad that yes, he had done the chores. Alex heard the emotion that was so close to breaking into tears, but he also knew that Howie was hanging in there, making an effort.

"Let's take turns doing exercises. We've got a few hours until sunup, but we'll make it."

"Okay."

Alex had Howie lie on his side and leave as much room as he could, and then Alex did pushups. When he was finished, he said, "I only did twenty-one. That's all this poor old body could manage. See if you can do more."

And Howie, so lean and yet strong, did do more. He even bragged about it, which was a good sign.

After the pushups, the two lay next to each other. "We'll do some more in a minute," Alex said. "I feel a lot better. Don't you?"

"Yeah. Some."

"What would you be doing if you were home right now?" Alex asked. He knew he was taking a chance. He didn't want to make the poor kid homesick, but he did want to remind him of the things that were worth living for.

"What day is it?"

"I'm not sure. We got trucked up here on Monday, and that was the eighteenth. How many nights have we been dug in?"

"This is the fourth night."

"Okay. So that means it's Friday, the twenty-third. That's Joseph Smith's birthday. I'll bet you didn't know that."

"Nope. But I do know who Joseph Smith is. I did learn that much about your church."

"So what would you be doing today, back in Boise?"

"Just working somewhere. When construction shuts down in the fall, I always found some kind of work inside somewhere."

"What about Christmas? Would you have all your shopping done?"

Howie let out a little gust of breath, maybe a laugh. "Prob'ly not. I'd usually buy something for my little brother, but I almost always left it until the last minute."

"Didn't you get anything for your mother or your sisters?"

"Naw."

"How come?"

"I don't know. My family never went in much for all that. They're getting a little more that way, but during the Depression, when I was growing up, we hardly got anything. And you know, my sisters are married. I don't know why I didn't get anything for my mom."

"Next year you will. We might all be home by then."

"I think I will do that." Then, after a few seconds, he asked, "Do you really think we'll be home by then?"

"I think the war in Europe will be over by then. I don't know about Japan." But now Alex realized he'd taken the conversation in the wrong direction. Neither one of them needed to think about how many nights in foxholes they might have ahead of them. "What are you going to do when you get back home?" Alex asked.

"I don't know. Just get a job. I can almost always find a job welding, if nothing else." The shivering was getting worse, and he was beginning to sound distracted again.

"You want to get married, don't you?"

"Sure. Sooner or later. But . . . I don't know."

"What?"

"We're all going to get killed, aren't we?"

"No."

"Aren't we in an awful mess?"

"Sure. But that doesn't mean we'll all get killed. We can keep holding out. That's what us paratroopers do. Isn't that what they told you at jump school?"

"I didn't think it would be like this."

"None of us knew what it would be like," he said. "There's no way to be ready for it."

"I'd hate to have my little brother find out what kind of soldier I've turned out to be."

Alex was suddenly at a loss. There was almost no right thing to say. There was something so innocent and plaintive in Howie's voice that Alex was tempted to wrap his arms around him, hug him like a little brother, and tell him not to feel bad. But that was the worst thing he could do. "Howie, don't start that self-pity stuff again," Alex said. "Just get through this night, like the rest of us. And when the shooting starts, pull the trigger. You can't *think* about everything. Isn't that what I keep telling you?"

Howie didn't answer. He lay still for a time, his breathing a little too loud, as though he were straining to control his emotions, or maybe just dealing with the cold. Finally he did say, "When I was a kid, I went hunting for jackrabbits with my dad."

"I thought your dad ran out on you."

"He did. But every now and then he'd show up and want to be my big buddy. So this one time, he wants to show me how to hunt. It took me a long time just to hit a rabbit with a .22. When I did, the thing started flipping around and screaming. I never knew a rabbit could make a noise like that." He hesitated and breathed hard again. "I was only about ten or eleven, something like that, and we'd always raised rabbits and killed them to eat. I never thought nothing about it. But this ol' jackrabbit was wild with pain, I guess, and flopping all over the place. So my dad said, 'Shoot him again. Put him out of his misery.' But I couldn't do it. He finally did, but then he looked at me and saw I was crying, and he really lit into me. He told me not to be a bawl baby. It was just a jackrabbit, not worth worrying about. But I never hunted after that. I'm the only kid I knew from up around Boise who never wanted to hunt deer and elk and all that. Part of it was, though, if I did go, I didn't want to go with my dad."

"It doesn't matter," Alex said, but he hardly knew what he meant. And then he did put his arm around Howie.

For a long time they lay like that, until Alex said, "We'd better do some more pushups."

They each took a turn again, and then they lay still. Alex kept repeating in his mind, like a mantra, "Don't think. Don't think. Just get through the rest of this night." But thoughts of Anna kept working their way past his resistance. The twenty-third was the day he had intended to arrive in London.

He knew he had to get Howie talking again—and occupy his own mind that way. Howie had played baseball when he was growing up, so Alex asked him about that. And then they talked about the major leagues, all the great players who were in the military now: Joe DiMaggio, Bob Feller, Ted Williams, Enos Slaughter, Red Ruffing. After that they did more pushups, and then they talked about boxing, about Joe Louis, Jack Dempsey, and Sugar Ray Robinson. And eventually the sun did start to rise.

All the men in the squad got up early and got some breakfast in themselves, but after that they didn't want to go back to their foxholes. Howie looked anything but strong, and his face was gray, as though a layer of skin was frozen. Most of the men had moved into the woods, out of sight from the open field in front of the forest, and they were talking, tramping, moving to try to stay warm. Then, without warning, Alex heard the whistle of incoming artillery, and he shouted, "Get to your holes!" He ran for his own foxhole, realized he was too far away, dove into the snow and flattened himself as best he could.

A shell struck a pine tree not twenty yards away and sent limbs and shrapnel flying in all directions. Two more hit quickly after that, each a little farther away from Alex, so he jumped up and ran again, and crashed through the opening in the limbs into the hole. He landed on top of Howie, who had apparently never stopped running, even when the shells had struck.

They squirmed into a better position but remained rolled up, each hugging his own knees. For a solid hour their position took a terrific pounding. The sound of trees ripping apart, exploding, was paralyzing. Alex could feel the suck of the concussion at times, even feel the burst of heat, and with it the whirring sound of shrapnel in the air. He kept watching Howie, who was not complaining, not whimpering, as he'd done in Holland. Instead, he was stone-faced.

"We're all right," Alex would say after each round of explosions. "Nothing's going to get to us in here. The shells are blowing up in the tops of the trees." But of course that wasn't always true. Some of the shells were shaking the earth as though a volcano were erupting nearby.

When the shelling finally stopped, Alex told Howie, "We're okay now. You just stay right here. I'm going to check the men."

"All right," Howie said, but nothing more. Alex thought he understood what Howie was doing. He was trying not to think, not to feel. He was following Alex's advice.

Alex discovered that a shell had broken up a tree almost on top of Pozernac and Gourley. Debris had penetrated their cover, and Gourley had been nicked by a hunk of shrapnel, just above his knee. He had already bandaged it, however, and he said he didn't need a medic.

Alex got one anyway, and then the men waited and watched for movement in the fields in front of them. Nothing happened for more than an hour, but then the pounding of artillery began again. That pattern continued the rest of the day and into the long evening. It finally let up during the night—and mercifully, the night wasn't quite as cold—but Alex expected an assault at first light. This bombardment was probably to soften up the sector before an attack.

Alex could see the nervousness in the men now. They ate from their rations again, but they didn't head into the trees for long, except to hurry to a latrine and back. There was more strain in their voices. Maybe today—Christmas Eve—was the day they would die. But no one talked about what day it was.

Alex took the early watch at the outpost himself, and he took Howie along with him. They scanned the snow for any movement, expecting any second for the attack to come, but it didn't. Alex could feel his nerves ready to break. The cold, the dread, the constant realization of the trap he and his men were in—all of it was building up.

Nothing happened all morning, however, and even the shelling in their area had stopped. Alex finally got word that he should report to the headquarters tent. When he got there, Lieutenant Owen assigned him to take a patrol out to make contact with the Germans. "We don't know what we've got out there," Owen told him. "Everything seems quiet, but we could have Krauts moving in on us, maybe even trying to breach our lines. They're not coming up the road from Foy or across the fields, but they could be infiltrating through these woods on our right flank." He pointed to a wooded area on a map that extended along the railroad line. The name of the forest, printed on the map, was the *Bois Jacques*. "We need to go in there and find out what's happening."

So Alex walked back to his men and called them away from

their holes. "We're going out to make contact," he said, trying to sound confident. "We need to find out what's going on in that stand of trees that runs along the railroad tracks on our flank. That's the only cover the Germans have in this sector. We can spot them if they come at us any other way."

Alex looked at Howie, who didn't nod, didn't accept. He merely stared straight ahead. But then, no one was excited about a patrol like this. It was always one of the most likely ways to get shot. A couple of the men cursed, and Pozernac said, "That's a bad spot in there. You can't see a thing. We'd better not get scattered out to where we can't see each other."

"That's right," Alex said. "We have to keep each other in sight at all times." He looked at the three young guys. They nodded, seeming willing, but Alex also saw the anxiety in their eyes. This was their first real action, and he knew the adrenaline had their hearts pumping.

Alex led out, and the men followed, in file. He stayed in the trees until he reached the railroad tracks, then he turned left across a clearing and into the *Bois Jacques*. As he entered the trees, he could see more clearly why Pozernac had been so concerned about getting scattered. The soft snow stopped sounds from carrying, but the larger problem was that the forest had been cut, the trees replanted, all in rows. They were the same size and shape, so every part of the forest looked alike.

"Let's move up in a double column," Alex whispered, "two by two. But keep in visual contact with the men in front of you. We don't want to get guys lost in here. Campbell, I want you to move ahead of us and scout the area. Bunched up like this, if we walk into something, we could get ourselves into a mess."

Campbell nodded and then stepped forward.

"It's your lucky day," Duncan said, and he laughed. Campbell glanced at him, but he didn't smile. He looked grim in his muddy field jacket and with his six-day growth of whiskers.

"Don't move out too far, too fast," Alex told Campbell. "I want to be able to see you."

Campbell walked ahead, crouching and moving in short runs, hiding behind a tree each time he stopped. He looked back at times, too, to make sure he could still see Alex.

Slowly the squad worked its way through the woods, following Campbell. There seemed to be no sign of enemy troops, and Alex, working to get through the snow, was warming up, feeling better. And then the sound of machine-gun fire cracked through the air, sending a hail of fire through the trees. Campbell disappeared. Alex hoped he had only dropped into the snow for cover. But silence followed, and nothing moved.

"I'm going up," Duncan whispered.

"No. Stay put."

But all was silence. Alex waited and watched, breathed steadily, expecting hell to break loose any moment. Five minutes passed, and Duncan finally said, "I gotta get to Campbell." He made a quick dash ahead before Alex could say anything.

Duncan drew no fire, and he worked his way forward in quick dashes. Then he crawled under a pine tree. Alex couldn't see what was happening at that point, and he hated the quiet that followed. He was about to move his men up when he saw Duncan crawl out from under the tree and wave the men back. At the same time, the machine gun fired again, and Duncan dropped onto his face.

Alex waited, unsure what to do. But after a minute or so, he saw that Duncan had begun to crawl, flat on his face in the snow. He worked himself around another pine tree, and then he suddenly jumped up and ran hard. As he approached Alex, he shouted, "Get out. There's a platoon, maybe a whole company, in the field just beyond these trees. They're ready to move."

"What about Campbell?"

"He's dead."

Alex and the others fell back quickly, working hard to

trudge back to the perimeter they had been protecting, back to their foxholes. Alex headed straight on to the headquarters tent. He told Wells about the German troops, and Wells called in artillery fire. For about twenty minutes the sound was deafening, but heartening, as the position below the trees took a terrific barrage of fire.

When it was over, the men waited, still expecting the attack. But it didn't come, and that meant the artillery had driven the Germans back. So Alex climbed out of his hole and walked to Duncan and Bentley. "Do you want to go with me?" he asked. "I'm going after Campbell."

"Yeah," Duncan said. "I was just thinking the same thing."

He climbed from his hole, and then he added, "He took a bullet in the forehead. He didn't suffer."

Alex nodded. "Well . . . that's good," he said. And automatically the words ran through his mind: "Don't think about this."

Alex and Duncan went after the body, but Alex didn't look at Campbell any more than he had to. He helped carry the body back behind the line, and then he returned to his foxhole. "How're you doing?" he asked Howie, who was standing up in the hole, the pine boughs pushed back from over the opening.

"I'm all right," Howie said, with no emotion.

"Were you okay during that patrol?"

"Yeah. Pretty much."

Alex looked out across the fields and then to the right, toward the trees where Campbell had died. He wasn't going to think about that. Couldn't. But the snow, the pretty scene, seemed to remind him again that it was Christmas Eve.

"At least it's over for Campbell," Howie said. "He doesn't have to do this anymore."

"Let's eat something."

That evening Alex and Howie huddled close and shook. It wasn't the worst of the nights, but it was bitterly cold, and it promised to last far too long. And then, late in the evening, Alex heard one of the men begin to sing. It took Alex a few seconds to realize that it was Pozernac, who didn't have much of a voice. He was singing, "Here comes Santa Claus, here comes Santa Claus, right down Santa Claus lane."

"Hush up," Alex called out.

Pozernac hesitated long enough to laugh, and then he started again. "Vixen and Blitzen, and all his reindeer—whatever are their names."

"Pozernac, that's enough," Alex said. And this time the singing did stop. "What's wrong with you, Sarge?" he yelled. "Don't you know it's Christmas Eve? I want Santa to come down my chimney. I asked him for a pretty girl to keep me warm in here. I think I'm going to get Betty Grable."

"I want the Andrews Sisters—all three," someone else yelled.

Alex knew the noise wasn't wise, but he called back to Pozernac, "Cuddle up with Gourley. He's warmer than a skinny little girl."

"Yeah. But he's not a very good kisser."

Duncan was yelling now. "You would know."

But all this seemed a little strained, as though the men were trying too hard. Silence returned, and now Alex knew that the men were thinking about the very thing they had refused to mention all day. It was "the night before Christmas," and everyone had memories of that.

Maybe five minutes went by, and then a better voice, a stronger one, began. It was Duncan. "I'll be home for Christmas," he was singing, and Alex didn't tell him to stop.

By the time he had finished, the silence was almost frightening. But then Duncan began to sing "Silent Night," and the other men joined in.

Most of the men weren't particularly good singers, but their voices blended pretty well in this silent night—with no artillery coming in. By the time they were finished, Alex could feel the pain, as though it were hanging in the cold night air.

He knew he couldn't let go. He held on tight, tried to make his mind blank. But his body was rigid from the attempt.

"I keep thinking about Campbell and them sisters of his," Howie finally said. "He had a girl waiting for him too."

"Don't do it," Alex said. "Don't talk about it."

"But he was such a good guy, and I keep wondering when his family will find out—and how they'll feel about it."

"Private, listen to me. I don't want to talk about that. And you shouldn't either. Let's try to get some sleep before it gets really cold."

"Okay. I know what you mean."

Alex stretched out in the foxhole, next to Howie. His body and mind were spent with exhaustion, but he couldn't sleep at all. "Silent Night" kept running through his head, the words, the tune. And thoughts of London. Finally he said to Howie, who was obviously awake, "Howie, look at it this way. This could be the worst night of our lives. If we can get through this, we can get through anything."

"That's what you told me that one night back in Holland."

"Well . . . yeah. But this one might be a little worse."

"No. That one was worse for me. I'll make it through this one."

"All right. Good. Me too."

And so they didn't try to sleep. They talked about basic training and about jump school—about anything that they had in common. Anything but Christmas.

2 9

Anna Stoltz and her mother received a gift for Christmas. On Christmas Eve, Anna got word at the OSS offices, from one of the agents, that her father had made contact, and he was safe. The man wouldn't admit where he was, but when she asked, "Is he in Germany?" he didn't deny it, and his careful reaction told her she was right. She didn't tell her mother that part, but she did bring home the word that nothing had happened to him; he was merely delayed.

This news was an enormous relief. Over the past few weeks the tension for Anna and Sister Stoltz had constantly increased. It was terrible to wait, but at least they knew Heinrich was all right for the present. What they didn't know was why he was delayed and how much danger he might be in. And they also knew nothing of Peter, and that continued to be a terrible worry.

In addition, Anna had something new to concern her. She had learned in recent days that the 101st Airborne had been drawn into the fighting in the Ardennes Forest, in Belgium. Because of the bulge in the line created by the German offensive, newspapers were calling the action the "Battle of the Bulge." And the news was frightening: the Americans in Bastogne—the entire 101st Division—were surrounded by

German forces. Supplies were limited, and the cold was punishing. As Christmas approached, all of England and America—all the world—was waiting to know the fate of these soldiers, who could easily be overrun, any day, destroyed or taken as prisoners.

Anna had received word from Alex the week before that he might be able to make it to England for Christmas. She had been excited about that, had thanked the Lord many times, and now it had all been taken away. She had not yet heard any direct word from Alex, but there was no doubt his leave had been canceled. Anna's disappointment was so intense that she had to fight every second not to despair. But she couldn't do that. Her mother needed her too much, and even the Dillinghams needed some cheering up. They were missing their home, their former life, so very much. They had hoped to spend Christmas with their son Arthur and their grandchildren in Manchester, but Arthur, who had been wounded in Africa early in the war, had written to say that he was being recalled to the Royal Air Force. England was in desperate need of pilots, and Arthur was considered well enough now to fly again. The Dillinghams, the couple staying with them, hadn't expected anything like that, and they, too, were very worried. The pilots who were bombing Germany didn't have a long life expectancy these days.

For Anna, all the anxiety was almost too much. Alex was in more danger than ever before. She lay awake at night and wondered how cold he was, whether he had enough to eat, whether he was in immediate danger. She had seen newsreels of battles, watched the explosions as artillery fire crashed among the soldiers. She hadn't yet heard anything from Alex, but she had to assume he was living out in the open, in a foxhole, just as he had in Holland, and she wondered how much terror he was living with.

Sometimes Anna had admitted to herself that Alex's chances of surviving might not be very good. But now, with the newspapers and radio constantly blaring the news that the Americans were in trouble in Bastogne, she knew that bad news could arrive at any time. She had once told Alex that she would rather be married to him, take the chance of losing him, and at least know that he would be hers in the next life, but all she could think now was that she wanted him back, whole. She wanted him to hold her again. She wanted to go with him to Salt Lake City, to meet his family. She wanted a life with him.

But Anna stayed busy with her work, and she laughed as much as possible. She found humor where she could, and she tried to lift her mother whenever she found a way. True, at night she sometimes lay in bed and cried, but she hated self-pity in others, and she wasn't about to tolerate it in herself.

Recently Anna and her mother had received a Christmas card from Brother and Sister Thomas. Sister Thomas had written a nice little note, wishing them well and expressing her great desire to meet all the Stoltzes as soon as possible. Another letter had come from Bobbi. Alex had told Anna all about this sister he loved so much. And Sister Thomas had told Anna about Richard, who was missing in action. But Bobbi's letter was full of gratitude and hope. Richard was safe, she said, and she wished the same for Peter.

Bobbi had written the letter before word had come about Alex being pulled into the battle in Belgium. Nonetheless, the part of the letter Anna kept rereading was the conclusion:

Anna, I'll never forget the first time Alex told me about you. He said, "She's so beautiful, it hurts to look at her," and he told me he felt sure the two of you would end up together—that God had given him that affirmation. I used to think that if I prayed hard enough, nothing bad would ever happen, but now I understand that life is all about surviving hard times. I know these are difficult days for you, but I also believe you and Alex will be back together before too much longer, and then, more than anything, I want to meet you and know you as my dear sister.

Anna did want that. She had never had a sister, and she

longed to experience that kind of closeness with Bobbi—and with all of Alex's family. Life was so full of dread and worry, it was true, but it was also full of hope, if only she could get back those she loved so much.

Christmas morning was not easy. The Dillinghams were optimists by nature and rather lighthearted in the way they approached life. But their discouragement was obvious that morning. Edward had only said it once, but Anna knew it was on his mind all the time now: "We had thought the worst of the worries was over for our family."

As it turned out, however, everyone had managed to buy some little thing for everyone else, and the exchange was good fun. Sister Stoltz had baked a German *Weinachts Stollen*, the traditional Christmas cake. She served it with an herbal tea, and everyone liked it very much.

"Thank you so much, deary," Mrs. Dillingham told Sister Stoltz. "It's such a lovely thing to have a little sweet now and then. I can hardly remember the days when we had so much—and hardly appreciated it."

Sister Stoltz, whose English had improved a great deal since the Dillinghams had moved in, told her, "Maybe the war makes us learn something."

Mr. Dillingham sipped at his tea. "I think I've learned quite enough to last me for a time," he said, and he chuckled, his voice sounding warm. He had a way of dropping his head when he looked at a person, as though he had to do so to see over his big nose, but it always made Anna feel as though he were going out of his way to look closely, to make a clear connection.

Anna had gotten used to the way the English thought and spoke. She liked Mr. Dillingham's understatement. Surely everyone in the world had learned enough to last for a long time, she thought. She knew that people had a way of forgetting quickly, but this amount of suffering had to stick with people for generations to come, it seemed.

It was a quiet day, and the good humor of the morning gradually slipped away, at least for Anna, toward a disappointing melancholy. She always wanted too much from Christmas. She remembered the enchantment of the day from her childhood, and she often thought of the year when she had been sixteen and Alex had been a missionary in her home. She also remembered that one wonderful year, during the war, when the Rosenbaums had still been safe with her family. But those thoughts were not helpful, and so she told herself to be thankful she had escaped Germany and that she was married to Alex. She went to her bedroom, read Bobbi's letter again, and then knelt and prayed that Alex was all right today, that he would find some comfort in spite of the conditions he was living in, and that he would live to return to her. Then she prayed for her brother and her father. She only allowed herself to cry for a minute or two.

Then she sat on her bed, and for a time, like Mary, she pondered the secret in her heart. In October she had suspected she was pregnant. By November she had been certain. She had wanted Alex to be the first to know, and so she had written him in Holland. But in his latest letter he had not mentioned it. The last letters she had sent to Holland had apparently not caught up with him in France. She had told him again, now, but she didn't know whether these new letters had reached him before he had gone into battle. Perhaps he still didn't know that he was going to be a father.

Anna had thought of telling her mother that morning, but she feared that the news, in spite of its loveliness, would also add another worry to her mother's mind. It was also still something Anna wanted to hold for Alex. She wanted to feel that the two had shared this wonder with each other before they passed it along to others.

Anna had been lucky so far. She had felt an occasional wave of nausea but not the debilitating morning sickness she knew some women suffered. And yet she was almost disappointed. She longed for a sense of change within her. She wanted to feel the life that God was creating. And at the same time she also wondered, would the war end in time for Alex to come back to her, so he could be with her when her time came? And always, virtually every minute of the day, a haunting question was lurking in her thoughts: What if he never gets a chance to see his own child?

But she refused to dwell on that. She touched the palms of her hands against her abdomen, over her womb, and she shut her eyes. "I love you," she whispered. "We'll be all right." She meant the baby, of course, but she also meant Alex. She had to trust that somehow the three of them would have a chance to share their lives.

* * *

Peter was sitting in the cellar of a bombed-out building. The cold was paralyzing outside, but the cellar wasn't quite so bad. He was wearing his heavy coat and had wrapped a blanket around his legs. He had eaten a tin of applesauce, the only food he'd had in the past twenty-four hours and the best food he'd eaten in weeks; now he was merely staring ahead, feeling some sense of relief to be out of the cold, to have eaten a little, not to be under fire. But he was too exhausted, too emotionally and physically spent, to feel much of anything but the numbness that filled his brain.

Hans was sitting next to Peter. "Someone said it's Christmas," Hans said, absently.

Peter didn't know whether that was right, but a defense inside him responded quickly. He pushed the idea away.

Life had become a long series of momentary stops laced with firefights and bombardment from airplanes, big guns, tanks, and then another hard run through the snow. Everywhere around him, on every road and lane, were thousands of refugees. All across Latvia and Lithuania—and surely Poland and East Prussia, too—the people had been fleeing from the constantly moving front. The Russians made little distinction between soldiers and civilians, nor was that easy to do. Often the refugees, both men and women, picked up the rifles of fallen Germans and fought for the sakes of their families.

The death and devastation were beyond anything Peter ever could have imagined. Whenever the skies cleared, fighters and dive bombers wiped out whole villages. The ground troops then followed and burned everything in sight. Tank crews gunned down civilians—women, children, everyone—and then rolled over their bodies, smashing and breaking them.

Peter had seen so much horror that there was no reacting anymore. He had struggled to get by on meager rations, had known almost constant hunger, but around him he had seen refugees drop and die beside the road, eaten away by fatigue and hunger. Some carried dead babies with them, and then buried them when they felt safe enough to scratch a shallow hole in the frozen earth. He had watched refugees kneel and pray over these makeshift graves and then hurry on.

The fleeing German troops had reached Memel, in Lithuania, on the Baltic. It was a trap, a cul-de-sac, but there had been no other direction to retreat. Germans were trying to evacuate hundreds of thousands of refugees by way of the sea, and the soldiers were now called upon to hold the perimeter around the city until the civilians were able to escape.

The talk, of course, was that the soldiers would follow, but the men knew better. Peter never thought in terms of hope anymore. It wasn't that he had given up; that required thought. He simply accepted the reality that death would come before much longer. Every day he saw soldiers die, and even though he still screamed when artillery shells struck close, that didn't mean he hoped to avoid the shell or bullet or grenade that would finally take him. His screams were merely a reaction, like the wailing that scared him from his sleep some nights. He would awake, startled, thinking someone had screamed, and then know that the noise had come, was still coming, from himself. Sometimes Hans would also roll up on his side and shriek, and then begin to cry, or even laugh. Everyone understood; every soldier did it at times. The terror would simply build up until it had to come out in some way.

Long lines of civilians waited all day for ships, boats, barges, anything to carry them out of the trap and along the coast to East Prussia. This was only a momentary salvation, since the front was steadily pushing west, but the voyage would get the refugees behind the front lines again, and then they could continue their flight. As the people stood in lines, however, Russian airplanes would dive out of the sky and strafe or bomb not just the city but specifically the people. Little was left of the town of Memel. All was leveled, smoldering, and so the last target seemed to be the refugees themselves.

Peter had watched as the people stayed in their lines even though they knew full well they would draw attacks. They saw no answer but to climb on the next boat, or the one after that. When the airplanes struck, and people fell, others would tend to them or drag the bodies away, but then, immediately, the lines would form again. And after all that, the ships were often attacked, and those who had survived the wait in the lines would die in the icy water.

But Peter didn't react to any of this. The human body, he now understood, was very delicate. It could be pulled apart, crushed, broken. And when it lay in the mud, with the blood pumping from it, he had never seen anything escape, no soul. He remembered what he had believed just a few months before, and he didn't deny any of it. For him, it was one reality, gone, and this was another. In this new state of mind, life had very little significance, and death none at all. One day he had seen an older couple standing next to a heap of bodies. The man had picked up a rifle from a fallen soldier. He had appeared pleased and excited to find such a prize. But then he had calmly turned to his wife. She waited, quietly, as he fired a bullet into her chest. She had been thrown backward by the blast before she folded in on herself and dropped. Then the man had turned the rifle on himself, bending over and aiming it between his eyes. Peter saw the man's head burst, but he didn't look away. It was nothing new to him, and he understood. They were old and tired of running, starving. It seemed a sensible choice.

And still, he wanted to live. He didn't believe he would, but something inside him said that he wanted to survive at least another day. A week before, his company—or the remnant of it—had been sent south to take on the Russians and stop the pincer movement that was gradually strangling the troops in Memel. They had caught the Russian troops by surprise, and they had driven them back six miles or so. But ultimately their numbers, their equipment, and their weapons had proven inadequate. When the Russians attacked their flank, the Germans were strung out and had to make a desperate flight, mostly at night, back into Memel. Almost all of Peter's friends had been killed or taken captive. In the chaos, Hans and Peter had lost track of Helmut. He was probably dead. And so were many of the veterans who had lasted through five long winters of this war. Next to those veterans lay the fourteen- and fifteen-year-olds who had lasted only a few months. Peter had seen these boys fall, scream for help, cry like little children, and he had stopped to help when he could. But finally he'd had to keep going or die himself. And now, sitting in this basement, he knew what he should have done: stayed, made some boy's last minutes a little better, and then died with him. What appealed to him was the idea of dying with a bit of honor instead of being blown apart in this cellar by a sudden blast from an artillery shell, or dying of starvation and exposure to the cold, the worst possibility of all.

Hans leaned toward Peter and put his hand on his arm. "If I could be home for Christmas one more time in my life," he whispered, "I wouldn't complain."

Peter looked at Hans's hand, the gray skin of his wrist where his glove and sleeve didn't quite meet. Hans had suffered with frostbite time and again. His hands and feet were in terrible shape. Peter had suffered that way too, but not as severely as Hans.

Peter saw no chance that a miracle would somehow lift Hans out of all this and carry him back to his Black Forest village for another Christmas. What he did feel was pain for Hans, and that was almost like life. That hint of life caused a picture to form in his mind: a Christmas in Frankfurt, with a tree in the living room, and Elder Thomas and Elder Mecham singing American Christmas songs. He saw Anna, his pretty sister, so taken with Elder Thomas, and his mother, so happy. Peter had loved those elders, had wanted so badly to be like them. He hadn't had any idea then that his body was breakable, that his spirit could be crushed with his body. He hadn't imagined any such reality as he had discovered here in this war. For the first time in a long time he actually wished he could travel backward to that time. What he didn't believe was that there was any chance he could move forward and get there again.

He told Hans, "We'll get through. We'll be all right." But he didn't look at him. He knew that if they looked in each other's eyes, they would see the truth.

* * *

Alex and Howie had walked through the woods to the headquarters tent. They were taking their turn at receiving the Christmas dinner that had been brought to them on trucks from Bastogne. As much as possible, everyone would receive turkey and mashed potatoes today. Even cranberry sauce. It was all from a can, and no longer hot, and was worse tasting than some of the choices in a K-ration box, but the idea of it was appealing. There was no table, no chairs, so the men hunkered down next to the tent to avoid the wind a little, and they ate from their mess kits.

"Just like Mom's cooking," Alex said, and he laughed.

"If this is how your mother cooks, don't invite me over for dinner," Howie told him. He sipped at some hot coffee.

In a few minutes Duncan and Curtis came out of the woods and walked toward the tent. "How is it?" Duncan asked.

"You don't want to know," Howie said.

Alex liked to see Howie joking, talking.

Duncan and Curtis got their food and then returned. They crouched next to Alex and Howie and began to eat. The snow around the tent was trampled down, but sitting on the ground would be a mistake in this cold. More supplies had been dropped that morning. Some blankets had reached the men— although not nearly enough. At least Alex's squad had received one for each foxhole. That would help a little, but the men needed coats and underwear and galoshes. They understood the difficulty of supplying an entire division, but they were tired and angry—and so they cursed the army for all the foul-ups. Everyone believed that the support troops stole the best of the supplies and cared little for the men on the front lines.

"Listen to that shelling," Curtis said. "Someone's taking a beating."

The sounds were coming from the distant south, on the opposite side of Bastogne, and it seemed incongruent that the Germans would interrupt their own Christmas to make a thrust of this kind.

"Do you know who that is returning fire for our side down there?" Alex asked.

"No," Duncan said.

"That's the 969th Field Artillery Battalion—a colored unit."

Duncan grinned. "Glad they're here," he said. "I hope they keep the Jerries out. If they break through our line somewhere, we're all in trouble."

Alex had thought a great deal about that. He knew that the entire division could be placed in a position where surrender would be the only option. He didn't want to die, of course, but the idea of being taken prisoner was almost as bad. "What did you think of what McAuliffe told the Germans?" he asked.

The men laughed, and Curtis said, "I can just see the German generals asking each other, 'What does *zis* mean? Nuts?'"

Every soldier had received a Christmas greeting from General McAuliffe, who had been left in command when General Maxwell Taylor had been called to Washington for meetings just before the "bulge" had broken out. McAuliffe was better liked than Taylor anyway, and his greeting, although a little too full of bravado, had included a story the soldiers loved. The Germans had apparently sent a representative to the American command, and he had offered the 101st a chance to surrender. General McAuliffe wrote to the men that he had sent back a one-word response: "Nuts!"

McAuliffe had also wished the soldiers a Merry Christmas, and then he had said, "What's merry about all this, you ask? Just this: We have stopped cold everything that has been thrown at us from the North, East, South and West. We are giving our country and our loved ones at home a worthy Christmas present, and being privileged to take part in this gallant feat of arms, we are truly making for ourselves a Merry Christmas."

"I like what he told the Krauts," Duncan said. "I don't want to give up. But all that Merry Christmas stuff was a little hard to take. If I was living in some hotel in town, sitting down to three good meals a day—and some good whiskey—I might feel pretty merry myself."

"He's in the same trap as the rest of us," Alex said. "He knows he's blowing some smoke at us, but he also wants us to keep our spirits up." Alex had finished eating but was still sipping some warm water into which he had poured lemon crystals from his K rations. It tasted terrible, but it felt good inside. His legs were getting tired, though, so he stood up.

Duncan laughed. "Hey, we're paratroopers. We don't need no rah-rah speeches. We love this stuff—surrounded, fighting off the enemy from all sides. Not enough food or ammo. Ready to fight with our bayonets and bare hands. That's what we live for."

Curtis stood up. He looked at Alex. "Remember that speech Summers gave us on the first day at Toccoa—when he kept yelling for us all to quit right then and there?"

Alex looked down at Howie. "Yeah, that's one thing you missed," Alex said. "Summers told us, the first time he ever saw us, that we were a bunch of idiots to sign up with an airborne outfit. We were sure to die if we stayed on."

"We got some of that same stuff on our first day too," Howie said.

Now Duncan stood, and Howie. The men created the four sides of a square. Alex thought how ragged they all looked, caked with mud from head to foot.

"Summers was right," Duncan said. "We *were* stupid to stay on." But he laughed.

"I wanted to quit so bad," Alex said. "The only reason I stayed was that I didn't want the rest of the guys—especially you, Duncan—to think I was a quitter."

"That's the same reason I stayed," Curtis said.

"Hey, I was talking so big, I had to stay," Duncan said, and he laughed harder than ever. "But I was shaking in my boots. I wanted to catch the first bus home."

"I would have," Howie said. "If there had been any way I could have gotten out of there—and kept my head up—I would have walked out that very first day."

Alex wasn't really surprised by any of this; he was only surprised that everyone could say it now. "I've never liked all the big talk about paratroopers being supermen," Alex said. "But I do like what happened to us at Toccoa. We worked hard, and I think that's helped us make it through."

But that only brought to mind the men from the squad who had been lost, and he knew that Curtis and Duncan were thinking the same thing. "We didn't have any idea what we were heading into," Curtis said.

And Duncan said, "Remember that flight across the channel, on D-Day, everyone so scared they were puking? Me and ol' Rizzardi, we were telling you guys, 'Look out, here we come,' but I was sitting next to him, and he was shaking just as hard as I was."

Alex looked down at the ground. "Have you heard from Rizzardi?" he asked.

"Not for a while. He didn't quite say it, but what I got from between the lines was that he'll be in a wheelchair the rest of his life."

"Sometimes I think about all those guys," Curtis said. "Cox, McCoy, Huff, Campbell—the guys who started out with us and are dead now."

"Six of our original guys are either dead or hurt real bad," Duncan said.

"And the three of us right here have all been hit," Curtis said. He touched his arm, which was still bandaged, under his coat.

"Withers, from my group, is dead," Howie said. "And Sabin took a hit."

No one looked at each other, and for a time no one spoke. Clearly, the next few days were going to be crucial for the rest of the men, but no one said so. No one needed to.

It was time to get back to the line so some other guys could have their Christmas dinner, and so the four soldiers washed out their mess kits, and then they walked together back to their foxholes. The silence that had set in continued as they tromped through the snowy pine forest. But at the foxhole, Howie said, "Well, that was Christmas. Sure was nice, wasn't it?" He laughed quietly.

The two got back into their foxhole, facing each other, and they wrapped the blanket around their legs. Above their heads was an opening in the pine boughs—a circle of blue sky.

"While it's quiet, we'd better change our socks and rub our feet," Alex said.

"Oh, man, it's too cold. I don't want to do nothing like that."

"We've gotta do it, Howie. You don't want frostbite—or trench foot. Take your boot off, and I'll rub your foot for you."

So Howie pulled off a boot. It was awkward to do that with both of them in the hole, but they were warmer there than they would have been outside. Alex rubbed Howie's foot, then helped him get his other boot off and rubbed that foot. Then Howie did the same for Alex. They were a little embarrassed and laughed about it, but when they were finished, Howie said, "Well . . . Merry Christmas."

"In Bible days, the people used to wash each other's feet," Alex said. "Even Christ did that for the apostles. I guess this is sort of like that." He had meant it as a little joke, but it hadn't come out that way.

Howie nodded and said, "Yeah. I guess so. I was going to get you something else—but I didn't get a chance to go shopping." He smiled, and the two looked at each other for just a moment. Something in Howie's smile always made Alex think of Gene. The thought, this time, was almost too much for Alex.

* * *

Brother Stoltz was visiting with a young family, the Steurers, members of the Church in Karlsruhe. They lived in a tiny apartment that had once been badly damaged in an air raid. It was patched together, but the walls had never been repainted, and the draftiness spoke of gaps in the building somewhere.

Sister Steurer was a lovely woman—tall, with soft blonde hair—and she had made a nice dinner from what she had: a chicken and some potatoes. But it didn't take Brother Stoltz long to realize that he had made a mistake in visiting them. The Steurers had two children: a pretty little blonde-haired daughter named Gerta, who was eight, and a busy little boy of four, named Klaus. Brother Stoltz saw his own children every time he looked at them.

Sister Steurer had taught Gerta and Klaus a song for "a little entertainment." After dinner she had them stand together and in sweet if somewhat off-key voices sing, "*O Du Fröhliche.*"

Brother Stoltz tried not to cry, but he couldn't help it, and once the tears began to flow there was no stopping them. After the children stopped singing, little Gerta said, "We're sorry, Brother Stutz."

"No, no," he told her, and he took her in his arms and hugged her. And then he hugged Klaus, but when he did, he lost control again and began to sob.

The little boy stepped away, confused, so Brother Stoltz told him, "I'm sorry, Klaus. But I have a son, like you. He's grown now, and he's in the war. I'm very worried about him."

The children seemed to understand, but Brother Stoltz couldn't seem to get control of himself. Soon after, he made excuses, then went back to his boarding house. He was grateful that he had been able to reach his OSS contact, who had used the Joan/Eleanor radio system to relay a message to a high-flying Mosquito airplane. Brother Stoltz had relayed Georg's information, and he had requested that his wife be informed that he was all right. He hoped that had happened. Now, if there were only some way to reach Peter. There, in his little room, he got down on his knees by his bed, and he pleaded with the Lord to let his son return to him.

What happened was anything but what he expected. A wonderful, calming peace came over him. He felt a reassurance, a trust that he hadn't known during all this time that Peter had been missing. He cried again, but this time out of relief and gratitude.

It was such a hard thing to trust for certain, to know. Maybe it was only his wishful thinking that had brought on the sensation. But the feelings were as real as anything he had to cling to. And so he lay down on the bed and told himself if he ever relied on the Spirit in his life, to rely on it now. "He's alive," he said aloud. "I'm going to see him again. Isn't that what you told me, Lord?"

Again he felt the calm, the peace. It had come twice, and so Brother Stoltz accepted it, refused to let his skeptical side tell him otherwise. "Merry Christmas, Peter," he whispered. "Merry Christmas, Anna, Frieda."

Christmas was quiet at the Thomas house. There had been plenty of presents for LaRue and Beverly, and the girls had been able to buy a nice gift for their parents, too. They had combined their money and bought a framed print: a painting of the Salt Lake Temple on the day it was dedicated. "It's about time we got rid of that dog on our wall," LaRue told her parents. "That poor old thing has been howling in the snow since before I was born."

President Thomas didn't say a word, but LaRue knew very well what he was thinking. He didn't like change, and that dog was part of the house. She already knew that the new print would end up in his office, or upstairs somewhere, maybe in her parents' bedroom, but it would never replace the old dog.

That night, however, after the extended family had left and the house was quiet again, President Thomas did something he usually didn't do. He admitted that he wasn't going to replace the dog, but then he explained why: "LaRue, when Wally comes home, I want him to find everything just the way it was. I have a feeling that every day of his life he pictures his home and imagines what it's like to be here. And I'll bet that poor old dog, as you call it, is one of the things he never forgets."

LaRue was actually touched by that thought. "Well, okay,"

she said. "That *is* right." But then she laughed and added, "but I'm only giving him a week or two to be home, and then I'm dumping ol' Shep in the garbage can."

"You will *not*," Bea Thomas said, but she laughed. "The only thing I want to get rid of are those stars in the window. Sometimes I think of throwing them away now. They used to be a badge of honor. Now they just seem a bad reminder."

There were still three blue stars in the front window, but there was also a gold one—the symbol of a family member fallen in the war.

Beverly and LaRue were sitting on the floor. Bev had received a new paint set for Christmas. To LaRue it seemed a child's gift, but it was one of the things Beverly had wanted. She seemed to have little, if any, talent at painting, but every year she wanted a new watercolor set. Now she was looking through the box, checking to see what colors of paint she had. "Dad, what was Uncle Everett talking about today? Is Alex surrounded?"

LaRue had seen it in all the papers the past couple of days, but Beverly never paid much attention to the news, and her father and mother rarely said anything to worry her about such things.

"It may not be as bad as it sounds," President Thomas said. But he was holding the paper, and LaRue had seen the headlines: "Nazi Tanks, Infantry Again Push Forward." And under it: "Christmas Finds U.S. in Solemn Mood."

"What's going to happen to him?" Beverly asked.

"He'll be fine. His division got called into this new battle in Belgium. And the Germans are all around that area. But . . ." LaRue could see how hard he was searching for something he could tell Beverly. "But paratroopers can handle something like that. I think Alex will come out all right."

This last had sounded anything but confident, and Beverly seemed to sense that. She looked up from her paint set. "You always told me Gene would be all right," she said.

President Thomas looked away for a moment, let the paper drop into his lap. And then he took his reading glasses off. "Beverly, I did think Gene would get through . . . but he didn't. I think Alex will now, but I can't promise anything. You know that."

Beverly clearly didn't like his answer. She ducked her head for a moment, and then she said, "I don't see why they make him stay in the war so long. My friend Linda had a brother in the war. And he got to come home."

"Every situation is different, honey," Mom said. "The boys go to lots of different places, and some are needed longer than others. Are you sure Linda's brother isn't just home on furlough?"

Beverly didn't answer for quite some time, and when she did, her annoyance was only more pronounced. "Alex hasn't had a furlough for two years," she said.

"He did. But he was far away, in England. That's when he got married."

"He got shot, and he still had to go back to the war. Some boys, if they get shot, get out of the army."

Beverly was thirteen now, but LaRue was always amazed at how young she acted at times. "That's because they get worse wounds than Alex had," LaRue said. "Is that what you want, for him to get hurt really bad?"

Beverly didn't respond to that. "I just want him to come home," she said. "And Wally, too. And Bobbi."

"Alex and Bobbi signed up for the duration of the war, plus six months," Sister Thomas said. "That's the promise they made, and there's no going back on it."

LaRue wondered how much longer the war might last. She had always hoped that Bobbi and Alex would come back and be exactly the same. It seemed strange to think that Alex was married and that Bobbi had found a man she wanted to marry. That changed everything: strangers in the house, and Alex and Bobbi only there for a visit. She had wanted a little time with everyone together again, just the way they had been before the war.

Beverly was apparently thinking the same thing. She replaced the cover on her paint set. And then, seeming frustrated but trying to sound mad, she said, "I want Gene to come home too. And he never will."

She got up and tramped up the stairs. LaRue knew that Beverly was going to her room to cry—and didn't want to do it in front of the others. But LaRue had tears in her own eyes. Sometimes she thought she was over feeling bad about losing Gene, and then it would hit her again that he was gone, just gone, and she would never see him, never talk to him again.

Sister Thomas waited a few minutes, and then she got up and followed Beverly up the stairs. LaRue knew that her mother had given Beverly a little time to cry, and now she was going up to console her. It's what she always did.

But once her mother was gone, LaRue controlled her voice and asked her father, "How bad of a situation is Alex really in?" And of course she liked the idea that she was old enough to hear the whole story, even though Beverly needed to be treated with special care.

"I don't know, LaRue," President Thomas said. "It sounds like our troops are holding their own all right. I suspect reinforcements will be sent in to back them up. Some say that General Patton will march the Third Army up to Bastogne, but no one knows that for sure."

"Does Alex have enough food? I heard on the radio that we weren't getting any supplies to the men."

"Airplanes have dropped some food in now. But I don't know how short on supplies they got before the skies cleared. It might have been a little tight for a while. It's very cold there, too."

"Is Alex out in the cold all the time?"

"I would think so. Unless they've taken over some houses,

or something like that. It's just so hard to know what's going on until we hear from him."

LaRue liked all this honesty. Her father was talking to her like a grownup, and she really needed that from him.

"I will say this," President Thomas said. "I was just as worried about you—when you were hanging out at the USO club all the time—as I am about Alex right now."

"Really?"

"Alex's life is in danger—just like it has been all along. But to me it seemed as though you were casting aside everything I've ever tried to teach you—and that scared me to death."

LaRue was stunned. The comparison seemed so out of balance when she thought how much she feared for Alex's life all the time—especially since Gene had been killed. "Dad," she said, "I didn't do anything very bad—not like you worried about."

"That's good, honey. And I've felt a lot better about your choices lately—not just that you aren't going down there, either. You've seemed more mature."

"I wish I felt that way."

"You don't?"

"Not really." She got up from the floor and sat on the couch, across from her father. "The other night, at the Christmas dance, I was embarrassed that I was wearing an old dress everyone had seen before. I was so mad at myself for not getting a new one—after you and Mom had already said I could."

President Thomas laughed. "Well," he said, "I don't suppose wanting a new dress is such a bad thing."

But LaRue knew that her father was missing the point. She had come home from the club on the night Ned had told her the truth about herself, and she had really wanted to become a better person. But by the next day she had already regretted the loss of the new dress. "Dad, do you think people can change?" she asked.

"What do you mean, 'change'?"

"Change who they are—the kind of person they've been."

"Most people don't change a whole lot, I guess. Not fundamentally. But everybody can improve. Especially young people."

"You always say that I'm self-centered. But I don't know what I can do about it."

"Admitting to it sounds like an awfully good start."

LaRue leaned her head back against the couch and looked up at the high ceiling. She saw a little cobweb in the corner of the crown moldings. She hated cobwebs, and she thought for a moment of going after a broom to reach up and brush it away, but she didn't do it yet. She was still thinking about herself. That night at the dance, she had teased Reed Porter, flirted, kept him flustered all night. He was nuts over her, and she knew it—and she knew how to entice him—and yet that whole evening she had thought of Ned, who was gone now. Ned had really loved her, and Reed was just a boy who thought she was cute.

"Dad, I might marry Ned someday."

President Thomas had begun to look at his paper again. Now his eyes drifted slowly back to her. "Is this a test?" he asked, and he took his glasses off again.

"No. I'm serious."

"Well, you're fifteen. I think you'll meet quite a few boys you like between now and the time for you to get married."

"I know. I might change my mind. But I'm going to decide for myself."

"Oh, I have no doubt of that."

"Dad, I need to change, but so do you."

He laughed. "I believe you've also mentioned *that* before."

"I know. But I don't just mean that you have to stop being so bossy." She smiled and waited.

Her father's eyes closed for a moment, and he shook his

head just a little, as though he were thinking, "Dare I ask?" But he did. "What else is on your list?"

"You think you're better than other people—especially people who aren't Mormons."

LaRue saw immediately that she had stung him—more, really, than she had intended. His smile faded, and he said quietly, "What makes you say that?"

"You didn't know Ned, but you made up your mind about him. He's actually a better person than I am."

President Thomas sat still. He was quiet for a long time, and LaRue began to wish she had not been so blunt. But finally he leaned forward and set his paper on the little table next to his chair. Then he looked at LaRue intently. "Between you and your mom, you've given me a lot to think about lately," he said.

LaRue heard the pain in his voice, and she was surprised. She had never expected him to take her words so much to heart. "Dad," she said, "all I mean is, we shouldn't be too quick to judge people. That's just what it says in the Bible."

He smiled just a little, and suddenly her own insolence struck her. How could she think to instruct *him* about the content of the scriptures? "I know very well what you mean, LaRue. And I do plan to have a good look at myself. But remember, too, if a father is suspicious of people at times, that could have something to do with his desire to protect his children."

"I know, Dad. I understand that." She thought how rough she had been on her father over the past few months, and sadly, how right he had been about her at times, however much she hated to admit it.

"This adventure never ends, does it," President Thomas said.

"What adventure?"

"Raising kids.

"I guess not." Then she added, "Dad, I do love you. And it's nice to know you were so worried about me." She got up and did something she hadn't done in a long time: she kissed him on the cheek.

And he did something that took her by surprise. He pulled her onto his lap and held her, as though she were still a little girl.

What LaRue wished at the moment was that she *could* be a little girl again. On New Year's Eve she had another date with Reed, and this time there was just no way she could go without a new dress. She already had plans for bringing up the issue with Mom that evening, for arguing that the after-Christmas sales presented a very "practical" opportunity for a purchase. Then she would send Mom to negotiate the deal with Dad. It crossed her mind now, sitting on her father's lap, that she might cut out the middleman and go straight for that dress right here and now, while he was feeling good about her.

At least she didn't do that, and so she had just a little something to congratulate herself about. But what she knew was that she hadn't changed much, if any, and she wondered whether she ever would.

* * *

Later that evening Lorraine Gardner, Wally's old girlfriend, showed up at the front door. Mom greeted her, hugged her. "It's so good to see you," she said.

Lorraine stepped in. "I'm just home for the holidays," she said.

"I saw your mother a couple of weeks ago. She told me you're still in Seattle. And she said you were engaged. Congratulations." Lorraine nodded and seemed just a little awkward, but Sister Thomas didn't want her to feel that way. She took her hand and looked at her ring. It was a simple gold ring, with only a few stones. "That's so pretty," Sister Thomas said. "It's a lot like mine."

She held out her own hand, and Lorraine looked at it. "It is," she said, but nothing more. And the awkwardness seemed to increase.

"Come and sit down. Everyone will want to see you." And so Sister Thomas called the girls downstairs, and she took Lorraine into the living room to say hello to President Thomas. After all the greetings, Lorraine sat on the couch, with LaRue and Sister Thomas on either side of her. Beverly sat on the floor next to her father's chair.

LaRue said, "Lorraine, you're beautiful. You get prettier every time I see you."

It was what Sister Thomas was thinking. Lorraine still had that lovely figure, but something in the confident way she moved, the natural assurance about her, made her seem so grown up and poised. "Oh, LaRue, don't tell me that," Lorraine said. "I'm like a thorn among the roses alongside you and Beverly."

Sister Thomas knew that Lorraine had said exactly the right thing. Everyone always spoke of LaRue's beauty, but few noticed the delicate, less striking attractiveness in Beverly. Lorraine had not seemed to strain to include Beverly, however, and Sister Thomas saw Beverly glow with the attention.

"Have you heard anything from Wally?" Lorraine asked.

"No. Not a word this whole year," Sister Thomas told her.

"That must be terrible for you."

President Thomas said, "Our soldiers are finding very few prisoners of war in the Philippines so far. Most have been shipped to Japan."

"Does anyone know anything about the conditions there?"

"The only thing we hear," President Thomas said, "is that they are put to work—in mines and factories. I'm sure they have to work very hard, but if that's the case, the Japs would have to feed them pretty well." President Thomas chuckled quietly and then said, "Maybe Wally has learned to work. That's not something he was very good at."

Lorraine smiled. "I've thought a lot about Wally—and the way he was. He was under a lot of shadows. Yours. And Alex's.

Even Bobbi's. I don't think he knew how to live up to all the things everyone expected of him."

"That's exactly right," Sister Thomas said.

President Thomas nodded. "I'd do some things a little differently if I had another chance," he said. He glanced at LaRue.

"I would too," Lorraine said.

It seemed to Sister Thomas a strange thing for an engaged girl to say, maybe even inappropriate. "Lorraine, tell us about your fiancé," she said.

"He's a Lieutenant, junior grade, in the Navy. Right now, he's stationed on Guadalcanal, and he has a nice, safe desk job."

"I guess, even if you were married, you couldn't have gone there with him?"

"No. He wanted to get married before he left, but . . . I don't know. I just felt like I'd rather wait until he got back."

"I can understand that," Sister Thomas said.

"If you hear anything at all about Wally, could you please let me know? I'll leave my address with you."

Sister Thomas gave Lorraine a sheet of paper, and she wrote down the address, and then they chatted about Seattle, about Lorraine's work, and about LaRue and Beverly and the rest of the family. But Lorraine didn't stay long, and when she left, she stood at the door and hugged Sister Thomas, held her a little longer than Sister Thomas expected, and she said, "I love your family so much. I hope you can all be back together before too much longer."

* * *

Afton Story was spending Christmas day with the Nuanunus. She hadn't broken the news to her family yet, but she had now admitted to Bobbi that she was planning to marry Sam. Bobbi was happy for her. And yet sometimes she wondered whether she had done too much to talk her into her choice. Afton and Sam would be facing some hard challenges.

Bobbi had still not had a letter from Richard, and she was worried about that. But he was alive. And more than that, she felt some sense of protection, some sense that God had blessed her, granted her desire, and the only appropriate response was gratitude. If only she felt as sure about Alex. The world was watching and waiting to see what would happen to the men in Bastogne, and Bobbi dreaded every day the possibility that she would receive bad news.

Bobbi and Ishi and the kids had dinner together at Ishi's house. Little David loved Bobbi, and the two of them played on the floor after dinner. David had a little collection of wooden cars and trucks, and he liked to make loud noises and push the cars around. Bobbi built little bridges out of blocks, which David knocked down more often than not as he tried to cross them with his vehicles. Bobbi would pretend to cry, but that only made David laugh. He was an intense little boy, almost wild at times, and sometimes, even at his age, he intimidated his shy big sister.

After a time, Bobbi got up and sat on the couch, and Lily came to her, sat next to her. "My dolly is tired," she told Bobbi. "She needs to sleep." The doll was wrapped in a pink blanket. Lily began to rock her, with a little more bounce than a baby might really like.

"Nice and soft," Bobbi said. "That's what puts a baby to sleep."

David looked up. "It's just a doll," he said, as if to explain to Bobbi that she needn't worry.

Bobbi and Ishi laughed. Ishi was feeling some relief herself these days. She had heard from Daniel a few days before, after hearing nothing for a long time. His unit had been pulled out of Italy and was now in southern France. He couldn't tell her much about what was happening, but Ishi thought he might be in safer circumstances than he had been in the mountains of Italy.

"Remember last year, on Christmas?" Bobbi said. "We all hoped the war would be over by now."

"Well . . . it's a lot closer."

"I don't know, Ishi. This new push by the Germans really worries me. It seemed like they were almost finished off, and look how they've come back strong again."

"You're worried about your brother, aren't you?"

"Sure."

"I feel sorry for his wife."

"I know. That's what I keep thinking. I love her so much, and I've never met her. She sent me a sweet letter, in such correct English. She said, 'Alex should not be a soldier. He loves people too much.'"

"The sad part is, that's true of so many of these boys out shooting at each other. No one should be a soldier."

Bobbi nodded. She thought of Richard the same way. What he had seen in the war had hurt him so much. She wondered what more he had been through now, and what it had done to him. "I wonder what Richard will be like when I see him again," she said. "Ishi, sometimes I get so scared. I don't really know Richard very well. I'm not even sure anymore what made me fall in love with him."

"That's not how you'll feel when you're with him again."

Bobbi wished she knew that for sure. She also wished she knew what was happening. If Richard was in a hospital, he was obviously hurt in some way. She remembered how much he feared the idea of being mutilated. The telegram had been so neutral, so incomplete—and since then she had heard nothing. Maybe his injuries were bad enough that he wasn't able to write.

"I feel a change in Daniel's letters," Ishi said. "He started out so devoted to winning the war for his people, for democracy— all those things. But now he never speaks of anything like that. I can't tell what he's thinking. It's like he knows something now that he doesn't dare say to me."

"Maybe that's how we all are. I've seen things in the hospital, heard talk, learned things about people. Maybe I'll be a little better for it in some ways, but I'll never be the naive kid I was when I came over here."

"There are so many kinds of costs," Ishi said. "Just think about these years Daniel and I have lost—and think about Lily and David. During these important years of their lives, they've never even seen their father. He's a picture to them. That's all they know of him."

"Ishi, I hope, in a way, that Richard's injuries are serious enough that he won't have to go back into action. What if he has to go back—and get in on the invasion, when we go into Japan?"

"I have relatives in Japan, Bobbi. What am I supposed to hope for? I lose on both sides of this war."

That was easy for Bobbi to forget. She could only imagine what Ishi had to go through, every day hearing the ugly epithets about the "Japs," constantly seeing the ugly caricatures in the newspapers. Ishi was experiencing an element of the war that other Americans would never know.

But Bobbi was still thinking about Richard. If he was hurt too seriously, maybe his life would be full of problems. Maybe his heart had been changed somehow, too. But if he wasn't hurt badly enough, maybe he would be going back to sea. Maybe Bobbi's worry and the waiting would only start again.

"Well . . . Merry Christmas, anyway," Ishi said. "A year ago we would have been very pleased just to know that Richard and Daniel were still alive. We do have that. Maybe next Christmas we'll be with them."

"Maybe so." Bobbi touched Ishi's arm. "And no matter what this war has cost us, maybe it's taught us some things, too." She didn't say it, but what she thought about was the afternoon when the telegram had come. She was not a woman of great faith, but that day she had felt God with her before she ever opened the envelope. That was something she could build a future around, no matter what else came.

* * *

Wally had to work in the mine on Christmas Eve and again on Christmas Day. There was nothing different about such days. The routine didn't change. But Wally longed for something—just a little extra food or some other indication it was a special day. But there were no packages from home, no letters, not even a sign that the guards or his supervisor knew what day it was.

So Wally decided, on a sudden impulse, to do something himself. When lunchtime came, he walked to Kiku, bowed, and then said, "Merry Christmas."

Kiku didn't understand. He shook his head, looked curious.

"Merry Christmas. I want to give you a gift. You don't kick me anymore, and I want to thank you for that."

Again Kiku looked confused.

"I'll work during dinnertime today. You'll get a little more done. And you like that." His tone was friendly, and when he finished, he bowed again, something the prisoners usually only did when they had no choice.

Kiku shook his head. He asked something in Japanese, something Wally couldn't understand. Wally smiled, and then he picked up a shovel. He pointed to some loose rock the men had broken up that morning. "I'm going to shovel this rock during dinnertime. I won't take off time to rest," he said. And then he began to shovel.

The other men were watching. Hernandez said, "Don't do it, Wally. He doesn't understand. And he sure won't appreciate it."

"That's all right. I want to do it."

No one else joined in, and Kiku, clearly baffled, walked away and left the men as he always did at lunchtime. Maybe he thought Wally was bargaining, hoping to get an early release that afternoon for his crew. Or maybe he knew about Christmas and finally made the connection. In any case, when he returned and found Wally still working, he approached him, stood before him, and this time he bowed. This was certainly his way of accepting the gift.

That was all. The day didn't end any earlier, and Wally was so exhausted he could hardly make the march back to the camp that night. But he felt good.

3 1

Peter, with a small remnant of his company, had retreated again. They were still in Memel, in Lithuania, but they were closer to the bay, pinched in by the Russian forces. They had found a damaged pillbox to hide in. The gun was destroyed, but the reinforced concrete provided some protection against the shelling. Still, the January cold was now a greater threat than the artillery fire, and the pillbox was more exposed to the air than the cellar, their last refuge, had been. By now the civilians were mostly gone, either dead or actually evacuated by German boats. Some of the soldiers had been removed too. But every time another boatload left, the odds for those remaining grew worse, with the Russians moving closer and fewer Germans to defend the position.

Peter was sick. There was very little to eat anymore, and the perpetual cold stole the life from all the men. But now, deep in Peter's chest was a constant, dull pain, like the pressure of an expanding balloon. He had been coughing for some time, spitting up blood, but now his body was giving up. The energy to cough was too demanding, it seemed, too fruitless, and Peter's will to live was almost gone. He moved about in a state of groggy confusion, or, more often, sat with his eyes open, more or less asleep, not really seeing what was in front of him.

Sergeant Gottschall, Peter's latest leader, believed that the Russians had made up their minds to end the standoff in Memel. Peter only knew that the intensity of the artillery fire, the pressure from tanks, had intensified in the past twenty-four hours. The bombardment, which had gone on all day, was as intense as anything Peter had been through. Now it was night, and the explosions were lighting up the sky, the sound rumbling from a distance at times and then crashing all around the pillbox where Peter lay, rolled up, shivering with fright. The close strikes would crack like lightning, suck the air from his lungs, shake the ground, reverberate through his ribs. Twice during the night the pillbox had taken direct hits, the concrete shattering and debris cascading onto the men, but the structure had held together. Peter had felt his body take a pelting from the flying chunks of concrete, but the pain inside him was so deep that surface pain hardly seemed significant.

When the barrage had finally let up, Peter wondered whether he was better off to have survived one more time. Alfred Webber, a veteran of most of the war—one who had survived a thousand experiences just as bad—had been killed this time by flying shrapnel. A little piece of steel had found its way just beneath the edge of his helmet and had torn through his temple and into his brain. So many bullets had whizzed by this man before. He had even been seriously wounded twice, but now half an inch had made all the difference. Peter stared at the man's body and wondered what it felt like to finally be dead. Peter's mind had become elemental now, and he didn't search for what he had been taught. He only stared at the bulk, the flesh, that lay there in a heap, and it seemed to him that the cold couldn't penetrate, that pain was ended.

It was almost morning when Hans said, "Peter, I'm going to kill myself. I don't want to wait for the Russians to do it for me."

Peter had thought of doing the same thing himself, but this shook him. "No," he said. He didn't have the energy or the clarity of mind to say more. But he did move enough to get hold of Hans, to look into his eyes. The first light of day was dawning, and he could see Hans, his emaciated face, his hollow eyes. "No," he said again. And Hans nodded. Maybe it was what he wanted to hear—at least that much concern for him.

Sergeant Gottschall was up barking soon after that. The man had more drive than anyone Peter could imagine, and through his sheer stubbornness, he was trying to keep these few men—now only fourteen—alive. "We must take up our positions at the outpost," he told the men. "The Russians will be coming this morning. You know they will."

Surely all the artillery fire was a precursor to a ground attack. What wasn't clear was what the sergeant thought the few Germans left in Memel could do against another major thrust. Still, Peter pulled himself to his feet. The most meaningful thing left in his life was the leadership of this man, who kept on fighting no matter what he faced. Peter never worried about killing now, never wondered whether anything was right or wrong. His only decision was whether to keep trying.

He walked through the hazy, frozen air. His tattered boots squeaked as they crushed the ice-crusted snow. At the outpost—a trench that extended along a road—Peter sat down, his body trembling from the effort, and, of course, from the cold. It would be a terrible morning.

"We'll die today," Hans said.

It certainly did seem likely, but it had seemed likely for such a long time that Peter didn't say anything.

"Tanks will be coming before long. And there's not one thing we can do about it. We hardly have enough ammunition to shoot at their soldiers. What can we do against tanks?"

"My name isn't Stutz. It's Stoltz," Peter told Hans. It was something he had wanted to say for a long time.

"What do you mean?"

"I lied. I told you a false name. I used this name for the army, too."

"But why?"

"It doesn't matter. But I want you to know my name."

Hans was gray, the color of the whole world now. His eyes had lost their tint, like his faded uniform, and his freckles were gone. Everything was lost in the haze, the frozen air. Hans looked like an old man, with sunken eyes and bones for a face.

"You've always kept secrets, Peter. Why?"

"There were things that happened. Before all this. But it doesn't matter now."

"Of course it matters. We're the only ones left. You and me. It matters."

Peter understood Hans's meaning, but he didn't have the energy to explain. He knew that he had always possessed a secret that would make Hans hate him, and he couldn't reveal that. But at least today, if it was going to be their last day, he had wanted Hans to know his name.

"You never wanted to fight in this war—not the way the rest of us did."

"No. I didn't."

"Tell me why, Peter. Who are you?"

"Hans, I can't."

"You need to tell me something."

"I don't love the Führer. I never did." And then Peter searched for some way to explain. "My family tried to help a Jewish family. There was a little boy. Benjamin. The Gestapo took him. Maybe they killed him. That was wrong, Hans. That was wrong." Peter was gasping for air. The words had cost him in strength, in breath, and the memory was too much for him. It called to mind a self, a time, that no longer seemed real.

Hans was staring at Peter. But there was no hatred in his eyes. "You should have told me before," was all he said. He didn't seem to care about the rest.

They sat next to each other after that, their shoulders against each other. And Peter felt a little better. He was glad that Hans knew his name. When someone shouted, "Tanks!" he felt the old terror, the conditioned instinct, but at least his secret was out, and Hans was still his friend. He and Hans didn't stand up. Peter knew that when his sergeant commanded him to do so, he would try, and he would shoot his rifle, if the thing would fire in this cold, but what he couldn't do this time was run again. There was little room left for retreat anyway, the harbor not all that far behind them.

So the tanks would come. And that would be the end.

When artillery fire began again, Peter was vaguely surprised. Usually the fire ended when the tanks and the riflemen appeared. Then he heard Gottschall shouting, "Those are our guns. Look what's happening. They're hammering the Russian positions."

That made no sense. The Germans didn't have any guns. Hans got up and looked. "Ships!" he said. "Our ships."

Peter had a hard time believing such a thing was possible. In his mind, all German forces were in disarray, on the verge of destruction. It was hard to imagine that from somewhere, battle ships could be dispatched to the Baltic, sent to defend the troops. Did someone—Hitler or some general—actually think that Germany could still win this war?

"They're blasting those Russian tanks," Hans said with life in his voice, as though he had returned from the dead. "The tanks are pulling back."

But Peter knew the truth. The Russians still had massive forces out there waiting to attack—more than any pair of ships could stop for very long. This was not salvation; it was only prolonging the inevitable one more time. Peter felt the same relief Hans did, the release from the immediate horror that had lain beyond their trench, but he also knew he didn't have the power to pull himself up many more times. So what had he gained? He tried to cough, tried to clear himself of some of the congestion within him, but his chest had turned to rock, and nothing was letting loose.

The men who were in better shape seemed to find new hope in this artillery fire, and they responded. German soldiers who had been hunkering down by the bay, hoping for a boat to take them away, returned to their outposts, to the trenches, and that day the fighting continued. Peter even got up and fired his rifle for a time. And the tanks held off, probably because the Russians didn't want to bring them out to be fired on by the German ships.

That night Peter and his friends returned to their pillbox. Peter lay on the concrete floor, the cold penetrating him, and he wished for the blankness he had once associated with sleep. But then, sometime in the middle of the night, he heard, as though part of his confused dreams, a voice—his sergeant's voice: "Up. Everyone up. There's a boat in the harbor. If we can get there first, we can get out of this hellhole."

Peter couldn't do that. His sickness no longer had any symptoms, only the dead weight of his body and the rock in his chest. But he knew he couldn't get up and run to the harbor. Hans was pulling on him, however, and then someone else, and he managed to keep his feet under him as they pulled him from the pillbox and down a cobblestone street. He hardly knew what was happening, but he was moving, and his body, under this exertion, seemed to be waking up a little, hurting more.

They were at the water's edge with a wild crowd of shoving, frantic soldiers when the word began to spread. "They're not taking soldiers. They're only taking food."

"What?" Peter couldn't grasp this.

Apparently the German headquarters had been passing out cans of food slowly, hanging on to enough to continue rationing to the men. This food was needed somewhere south, where soldiers were starving. The next boats would pick up the men, but the food had to be gotten out while there was someone left to defend the position.

"That's crazy!" Hans was screaming.

Peter slumped to the ground.

"They're sacrificing us for someone else to live. Why? What makes them any more valuable than us?"

"Be quiet, Hans! That's enough." This was Gottschall, shouting into Hans's face. "They sent us gunships today. They saved us. Now we can fight another day, and then they will pull us out."

"Peter is dying!" Hans shouted. "Can't you see that?"

The sergeant dropped down on his knees, and he grabbed Peter and shook him, sending waves of pain through his body. "No you aren't," he shouted into Peter's face. "Don't let anyone tell you that."

Peter was relieved by Hans's words. It was as though Hans had given him permission. He felt himself drift away.

When Peter awakened, he was back at the pillbox. He had obviously been carried there. "Peter, Peter," Hans was yelling to him. And he was slapping him, rather sharply. "Don't give up. Boats are coming. Maybe today. You have to eat something. And drink."

Peter hardly knew what he wanted most—to live or to die—but at least something in him said he should try. And so he ate a few bites of something foul tasting—maybe a rotten potato. And he sipped at a warm drink, a tea of some kind. He could hear the rumble of artillery and mortar fire, but he was able to slip away from his fear now and return to the oblivion he longed for.

That night he awakened, and this time Hans was pulling him to his feet again. "We've got to move down to the water. We have to be ready if a boat comes for us."

Outside the pillbox, the pounding of artillery was incessant, the shattering of buildings, the scattering of debris. The dark was full of dirt that filled up Peter's lungs as he tried to get his breath. He couldn't imagine going out into all that.

"It's our only hope, Peter. If we don't get out tonight, the Russians will overrun us in the morning. Even our ships won't be able to hold them off."

That was certainly true. Peter found a little reserve in himself that he hadn't thought was there. With Hans's help, he got to his feet. But outside, try as he might, he couldn't make a run for it. He could only stagger along with Hans's support. The two walked straight down the street toward the harbor, and all around them the explosions were crashing, the concussions thumping through the town, off the walls, drawing away all the air.

"Just keep going. Keep going," Hans kept saying.

Then a shell struck a building next to them. There was a tremendous flash, and a wall of bricks knocked both of them to the ground. Hans went down on top of Peter, and Peter heard him moan. He had taken the brunt of the blow.

Peter struggled, found some strength, and rolled Hans and some of the rubble off him. "Hans, can you hear me?" he shouted into his face. The explosions kept booming, lighting Hans's face, but he was unconscious. His head was bleeding. "Hans! We've got to get up. Come on."

Peter struggled to his feet, and he pulled Hans to a sitting position. But he couldn't do more than that. He dropped to his knees. Another explosion rocked the area, the concussion slamming Peter down across his friend. Peter gasped for air, tried to think what else he could do. And finally he turned to a power he remembered. "Lord, please," he said. "Help me get Hans out of here."

He got up, pulled Hans to a sitting position again. "Can you hear me?" he yelled into Hans's face.

Hans nodded. His eyes came open just a little.

"You've got to get up, if you can. I'll help you."

He pulled Hans by the arms, and Hans found enough strength, with the help, to get to his feet. Peter bent and let Hans fold over his shoulder, hefted him, got himself upright, and then staggered under the weight but began the walk to the harbor.

* * *

When Peter awoke, he didn't recognize anything around him. He tried to sit up, but Sergeant Gottschall appeared. "Stay down," he said.

By then Peter felt a strange motion, as though the earth had begun swaying under him. "Where are we?" he asked.

"On a ship. We're safe."

"Where's Hans?"

"He's on the ship too."

"Is he all right then?"

"He's alive. But he took a terrible blow to his head. He's not well."

"How did we get here?"

"You carried him. You got him to the dock. Then we helped you both get on board."

"I don't remember."

"I know. Be thankful for anything you can't remember."

"Where are we going?"

"Pillau, they say. That's in East Prussia, well ahead of the Russians for now."

Peter felt the weight of a blanket on top of him, but he was very cold. Inside his chest was the familiar block of weight. Throughout his body he still felt the same weakness, death trying to work its way into his head. "I think it's too late for me," Peter said.

"You picked up your friend and carried him here. There's still something left in you."

Peter felt a tremor go through his body, and then a power, like heat. It was something he hadn't felt for such a long time. He had prayed, he remembered, and afterward, he had carried Hans. That was real. Peter began to cry. The tears dribbled from the corners of his eyes and down his temples. Something seemed to be breaking loose inside him now, the return of hope changing everything. He began to cough.

Aboard ship there was no medicine. But the sergeant watched over Peter, kept him warm, fed him a little. By the end of the long day, the ship arrived in Pillau. Conditions were not much better there, but at least Peter was placed in a little hospital. And a nurse fed him a broth that heated him up inside. The coughing was wracking his body now, but the congestion was breaking. He felt more strength, and also more sickness, but he knew that was good.

In the same little hospital, with men crowded in everywhere, Hans lay still. His head was wrapped in bandages, and his right arm was held in a bloody sling. Peter could see him from across the room, but he was too weak to go to him. He kept watching, however, and on the third day Hans moved, and then he cried out. Peter responded immediately. He pulled himself off his cot and walked to Hans. He took hold of his hand. "It's all right. You're in a hospital," he said.

Hans's eyes looked wild. "I hurt," he said, not naming the place of his pain.

"I know. We got a building blown onto us."

"What?"

But Peter could see that nothing was clear to Hans now. And it was too much effort to go back and tell it all. "You need to rest."

Hans kept staring, obviously working to understand. "You don't love the Führer, Peter. But I do."

There were men in the room who were awake and well enough to hear these words. But that didn't frighten Peter. No one cared anymore. Or at least he couldn't imagine that they did—not in this filthy old building, where the smell of gangrene and death filled the air. "I know you do," Peter said.

"Peter, you *must* love the Führer. It's the only reason for all this."

"I know. It is the only reason."

"We have to fight. We have to stop the Russians. For the Fatherland. Don't you know this?"

"Yes."

"Why else did we do this? Tell me that, Peter."

"Just rest now. You're getting better now. You'll go home. Next year, at Christmas, you'll be home."

"No. I must continue to fight. We must drive the Russians back. Do you understand? We must make this sacrifice—for our people. Peter, you must join your heart to this cause. You have never done that." Hans tried to push himself up, but the effort was too great, and he dropped back immediately, and then he groaned and his eyes rolled back.

Peter watched Hans slip back into unconsciousness, or sleep. But a woman—a nurse's aide—finally came, and she told Peter to get back to his bed. "If you're well enough to run around this way, we'll send you back to the battle. We need the bed, you know."

Peter returned to his cot and lay down, spent from the effort, but all that day and night he watched Hans, who was sometimes awake, screaming out in pain or talking wildly, demanding his uniform, his rifle, so he could return to the battle, and sometimes asleep and moaning.

A medic came through the room late in the day. Peter asked him, "Please, can you get something for my friend? He needs morphine."

"We have nothing," the man said without emotion.

"What can you do for him?"

"Nothing. We set his arm. We wrapped his head. But there's nothing more to do. He's injured inside his head and inside his body. He won't last much longer."

"No, no. He's getting better. He's much better than he was at first."

But the man didn't answer. He merely walked on to the next cot.

Ten days passed, and Hans continued to sink, never again returning to consciousness. Eventually his breathing was barely discernible, and Peter could see what was coming.

There was so much that Peter didn't understand. Back in Memel, after Hans had been injured, Peter had finally turned to the Lord. But his prayer had been for Hans, and it was Peter's life that was being saved. With so many dying, everywhere, Peter wondered, had the Lord actually taken an interest in him? Maybe not; maybe all this was pure chance. And yet, when he shut his eyes and tried to remember the renewal he had experienced back on the ship, he felt the warmth spread through him again. What came to mind was his father, his voice, and a distant memory. As a little boy, he had fallen down and hurt himself, and his father had picked him up and held him, had whispered in his ear, *"Ich liebe Dich, Peter."* I love you, Peter.

He heard those words now, and he believed they were still true. He believed that in spite of everything, his father still loved him. He didn't know why some were dying and some living, but he believed what he had stopped believing, that he could still be loved.

Every day Peter became stronger. His body was fighting off the bronchitis, or whatever it was, and with no medicine, that did seem a miracle. He was far from well, but he knew he would soon be moved to a camp, and then he would be allowed to recover for a month or so—but no longer. Once he showed signs of strength, he would be trucked back to the front, or maybe the front would catch up with him before then.

But Peter was not going to fight again. He had run to the army to save his life, and he had almost lost it. Now he needed to get away. In all the chaos, he knew how to do it, too.

When Hans took his last breath, Peter was with him. He felt sorrow, seeing the end finally come, but anger also swelled in him. He cursed Hitler, whom Hans had loved to the end.

Peter also had a plan. He slipped the blood-stained sling off Hans's arm. Then he straightened both arms at Hans's sides before he pulled the blanket over his face. He took the sling back to his own cot, where he stuffed it under his blanket. Others in the room saw him do this, but they seemed not to wonder, or certainly not to care, why he had done so.

Peter walked to the door of the room and called out, "A man has died in here."

A nurse came down the hall, walking resolutely, her eyes almost as empty as those of the patients she cared for. "It's Rindelsbach. The one with the head injury."

"Yes," she said. "I knew it would happen today."

"I'm ready to go back and fight," Peter said. "I want to get back to the battle—to avenge my friend."

"Yes, yes. But I need to get help to move this boy." She turned and left.

When a medic came by, Peter told him that he was ready for battle.

"No. You need more time," the man said. "But we can move you to the recovery camp, if you feel well enough."

"I do."

And now Peter had what he needed. The next morning, he received a shabby uniform, one that some poor soldier had probably died in. And he received a coat, which is what he wanted most. Before he left the room, he pulled the sling from his bed and stuffed it into his pocket. Then he walked to the door, where he stopped and looked around. "My friend Hans was just a boy," he announced to the men in the room. Those who were awake enough to pay attention looked up. "He loved the Führer. He fought for him. And the Führer *killed* him. He was only a boy, and Hitler—that madman, Hitler—stole his life from him. He's trying to do the same for all of you."

There was no reaction. The men looked at Peter as though he were one more anomaly in a world gone mad. What did they care what he thought? Maybe they agreed with him, but it was apparently not worth bothering to say so.

Peter was supposed to go to the front of the building, to wait for a truck to pick him up—along with others who were being transported to the camp. But it didn't occur to anyone to watch him, to make certain he got on the truck. So he walked out the door and kept walking. Once he was well down the street, he got out the sling and placed his arm in it. The blood was certainly real. No one could doubt that.

Peter kept walking, taking on a limp, until he found the edge of town and a little road. Refugees, in a steady stream, were walking or pulling carts, some even riding in horse-drawn wagons. Peter didn't know where he would get his next meal, and he had no idea where he was going, but he walked with the refugees. He would take his chances as a deserter, but he was never going back to die in this war. More important, he was never going to kill again.

3 2

For some reason, the Japanese guards and the supervisors in the mines were mounting the pressure on the POWs in Wally's camp. Some of the prisoners claimed it was because the war was coming to an end and the guards were frustrated to know they were losing. Others claimed it was retribution for the way America was bombing Japan. But Wally had his own theory. He felt that those who operated the mines were under increasing expectations to produce. The supervisors knew no other method to get their work done than to pass the pressure on to the prisoners—mainly in the form of longer work days and more harassment at morning roll call.

It was best for Wally to think that way. It gave him a way to forgive the supervisors—to tell himself that they weren't instinctively cruel. Since Christmas, he had been making a stronger effort to control his hatred. But it was not easy.

In some ways, the mine was the best place to be these days. Deep in the mine, the temperature was constant. After work, however, the prisoners would return through the snow to their barracks, which were not heated. They would huddle together, with all their clothes on, and try to sleep. But they got little rest, and on the coldest nights it was all they could do to survive.

The long workdays, the inadequate food, and the cold were wearing down men who had already survived so many other horrors. Some were dying. One man, knowing that he was not going to make it otherwise, let a train car in the mine roll over his feet and cut off his toes. The pain was terrible, but it saved him from the drudgery that was gradually sapping the life out of him. Wally thought maybe the man had been smart; he appeared to have saved his life.

One day, early in 1945, when Wally walked into the mess hall after work, he saw four men standing on a table in the center of the building. They were naked, and each was holding a carrot. Wally found Chuck and sat down next to him. "What's going on?" he asked.

"They swiped some carrots. Everyone's betting that Langston turned them in. But there are other guys who would have done it. Honeywell, for one."

Wally looked at the four men, obviously tortured by the cold, and standing in front of everyone. He could see them quivering, the skin on their legs and arms turning blue. "Who are they?" he asked.

"I don't know any of their names," Chuck said. "I heard that two are Brits, one an Aussie, and the little one, on the end, an American."

"How long have they been up there?"

"An hour or so. Something like that."

Wally tried not to look anymore. He sat and ate his rice. But he told Chuck, "How can you starve men and then punish them for taking a carrot? It's at times like this that I think there's nothing wrong with hating these guards."

"I know the feeling," Chuck said. "But I don't know how I'd think and act if I'd been brainwashed and trained in the Japanese army."

Wally was bending over his bowl of rice and scraping out the last few grains. "Maybe that's right," he finally said. "But these guys take joy in what they do."

Chuck leaned over close to him, his elbows on the table. "Look, Wally," he said, "I'm not doing any better than you are. I feel the same way. But when I try to pray, I feel like everything's not really right inside me. And if I want the Lord to get me through this, I need to behave—or at least try to behave— the way he tells us to."

It was the same guilt Wally often felt. "I know what you mean," he said. "But you're way ahead of me."

"No. I don't think so."

There was a stir, and Wally looked around. The four naked men were being allowed to get down from the table. Wally hoped they would also be allowed to dress. He knew they would be placed in solitary confinement for a time—probably without food.

However, they were marched through the hall, and when they reached the door, the guards motioned for them to walk outside into the snow in their bare feet. One of the guards, a man in a heavy coat and high boots, gave each of the prisoners a hard shove as they stepped through the door. The little American stumbled and fell onto the snow. Then the door closed, and Wally could see nothing more.

Wally couldn't think of a way to forgive that kind of behavior. He finished his rice without saying another word, and when he left the mess hall, he saw the four men, still holding the carrots, still completely nude, standing in front of the guardhouse, up to their ankles in snow.

A few days later, Wally heard that the men had been forced to stand in the cold all that night. The two Englishmen had died. The American, according to what prisoners were saying, was going to lose his legs up to the knee. Wally, of course, was not surprised by any of this, but at a time when he was trying to get control of his own hatred, he found himself wishing he could force those guards to suffer some of their own brutality.

When the tenth day of work came, most of the men had the day off. But that was a mixed blessing this time of year. The prisoners needed the rest, but spending all day in the cold barracks was miserable. Wally was almost glad he had drawn duty for the day and would be inside the mine where the temperatures were less uncomfortable. On this extra day, however, he wasn't working with Kiku. His supervisor was someone he didn't know—a quieter, less intense man than Kiku.

Wally worked hard all morning. He was drilling and breaking rock with a bulky old jackhammer that had a way of bucking and slamming against his body as he tried to keep it under control. After a couple of hours on the thing, he was dead tired. The foreman saw him taking a rest and walked over. He pointed to one of the other men and motioned for Wally to turn over the hammer. Wally was relieved. The only problem was, the supervisor was obviously hoping to salvage a little of the day for himself, too, and he wasn't about to let Wally continue to rest. "Kabok," he said, and pointed deeper into the mine shaft. Then he pointed at a man named Fred McPherron and repeated the order.

Wally knew what the supervisor meant. Kabok was the word for the timbers used in the mine. They were in short supply, and so the foremen would often send the prisoners into caved-in areas to salvage the big logs. It was dangerous, but so was almost everything else in the mine. Wally was a little irritated by the supervisor's insistence that he leave immediately, but otherwise he didn't mind. Once he and Fred were out of sight, they could move at their own pace and not be pressured to hurry.

And so the two walked into the dark, with only their lanterns to guide them. They each carried a shovel. "The only timbers left back in here are buried deep," Fred mumbled.

"I don't care. We can take our time."

When they came upon a place where the shaft had collapsed, they found one end of a timber sticking out from under the rubble. "Should we try to dig this one out?" Wally asked.

"Might as well," was all Fred said, and they began digging, not pushing hard but working steadily.

"This thing is waterlogged," Fred said, once they had uncovered a good share of it. "It's going to be heavy as lead."

"Do you think we can carry it?" Wally asked him.

"Yeah. Probably. It's going to be a job, though."

"We'd better get it out. If we're back here too long, and we don't have anything to show for it, that supervisor is going to blow a cork."

Wally turned toward Fred, who was leaning on his shovel for a moment, conserving a little energy. "This guy ain't so bad," Fred said. "Not usually anyway. I've worked with him for the last month or so, and he's pretty fair. But he's antsy today. They always are when they have to miss their day off."

"It's the only thing they have to look forward to, the same as us."

"I don't think they're much better off than we are, either. I've seen these civilian workers fill their lunch buckets with pieces of coal. You gotta figure that much coal ain't going to burn very long, and yet these guys are willing to take the chance of getting caught. And you know they'll pay a terrible price for that."

"One night, after work, I saw a guard get caught," Wally said. "The two-stripers beat him half to death."

"This whole country is getting bombed all the time. The people are getting to the point where they're real bad off."

"How much will they take before they give up?"

"I don't know, Wally. I don't think they ever will. I figure our boys will have to bomb this island until no one's left."

"Including us?"

"Maybe." He cursed. "I do worry about that. I hope there's some way those bombers know where we are."

It was something the men often speculated about. At least they were away from a strategic military site, and the mine didn't seem a high-priority target. That made them feel they were not likely to get hit by a stray bomb.

Wally and Fred knew better than to chat very long. And so they went back to work, lifting larger rocks away with their hands and shoveling out the dirt and debris. Eventually they were able to lift one end of the log, work it loose, and then drag it out. It proved to be every bit as heavy as Fred had predicted, but they each got on an end, and they hefted it onto their shoulders, left their shovels behind for the moment, and began the long walk back through the mineshaft.

They had walked maybe a couple of hundred feet when Wally felt himself begin to stagger under the weight. "I need a break. Let's drop it," he gasped. They let the log roll off their shoulders and thump onto the floor. Then Wally sat down on top of it. His shoulder was aching. "I just don't have the strength I used to have," he said.

Fred swore again. "That thing weighs as much as the two of us put together."

"You mean two hundred pounds?" Wally asked, and he laughed.

"That's about it," Fred said, but then he added, seriously, "It wouldn't be easy for any two men to carry—even ones who got a decent meal once in a while." Wally could hear Fred's breath coming hard, the same as his own.

Maybe two minutes passed as the two continued to get their strength back, and then a light appeared. Someone had come out of a connecting shaft, around a corner. Whoever it was, was walking straight at Wally and Fred. They both stood up immediately.

As the man walked closer, Wally saw two stripes on his lantern. He was a manager, and he had begun to shout in Japanese. Wally knew that he and Fred were being accused of hiding out and sitting down on the job. They waited as the man came nearer. He was a clean, sharp young man, handsome, but he was extremely angry.

Wally pointed to the timber. *"Kabok* very heavy," he said. And then he made a motion to portray the difficulty of hefting such a large log. But clearly the man wasn't convinced. He shouted, *"Ki wo tsuke!"* Attention!

Wally came to attention, all right, but just as he did, the man struck him with his fist, hard in the face. Standing so upright—and unprepared—Wally was thrown backward, over the log. As he fell, he twisted enough not to land square on his back, but pain exploded through his shoulder and the side of his head. He felt something in his mouth and realized that this two-striper had broken one of his back teeth.

Wally snapped. He spat out the tooth, cursed the man, and then jumped to his feet. Three years of pent-up fury suddenly let go, and this time he didn't stop himself.

Wally charged toward the man, but as he did, Fred grabbed him. Wally fought against his grasp and shouted, "Let me go. I'm going to kill him."

"Are you crazy?"

Wally threw an elbow into the side of Fred's head, once, twice, and then pulled free. He lunged toward the manager, tried to grab him by the neck, but the man jumped back and then spun away. Wally took a step to pursue him, but Fred grabbed him again. The manager suddenly bolted. He dashed into the dark, as Wally screamed at him, cursed him in language he hadn't used in a very long time.

"Shut up, Wally," Fred shouted in his ear. He tried to grip his hand over Wally's mouth.

Wally pulled loose again, but he knew it was too late to chase the guy.

"We're in *big* trouble," Fred said, and Wally heard the terror in his voice.

"Not you. Just me."

"That's not how it works around here. You know that."

Wally did know, but he couldn't get himself to care. He only wished he had moved immediately, that he had knocked the man down so he could have strangled him to death. Then he could have dragged him to some dark corner of the mine and buried him. "When they come for me, I'm going to fight," Wally said. "I'm not going to sit still for another beating. They'll kill me, but I'm going to take someone with me if I can."

"That's just stupid. Why come this far and get yourself killed now? You've gone through plenty of beatings before. All that guy did was hit you."

"I don't care. I'm not going to take it anymore. I've had enough. They have no right to treat us that way."

But all the effort was robbing Wally of his energy. He felt the rage seeping away, the tiredness returning. And already he was feeling the guilt. For a few seconds it had felt so good to allow himself the anger and hatred, but all that only showed what a weakling he was—and how stupid he could be. Fred was right. Why put up with so much for so long, only to throw away his life now?

"The first thing we've got to do is get this log carried to our supervisor," Fred said. "We need him to report that we were doing the job he sent us to do."

"What difference does it make?" Wally asked. "These guys don't care about justice. They won't try to find out whether we were really being lazy or not."

Reality was coming clear to Wally now. If he survived the beating that would be waiting for him, other punishments would follow. He could be left out in the cold, naked, like the four men who had stolen the carrots. Or he could be thrown into solitary confinement without food. Recently a prisoner had been left in solitary for twenty days. Every day, rather than comply and beg for food, he had spat in the faces of the guards. He had had his victory, of sorts, and had never given in. He had also died.

Wally saw no way out. What he did know, however, was that Fred, with some luck, might not be treated as severely. He had, after all, held Wally back. So Wally lifted the log, and he struggled down the mineshaft with it. He was doing this for Fred, not for himself. His ordeal would be waiting, no matter what he did.

When Wally and Fred reached their crew, they dropped the log, and then they bent and grabbed their knees, both needing to recover from the strain. The supervisor began to chew them out. Wally didn't know what he was saying, but it was the usual nagging. Clearly the man didn't know what had happened.

There was nothing to do but wait for the next shoe to drop. Maybe someone would come for him, down in the mine. More likely, the two-striper would be waiting, with others, when he left the mine at the end of the shift. And Wally was calm enough to be frightened now. He feared the beatings, the pain he might have to pass through, and he feared death. He had lived with the idea of his own death for so long that he didn't panic. He could even accept the idea that if his life was over, maybe a better one lay ahead. But he didn't want to leave the earth this way, in failure. He had succumbed to his own hatred, the very impulse he had hoped to overcome.

"I'll try to keep you out of this," Wally told Fred later as they got off the train.

"I guess you've changed your mind about fighting them, then," Fred said.

"Oh, yeah. Look, I'm sorry I lost my temper. Sorry I got you into this."

Fred didn't say anything. What was there to say? Wally knew how afraid he was. He was a big man, had once been a very strong man, but he had to know, just as Wally did, that he might be on his way to his death. Wally felt that regret more than any other—that he had put Fred in such jeopardy.

The shift had been shorter than usual, but the January sun was already setting. The opening to the mine was fenced in, with only one gate, and by it was a guard station. That was where Wally expected the manager to be waiting for him.

He decided to walk ahead of the others, and away from Fred. Maybe he could pull all the retribution toward himself and Fred could pass through the gate without a problem. Wally felt as though he were walking a gangplank, about to be plunged into a sea of pain. As he approached the guard station, he kept saying, in his mind, "Help me, Lord. Help me to get through this."

And then he saw the manager, recognized his frame, his stance. In the twilight, Wally saw the crisp lines of the man's cheekbones and jaw, the resolution that seemed sculpted there. The young man stared hard at Wally, not with anger but with authority. This seemed a statement, and it said to Wally, "You are mine. Be ready for what is coming."

But the expression didn't change. Wally reached the man, kept looking into his eyes, and then in an act of submission that seemed natural, stopped in front of him. The man gave Wally the slightest nod but nothing more. He didn't speak, didn't move. Wally waited another second or two, and then he walked on.

It couldn't be that simple. What was he waiting for? When would the two-striper come after him? And yet, that nod, that look, seemed calculated to say something. Wally worried that he was fooling himself, but the manager seemed to have been saying, "It's over. I'll leave you alone, and you leave me alone." But why?

Fred caught up to Wally. "What's going on?" he asked.

"I don't know. He nodded to me. But that's all."

"Maybe he's ashamed he ran from you. That might be a loss of face, in his mind."

"Or maybe he's just waiting. He might come after me tonight."

"Why would he wait? Back there he had all those guards. If they were going to grab you, that would have been the time."

"I don't know. You can never figure these guys out."

Nothing happened that night. In fact, three days passed,

and Wally didn't see the man. But then one night he was at the gate again, and Wally's confidence, which had been growing, disappeared. Once again, however, the man stared at Wally, and this time the nod was more discernible, as though he were saying, "Our compromise is still in place. I'm not going to bother you."

That night, in the cold barracks, Wally speculated with the other men about what had happened—why a man in the manager's position would let Wally off that way. No one understood, but the popular idea was the one prisoners liked to give for everything these days. The war was coming to an end, and this man—opposite of the others—was being careful so he wouldn't be held up for war crimes when the Allies took control of Japan.

Wally wasn't convinced. He was lying on his mat that night, kept awake by the cold and the gnawing disappointment with himself, when the truth hit him—or at least an idea that rang true to him. What seemed to make sense was that the manager had known he was wrong, and that he, too, was ashamed of himself. Like Wally, he had acted rashly. He had struck down a man for no reason, and he was sorry for it. When he had seen Wally's rage, he had understood it. He had said to himself, "How would I react if someone treated me that way?"

That had to be the answer. It was the only idea that made sense to Wally. And it was by far the most useful way for him to think of it—because it turned the man into someone he could understand, even forgive. Wally knew how completely he had failed when he had made his move to kill the man. He also knew that if he was ever going to get on top of his anger and resentment, he would have to think of the guards and supervisors as people like himself: weaklings, giving way to the worst of human impulses. If he had been ready to commit a murder, how could he judge anyone else?

But it was all a little too abstract and rational. He could

pardon this man who had acted with some fairness, but forgiveness for all the others wasn't in his heart. When he thought of his good friends Warren and Jack, who had died so needlessly back in the Philippines, the bitterness returned to him like a nasty aftertaste. Maybe this one manager had regretted his rash act, but that didn't diminish the stored-up resentment Wally felt. He might make it through this nightmare, and he might return home; he might even be a stronger, better man in some ways. Maybe the Lord could forgive him for his momentary intent to kill. But what bothered Wally most as he lay there on that cold floor, without so much as an extra winter blanket, was that he saw no escape from the hatred he was harboring. However often he told himself that his anger was his own problem, he knew what he really believed: that these guards had planted that hatred in him. They had won in both ways. They had not only put him through this agony and humiliation; they had also filled him with so much rancor that it was likely to distort his entire life.

33

On the day after Christmas, Patton's Third Army—the 4th Armored Division and two infantry divisions—broke through from the south and opened up a supply line to Bastogne. That, of course, was good news for Alex and the men of the 101st, but all of them ruffled a bit when the tank men suggested that they had ridden in like the cavalry to save the beleaguered paratroopers. "We were doing just fine," was the usual response. "We're used to fighting behind the lines."

Actually, very little changed for Alex. He and his men received underwear and galoshes, and a better supply of ammunition and food—but the flow of supplies had begun with the air drops, before the breakthrough. The men were still dug in at the crest of the hill above the village of Foy. The cold was worse than ever, the snow deeper, and every day, at unpredictable times, the men were hit with fire from German 88s. The shells came quickly; only in the last few seconds before striking could the men hear them. But every soldier knew the high-pitched whine, the hissing sound, and the final whoosh just before the explosion. The shells crashed through the trees and sent jagged spears and chunks of metal slicing through the forest. There were also nightly patrols, and by now all of the men had had turns at crawling about in the snow, trying to locate the German forces. Almost every night men had been shot at, sometimes wounded, sometimes killed. In all, the 121 men of E Company who had been trucked to Bastogne were now down to fewer than 100. Seven, including Campbell, had been buried in shallow, temporary graves in the hardened ground; the others had been wounded and pulled into improvised hospitals in Bastogne. With the encirclement broken, at least some of them could now be evacuated.

With the arrival of Patton's forces had come newspapers. The men of the 101st were surprised but rather pleased to learn that they had been the focus of worldwide attention. As the German "bulge" had pushed through the Ardennes, one little circle of Allied control had remained on all the maps in every newspaper, and that was Bastogne. Headlines spoke of the "Battling Bastards of the Bastion of Bastogne." Alex had to laugh at the idea. No one back home would ever understand what it had really been like. It all sounded as though the men had fought to the tune of war songs, their chins held high in the air—not hunkered down in foxholes, fighting the cold as much as the Germans.

The added clothing and blankets did help, but after the misery in Holland, and now these two numbing weeks in frozen foxholes, Alex felt dazed more than frightened. When artillery fire came, he hated the fear, the sound of it, but more wearisome were the nights, which seemed to end only in time to begin again. He found it difficult to imagine ever being truly warm again.

Alex could see what was happening to his men, too. The cold, with the intermittent periods of horror and the daily death, was taking a toll. The men were caked with mud, and none had had a shower for two weeks, but it was the look in their eyes that was unnerving. Alex often saw a kind of vacancy behind those eyes, as if the men had learned, like Alex, not to think, not to hope, not to do anything but stay alive another day. They laughed at times, talked into the night, told stories, and seemed to keep their spirits up, but in odd moments Alex would glance at a man and see his eyes take on an empty, hollow look that seemed a mirror of what he was feeling inside himself.

During those terrible weeks in the mud and rain in Holland, and especially here in these woods, Alex's way of thinking about the war had changed. He could hardly remember his view of things back when he had signed up to satisfy his conscience, but he rarely thought of politics anymore, of world domination, of evil Nazis. What he thought of was surviving—and keeping his friends alive. He wanted to see Curtis make it, and Duncan, Gourley and Pozernac. Most of the old Toccoa group was gone now, and he didn't want to lose any more. He also wanted these young men, the replacements, to make it home to their families.

He wondered at times, even if he and his friends survived the coming battles, how deeply they had been changed. His worst fear was that a spirit had been robbed from him that would never come back. He didn't feel anything holy inside himself anymore. He didn't blame himself for the killing, but he blamed the killing for what it was doing to him. He wondered what he would be like when he returned to the world where killing was wrong, as it always had been, where civilization shaped people's behavior, not survival instincts, not this ugly spirit of vengeance that the men tried to foster in themselves—to justify what they were doing.

But he never spoke of these things with the other men. He had made a careful attempt once to tell his father what he was feeling, but he had found himself unable to express the seriousness of his concerns, and his father's letter had come back from that other world, where people didn't understand anything about war. Dad had told him about a conversation with President J. Reuben Clark. President Clark had talked about the terrible influence of war and had said he was sorry if he had pressured him too much to keep the Spirit. The main thing was merely to "do his best" and come home with a testimony. Alex appreciated that, but he had to wonder, did his father or President Clark have any idea what he was actually dealing with?

Alex had made up his mind now that he would never mention the subject at home, if he ever got there. And for now, he tried to keep his mind occupied with other things. His sense of loss, however, was always with him, and behind it all was a self-doubt and disillusionment that he had never known in his life. He felt damaged inside, as though a malignancy were growing in him. He would have to find a cure someday—if a cure was possible—but for now, he couldn't deal with it, and he wouldn't.

On New Year's Eve, the Americans launched a huge volley of fire from every artillery gun. This was a way of telling the soldiers—both American and German—that the Allies had held their own, and the time for counterattack was at hand. Alex felt certain that the major push by the Germans had been stopped, and he was thankful that his men hadn't come out of it any worse. Some of the battalions had fought in bloody battles and had been decimated. The soldiers in the Second Battalion—Alex's unit—had suffered, but so far they had not been thrown into the worst of the action. The only problem was, Alex was sure that couldn't last much longer. Third battalion had had to pull out of Foy, and the town was now occupied by Germans. Now the place would have to be cleared, since it was on the main road to Noville, a town that would have to be retaken as the Allies tried to force the Germans back from the bulge.

New Year's Day was relatively quiet. Late that afternoon, however, word came that Second Battalion, along with a couple of other units, would make a thrust in the morning to clear the *Bois Jacques.* It was the first step the Americans had to take before attacking Foy.

That night German bombers struck. This was something

that hadn't happened often, since German air power had been reduced to a minimal force. All the same, bombs fell into the woods that night and made huge craters in the earth. Men in the battalion—even in the company—died again, but Alex's squad made it through safely.

However much Alex hated life in a foxhole, the idea of moving out was even worse. The great advantage the 101st had possessed until now was that they had been staying put while the enemy had had to attack, out in the open. Movement was slow in all the snow, and men in the fields made easy targets. Now it was the Americans who were going to be on the march, and the Germans who could dig in and hold on.

At first light the troops lined up and got ready to go. They crouched in the snow, which crunched each time someone moved. Alex could sense the fear around him, felt it in himself. His breath was coming in short, tight tugs. He could hear the occasional clank as a man shifted, causing a trigger housing to scrape against a belt grommet or the subtle rub of a pistol handle against the canvas cover of a canteen. There was a no-smoking order, the little flames a sure signal to the other side, but this clearly added to the tension. "I could sure use a smoke," he kept hearing men whisper.

Finally the whispered order came: "Move out." The soldiers knew the routine: they were to form a long skirmish line and sweep through the woods. They were to engage any German units they contacted and drive them back. This could end up a simple operation or a terrific firefight; there was no way of predicting which.

The men moved forward, crouching. Alex could see the others in the yellow light of morning, a long line on either side of him. Howie stuck close to Alex, but as they entered the trees, they found, as they had the time before in these woods, that it was difficult to keep contact with the rest of the line. The forest was thick, and the snow muffled the sounds. Many of the men had white cloth draped over their uniforms as camouflage. At times Alex could see no one but Howie, not even the other men in his squad, and it was difficult to know whether he was walking ahead of or behind the rest of the men in the company.

The going was very slow in the deep snow, and the tension kept building. The woods were peaceful, beautiful, with the snow on the pine trees, but each tree was a hiding place, and a sniper could be hidden in any of them. Alex and Howie walked at least a couple of hundred yards into the woods without seeing any sign of the enemy, and then machine-gun fire opened up. Alex dropped onto his stomach. He realized almost instantly, however, that the fire was coming from a point well to his right. The men out there were meeting some solid resistance. He doubted that anyone in his own company was in on that. There were three battalions strung out along this extensive battle line.

Alex got up, as did Howie, and they worked their way forward again. Alex was careful about moving past trees. Brushing a limb could release a load of snow on his head, but even more important, the sudden movement could alert a sniper or a machine-gun team. It was eerie out there, knowing that hundreds of Americans were with him, but feeling quite alone.

Alex was sweating now, and breathing hard. Each time he stepped, his feet plunged deep into the snow, and it was work to pull his galoshes loose and take the next step. He was weighed down with his heavy clothes, his rifle, his pack, all his ammo and equipment.

When American artillery began to fire, the whistle of shells, the explosions in the distance were comforting and disturbing at the same time. It was good to add the artillery pressure on the enemy, but Alex knew that the Germans would return fire. And just as he suspected, when the 88s did open up, they were not directed at the American artillery. The enemy knew what had to be coming, and they zeroed in on the woods. Suddenly shells started dropping into the trees, and Alex dropped down again.

The next few minutes were paralyzing. There was no foxhole to run to, nothing to do but lie in the snow and hope for the best. "Stay flat," he yelled to Howie. "You'll be all right." But that all depended on how close the shells struck; both of them knew that.

"Medic!" Alex heard someone scream. "Help me. I'm hit. Bad!"

Alex kept his head down as the bursts continued. He could hear the sound of breaking, shredding trees, and the disturbing sound of men screaming in pain. But the artillery stopped after only a few minutes. Maybe the Germans were too unsure of their target. "Let's go," he told Howie, and they got up and ran. There were more shouts by then, more men calling for medical help. The Germans had been on target and had made a big mistake not to keep the pressure on.

Alex didn't know how the line was advancing, but he began to hear more machine-gun fire, and he knew that American troops were coming onto German outposts. Then up ahead and off to his left, he heard a machine gun open up, and he saw the flash of muzzle fire. He dropped, but he knew the shooting was aimed at the men directly in front of the gun. "Howie, we need to work our way over there and help those guys—see if we can get some grenades in on that gun."

"Okay." Howie moved with him. They crawled through the snow, inching their way toward the machine-gun emplacement.

And then a series of explosions went off. Alex looked up to see that other soldiers had gotten close enough to throw grenades. When the smoke cleared, he saw two Germans running through the trees. Rifle fire was popping behind them, and one of the men went down.

It was getting lighter now, and Alex could see Howie's face

clearly. "That took care of that," Alex said, and he saw the relief in Howie's eyes. "Let's keep moving."

The hard walk went on for hours, and Alex was careful to wait and watch at times, never to move too far without checking out the possibilities ahead. But all the heavy action seemed to be on the flanks, and Easy Company was moving straight down the middle of the woods. Alex was able to see other men in his squad more often now, but at one point a sniper held them down for several minutes. The men kept inching forward, crawling, looking for the source of the fire, and finally Gourley was able to spot the man, up in a tree. He squeezed off a round and then shouted, "I got him. Knocked him right out of that tree."

Gourley hated Germans, loved to kill them. He and Pozernac never seemed to doubt themselves or second-guess what they were doing.

The line moved ahead again. The squad met no further resistance in its sector, and by early afternoon the men made it all the way to a logging road, where they had been instructed to stop and recreate their line. A few men had arrived ahead of Alex and Howie, and all his squad soon arrived. Alex moved up and down the line, checking to make sure everyone was all right. "That was a cakewalk," Pozernac told Alex. "We lucked out again. Guys were catching hell on both sides of us."

"We're not finished yet," Alex told him.

During the rest of the afternoon, patrols went out searching to find pockets of resistance in the forest beyond the logging road. From all appearances, the Germans had cleared out, however, and as darkness approached, Alex got the command from Lieutenant Owen to have the men dig in for the night.

With all their equipment, and walking through the deep snow, the troops had worked up a sweat, but during these hours of waiting, they had gotten cold. Digging through the snow into the hard ground was a difficult job, but at least the movement was better than sitting around.

The men were working to break their way through the frozen earth when the hiss of artillery filled the woods. Everyone dropped. A couple of shells exploded just beyond their position. Everyone waited for more, and when nothing came, they started digging again, much harder. That pattern followed well into the evening. The Germans never set up a cannonade of fire, but at odd times they would fire a few shells. Some of the men were making trips into the woods to cut tree limbs, and every time the 88s opened up again, there was a mad dash back to the foxholes.

After all the work, with a good deep hole and limbs to cover it, Alex and Howie lay side by side, hoping to get some sleep. But once they stopped working, the sweat from all the digging seemed to turn their bodies to ice. Alex was shivering violently, and he saw no hope that he could get any rest. Thankfully, the guns didn't fire all night, and at times he drifted into that half-sleep that had become so familiar to him. It was sleep that never really disconnected him from the passing of time, from awareness of the cold, the place, the danger, and it was a night long enough to seem a week. Eventually he and Howie gave up, sat up, even talked some—but there was so little to say. Alex wondered what would come next. Chances were, they would push ahead again, dig in again. But more men would probably die that day.

As it turned out, however, word came down from Wells—now Captain Wells, since his promotion had come through—only to hold the position for now. So the men ate breakfast from the K rations they were carrying, and they waited. Some worked at deepening their foxholes, covering them better, but all was stasis. Everyone kept asking, "What now?"

During the day, some of the troops, probably the units that had been pounded hardest the day before, were pulled out. Replacement platoons were sent in. The replacements were heading to their positions in the woods when some of them decided to cut across a snowy field. The Germans apparently spotted them, because they opened up with artillery fire. But they didn't shoot at the men in the field. They fired into the woods where they could see that the men were heading.

Alex and Howie were close to their foxhole, and they dove in as soon as they heard the sound of the shells. But with the first explosion, Alex knew the game had changed. These were big shells, probably 170s, and they seemed to rock the planet itself when they blew up.

For maybe half an hour—a stretch of time that seemed destined never to end—the big guns pounded the position. The earth rolled like waves on an ocean. The eruptions, the tree bursts, the furious blasts were beyond anything Alex had experienced before, and he had never been this terrified. The explosions were like volcano bursts, like earthquakes. The air would suck away, empty Alex's chest, actually jerk him and Howie off the ground and pull them halfway out of their hole. Several times the impact was so close that the debris blew over their heads like the rubble in a hurricane, tossing away their cover and filling their hole with dirt and rocks. Alex had no doubt that he was about to die. It seemed impossible that anything could live through this.

But then it all stopped.

Alex waited, his breath holding, and finally he looked at Howie, who was obviously in a state of panic. "Is it over?" Howie asked.

"I hope so," Alex said. "I can't do that again."

"*You* can't?"

Alex didn't answer. He knew he had said the wrong thing, but it was what he felt.

"I heard you praying, Sergeant."

"What?"

"You were praying."

"Me?"

"Yes. Didn't you know?"

"No. I mean . . . I didn't know I was talking out loud, I guess."

Howie nodded. But it seemed important to him. "I didn't know you could get that scared," he said. "As scared as me."

There were no more shells, but the shouts of wounded men were everywhere now, up and down the line. Alex got out and ran to the nearby holes to check his men. He was relieved to find them all right, but he also saw how deeply shaken they all were, even the veterans.

Buckley and Ling were in a hole together. Alex saw how overawed they were. "What was that they were sending in?" Ling asked.

"It was something big. It must have been their 170s. That's the worst artillery barrage I've ever gone through."

Ling nodded, as though he were glad to hear it. "If they keep coming back at us with those . . ." He didn't finish his sentence. What he meant was obvious enough.

"Just do what you did this time. Stay down and ride it out. Unless they put one in your hole, you'll be all right."

But he had heard the cries for help, the screaming, and so had Buckley and Ling. They knew without looking that these shells were making huge craters, reaching a much wider radius than the 88s did.

Buckley was looking up at Alex, wide-eyed, all the color gone from his face, and seeming even younger than he was. He was too tall to fit into a foxhole very well. He looked awkward, crouched the way he was. "Do you think we'll move out today?" he asked.

And, of course, that was the other question. It was one thing to ride out artillery fire in a hole. It was another thing to go back into the woods and get caught by those big guns. "I don't know what to expect," Alex said. "But sooner or later we have to clear Foy out. That's that little town just beyond this forest."

Alex saw it in their eyes, the realization that eventually

came to every replacement soldier: the reality that he was likely to get hit, sooner or later. And then the other questions always followed: Will it come today? How bad will it be?

When Alex talked to Duncan and Curtis, they looked worn out, weary of it all. Duncan said, "I don't like that big stuff." And he wasn't ready to make any jokes about it.

Curtis said, "Alex, have you got a minute? There's something I want to talk to you about."

"Sure. Come back with me. I'll send Howie over here with Duncan for a few minutes. I don't think we should spend much time out of the holes."

And so Curtis ran with Alex the thirty meters or so, and Alex asked Howie to trade holes. Howie looked a little confused, maybe even worried. Alex knew how much he depended on the idea that Alex was going to get him through. "It's just for a few minutes," Curtis said.

And so, when they jumped into the hole and sat down, facing each other, Curtis was quick to say, "Alex, that scared me. Me and Duncan took a couple of hits that were way too close. A few yards closer, and we'd be gone."

"I never felt anything like that, Curtis," Alex said. "I hope we don't get that big stuff all night."

Curtis nodded, but he said, "If we make a move on Foy, a lot of us could die anyway."

"Maybe. It's hard to say."

"There's something I need to talk to you about." Curtis hesitated, gathering his thoughts. "We've talked a lot about your church, and I believe what you've told me."

Alex nodded.

"Is there any way you can . . ." He hesitated and smiled. "Sign me up to be a Mormon, or something like that?"

"Is that what you want—to join my church?"

"I guess so. I probably need to learn a little more about it. But I keep thinking about that place you told us about. If I die, that's where I want to go."

"Curtis, you're one of the honest in heart. If you were to get killed, you'd be taught the rest of the gospel, and I know you'd accept it. So you have nothing to worry about."

"Okay. Good. But I'd feel better, I think, if I could join up now."

Alex laughed. "I'd have to fill this foxhole with water and baptize you. I don't have that much water in my canteen, and I don't think you'd want to get quite that wet, out here in this cold."

Curtis grinned. "No, I guess not." But the smile soon faded, and he said, "Alex, I'm not holding up too well. I'm not a very good soldier. It's too bad I didn't get hit a lot worse—back in Normandy. Then I could have stayed out of this."

"I've thought the same thing myself."

"But you do a lot better than I do."

"Not really. I remember what we've been trained to do, and I carry out an operation, once it's started. But after, I have trouble. You know what I was thinking about back at the hospital, in England. That stuff is still in my head."

"I didn't know that, Alex. You never say."

"A guy can't say anything out here. You know that. But we all have stuff going on in our heads."

"Artillery makes a guy religious." He tried to smile but didn't come up with much.

"Not always. Some guys *blame* all this on God."

Curtis's eyes were sunken. He looked ten years older than he had when Alex had first met him. The stubble on his chin was light, scattered, but the cold and exposure had taken a toll on his face. His skin looked leathery and pale. "Alex, I've always been scared, but this is worse. I just feel like my time is running out."

"Everyone thinks that. The longer we're out here, the more we think the odds are running out on us."

"Aren't they?"

"Not necessarily." But it wasn't much of an answer. Alex

wanted to offer something better than that. "Curtis," he said, "I can't baptize you right now, but I could use my priesthood and give you a blessing."

Curtis's head came up. The eagerness was clear in his face. But Alex immediately doubted himself. He wasn't at all sure he was worthy to give a blessing. And he wasn't sure what he could promise. "Curtis, I don't think I can tell you that you won't be killed."

"No. I understand that."

"But I could ask God to be with you and help you through the hard things ahead."

"Sure. That's all I want."

"But Curtis, I have to be honest. I haven't felt God with *me* lately. Maybe I'm not the right one to do this."

"Alex, if anyone is, it's you."

Alex was touched by Curtis's words but not convinced. Still, he wanted to do this for his friend. He had Curtis remove his helmet, and then he placed his grimy hands on his matted hair. He blessed Curtis with the faith and confidence to deal with his fears and to accept the will of the Lord. Then he blessed him to understand and know the truth of the gospel, whenever he would hear it in its fullness. "Lord, bless him for his goodness. Touch his heart, and let him feel thy presence," he concluded.

When Alex removed his hands, Curtis began to cry. Alex pulled him close, held his face against his chest. But Alex didn't cry. He wished that he could. What scared him was that he felt almost nothing. He had trained himself over the past few months to hold everything outside, not to let any of his conflicting emotions overcome him. Now, when he wanted to feel, there was nothing there, not even faith. Curtis was the one who had the Lord with him now. What Alex feared was that whatever he faced in the next few days, he would have to face alone.

34

A lot of men in E Company had been hit during the heavy barrage with the 170s, and a couple of men were broken emotionally. A sergeant who had been wounded in Normandy and had survived Holland went to pieces. His squad got ripped apart, almost all of them wounded, some killed, and he lost control. He ran through the woods, screaming for medics. He finally ended up at an aid station, and he didn't return.

If some had cracked, everyone else was close. The men stayed near their foxholes, and they waited for the next cannonade to begin. But the big guns had sighted in on another target. Alex heard their thunder, and then he breathed easier when he realized that the aim had shifted to another sector. Fortunately, too, the company was not sent into Foy immediately but was allowed to hold its position for another day. Then the men were pulled back into reserve. They were still out in the cold, but at least they were away from the front line. Alex knew that his men were worn out and nervous, but he hadn't lost anyone, and the other squads in the company had all taken casualties.

The company was receiving replacements now: young kids who had landed at LeHavre just a few days before and had been transported by train or truck directly into the battlefield.

Most of them acted cocky, but Alex could see their apprehension.

He was glad he wasn't getting any of them. His replacements had seen a little action now; they understood what they were up against.

The fighting around Foy was raging now. Word came back to the men in E Company that the rest of their battalion, along with other troops from the regiment, now occupied a U-shaped perimeter on the west, south, and east sides of town. But they had attacked several times, and each time they had been thrown back, taking heavy casualties.

E Company got four days out of the action, but no real rest. The men were still battling the cold, their own filth, trench foot, minor wounds, illness, and more than anything, the dread of what lay ahead. And then, on the morning of January 9, they were sent back into the battle. The first assignment for the company was to clear another section of the *Bois Jacques*. They spent a hard day slogging through the deep snow. As it turned out, they met no resistance, and Alex had to think that was lucky. It was hard to keep their rifles dry and functioning, especially automatic weapons, in the cold and wet. Hiking in the snow was also exhausting, and it was easy to let down and not watch closely. If a machine-gun team or a sniper had been waiting for them, the men would have been easy pickings.

By afternoon, the company had reached the road it was pushing toward, and then came the miserably hard task of digging in all over again. Chipping through the first few inches of ground, under the snow, was slow going, but the last thing the men wanted was to be exposed to artillery fire, without cover, or to be out in the weather during the night. Alex and Howie battered away at the ground until neither one had much strength left, but the work got easier as the hole deepened. Alex knew very well that all this work was only for a one-night stay, and he knew some men might give up and settle for a shallow hole, so he moved among his squad, telling the men to keep digging until they had some genuine protection.

By the time the men finally got settled in enough to take time to eat, the sun was low in the sky, reflecting a golden glow off the snow, making everything look lovely. Some of the men were making trips to the woods, cutting and hauling back limbs for cover. And then the whine of artillery shells was in the air. "Incoming!" men shouted. Alex and Howie were sitting on the edge of their foxhole, eating. Howie jumped in, but Alex took a quick look around first. He saw men running hard toward their holes, and he hoped that the artillery wasn't accurate. He ducked down just before the first shell struck. He could hear—and feel—that it wasn't far away. And then a deafening barrage continued for maybe ten minutes. The Germans had opened up with a "Screaming Meemie," as the Americans called them. This was the *Nebelwerfer*—the "fog thrower"—a weapon that could fire hundreds of shells at a rapid pace. The multi-barreled launcher set off terrific screeching noises, like a tirade of sirens.

When the noise stopped, Alex stood up and looked down the line. He didn't hear anything from close by, which was a good sign, so he waited a little longer to make sure the Germans weren't about to fire again. When he finally did go looking, he made a run to Curtis and Duncan's hole. The two of them were standing up, looking okay. "Man, I almost got caught out there," Duncan said. "I had to make a long run for it, and there were shells dropping in all around me. Buckley and Ling were yelling for me to jump in with them, but I figured they didn't need another guy, so I just kept coming."

"He jumped in here with those size-12 boots of his and landed right on me," Curtis said jokingly. But neither man smiled. They both looked spent.

"Some shells hit close, didn't they?" Alex asked.

"Real close."

"I'm going to check the other men." He hurried toward the next hole, but halfway there, he saw a crater, and dirt scattered over the snow. The light was dim, and he didn't want to believe what he was seeing as he came closer. A boot was sticking up from the crater. Alex jogged the last few steps and dropped onto his knees. It was Ling and Buckley. They had taken a direct hit. They were broken in pieces, scattered, mixed with the dirt and snow. And blood was everywhere.

Alex jumped up and spun around. He could see Duncan and Curtis, standing up in their foxhole, the sun behind them. Even in silhouette, he could sense their reactions, their realization.

Alex knew there was no point of calling for help. He would let the medics deal with the wounded who could still be helped. Someone could also try to find Ling and Buckley's dog tags, gather something together to bury, but Alex wanted nothing to do with any of that. He was wondering whether he would vomit. He had seen bodies broken and shredded before, but not quite like this. These were just boys. These were the kids he was responsible for.

Pozernac had walked over. He put his hand on Alex's shoulder, but he didn't say anything.

Alex took a long breath, and he swallowed. Then he said, "You'd better get back to your hole. About now is when the Germans like to hit a second time."

"The other men in the squad are all right. I just checked on them."

"All right." Alex walked toward his own hole. When he reached Duncan and Curtis, they were waiting, looking up at him. "There's nothing left of them," he told them.

"That's the hole I almost jumped into," Duncan said.

"I know."

"Buckley was telling me yesterday that he had a girl back home. I think they were engaged, or at least—"

"Don't talk about it," Alex said. He walked back to Howie and told him the same thing. Then he got down in the hole and tried to follow his own advice. But Alex didn't sleep that night. What he had learned earlier that day from Captain Wells was that E Company had been chosen to lead the charge into Foy in the morning. The entire Second Battalion was to move west, line up directly south of Foy, and then make a charge across an open field of snow, straight into the machine-gun and mortar fire that would certainly come from the town. And E Company would be out front. The Germans occupied all the stone houses in the little village, the barns and chicken coops. They would have cover, and they would hit the lead company with everything they had. Men were going to die in the morning, and it seemed very likely that more men in his own squad would fall.

Alex wanted to sleep, but when he closed his eyes, the images of limbs and blood returned, so he kept his eyes open and stared into the darkness. Late in the night he seemed to hit bottom, reach a level of despair he had never known before. He found himself screaming, inside his head, trying to keep the thoughts away, the pictures. But his mind kept racing. He thought of losing his life, of letting Anna down. He thought of seeing more of his men shot up. But behind it all was a general sense that all of this was never going to end, that this winter would go on and on, and the cold, the shelling, the death, would never let up.

What he knew instinctively was that he must not let this panic and fear penetrate his soul. He had to keep moving forward, doing what was required of him. He had to get out of the foxhole in the morning, take what came, and do the same the next day and the day after that. If he thought about it, imagined it, he couldn't face it.

He also knew that he was drawn toward death, as an escape, and it was hard to find some reason to want life. But that much of Anna was in him, a sense of what he owed her. So there was nothing to do but accept the horror. He just couldn't live through it tonight, in his head, and then face it again, in the daylight. So he tried to rattle his head, bang it against the side of the foxhole, anything but let the thoughts keep coming.

That only worked so long. Finally he gave way. He let himself visualize the crater, see the two boys—the broken parts of them. And then he saw the charge his men would make in the morning, watched it over and over. At least the repetition seemed to dull his anxiety, wear him out, until he entered a state that was similar to sleep.

Very early, however, long before first light, he was awake again. So was Howie. Alex could tell that Howie's breathing was strained, that the fear was in him too.

"How are you doing?" Alex asked him.

"Not too bad. I think I can handle it this time."

"Good. But play it smart. Don't try to prove anything."

"I won't."

"Did you sleep?"

"Yeah. Some." And then without explanation he added, "I sure wish our mail would catch up to us."

"Why?"

"I don't know. In the night, when I can't sleep, I just think a lot about Mom, and everyone back home. My sister told me way last fall that she was sending me a Christmas package."

"You'll probably get some nice warm undies—just in time for summer."

"Yeah. That's about right." He hesitated again, and then he said, "One time you asked me why I didn't buy Christmas presents for my sisters. I was thinking about that during the night. When I get back, I'm going to do that kind of stuff. My family needs to be more like yours."

"Every family has its problems. I wasn't very close to my brother—the one who's a POW. That's something I want to change."

"That's the only good thing about this mess out here. Maybe it makes you appreciate a few things."

"Yeah. It does do that." Alex's mind was drifting back to

what lay ahead. He knew he had to get the men up and get them moved into position. So he pulled himself out of his hole, out into the brittle air, and worked his way around to the other foxholes.

The men ate a little—most of them not really very hungry—and then they fell in as a platoon, and they moved in a line silently through the dark to a position at the top of a little hill, east of the woods they had been clearing. At the bottom of the hill, to the north, only about two hundred meters away, was the village of Foy. There were snow-covered haystacks scattered across the field, and a few little groves of trees, but nothing else would provide cover. The men would not be able to move very fast either, with the deep snow hampering the charge.

For two days German trucks had moved in and out of Foy, on the road from Noville. These could have been supply trucks, hauling in ammunition, but they could also have been troop carriers, bringing reinforcements to the German forces. No one knew for sure.

The men of E Company spread out in a skirmish line along the edge of the woods. First Platoon was on the left flank. Second Platoon, with Alex's squad, was directly in the middle, with Third Platoon on the right. Headquarters Company had set up machine guns on each side of the line.

As the sun began to rise, the distant hills glowed silver, but the slope in front of the men was gray and flat. The cover fire began. That was the signal for the troops to make their move down the hill. Alex led out, and he tried to keep a hard, steady pace. It was foolish to try to run in this snow.

There was sporadic rifle fire from Foy—nothing more—and that was a good sign, but the men had a long way to go. Alex knew the action would heat up as they got closer. It was hard going, but Alex slogged along, hoisting his knees, moving as fast as he could. Howie was next to him. When First Platoon, on the left, reached a barn and some outbuildings about halfway down the hill, Alex heard some shooting and the burst of a couple of grenades. He didn't know exactly what was happening over there, but in the center of the line, Alex saw Captain Wells head toward some haystacks that were maybe seventy or eighty meters from the first buildings in Foy.

"This way!" Wells called out, so Alex and his squad, with the rest of the platoon, fought their way through the snow toward one of the haystacks. Small-arms fire was still popping, here and there, but still no mortars, no heavy machine guns.

"We've lost our left flank!" Captain Wells yelled. "Hold right here for now!"

"That's crazy!" Duncan told Alex. "We've got to keep going. If we sit out here, we're easy targets. They'll zero in on us with mortars."

That was exactly what Alex was thinking. Wells was such a fool. "Captain," Alex called out, "First Platoon went into that barn. They're all right. We need to keep moving."

"No! Hold where you are."

Alex could see the man's face, full of confusion and fear. He was crouching behind the haystack to Alex's right, and he obviously had no idea what to do.

In another few minutes, First Platoon, led by Lieutenant Atwood, charged down the hill from the barn and caught up, but they moved in behind haystacks themselves, and Wells still gave no command. Alex was frantic. He knew that in a charge of this kind, speed was everything. The snow had already slowed the men far too much.

"Atwood!" Captain Wells finally yelled. "Take your men around to the left, flank the town, and attack from the other side. We'll give you cover fire from here."

Duncan cursed. "That'll take forever. We'll all be dead by the time they get into place."

"Captain," Atwood yelled. "We're supposed to go straight in. If we try to—"

"No! Move out! Do what I told you!" Wells shouted back. "Let's get some machine guns going."

So Second and Third platoons started some covering fire from the haystacks, and First Platoon took off in single file around the west side of town. They took a path that led past some trees, which they used for cover, but the trees were spaced out enough that they were of little help, and small-arms fire—rifles and machine pistols—began to cut the men down.

Alex could see the men dropping. Those who weren't hit were pinned down. They had no chance of continuing their flanking move around the town.

Duncan was cursing again, and now Lieutenant Owen was yelling, "We need to go, Captain! We can't sit here!" But Wells seemed petrified. He didn't answer, didn't even move.

By now machine-gun fire had begun to crack and rattle from the buildings in town. Alex knew things would be tough from here on in. The Germans had recovered from whatever surprise might have been on the Americans' side. Mortars would be striking soon, maybe even artillery fire. Alex and his men were going to die out in this field because a stupid officer didn't know what he was doing.

Still Wells waited, and he responded to none of the calls from his other officers. Several crucial minutes went by, and then Alex saw Lieutenant Nichols, a platoon leader from D Company, running down the hill, fighting his way through the snow. Bullets popped overhead, but the man kept coming. When he reached the haystacks, he was breathing hard, but he shouted, "Captain Wells, I'm taking over. Captain Summers sent me."

Nichols was tough and smart, and all his men spoke well of him. He immediately started shouting out commands as he ran from one haystack to another. He got a mortar team to hit a haystack close to town, where two snipers were apparently hiding, and then he got the machine-gun teams set up and firing. "All right, men!" he finally shouted. "We need to get to those buildings. Don't stop again. Let's go!"

And he dashed out first. Lieutenant Nichols was a powerful, athletic man, and he used his long legs to lope through the snow faster than Alex thought anyone could. But Alex went hard, too, tried to pull his men along with him.

Mortar fire had opened up now, and snow and ice and earth began to erupt across the field. Alex saw German tanks maneuvering toward the edge of town, and then he saw their big guns begin to burst with fire. The noise and confusion was tremendous, with machine-gun fire from both sides, mortars thumping into the town from the haystacks, and fire from rifles, grenades, Tommy guns, bazookas. Tracer bullets were streaking through the air, whizzing past him.

Ahead, Alex saw the muzzle fire from windows and alleys, but he kept going. When he got close to the nearest building, a stone house, he dropped down and tossed a grenade at the front door. When the explosion blew the door away, he jumped up, ran to the house, and this time rolled a grenade inside. The blast shook the house, filling it with smoke, but Alex ran in, Duncan with him. They checked for Germans downstairs, and then heard machine-gun fire upstairs. Alex charged up the stairs, pulled the pin on another grenade, and rolled it into an upstairs room. He heard a shout of panic, movement, and then the burst. As soon as the smoke cleared a little, Alex and Duncan charged, their rifles ready. Two Germans were down on their faces, both apparently dead.

Without saying a word, Alex ran back down the stairs. He and Duncan, with other men from the squad joining them outside, ran behind the house. Alex could hear another machine gun close by, and then he spotted the house, down the street to the right, where fire was coming from an upstairs window. Alex shot with his M-1 several times, and so did some of the others, but the angle was wrong, and the shooting from the window continued.

Alex knew he had to get to the house with the snipers. He ran across the street and then stayed close to the buildings as he moved in under the fire. Once again, he led his men into the house and up the stairs. Another grenade took out the machine-gun team.

As the men moved back outside, Alex saw the Panzers, three of them, rumbling away from town, with perhaps a platoon of men alongside them. The Germans were falling back from Foy, north along the road toward Noville. Alex and his men fired a few rounds toward the retreating platoon, but Alex was more concerned about any enemy left in the houses. He led his men through the little main street. They checked one house after another. But they were finding nothing, and Alex was enormously relieved. The operation had gone much better than he had ever expected. Clearly, most of the Germans had abandoned Foy the night before. There had been only a skeleton force there to fight a rear-guard action. If the company had kept moving in the beginning, instead of holding up the way Wells had commanded them to do, E Company would have taken hardly any casualties.

Clearing houses took some time, and some of the men had taken prisoners, who had to be guarded. In all the confusion, there had been some scattering. Alex realized that he'd better round his men up and account for everyone. He had known at some point that Howie wasn't with him, but he hadn't had time to deal with that. "Where's Howie?" he asked now, but none of his men knew. Alex hoped Howie hadn't lost his nerve and stayed back at the haystacks.

When Alex spotted Davis walking down the street toward him, he waved him over and then asked, "Did you see what happened to Private Douglas."

"I saw him get hit and go down," Davis said. "Right after we came out from behind the haystacks."

Alex felt stunned. He had to find him, make sure he had

gotten some medical help by now. "Stay here," he told his men. "I'm going up to look for him."

Alex ran through the town and then trudged up the hill through the snow. As he neared the haystack, he saw a man lying face down. And then, as he took a few more steps, he recognized Howie's muddy field jacket.

Alex stopped. He didn't want to deal with this. But then he told himself that the boy might still be alive. He hurried forward and dropped down by Howie, rolling him over. "Howie!" he shouted, and he slapped his face. But there was nothing there, and Alex knew it. Howie's chest was covered with blood, his face pallid, almost blue.

Alex's body seemed to shut down, his breath coming to a stop, even his pulse. This couldn't happen. This just couldn't happen.

"Howie, come on. Don't," he said, hardly knowing what he was saying. And then, "I'm sorry. I'm sorry." He sat down in the snow, pulled the boy's body onto his lap, and embraced him. "I was going to get you through."

But the enormity of that lie struck Alex now. He'd had no right to make such guarantees. There was no protecting anyone out here.

He wanted to feel something—rage perhaps, at least with himself. But he sat there on the hillside, holding the boy, and the only thing he felt was the ice in his chest.

After a time he saw his men coming to him, Duncan leading the way. They tromped up the hill and stood around him, but no one said anything. No one smoked; no one spoke of eating. They simply waited.

Alex didn't know what to do. He had to put Howie down, had to get on about his business. He was the squad leader, and the younger men didn't need to see him locked up like this.

Duncan finally muttered, "At least he died quick."

It was what every man hoped for. He would rather take a bullet in the heart than to have a leg ripped off by a mortar or a shoe mine and have to bleed to death in horrible pain. Still, to Alex, it hardly seemed a compensation.

Davis said, "I saw him come out from behind that haystack, and then he stopped. He raised his rifle and aimed at something. Then I saw him go down, straight on his face."

"Did he fire his weapon?" Alex asked.

"I don't know."

Alex laid Howie down, and then he got hold of his rifle and yanked it out of the snow. He sniffed the barrel and knew immediately that it had been fired. "We taught him to kill—just in time to die," he whispered. He tossed the rifle back onto the snow and then slammed his fist into his thigh.

Curtis dropped down next to Alex and put his arms around his shoulders. "You did what you could do," he said, but Alex felt the weakness of that. What he could do was nothing at all.

Alex got up. "Duncan, go find us a house," he said. "We'll sleep inside tonight."

"Yeah. All right. What are you going to do?"

"Just stay here for a minute."

"All right." But no one moved. "Deacon, don't put this on yourself."

"Why don't you come on down with us now?" Curtis said. "There's nothing more to do up here."

"I'll be down in a few minutes."

So the men walked back down the hill into Foy. Alex picked up Howie's rifle and stuck it, barrel first, into the snow. He set Howie's helmet over the butt of the rifle, and then he looked out across the valley. The sun was up now, and the snow was glistening, as though this were just a nice winter day in Belgium. What Alex knew was that the pretty morning had brought one more horror to pile on top of all the others, to fill his head with memories he would have to live with forever.

He wanted to cry. He thought it would do him some good. But he had worked too hard, too long, to keep everything out, and he had become good at it. He felt like lead now, like a statue, cold and hard and heartless.

He looked down at Howie again, and he thought of the young man's mother, who had worked so hard all her life to keep her family going. He thought of the sisters Howie had planned to buy Christmas presents for—next year. He thought of the dance hall in Boise, and Howie deciding to sign up with the paratroopers so he could be a war hero and impress the girls. That was plenty to cry about, but Alex couldn't do it. So he walked down the hill, and he thought how much Howie would have liked getting inside a house to sleep warm for one night.

35

It was almost three weeks after Bobbi had gotten her telegram from the Hammonds that she finally got a letter from Richard. His hands had been burned and were still wrapped. "I don't really know how bad my hands are going to be," he told Bobbi. "The doc here wants to send me to your hospital. I guess your burn ward is better than the one here."

He didn't say exactly how he had gotten burned, and he mentioned only briefly that after his ship had sunk he had made it to land, in the Philippines. "That was a very hard time," he said, but he gave no details. In fact, the letter seemed rather impersonal. Part of that, surely, was that someone—a nurse or a Red Cross volunteer—was writing it for him, but Bobbi was left confused and a little worried. There was no expression of feeling for her, no hint of what his plans were—or how she might fit into his future. He did say, "My doctor told me I'll probably have to have some surgery." And he said, "I won't be going back to sea. I guess I'll be leaving the navy at some point."

Only at the end did he drop a little hint as to his feelings. "Bobbi," he said, "I hope you didn't go through too bad of a time while you were waiting for word. There was nothing I could do to let you know I was alive." But then, just when

Bobbi was expecting some expression of affection, he only said, "I hope I do get transferred to Pearl. We need to talk things over."

What did that mean? Bobbi didn't like the hesitancy. The last time they had seen each other, they had made promises. Why couldn't he at least say that he was still committed?

Bobbi took the letter to church with her that Sunday. She shared her news with Ishi and with Sister Nuanunu. After sacrament meeting, everyone wanted to talk to her. "So I hear you and Brother Hammond are going to get married," Brother Nuanunu told her, and he grabbed her in his big arms and hugged her.

"Where did you hear that? The letter said nothing about it."

"My wife said he wants to talk to you when he gets here. We know what that means." He laughed in his big, mellow voice.

Others were coming. Everyone wanted to hear about Richard, what his injuries were. They had all felt Bobbi's gloom during those weeks when he had been missing, and the telegram had brought enormous joy to everyone. Now they were hoping that he was well. Every family in the ward had been affected in some way by the war, and there were so many sad stories. When something turned out right, it was something to celebrate. Even the haoles in the ward had learned from the locals to extract all the joy they could from good news.

But Bobbi felt strange about all this enthusiasm. What if Richard made it to Hawaii and the members talked to him the same way? Would he think Bobbi had made false claims? She told Ishi about her worries, but Ishi only said, "Richard knows you better than that. You always worry too much, Bobbi."

"You worry as much as I do," Bobbi told her.

"I know. But I still have good reasons."

Bobbi knew what she meant. Ishi hadn't had any letters from Daniel for a couple of weeks, which wasn't unusual but was always a concern. Bobbi had read about the "four-four-two" in the newspapers, the bloody battles they kept getting involved in. She knew there really was plenty to be worried about—and she pitied Ishi. At least Richard was out of danger, however badly he might be injured.

Afton was going to dinner that afternoon with the Nuanunus, as she usually did these days. In recent months, military policy had changed, and nurses were allowed to marry, but there was no way for Afton to leave the navy until the war was over. A marriage date was still up in the air, mainly because Afton was hoping to receive the blessing of her family. She had mentioned Sam, very carefully, to her parents, but hadn't hinted yet that she was serious about him.

Bobbi was also committed to the navy for the duration, but there was now a new complication. She had volunteered to serve on a hospital ship, and her paperwork was in process. Lieutenant Karras claimed it was too late to cancel the transfer. Bobbi could be the one at sea before long, with Richard home, waiting.

Bobbi and Ishi, with Lily and David, were on the bus, on the way to Ishi's house. "There's one thing I *am* still worried about," Bobbi told Ishi. "I don't know how bad Richard's hands are, and I don't know what he's feeling about that. His letter was so reserved and careful. It sounded like he wanted to hide his feelings."

"What if his hands are really bad?" Ishi asked. "Would that make a difference to you?"

"I'd feel bad for him, Ishi. Of course. But I thought he was dead, and now I have him back. How could I complain about some scars?"

"But what if it's more than scars? What if he's crippled for life?"

"We can deal with that—together."

"I think that's true, Bobbi, but I've seen men come home badly wounded, and their wives haven't stayed with them.

Maybe sometimes the man is changed so much—and bitter—that you can understand why it happens."

"But look how many girls don't even stay true to their husbands while they're gone to war," Bobbi said. "I'm not going to abandon Richard just because he's injured; that's not the problem."

"What do you mean? What problem?"

Bobbi glanced at the children. David was standing up in his seat, leaning against the window and looking outside, but Lily was listening intently to Bobbi and her mother. Bobbi chose her words carefully. "I just don't know what it will be like when we see each other. We only knew each other such a short time. And now his letter seems so distant. What I want is just to love him and help him heal, but I'm not sure that's what he wants from me. Maybe he regrets the things he told me before."

"I don't think so, Bobbi. I think you'll both know how you feel when you see each other."

"I hope so."

The week that followed seemed long and slow, and every day Bobbi hoped for another letter from Richard. She wrote him each day, and she tried to make him feel that nothing had changed for her. But she heard nothing more, and she had no idea what that meant.

On Thursday morning Bobbi was doing some paperwork at the nurse's station, outside the burn ward. "We're getting some more patients in today," one of the nurses said. "I don't know where we're going to put them."

Bobbi wondered the same thing, but she didn't give the problem any further thought. She made her rounds and was busy for the next couple of hours. She was carrying a basin of water and using her backside to push back the swinging door to the ward when she saw a little collection of men coming down the hallway, some being pushed in wheelchairs, others walking. She noticed a tall man among them, walking upright and holding his hands, which were wrapped in bandages, folded across his chest. And then she realized. "Richard!" she whispered.

He saw her at the same time, and he stepped outside the group—but he didn't hurry to her. Bobbi set down the basin and took a couple of quick steps, and then she slowed. She didn't want to make a scene, and she sensed that Richard didn't want that either. She saw a look on his face that seemed closer to alarm than joy, and she didn't know what to make of it. She stopped in front of him and waited to see what he would do.

Her breath held as he looked at her. She knew his reserve, knew how private he was. At the same time, she also knew what she was feeling. What she remembered, felt again, was his goodness. And then he reached for her with those big, bandaged hands. She stepped to him, and he took her in his arms.

Bobbi began to cry. She felt as though she were being swallowed whole. It was too wonderful to believe that he was finally there, that he was actually holding her. She felt him crying too, felt his breath on her hair. "I didn't know if I would ever see you again," he whispered.

Bobbi had so many things she wanted to tell him, but she was crying too hard. It took her at least a minute to realize that the people in the hall had all stopped and were watching. Some of her friends had begun to gather round. She finally pulled away enough to look at him again. She saw how gaunt he looked, and she sensed that he had been through a much worse ordeal than he had admitted in his letter.

"Are you all right?" she asked.

He didn't seem to know what to say. He pulled his arms back to his chest, as though the bandages had grown heavy—or his hands were hurting. "We need to talk," he said.

"I know. I'll make sure we get some time before the day is over." She still hadn't kissed him, and she wanted to, but she could see how self-conscious he was. He had come off the hospital ship in pajamas, a robe, and slippers, and now he was in the center of a little crowd.

Bobbi turned to her friends and said, "I'll introduce you all later. Right now, these poor guys need to get located somewhere."

"Oh, sure. You just want to get him alone," her friend Iris said. But everyone stepped out of the way and let him go. Bobbi did hear one of the nurses say, "He is *so* good-looking."

Richard had to be processed, and he ended up in one of the crowded rooms in the burn ward. After that, a doctor removed his bandages and had a look at his hands. Bobbi knew that, but she wasn't there—knew that Richard didn't want her to be. But it was a horribly long day, and it was only at the end of her shift that she finally went to Richard and said, "You have permission to go for a little walk, but you'll need a nurse to go along. I could do that—unless you've seen another nurse you like better."

He smiled a little but didn't joke with her. He only got off his bed. He looked toward his robe, hanging on a hook on the wall, and Bobbi quickly got it for him and helped him get it on. Then, as the two walked from the room, they listened to the inevitable teasing. "I never get treatment like that around here," one of the men called out. "What's the lieutenant got that I ain't got?" Obviously the word had gotten around.

Bobbi took Richard outside to the bench where she and Gene had once sat. When Richard sat down next to her, Bobbi hoped he would put his arms around her again, maybe kiss her, but by now she could see that he was holding back. And so she asked again, "Richard, are you all right?"

"Sure . . . but. . ." He took a deep breath.

"What? Just tell me what you're thinking."

"I'm thinking a lot of things, Bobbi. I'm not sure where to start."

"Start anywhere."

He nodded, but then he sat for quite some time before he said, "The doctor told me he wasn't sure he could save my left hand. He's going to keep me here for a while and maybe do some surgery. But he might send me on to Brigham City—of all places. I guess they have a hospital there that specializes in amputations. If they have to take it off, he said that's the best place to have it done."

"What about your other hand?"

"It's a little better. It . . ." Richard hesitated. "See, when I went into the water—when my ship went down—I made it to a lifeboat, and we reached an island in the Philippines. But the islands were still held by the Japanese, at least for the most part, and we had to stay in the jungle for a long time. My hands were burned bad, and there wasn't one thing we could do about it. I guess some of the tendons have locked up, and the scar tissue is really bad. Once they cut away at me for a while, they'll have a better idea how much movement I'll have. But I probably moved my right hand more than my left, and so that one stayed in a little better shape."

"How did you finally get out of the Philippines?"

"One of our guys walked a long way, worked his way through the jungle, and made contact with our troops. A boat came after us after that, and then we got put on a hospital ship. But I was on that island for almost three weeks, and then on the ship for most of another week. The navy didn't get word to my family until I reached Guam."

"You were in a lot of pain all the time, weren't you?"

"Yeah, I was. We didn't have much to eat, either. And we didn't know how long we might be there—or whether the Japs would find us. I wouldn't want to go through any of that again."

"But you made it, Richard. That's all I prayed for, for a long time. And then I gave up. But the Lord brought you back to me."

Again she saw the look she had noticed that morning, that hint of alarm. "Bobbi, I don't know what to say about the future right now. I need to find out what's going to happen to me."

"The worst thing that could happen is that you would lose a hand. That's better than losing your life."

"I guess. I'm just having a little trouble looking at it that way. I'm starting to realize all the things I won't be able to do. Do you understand what I'm saying?"

"Of course I do. But Richard, I see men in here every day who are burned so much worse than you are. I see men with their faces burned, their eyes gone, their feet burned off, their lungs ruined. It's hard to lose a hand, but think how much worse it could have been."

Richard nodded. "I know. I'm not ungrateful. But I don't know what my life is going to be like now. I don't know what I'm going to do. And, well . . . I'm not sure how you'll feel about everything."

"Oh, Richard, how could that matter to me now? I *love* you."

Tears spilled onto his cheeks. "Bobbi, that helps me a lot. I didn't want you to feel obligated."

"Richard, men are so stupid, I sometimes wonder how they manage to get their own pants on in the morning."

He smiled at that, and then he finally took her in his arms, and this time he kissed her. But he didn't say a word about a future together, and that concerned Bobbi. She could feel that he was still holding back.

* * *

Early one morning, on a cold January day, Wally got called to the parade ground. He and the other prisoners lined up in the usual roll-call formation. But something was different. It was earlier than usual, and the man who stepped to the front of the formation was the ranking American officer, a colonel named Guthrie. Wally was tired, but he always hoped that a change from the usual routine was an indication of good news, so he waited anxiously as the men fell in.

Colonel Guthrie called the POWs to attention, and then he told them, "At ease." Wally couldn't see him very well, out there in the dark, but he heard how upbeat his voice was when he said, "Men, all the officers in this camp are being transferred to another prison. We don't know why, and we don't know where we're going. But the promise has been that our conditions will improve. I know that doesn't seem fair, and I'm not telling you it is, but I do want you to think about what this might mean." He hesitated and then said, slowly and thoughtfully, "If the Japanese are starting to concern themselves with the conditions of their prisoners, maybe they're also starting to think this war could end before long."

A little ripple of approval went through the formation, men agreeing, saying, "That's right."

"We see the bombers go over sometimes, but civilians also tell us that this country is taking a terrible beating. Some say there is little left of Tokyo. Here's what I say. We told you on Christmas day that '45 was going to be our year. Now I'm telling you that it's coming true. Keep up your spirits. Carry on the way you have—with hope. This is the year we've been waiting for!"

Suddenly the men were cheering and jumping up and down, slapping each other on the back. They knew the guards would not like that. Some men might well take a beating for it. But it didn't matter. It felt great to let go.

Chuck grabbed hold of Wally. "Let's get dates and go dancing at Saltair this summer. How about it?"

What a thought. Wally wondered whether he still knew how to dance. "We need to put on a little weight if we want any girls to go out with us," he told Chuck, and they both laughed.

"I'll tell you what. That's a project I'd be happy to work on. You give me enough food, and I'll bet I could fill out real fast."

That was an even better thought: all the good food he could eat. And maybe it really was coming before long. Wally wanted to think so. All that day, as he worked in the mine, he imagined his arrival home. He tried to picture his family, how they had changed, how they would react to his return. And he also thought of Lorraine. She probably had a couple of kids by now; he knew that. But he still liked picturing her, imagining what it would be like to dance with her, or at least with someone that beautiful, that good.

But those thoughts brought back worries about himself. He could gain back the weight, get his strength back in time, and maybe have fairly normal health. What he didn't know was how a really lovely girl would feel about him. He had grown in some ways, and improved; he knew that. But he wondered how distorted he was, wondered how much resentment he would carry with him. And how would it show itself? Maybe a nice young woman would sense the rage that was stored in his heart and avoid him. Maybe that's exactly what she *should* do.

* * *

Peter had been walking most of the day, every day, since he had escaped the hospital in East Prussia. He didn't know exactly where he was, but he walked with refugees, and they said they were heading toward Berlin. Eventually he would take another route, head farther south, and see whether he could cross into Switzerland more easily these days. Or maybe France. Maybe he could surrender to Americans, or British, and then try to find out where his family was. But for now, he had to keep walking, as much as anything, to stay warm.

He sometimes saw German military police along the route. They were watching for soldiers on the run, and he wondered why none of these police ever stopped him. The sling around his neck, with Hans's blood on it, hardly seemed enough disguise, but Peter was well aware of what he looked like. He had lost so much weight that there was hardly anything left of him. His uniform was filthy, and if his eyes looked as dead as he felt inside, he must have seemed little more than a specter.

And yet Peter was more alive than he had been for a long time. There was an ember of hope in him. He thought he might live now, might actually survive this war. He believed that he had sinned, that he had done terrible wrongs, and he wondered whether he could ever forgive himself, let alone find forgiveness from his Father in Heaven. But in Memel, God seemed to have plucked him from an impossible trap, from certain death. Maybe it was wrong to think so, but it seemed as though God still loved him in spite of everything.

Something else was happening too. From time to time, he would discover himself filled with a feeling he hardly knew how to describe: comfort or solace, even strength. He didn't know whether it was from God, or what it was, but it sustained him, and it made him feel that his family would accept him, even though he had fought for the enemy.

He slept in haystacks when he could, and once in a barn, but most nights he camped with refugees, who built little fires and sometimes had makeshift tents they were carrying along. He could usually move faster than these people, so he rarely joined the same group twice—but that was best. He wanted no one to know him, to learn any of his secrets. He would stay on the run the rest of the war if he had to, and hope that the chaos would give him cover. If someone chose to shoot him, he would accept death, which was not nearly as frightening as he had once considered it to be. But he would never kill again.

* * *

Heinrich Stoltz was still working in the bakery in Karlsruhe. Not far away, in the Ardennes Forest, the Germans were being torn up and driven back across the border into Germany. It couldn't be long now before the Allied forces broke through the Siegfried Line, crossed the Rhine, and pushed toward Berlin. He had made up his mind that he was going to help them do it, too. He had made contact with members of a resistance group, and he had promised his help.

Brother Stoltz knew that once the Americans or British occupied his area, he could possibly get free to return to England. But if he did that, he would have to return without knowing anything more about Peter. German troops were being driven back toward Germany from the east, and he still wondered how he could locate his son. He had no plan, no real idea how he could go about that, but he prayed every day that the way would be opened for him. What he did believe was that Peter was alive, and that somehow the two would find each other.

And so he continued to speak to Peter, to whisper words of strength and confidence to him, to reassure him that he was loved and missed. "We'll all be together again," Brother Stoltz would tell him. "Everything will be all right."

* * *

Anna and Sister Stoltz had gotten no further word from the OSS about Brother Stoltz. But at least they'd had that one communication that had relieved their minds a great deal. Of course, they wondered if he was still all right. Each day Anna went to work and continued to translate, and with the extra money the Dillinghams provided, the four of them got by all right. Food was not in great supply, and it was expensive, but they knew that many people in the world were suffering much more than they were.

Anna went a long time without hearing from Alex, but eventually she got several letters at once, and she knew that he had survived the terrible time in Bastogne. But his letters seemed less hopeful than before. She had the feeling that he was trying to prepare her for the worst, as though he no longer believed he would survive the entire war. Every day she feared that the bad news would come. She prayed constantly, almost without stopping, it seemed, that he was warm, that he had enough food, that he would be protected in battle. But she already knew that he was receiving injuries daily, wounds to his spirit, and she only hoped that if she could get him back physically, she could help him return, in time, to the Alex she had met when he was the young, handsome missionary she remembered.

So far, Alex had not mentioned the child she was expecting. He had apparently not received her letters for quite some time. She wondered how he would feel about the baby. She hoped it would give him joy—and one more reason to get home safe. But of course, what she harbored was the fear that he would never have the chance to see his own little child.

* * *

LaRue no longer went to the USO club. She actually felt that she could handle it all right now and be a better friend to the servicemen who passed through. But she also knew it was a place that seemed to bring out the worst in her, and she didn't want that. She was still dating Reed Porter, and she had gone out on dates with two other high school boys since Christmas. But she found these boys, even though they were older than she was, immature and rather silly. She missed Ned more than she ever imagined she would. She wrote to him two or three times a week, and she got back letters even more often than that. Ned was as committed as ever—or maybe just very lonely. She had no idea how she would feel about him when she was old enough to marry, but she did know that she liked him much better than any other boy she knew.

No one at school knew that, of course. LaRue's girlfriends all predicted she would marry Reed someday. LaRue, however, flirted with lots of boys, and she was addicted to the attention. When she took a hard look inside herself—something she didn't actually do very often—she wondered whether she could ever marry at all. She wanted to *do* things in this world and not be overshadowed by a husband. She still suspected that Ned had been right about her, that she wasn't a very good person, and sometimes she felt ashamed.

Just when the demands for armaments had slacked off a little, the Battle of the Bulge had scared the government into believing that the war would last some time yet, and the orders for parts had picked up again. LaRue was more willing to work at the plant than she had been when she had been going to the USO so often. She liked having the money, whether she liked the work or not. And the truth was, there was still nothing LaRue liked better than spending money on herself, especially to buy nice clothes. Her dad still chided her about that, but she knew she turned heads when she walked down the hallway at East High, and that was a pleasure she couldn't resist. She was well aware of the truth about herself. She had discovered who she was, and she hadn't been very impressed. But it was quite another thing to change, and she wasn't sure she was doing much of that.

* * *

President Thomas was putting a lot of money away, and he was making more contacts around the city and state. Without running for office himself, he had become one of the powers in the Republican party. At the same time, lately he seemed a little less quick to assume that he had the whole truth on every issue. He admired much about President Roosevelt and had admitted a couple of times, rather grudgingly, that he might have been the right president for the time. What irritated him most, however, was that his wife was such an unabashed fan of Roosevelt, and especially of Eleanor Roosevelt. "If you run as a Republican," she had begun to tell him lately, "maybe I'll proclaim myself a Democrat and run against you. I hate to tell you, Al, but I think I can beat you."

He always joked with her about that, but in fact, he thought she probably could. She was a better speaker than he was, more exciting and interesting, less given to predictions of doom; and people knew by now that in many ways she was the one operating the plant that had brought so much money to the Thomases.

In more serious moments, however, Bea admitted that she had no interest at all in politics. What she wanted was to have her family home. Maybe Bobbi had found a husband now, and maybe this was the year her boys would come home.

* * *

A week went by, and Bobbi saw Richard often, but he was struggling. She knew how worried he was about his hand. But then one day he asked Bobbi whether she could take a walk with him at quitting time, the way she had before. She heard a change in his voice, some life, but she didn't want to get her hopes up. She was careful what she told herself all day.

When the two walked outside late that afternoon, they sat down on the bench where they had sat before, and this time Bobbi waited, didn't push the conversation. But Richard was quick to say, "Bobbi, the doc thinks I'll be able to keep my hand. He still wants to send me on to Utah, but I think as much as anything that's because he knows that's home to me."

"Richard, that's wonderful."

"Well . . . not so wonderful as all that. My hand may not end up all that useful. There'll be a lot of things I won't be able to do."

"Sure. And I know that's hard. But I still think you're blessed that you made it off the ship—and came back." She didn't dare say "came back to me" this time.

"I doubt I'll be able to pin diapers on a baby." He smiled. It was the first time since his return that she had seen his full, endearing smile, and she suddenly felt as though she were dissolving into the bench. "I don't see the problem," she said. "You don't have any babies."

"But I hope to have some someday."

"Really? My understanding is, having received some training—let's say, book learning—in human reproduction, that a man can't have babies all by himself."

Richard stopped smiling. "Bobbi, I'm going home, and you're the one going to sea before long."

"I'll be all right. And the war *will* end. *Someday.*"

"I have to find a way to make a living. You're used to having a lot of things, and—"

"Don't. Okay? Just ask me—before I ask you."

He nodded. "All right," he said. "Will you marry me? In spite of—"

But she didn't let him finish. She took over. She kissed him, and then she told him, "You know I will, Richard. You know I will."

* * *

After the battle for Foy, Alex slept in a house for a few nights. The men built a fire in a coal stove, and they had to crowd into the kitchen, but the warmth provided a kind of comfort they hardly remembered. And yet Alex still wasn't sleeping well. He was too accustomed to a mental vigilance, a half-awake mind that heard every sound, feared every move. He did feel more rested after some days and nights inside, but he needed months away from the battle, not days, and that was not about to happen.

When word came one night that the battalion was moving out the next morning, no one was surprised. The men in the squad sat together in that one heated room of the house, ate K rations, and talked about what lay ahead.

"This road to Noville, and then on to Germany, is going to be bad," Duncan told the men. "We're a long way from finished."

Alex looked at Duncan and Curtis. They seemed, now, his oldest friends. He had never exactly said it to himself before, but it occurred to him that he loved these guys—loved them as much as Elder Mecham, or any friend he'd ever had. He could hardly stand to think that they might yet be killed.

Late that afternoon the mail finally caught up to the company. Alex had a whole handful of letters, and he almost cried at the sight of them, the smell of them. He put them in order and began to read, slowly and carefully, savoring the sound of Anna's voice, which seemed so close when he read the letters.

In the third letter he came to the important news:

Your last letter was very dear to me, Alex. You told me how much you needed me and missed me. You said my letters were important to keep you going. I miss you so much, Liebling, and I like to know that you miss me the same way. Especially now, more than any time in my life, I want you close to me. I didn't want to tell you until I was certain, but I now know for sure. So I tell you in a letter, when I want to tell you, holding you in my arms. You are going to be a father. I hope that makes you happy. I hope this gives you more reason to be careful and come home to me and your little child.

Alex stared at the words, read them again and again. And with each reading, their power built inside him. He knew that this changed everything. He had to return from battle whole, well in body *and* spirit. He wondered what chance there was of that. He shut his eyes and asked for help.

But he felt nothing, no sense at all that the Lord was near him, and the disappointment was shattering. He leaned over the kitchen table and put his forehead on his arms. And then, without warning, he began to sob.

He wanted to walk away this instant, return to Anna, where he belonged. He wanted to be himself again, find in himself the worthiness to be a father.

A father. The word was overpowering to him. It felt sacred. But it also felt like an accusation.

In a minute, Curtis was there, with his arm on Alex's shoulders. "Are you okay?" he asked. "Did something happen?"

Alex looked up, his eyes still full of tears. "Anna's going to have a baby," he said.

He looked around at the men—battered, dirty soldiers—and he saw them stare at him, begin to smile. But Duncan leaned forward, put his elbows on his knees, and ducked his head. Then his shoulders began to shake, and tears began to drip from his chin.

Alex didn't know exactly what Duncan was feeling. But there was something about the idea of a baby—the softness, the freshness—that seemed inconceivable here, as though such delicate things no longer existed. The thought of getting up in the morning and starting down another road toward another battle seemed not only incongruous but impossible.

"I wish Howie had made it," Duncan said. "And Campbell. All those guys."

Alex was startled by the connection. He felt a little spasm run through his body. He knew what Duncan meant. This moment was something all of them should have shared. They were buddies. Suddenly the loss of all those friends, and especially his "little brother" Howie, struck him with force, seemed finally to reach his core. He put his head down again, and he cried out loud. Howie shouldn't be dead, he told himself. He was just a kid. A nice kid. What was wrong with a world where people gathered into armies and killed each other—killed young kids?

Alex cried for a long time, and no one bothered him. Nor was he embarrassed. It was something he knew that he had to do, and even as he touched the depths of his sorrow, he sensed some gratefulness. After all, he was remembering what it was like to feel human, and ever so slightly, divine.

The road to Noville and on to Germany would be waiting in the morning, but he needed this softness now, before he steeled himself again.

"Father," he whispered to himself again. "I'm going to be a father."

Virtually every day I hear the same questions about *Children of the Promise:* How many books will there be in the series? When will the next one be out? Maybe it's time that I give some "official" answers.

My outline calls for five books in the *Children of the Promise* series. Volume 4 will carry the story to the end of World War II. Volume 5 will be about the early postwar period when the soldiers returned and the healing began. If all goes as planned, number four will come out early in the fall of 1999, and number five at about the same time in 2000. I would write the volumes faster if I could, but trust me, it's all I can do to produce one of these books in a year.

What pleases me most is that so many people do ask. Thanks to all of you who write or call or tell me personally that you enjoy the books. The Thomases have become real in my mind—and dear friends. It's gratifying to have readers tell me that they feel the same way.

I want to say a word about the racial and national epithets that are used in this book. I have mentioned before my uneasiness about using the terms that soldiers and even civilians at the time used to name their enemies. I think readers understand that I'm trying to be accurate about the language that was used at the time—not approving. I would hope that all of us have come a long way in our racial attitudes over the past fifty years. But I also think we need to be reminded that racial prejudice was and is very real, and we shouldn't pretend that it wasn't part of American life in the 1940s.

I mentioned in an author's note in *Since You Went Away* some of the books I have found helpful. Let me add a few more to that list. Robert and Jane Easton published a collection of the letters they wrote to one another during the war. The book, *Love and War: Pearl Harbor through V-J Day* (University of Oklahoma Press, 1991) is touching, fascinating, and realistic. It takes a reader back to the era as few books can. It helped me imagine the feelings Alex and Anna would experience.

The most thorough history of the Battle of the Bulge is probably Trevor N. Dupuy's *Hitler's Last Gamble: The Battle of the Bulge, December 1944–January 1945* (HarperCollins, 1994). Stephen E. Ambrose's new book, *Citizen Soldiers* (Simon and Schuster, 1997), is a more compelling and down-to-earth account of the last European battles, including the Battle of the Bulge.

To learn about the war between Germany and Russia, read David M. Glantz and Jonathan House's *When Titans Clashed: How the Red Army Stopped Hitler* (University Press of Kansas, 1995). To *feel* what the war on the eastern front was like, the most powerful portrayal I know is Guy Sajer's autobiography, *The Forgotten Soldier* (Harper and Row, 1967; Brassey's, 1990). Peter Stoltz's fictional experiences are mostly based on accounts in Sajer's book.

One of the best books about the life of military nurses is *G.I. Nightingales: The Army Nurse Corps in World War II* (University Press of Kentucky, 1996), by Barbara Brooks Tomblin.

For an account of the Japanese American fighting units in World War II, I would recommend *Unlikely Liberators: The Men of the 100th and 442nd* (University of Hawaii Press, 1983).

If you think of World War II as exciting and romantic, as it is often portrayed in the movies, I would invite you to read two books that will awaken you to the realities of combat: Eric Bergerud's *Touched by Fire: The Land War in the South Pacific* (Penguin, 1996) and Gerald F. Linderman's *The World within War: America's Combat Experience in World War II* (Free Press, 1997).

One of my favorite research experiences is to sit in a library and read old newspapers on microfilm. History books are written from a perspective, but a newspaper attempts to make sense of its own time. I love to read the ads, the editorials, the society pages, even the comics. This, as much as anything, helps me feel what the forties were like. Try it. I guarantee that it's more fun than almost anything you're likely to see on TV.

I wish to thank those who have read *Far from Home* and given me responses: my wife, Kathy; my son Tom and his wife, Kristen; my daughter Amy and her husband, Brad Russell; my son Rob; my friends David and Shauna Weight and Richard and Sharon Jeppesen. Jack Lyon has been a painstaking editor, and Emily Watts has added her artistic guidance. Sheri Dew has continued not only to offer editorial advice but also to cheer me on with genuine enthusiasm, as has everyone at Deseret Book.

Let me also thank the managers and employees of the many bookstores that handle my series. Their response has been overwhelming. Time and again people tell me that they bought my first two volumes because bookstore employees gave them such high recommendations. Without that enthusiasm, these books would not have reached such a wide audience.

I have dedicated *Far from Home* to my son Tom; his wife, Kristen Shawgo Hughes; and their little son Steven. Tom has done a wonderful job, I feel—and many people tell me—of reading these volumes for the "book on tape" (and CD) versions. He and Kristen have also read the books in manuscript and given me their responses and suggestions. So far Steven hasn't done anything but delight me, but he's done that *very* well.